JESS B. MOORE

Saving Grace

for all the ones who are unsure
(it's okay to forgive yourself)

Contents

Acknowledgement	iii
Lola	1
Lola	10
Brandt	18
Lola	21
Lola	26
Brandt	33
Lola	37
Brandt	45
Lola	49
Lola	57
Brandt	64
Lola	69
Lola	76
Lola	81
Brandt	85
Lola	87
Lola	92
Lola	99
Brandt	104
Lola	108
Lola	117
Brandt	128
Lola	132
Lola	139
Lola	143
Brandt	148

Lola   152

Lola   158

Lola   162

Brandt   166

Lola   169

The Chapel   174

About the Author   184

Also by Jess B. Moore   185

Acknowledgement

Saving Grace is my fourth book. I can't seem to wrap my head around the concept of having put FOUR books out into the world! I self-published this one, but that doesn't mean I did it all by myself.
Big squishy thanks to my editor, Ellie, at My Brother's Editor. She's fabulous and fun and made editing a delight.

All the love in the world to my early readers. Without them, plot holes would swallow my books! Seriously.

I will never get over the awesomeness that is my cover illustrator, Nina Sibiratkina. I stumbled upon her work when looking for my Fierce Grace cover image, and then begged her to draw something for Saving Grace. I'm happily working with her to make covers for ALL my books now!!

Super cheers for my biggest cheerleaders. Alisha, Cindy, Amanda, I don't know if I'd still be writing if I didn't have your voices whispering in my ear to keep going! Having you in my corner is everything.

Eric, you're my one, and I'm so happy to spend my life with you. Elijah, there will be more bluegrass in the next one. Like, all the bluegrass. Lincoln, I know you don't prefer love stories, but hopefully one day you'll appreciate my books.

1

Lola

Isn't it time you stopped punishing yourself, Lola? My mother's favorite question. Always followed up quickly by, When are you coming home, Lola?

Never, and never, hadn't proven to be acceptable answers to my insistent mother.

What I did was unforgivable, and I would never stop punishing myself for it. That's the least I deserved. As far as going home, no thank you. I couldn't wholly avoid my family, as we lived in the same small town, but I hadn't gone back for a Sunday dinner in months. I rarely went out which cut down on the number of accidental run-ins. Shame still burned hot in my chest a year later, and I couldn't face the people who loved me.

I knew they loved me as surely as I loved them. There had never been any question. Until I'd sunk to an unthinkable low and realized I didn't know myself well. My confidence slipped, and I needed time to figure things out. Time away from all the people who had helped define me as a person. Time all by myself.

Texts and phone calls from my family were altogether a different issue. I read each message my brothers sent and listened to every voicemail my mother left. I loved them more each time they reached out, knowing they hadn't given up on me. I hated myself a little more each time, too, knowing they'd never un-see the filth on me if they knew the truth.

Not going home for Thanksgiving was the height of unacceptable according to my mother, who saw my absence as a direct slap to her motherhood. My family was outraged that I would choose to spend the holiday alone rather than with them. Like being treated as a pariah was a better, more suitable alternative. Not that they treated me any such way, as they had no clue what their darling daughter was capable of doing. No, I'd continue avoiding them, keeping them in the dark, and living in solitude.

I thought once I knew why I did it, and how I was capable of it, then I could face telling them the truth. Until then, I kept my secrets close.

The last day of school before Thanksgiving break turned hopeless - my class of five- and six-year-olds unable to hold focus more than a minute at a time. I doubt a single teacher at Fox River Elementary bothered to stick to a lesson plan that didn't include playing games and putting on a movie. Anything you tried to teach would be a waste of time and have to be retaught when the kids came back the following week. It was the first real break since the start of the school year, and everyone was itching for the days off. Honestly, even I had the attention span of an ant. The hours flew by, filled with coloring turkeys with glued on feather tails, watching *Free Birds,* and making sure all my planning and paperwork were completed by the end of the day.

I'd go home smelling of crayons, glue, and childhood-innocence, as usual.

Annabelle Dare sought me out, stopping by my classroom, as I instructed my students to clear out their desks. A timely and necessary activity before we lined up to leave. She remained my friend, due to her effort, not mine. A sweeter, more thoughtful girl, I had never known. She wore her emotions on her sleeve and went out of her way to be kind and generous. Easy to like if you could ever get in close enough to talk with her. I had grown up in Fox River, whereas Annabelle had moved to the area only a couple years prior, yet while my circle of friends dwindled, hers grew.

"Hey, Lola." She smiled at me with her glossy pink mouth.

"Hi, Annabelle."

"How's it going? Sorry I haven't chatted with you lately," Annabelle unnecessarily apologized. A habit we shared.

2

We'd said hi and exchanged pleasantries any time we saw each other at school. The last time we got together outside of school, a couple weeks back, was at the bluegrass jam in town. Annabelle had been going pretty regular and convinced me to pull out my Dobro and start attending as well. It gave me something to do, but I was guaranteed to run into my family there. Dad always showed up, being the primary upright bass player of the town - unless Beau MacKenna showed with his boyfriend Elliot, both of whom played bass. They all took turns. My younger brothers Wes and Seth sometimes showed too. Seth would sit with me, leaning in eagerly, and peppering me with questions, practically begging me to come around more. I couldn't always make myself face the ordeal.

"No need to apologize. Things are the same with me." I stared at Annabelle's pretty brown eyes and wished I didn't feel like the worst person on the planet. I wanted to tell her I was a dishonorable person and she shouldn't waste her time being kind to me. "You have fun plans for the holiday?"

When Vincent and I had split up last year, it had been shocking to everyone in our circle of friends. Annabelle had been the one to stop asking questions first and had made a point to keep me in the loop. I left everyone else to Vin, which only seemed right. I refused to put our friends in an awkward battle with divided lines and simply removed myself from the equation.

The kids were set to be released in ten minutes. The halls were falsely still as I stood in the doorway, keeping an eye on the chaos in my classroom as book bags were stuffed full, and excitement ran high. I had to work the bus line after school, then I would be on my own for five days.

Five days suddenly felt like a long time to be alone. Hollowness gaped wide inside me, but I ignored it with practiced ease.

"Yes, actually. We're settled into the new house, and we're hosting Thanksgiving! It's Emily's birthday this weekend, too." Annabelle tipped her head toward the precocious blonde kindergartener in my class. "Asher's family is coming to our new place for Thanksgiving slash birthday celebrations." She glowed. Happiness was palpable as it came off her. It smacked against my misery and turned to cinders before it could reach me. "What about you?"

"No," I said the word too quickly and saw the shock on Annabelle's face at my reaction. "No, I don't have any plans."

"Oooh. Come over!" Her excitement was a quiet thing. A tiny spark that begged for recognition. Too sweet; she was *too sweet*. "Really, Lola Gal, I'm cooking which means it will all be horrendous. Emily and her dad Hudson will be there, of course, and I know you adore Emily."

"Thank you. That's so nice of you to offer. I..." I didn't have a reason other than not wanting to intrude, which was clearly not a feasible argument. "I don't want to intrude."

"Nonsense." She linked her arm through mine. The physical connection startled me, but felt good, oh so good. I was so starved for connection it was maddening. I didn't pull away, not because I allowed myself to be comforted by this girl, but because I didn't want to hurt her feelings. "It will be great. Super casual. Cook something and bring it, or show up early and help me cook, or don't cook at all. Whatever you want."

I couldn't help but smile at her. The small movement of laughter in my chest was unfamiliar after endless months of deadening emotions, something that felt oddly like it might lead to happiness. The sensation caught me off guard and left me wobbly on my feet. Another of my cravings hit me hard: the need to smile and laugh, to relax and be myself. Not setting a time limit on my self-imposed solitary life, I didn't know when - if ever - it would come to an end. Yet, after a year, I found myself fighting it on some level, wanting to give in and move on from my transgressions. Leave the past in the past.

But had I learned anything? Did I know who I was yet?

The bell trilled, and classroom doors began to open. The car riders would snake through the hallways first before the bus riders made their way. I jumped at the sound of the bell, and Annabelle smiled at me again, like she thought I was adorable or something.

"Text me and let me know what you're already planning to make." I extended the offer, "I'll make whatever is left."

"I'm so excited, Lola. We're going to have so much fun!"

I wasn't as sure about that but kept the smile on my face. Hundreds of little feet trampled past sounding like a herd of buffalo in the echoing hallway.

"Thank you for inviting me." My voice trailed after her, lost in the mass of little bodies as they rushed to the exits.

Annabelle hurried off with a wave down the hallway until she caught up with Cara, a third-grade teacher with auburn ringlets. They smiled and laughed as they were swept along with the current of kids going to meet their rides home.

***

Sitting at home alone was something I had grown so accustomed to, it was no longer weird. When I had first moved into the house, the empty rooms and lack of other people had been its own sort of presence. It reminded me every second of the life I had left behind, screaming at me and scorning me. Then somewhere along the line in the last year, it became a sanctuary. After a day filled with children, to come home and sit in my quiet, still house was a reprieve.

I'd grown up with a fair amount of chaos in the form of two little brothers. Heathens, the both of them, rough and loud. When Wes came along, I was only three, and therefore didn't remember a life without him. My mother told a hundred stories of me watching over him, bringing him toys, and insisting on curling up beside him when he napped. But Seth, when he came into our lives, I was six, and fully believed he was mine. I rocked him, carried him, mothered him, and did everything I could get away with while our mother was busy with the house and having three children. By that time, Wes had started throwing fits, screamed too much for my liking, and disliked not being the baby anymore. A few short years later, the boys were best friends, and I was the older sister no-one wanted around anymore. They lived to mess with my things and to play tricks on me. Moving away from them - even while we were all technically adults - gave me peace for the first time in my life.

I craved it - my own house - the collection of chairs I'd arranged in the living room, the rugs that softened the floors, and the feeling like I belonged. Having my own place had become a gift. The opposite of what it was meant to be, as a punishment, and I warred with myself over it.

That was how I explained it to myself: going to Annabelle's for Thanksgiving was a better punishment than staying home.

At home, I could relax, and although my thoughts - flashes of what happened, and the shame that came along - were punishment enough most times, I had gotten used to turning them off and enjoying the creaking of the little wooden house. Each day that passed made it easier to forget what I'd done and who I had become. My vicious spiraling thoughts slipped away for sometimes days at a time. Only to come back and slap me so hard I could barely recover.

That was when I felt it, the lightning strike of need, the nearly irresistible urge to drown my thoughts with a drink. Or five.

To spend the holiday with people and to put myself in a situation that made me uncomfortable, it was a punishment of its own. Because afterward, I would have to walk away, and I would have to live with the reminder of what it could feel like to be surrounded by people who care for you.

Not that they cared for me. I would bear witness to the love they shared, and I would always stand outside that fire, and getting close enough to singe my skin was what I needed.

Turned out Annabelle wasn't kidding about the food. She had volunteered to take on everything. Her boyfriend Asher had to work up until the day and couldn't help with any prep. The other brother, Hudson, and his daughter, Emily, were bringing sweet potato casserole. Asher apparently planned to help her cook Thursday, but she said she'd rather he be able to spend time with his family, and assured him that she could handle it. Only she couldn't, poor girl. We swapped texts about traditional and nontraditional Thanksgiving foods. I ended up volunteering to bring green bean casserole and Hummingbird Cake.

I grew up not cooking for myself. Food always prepared by my mother, who took it on as her eternal duty to serve her family. Only after I moved away and lived alone did I start figuring out feeding myself. Without the internet, I would have lived on frozen burritos and dry cereal. As it was, I learned to make a few things. Usually on the weekends, with nothing else to do, I would choose a few recipes, then eat whatever I'd made throughout the following week. Green bean casserole, I googled and found was surprisingly easy. Hummingbird Cake was my grandmother's specialty, and I had her handwritten recipe, though I had never attempted to make it before.

As I pulled in to park at Annabelle and Asher's new house, nerves shook my chest and clouded my sanity. I didn't know Asher Grace well, much less his family, and I wasn't sure what to expect. I used to hang out with them before things went south with Vincent and me. It was always as a group, and Asher had always been quiet, intense, and generally kept to himself. Since then, I'd avoided most of the old crew. It was only my continued friendship with Annabelle - bless her heart - that remained a connection to the Graces.

Their newly rented house sat atop a small hill, and I wish I had worn flats to make the short trek, my ankles caving in the stupid heels I'd strapped to my feet. I balanced the cake plate on top of the casserole dish with my left hand, carried a bottle of wine in my right, and picked my way up her drive.

The cold wind turned my skin to ice, showing me what late November in western North Carolina had to offer. It had been a harsh summer and had turned to sharp cold with the fall. I hated the winter and dreaded the coming months. Stupidly, I'd left my coat in the car because it was hard enough carrying everything without the added bulk. I'd be inside except for the walk from the car, so I didn't figure it would matter. The wind ripped through my sweater, and I wanted to kick myself for not bundling up.

Standing outside their door, my hands ridiculously full, I debated putting the casserole slash cake tower on the ground to free a hand for knocking. I also contemplated using my toe to kick the door in lieu of knocking. Would the bottle of wine crack if I used it as a door-knocker?

"You need a hand?"

A male voice came up behind me, pitched purposely not to startle me. Being perpetually jumpy, I flinched in surprise anyway.

I spun to see the source where I found a guy with a startling number of tattoos, green marble stretching his earlobes, dark hair falling into his eyes, and a frankly imposing stature.

Brandt Grace.

He looked me in the eye, not staring, but not avoiding my mismatched eyes either. Most people stared for a second too long when faced with one blue eye and one brown. After they recovered, they tended not to look at my eyes again at all. Until they thought I wasn't looking. First impressions were generally awkward. Not Brandt, he didn't seem weirded out one little bit - but then we'd grown up together.

Obviously, I recognized him on the spot. The sight of him sent my heart crashing against my ribs and robbed me of my breath and my senses. We'd gone to school together all those years ago. But he was not someone I ran into as we lived in vastly different circles. My reaction was the same as it had always been when confronted with him - an immediate physical jolt shouting at me to pay attention to this man. My attraction to him knew no bounds and unfailingly brought on a bout of embarrassment, with pink cheeks and rambling words to go along.

Growing up, everyone had a secret crush on a Grace brother. A whispered admission followed by all the reasons it was a bad idea. (Unlike the MacKenna brothers whom we all proudly announced our crushes to one another and openly discussed).

Of the three Grace brothers, Brandt had the most deplorable reputation. The youngest, and the worst of the three of them. If by worst, you meant biggest liar and trouble-maker. I could never quite remember why people hated him, but talk around town about him was never of the good sort.

Talk of taking and maybe selling drugs. Getting kicked out of school before graduating. Burning down the back five acres of their land - back when they had land. There hadn't been a bigger troublemaker in Fox River except for Lucian Porter, who met an untimely end a good five years back.

"Hi." That was all I could manage. Brandt was beautiful if a dark angel that reeked of violence could be beautiful. Breathtaking was maybe a better word. "No. I mean, yes, I do need a hand."

"I'll take those." His offer came out softly, surprising me, and wrapped a band around my chest so tight air could no longer flow properly.

He scooped the casserole with the precarious cake balanced on top free from my arms. He smiled at me, and I forgot all the reasons I should have avoided him.

For a second, I imagined us in a different world - a whole other dimension - as friends or lovers, laughing softly together, and happily trusting him to always handle the tough parts with me, making life better.

But in this world, I shivered from the repulsive cold weather, we shuffled our feet in mutual awkwardness, and I knew Brandt and I would never have a future.

"Thank you. I'm Lola," I supplied, which he may or may not have remembered on his own. Best not to assume. "Annabelle invited me."

I watched his eyes - a mesmerizing shade of blue-green, somewhere between turquoise and sea green - as he inspected me. His full lips twitched like he wanted to say something or smile, but he didn't follow through. He stuck a hand out and rapped solidly on the door.

2

Lola

As the door swung open, I stared at the blood-red rose on the left side of Brandt's neck. It was beautiful, but in the same way he was, with thorns high along the stem and the promise of poison on the petals. An alarming and visually effective warning to stay away. My gut should have heeded the warning, rather than ache with desire.

"Lola. Brandt. Hey." Annabelle greeted us with three separate words. Disconnected. I knew she was expecting me, so I had to figure Brandt caused her panicked reaction. After a fast recovery of obvious worry, she shook her head and pulled her smile wider. "Come on in."

Brandt waited and tilted his chin toward the doorway, allowing me to go in first. Who knew he had manners? I was on edge and confused and not sure what to do with that, other than to drag my gaze away from Brandt's handsome jaw and focus instead on entering. The herbs from the stuffing suffused the air, along with the tang of cranberries, and it reminded me sickly of Thanksgivings at home.

My family would be cooking together: Seth helping too much, Wes talking more than contributing, our dad staying out of the way by piddling around the house and yard, and Mom doing the bulk of the work. She liked it that way, being in charge of the kitchen, and providing for us. They'd set a place at the table for me on Easter, hoping I would show up. Would they reserve my spot again today?

Shame slithered in, obliterating my nonsensical libido rush at being so near Brandt Grace, and keeping me in check. Yes, good, shame - that I could deal with.

I hadn't expected to see Brandt. Yet I couldn't be shocked, as it was his niece's birthday and a family holiday both. He belonged more than me. Annabelle shuffled her feet, twisted her fingers, and stared too much, not the least bit comfortable with Brandt showing up at her door.

Curious.

"Hud's on his way over." Annabelle's voice came out breathy and weird. She didn't look at Brandt, which was more evident than if she had looked at him. "Asher's... right there."

Annabelle pointed her finger at the big guy in the tiny kitchen. Asher looked intense as usual, tight shoulders and concerned eyes, chopping away at something I couldn't see from my position. He was attentive enough to his surroundings to quirk into a smile when his girl said his name. But Asher hadn't looked up. He stopped his chore, found a hand towel, and took a few steps all before he looked our way.

Asher wasn't as good as Annabelle at disguising his feelings.

"What the fuck are you doing here?" he asked with a growly voice, sending a chill down my spine.

Even knowing he didn't speak those words to me, they hit me and rattled my bones.

"Asher," Annabelle admonished. Probably on my behalf, her pretty eyes wide, and her teeth gnawing on her lips with worry.

Asher flicked his glance to me, a crease etched deep between his eyes. Asher was taller than Brandt - but not by much - and a couple years older. His dark hair was shaved close to the skin, leaving just the idea of dark hair. His eyes were crystalline blue, a startling cold shade, hard.

Brandt stood behind me, so I couldn't see his reaction. Stuck in the middle ground between their face-off was a dangerous place to be, charged with their energy and tension. It sent me stepping backward and into Brandt, who became an unexpectedly solid and comforting presence. He didn't move away or try to steady me, but the way he adjusted his weight to account for me gave me something like a feeling of assurance in him.

Curiouser.

"Sorry." Asher grimaced when I think he meant to smile. "Hi, Lola. Good to see you."

"Lola, you know Asher. This is his brother, Brandt." She cocked her head to the side, and her eyes were pleading with Asher to calm down and let go whatever his issue was with his brother. "Hudson and Emily will be here in a few minutes."

"Nice to see you again, Asher," I managed, although my throat had constricted and nearly choked me.

"We know each other, Annabelle," Brandt mentioned in his low, surly voice. "We graduated in the same class."

"Right. Of course." Annabelle laughed, and it was filled with nerves. "I forget how everyone knows everyone here."

"*Would* have graduated in the same class," Asher pointed out loudly, bringing the tension levels in the room to an all-time high. "Brandt didn't bother graduating."

I could feel the embarrassment roll-off Brandt in waves. He stood behind me, and I didn't have to see him to sense the powerful emotion. Asher shamed him in front of Annabelle and me, and it was nothing but mean. My respect for Asher fell dramatically at his poor behavior. I had to remind myself I didn't know the inside track of their history.

Annabelle gasped and looked like she might fall over.

"I'm just gonna bring these to the kitchen." Brandt came around me, lifting the dishes of food in front of him as proof he needed to fully enter the apartment. He had to skirt past his brother along the way.

"Right. Yeah, me too." I followed Brandt to the cluttered counters of the small kitchen which opened to the living room.

It was like we had swapped places in a dance. Brandt and I lingering in the false safety of the kitchen, wrapped up together in the yummy scents. Annabelle and Asher hovering by the front door, looking unsure.

The house was lovely, small but clean, plain white walls and generic blue-gray carpet but funky fresh decorating. The air rippled with the residual angst of the brothers.

"Brandt." Asher shook his head and his tight control coiled, a snake waiting to strike. "Come outside and talk."

"I don't think outside is a good idea." Annabelle looked up at Asher, and her face was a book written on love, splashed with pleading. "Hud and Em will be here soon, and I don't want her walking in with you two being ridiculous."

Asher looked like he didn't think they were, in fact, any such thing. However, he relented. I turned away to study the oven timer. But it's not like I could block out the friction around me. I was all too aware of Brandt still standing there with me like we'd actually come together.

"Take him to our room?" Annabelle suggested.

"Our room? No."

"Ash. God. Just take him in there. Or else get over it and don't talk to him. Whatever."

I turned back as I heard Annabelle approach. She studiously avoided looking at Brandt, which struck me as weird. Something was going on there, something between the two of them. Something she didn't want Asher to know about.

Not that I thought Annabelle would cheat on her boyfriend.

Not that anyone had thought I would cheat on mine. A familiar wave of shame doused me and brought me back down to my place in the depths of hell. The quick flash in my head of walking away from an unfamiliar bed to be sick in a stranger's toilet stole my attention for a moment.

"I'm so glad you came, Lola." Annabelle grabbed my arm, and her voice sounded pleading. She effectively pulled me from my spiraling thoughts and back to the situation at hand.

"Thanks for the invite." I miraculously remembered my manners and how to speak correctly.

Brandt held back laughter ineffectively, as it still seeped out in staccato breaths, as he faced his brother.

"Alright, alright, brother, lead the way," Brandt said. "Let's get this out of your system."

When I glanced at him, joking his way through the messy tension, there were massive storm clouds behind his sarcastic smile.

Brandt Grace defined complicated.

He followed Asher down a very short hallway until they disappeared behind a hastily closed door.

"Oh my god, I'm so sorry!" Annabelle vehemently whispered with a guilty look. "I didn't know Brandt was coming. Obviously."

"No worries." I kept my voice low, too. I tried to let her off the hook. Not like I really cared about her boyfriend's family drama. "What can I do to help? I mean, with the food."

She breathed a little laugh, and we tried notably hard to focus on the mess in the kitchen and not the one down the hall. Ingredients which would add up to equal roasted turkey, gravy, stuffing, and the rest of Thanksgiving covered her small kitchen.

"How did you even know where we live?" Asher's voice rose, and the hollow door didn't do a thing to block it.

"Well, shoot. This is not going how I planned." Annabelle spun around to lean her hips against the counter, food prep forgotten. "I'm opening the wine. You want a glass?"

"Nah, I'm good. You go ahead, though." I'd stopped drinking a while back. For reasons.

"Maybe Hudson told me." Brandt's tone bordered on placating, but he didn't back down.

"Maybe? What does that even mean?" Asher countered.

"It's a small town, brother, I know where a lot of people live. Fuck, Ash, you're embarrassing Annabelle and Lola. As far as ass-hole-ery goes, today it's you wearing the crown."

"You should leave."

The response was nothing or else too quiet to carry to us.

"So, they don't get along." I twisted my lips, not immune to how embarrassed Annabelle was over the fight.

I'd fought with my brothers over the years, but never with such venom, never with hatred or distrust oozing out in our words. But I didn't know the Graces well enough to judge or to understand. All I knew were rumors which were doubtful at best and outright lies at worst.

"Correct," Annabelle agreed with a sharp nod. "They do not get along. I don't know Brandt well. Actually, I don't know him at all because Asher thinks I should avoid him. But he never gives me a reason, and it seems so… over-dramatic." She explained, but it left me with more questions.

I finished chopping the veggies Asher had been prepping for a salad. I almost suggested Annabelle put on some music. Loud music.

"I hope Hud doesn't—" she started, before being cut off.

"Why are you working so damn hard to keep me away from her? What do you think will happen?" Brandt evidently gave up on holding back.

I had to assume *her* meant Annabelle. Who Asher was hell bent on protecting from any and everything, evidently including his little brother.

"You are unpredictable. You are a risk I'm not willing to take," Asher boomed at him.

I winced and peeked at my friend. She still worked at maintaining calm.

"Do you think they think we can't hear them?" I was back to whispering.

"I think they aren't thinking."

We shared a small smile and twin eye-rolls.

"I would never hurt her. And you know it." Brandt's voice was raw, from yelling or from emotion. Their control slipped a little more with each minute that passed. "What is this really about?"

"I don't know that. I don't trust you."

"Fuck you, Asher."

Silence, heavier and louder than their words, pressed in around us.

"I'm sorry! Have I said I'm sorry?" Annabelle's fingers clutched at my sleeve as she begged me to forgive this slight.

"What's Thanksgiving without super awkward family fights?" I nudged Annabelle with my elbow, my hands still enmeshed in shredding carrots.

She almost smiled. I didn't know anything about her family - maybe I'd said the wrong thing. Annabelle had mentioned her dad passing away years ago, never talked about her mom, and that summed up what I knew of her past. Kendra was her family now. And Asher, of course.

"You should join my knitting group, Lola Gal." Annabelle, in all her kindness, continued the charade of normal. "It's been the best decision I made in years."

She laughed, and I tried to picture her sitting with a group of older ladies, yarn in their hands.

"Kendra convinced me to go, and it's not what you think." Her voice lowered to a near whisper, as if the knitting group was a secret society. "We knit, obviously, but it's more than that, we're all—"

"You should go, Brandt," Asher pleaded again.

We stopped bothering with conversation and quietly listened in while they argued.

"I don't have anywhere else to go." Each word was strained, filled with the overflow of emotions, and tugged at something deep within me. "I want to be here for Emily."

I felt terrible for him. I didn't know him well. I didn't know the details of his history or why his brother considered him a risk and didn't trust him. Brandt was clearly hanging on by a thread in there, and I hated it for him. The ambush was over the top from my perspective.

"Go home." Asher was relentless.

"I can't."

An explanation didn't exist or came at a lower volume.

"I'm gonna go break this up," Annabelle announced, steeling herself with a nod and a deep breath.

I nodded back as my friend downed the last of her small pour of wine. She skirted around me and walked determinedly to what I had to assume was their bedroom. She swung the door open but didn't go in the room.

"If you two are done with the pissing contest, we could use some help. With Thanksgiving. With Emily's birthday party. You know, the holiday we are celebrating. Together. Because we are a family."

She ground out the word *family* as if she could make them feel that way by the sheer force of her saying the word. It took a godly amount of effort not to crack up laughing. Annabelle wasn't tiny, taller than me by a couple inches with curves to die for, but she wasn't big either. Next to those brothers: she was tiny. Itty bitty. She rolled right up to them, spewed her brand of polite

16

sarcasm, and didn't bat an eye about it.

"You're right. I'm sorry." Asher broke first. Which made sense. Thirty seconds near them and you could tell he was wholly devoted to her. "What can I do to help?"

"Go chop the stuff for the salad. Lola took over for you," she guilted him. Not that I minded chopping the veggies.

Asher tried to smile as he came toward the kitchen. I was able to smile back easily, because I was a practiced smiler. I could tell it hurt him to walk away, leaving his girl and his brother there. But he could see and hear reasonably well from the kitchen with the open floor plan. Unless they closed her door, which wasn't likely to happen. All hell would break loose.

"I'm sorry, Annabelle." Brandt's words were low. Private. I got the feeling I was intruding, a wave of unease along my skin. "If you want me to go, I'll go. I shouldn't have just shown up."

"You're welcome to stay."

Politely disregarding all the underlying strain, we all spent a few minutes pretending it wasn't painfully awkward.

3

Brandt

Hudson said to show up. Specifically, he'd said: *Fuck Asher. It's Thanksgiving.* Then I'd told him I couldn't make it, spitting out an excuse about trouble with my roommates. Not a lie. Not the full truth, as I found myself with nowhere to go on Thanksgiving Day. But it wasn't what kept me from wanting to show up to the family event.

Asher, he didn't bother speaking to me about the holiday. Didn't need a repeat of the last year, when he'd brought his prissy girlfriend, and she'd shown us all up with her overpriced gifts. I knew Annabelle didn't mean any harm and turned out she's a nice girl. But she'd also asked me to lie to my brother about my run-in with her. Turned to trouble when I opened my mouth about the stupid gift, and Asher and I ended up fighting like kids on the front lawn. Apparently, my brother thought I'd like to reenact the event every year, and didn't invite me to his house.

He and Annabelle had moved in together to a little house with window boxes and shit. Like Ash could hide behind them and people might forget where he came from. Wash the dirty Grace blood right off his reputation.

Trailer trash. Without the trailer. We'd heard plenty worse over the years, but that one kept circling around. *White trash* came in second for how folks of Fox River liked to describe the Grace brothers. Next they whispered about which of us they'd like to fuck. Usually Asher came out on top there, but in the last year with Ash off the market, I'd edged my way up the list. Too bad I

18

didn't care about whoring around with girls in town.

Thanksgiving didn't fall on Emily's birthday this year, but we always celebrated them on the same day. It had become tradition. One I didn't want to miss.

Plus, with my belongings packed in my truck, I needed a place to crash. Not that I expected to stay with Asher or Hudson, but they were about the only choices I had left. With a reputation like mine, people didn't invite you in unless they wanted something.

I fully expected Asher to be mad. To *react*. Asher loved to react, and I was ready for him.

I did not expect Lola Donovan.

Yet there she stood, at my brother's front door, looking adorable and out of place. Food balanced in her arms, no coat on despite the cold, and hair blowing all over the place. I kept my voice soft so I didn't scare her. And when she looked at me, I didn't shy away from her eyes. Damn, her eyes were gorgeous. Unlike anything you've ever seen: one bright blue, the other light brown. I remember the first time I saw her - on the bus on the first day of school when we were little - and I've never stopped looking for her since. I've drawn her face so many times over the years, trying to get it just right, I felt a wash of shame come over me as I stared at her in present time. I realized I hadn't gotten her right yet either.

I should have warned her to turn back and not enter the lion's den. Surely, she'd hung out with Annabelle enough to know Asher could be a raging jerk. But that didn't mean she knew I'd be the catalyst of Ash's poor behavior today. Of course, Hud would show up soon with Emily, and we'd all act like we got along beautifully. Fights and a lifetime of distrust swept away for the sake of Emily. She was the only saving grace in our damn lives, and I would never stop being thankful she came along.

Just like I thought, Asher pulled me aside to yell, to express how much he didn't want me there. Blaming why I shouldn't stay on Annabelle. Said he didn't trust me around her. Ha. I could have told him about that day with the cake last year, when Annabelle and I worked together, and how she didn't think I was the big bad wolf. But I kept her secrets and took the lashing my brother handed out one barbed word at a time.

He'd hated me since we were little. Because he stood in front of me and collected Dad's beatings. Because he knew I kept secrets for Dad. Or because he thought I was Dad's favorite. Asher didn't need a concrete reason for his distrust, yet he wore it proudly and shoveled that shit all over town.

"Go home," Asher snarled at me, hands on his head, eyes blazing, and patience gone.

"I can't," I spit back at him, but that only made him want an explanation. Lowering my voice so the girls wouldn't hear, I told him the abridged version. "Ed collects the rent each month, and I've given him my third, but he's claiming I haven't. Dylan's done with the both of us, and I can't go back. Okay?"

Before Ash could share his wisdom on my fuck-ups, Annabelle barged in. If she was good for anything, it was reining in Asher.

Dylan was friends with Asher, which had worked in my favor securing the room in his apartment. He was a paramedic and a decent dude. He never brought his girl Haley around but spent a shit ton of time with her. Ed was a loose cannon hiding behind a bright array of Polo shirts. He was neat, which was a plus, and talkative as hell, which was a big negative for me. I didn't mind moving out in general, but to have nowhere to go on a holiday weekend sucked.

I found it hard to concentrate as we waited for Hudson to show up, bouncing between ideas of where to stay the night, and listening to Lola's voice when she spoke.

My fingers itched for a pencil as I studied Lola's features and the smattering of freckles across her nose. She'd changed. Not just her face or her body, as she moved into her mid-twenties, but something deeper. The way she held herself, like she could hide in plain sight, and the way she cast her eyes down. It wasn't so we wouldn't stare at the strangeness of the color - because we weren't doing that - it was an active avoidance, tucking herself away.

4

Lola

Saved by the doorbell.

Annabelle jumped. Brandt snickered. Asher glared while he chopped the last couple bell peppers.

I opened the door because Annabelle had made herself busy in the kitchen and because Brandt was not making a move to do it.

If I thought I had prepared myself for the size and presence of the Grace boys, I was mistaken. I'd seen Hudson at the jam sometimes, or picking Emily up from school, and hanging around Asher. But we'd never officially met. He was the tallest and broadest of the brothers by far. His image was softened only by the lovely blonde girl who held his hand tightly.

"Hi. I'm Lola," I offered as I opened the door wide.

"Nice to meet you." He had a casserole dish in one hand, and his daughter's hand in the other. I could tell he wanted to shake hands or something to make it official. I just smiled and ushered them inside.

"Miss Donovan!!" Emily dropped her dad's hand and leaped at me.

"Hi." I had already said that. I focused on the girl. "Hi, Emily."

"You look like an angel today." She gushed at me, pure devotion pouring from her, and petted my white Angora sweater.

"Me? You look like an angel," I countered her, then to Hudson said, "Every day, in fact, she looks and behaves like an angel."

Her smile was wide and innocent between us.

"Good to hear, Miss Donovan," Hudson said with a solemn nod. His eyes skipped away from mine, unsure where to land in his effort not to stare at my blue-brown unmatched eyeballs probably. Or weirded out by meeting-the-teacher, which sometimes happened, and was especially common when meeting outside the classroom.

"Lola. At least for today," I offered to him with a nervous laugh. I wanted to ask if Emily hadn't mentioned the eyes, or if it was different seeing me in person, as Hudson continued to blink at me.

"Hey guys, come on in," Annabelle called out, and we all shifted around in the entryway while I closed the front door. "Look, Em, Uncle Asher and Uncle Brandt are here."

Not so subtle warning about the other brother. *Okay, going with it.*

But with Emily there, everything was different. No antagonism. No looks that could kill. The undercurrent of it ran so deep I could barely feel it down there. The little girl didn't seem to know what to do with herself. She ran around, giving hugs to everyone. Brandt scooped her up with practiced ease, and she ran her fingers through his floppy dark hair. Whatever issues they all had, they were put to rest while they doted on Emily.

I swear, my uterus skipped a beat as I watched Brandt with his niece. *Hello, biological clock, odd time to start ticking.*

Annabelle pulled out coloring books and crayons. Emily opened her little backpack to reveal a harmonica, a half-naked Barbie with knotted hair, a deck of playing cards, and a book about an American Girl Doll. The one with the pink dress and long brown hair.

Hudson never stopped watching his daughter. He was well over six feet tall, broad through the shoulders and chest, and clearly the oldest of the brothers. His hair was lighter, honey brown, and his eyes were caramel. The other two had the dark, dark hair and the light, light eyes. They still looked like brothers. Same mischievous smiles and keen, watchful eyes. Shared mannerisms that spoke of a lifetime together.

I wondered if people saw that when they looked at my brothers and me together. We looked similar, but I would have said we had nothing else in common. It's hard to see when you're on the inside.

"Are you family? Or just almost, like Aunt Anna?" Emily asked me, curious about why her teacher had shown up to a family holiday.

Aunt Anna, huh. Guess things were progressing nicely for Annabelle with the Grace family. Good to know, and I couldn't be happier for her. In the beginning, when she moved to town, and when Asher was still a punk, I wouldn't have guessed at their future. Then they got together, and it was like seeing a puzzle solved, all the pieces fitting together perfectly.

"I'm friends with Annabelle. We met at school - like you and I did." I didn't explain how I had no plans otherwise, and how my friend invited me out of pity.

"I've known her the longest," Brandt called out and winked when Emily faced him with shock.

"Really?" she asked, playing along perfectly.

"Yes, really." He pretend snarled at her, then they both laughed. "We met way back when we were in kindergarten."

We'd been in the same class every couple years, randomly thrown together by the system, or by fate. But I rode the bus with him every year. With all the Grace boys. I lived out in the boonies, too, where the rolling hills of farmland were far more prevalent than houses. My dad still worked the land, whereas their dad had sold off their farm, leaving them the small house and a legacy of disaster.

"Wow!" Emily looked back and forth between Brandt and me like she tried to picture us her age.

She sat down on the floor and motioned for me to do the same. I joined her as she handed me her American Girl book. Samantha, that was the doll's name, based on a girl raised in the early 1900s. Brandt stood by a front window which looked out over the freshly raked lawn. Hudson positioned himself at the bar, easily able to talk to Asher and Annabelle, but within earshot and range of Emily.

"Did you go to preschool?" I asked her while attempting to smooth the Barbie's tangles. I probably knew the answer, but couldn't recall at the moment.

"Yes. At Grayson."

I nodded but didn't comment. I didn't know much about the pre-k except it was in the rural outskirts of town. Opened in the last few years and ran more like daycare than a preschool.

"You really grew up here and went to school at Fox River?" Emily asked like she might not believe the story.

"Yes, of course." I talked with her, forgetting about everyone else in the room with us. I loved that about children, the way you could zero in and be in the moment. "I always wished I could go to Agnes Academy, which is an all-girls school about an hour from here."

"All girls?"

"Yes. No boys allowed." I used a tone meant for shocking her.

"Cool. Boys are dumb."

"Don't use that word, Em," Hudson called out. Emily's face scrunched up, but she nodded.

"Not all boys are dumb. Your uncles seem pretty cool," I offered, figuring it was the least I could do.

The room went too still. Without checking, I knew they were all looking at me, and listening to me. My skin went warm, which meant pink.

"They are cool. But they aren't boys anymore." Emily's nose scrunched. "It's different."

"Hmm."

"Why?" Asher called out from behind me. He was picking for information that Emily was all too willing to provide, but the whole exchange stayed unexplainably strained for me.

Why did this feel so darn awkward, was the question. Asher's attention had turned to Emily, and the others followed. Except Brandt. When I looked up, he watched me, his face giving away nothing of his thoughts.

"Because." She rolled her brown eyes, like her dad's, and it was funny on her sweet little face. "The boys in my class only care about Legos and Hot Wheels. Plus they always make potty jokes. None of them can even read."

Asher shook with laughter that I could hear despite his efforts to keep it under control. Brandt slid his gaze to Emily and smiled in a way that was more indulgent than anything.

Hudson sighed. "Most of the kids in kinder aren't reading yet, Em. We talked about that. Don't go around bragging just because you can do something they can't."

"Yes, sir."

"Well, I love to read. What's your favorite book?" The air went back to normal. Annabelle and Asher resumed their conversation about the turkey and her worries about it drying out.

Brandt was the only one still watching us, and I remained acutely aware of him. Of his watching eyes. Of his sinuous posture. Of his listening ears. My fingers longed to trace the curve of his ear, to feel the green marble that sat in the lobes, and to know the warmth of his skin.

"Bad Kitty. And Desperaux," Emily replied with pride.

I smiled and shook off thoughts of crossing the line of socially acceptable touching with her uncle.

"Bad Kitty books are funny." I was swept up in the outpouring of love that followed this little angel of a girl, and kept her my focal point - determined not to repeat my previous wayward thoughts of a certain man. "Desperaux is one of my favorites, too. Should we ban soup and bowls and spoons from your party?"

"Yes!" She jumped up and ran to the kitchen to deliver the edict to the others.

I had a feeling I had made things more difficult. I couldn't help it. I loved kids, especially kids who loved books. It was a weakness.

When I stood from the floor, I looked over at Brandt to find he was still looking my way. His face was a question I didn't know how to answer.

5

Lola

Thanksgiving slash Emily's birthday couldn't have been more perfect. The turkey didn't dry out. The green beans were too salty, but everyone ate them anyway. The marshmallows on the sweet potatoes burnt and it was Asher's fault, so naturally, we all gave him a hard time for messing up Hudson's dish. Emily ate more than a tiny little thing should be able to and followed that up with a nap on the funky orange sofa. Brandt kept quiet, there but not there, observing. He only seemed happy when he was interacting with his niece. By the end of the day, I was stuffed and sleepy and dreading the quiet emptiness that awaited me at home.

They skipped opening birthday gifts, Hudson claiming they'd open them later at home, without an audience. I knew enough to realize this was a new tradition after last year's party when Annabelle became a pariah for her lavish gift of Samantha the American Girl Doll. It had blown way out of proportion and nearly ended without Annabelle and Asher together. Thankfully they'd gotten past that mess and were happily living together in their new little house.

Brandt had been the first to leave. Saying a lavish goodbye to Emily filled with hugs and peppered with kissing and ending with tickling, then simply nodding to the rest of us on his way out.

I followed suit not much later. Hudson stayed to help clean up the mess Emily had made of the living room. Asher washed the dishes and chatted

Annabelle's ear off about how wonderful she had made the holiday. After saying thank you and goodbye, and after hugging Emily three times at her insistence, I made it out the door to the dark sidewalk leading to where I'd parked on the street.

My feet screamed at me with every single step, and I vowed to never wear heels again. In fact, I'd take them off and drive home barefoot, then drop the stupid torturous shoes in the trash as soon as possible.

Until then, I balanced dishes in my arms and wobbled down the steep driveway toward my car. Then I almost walked right into Brandt, sitting on the curb.

"You scared me! What are you doing?" I screeched at him after nearly jumping out of my skin.

"Sorry." He stood and reversed my view, going from below me to above me. In the yellow of the streetlight and the dark of the night, his tattoos were nondescript, and his eyes shone bright but lacked their brilliant color. "I'm sorry, Lola."

"Do you need a ride home?" I asked of him, still trying to process nearly tripping over him, and oddly curious why he remained outside his brother's home. Especially when he was unwelcome there.

He let out a brief and powerful jet of air before responding.

"No. My truck's there." He pointed to a spot along the curb, but I didn't bother looking. "I... uh, got kicked out of my apartment. I haven't figured out where I'm going yet." The admission cost him, and I hated to have pulled it from him.

His words were truthful, raw and open. The shock of hearing him say something so incredibly real to me, opened doors in my mind, flooding my head with ideas.

"Oh." I couldn't suggest one of his brothers with their palpable tension.

I'd always been one of those people - taking on problems and eager to help solve them. The one my friends turned to for advice, and the one offering up solutions when not asked for them.

"I have - had - two roommates. Dylan got pissed at me because... you know what, never mind. That's too much information, huh?" Brandt stuffed his hands in his pockets and shifted his weight, looking as uncomfortable as he sounded.

"It's okay. I mean, we've all been there, right?" Not precisely, but I understood his predicament, and didn't want him to feel ostracized by his current situation. "I have an extra room. At my place. You can stay with me."

"No." His response was knee jerk. A rushed and adamant answer. "I wasn't suggesting you should make an offer."

I laughed and shifted my weight along with the dishes in my arms. With the night, the cold had gotten bitter, and I shivered hard.

"I didn't think you were suggesting it. I'm offering." I was a crazy person. The guy who might be on drugs, who was absolutely intriguing, and who was on the shit list of my closest friend's boyfriend. Yeah. But the words kept falling out of my mouth. "I live in a house up by Early Creek, and there's an empty room. You may as well sleep in it."

"Lola." My name sounded like the start to more thoughts to follow. But he stopped there, with my name.

"Really, Brandt." I tried out his name on my lips because he had done the same with mine. It made us even. "Follow me home and stay the night. Or a few nights. It doesn't have to be a big deal."

"Asher would kill me," he admitted in a hushed tone. Another group of words which must have cost him to say.

"Asher doesn't have any say in what I do." Of that much, I was confident.

"Good answer." I smiled at the smile I heard in his voice. "But the fact is you're Annabelle's friend, which means Asher will want to be over-protective crazy with you, which leads to my imminent death."

He laughed, making the threat meaningless, and I laughed too.

"I'll take my chances." I rolled my eyes and waved a dismissive hand back at the house. "Besides, you said yourself: you've known me the longest. We're practically life-long friends."

"Something like that," he mumbled, sounding conflicted.

We had gone from nervous to fearless in a matter of minutes. Apologies and timid questions turned to requests and reassurances. I tamped down my physical attraction to Brandt. I had become a pro at ignoring men, and he would be no exception. It was part of the lifestyle I had adopted after my relationship with Vincent had blown up. Better off alone than hurting everyone who dared come near me. Better to learn from my mistakes, than to repeat them.

The tendrils of more, wanting to know him, wanting to comfort him, wanting him to reach out to me, were much more difficult to suppress.

"I'll follow you," he said, relenting.

***

I became acutely aware that I had never had anyone over to my house. Since I moved in last year, the only person who had been inside other than me, was the guy who fixed the heater when it went out in December. I'd been in the house for maybe a week, and the heat quit on me. I thought I'd just go without - I had space heaters and a thick warm robe, how cold could it get? I didn't last long; self-imposed punishment didn't include frostbite. The penalty was more of an emotional thing, requiring that I not let anyone close enough to me that I could hurt them. I could do that with a functioning heater.

Relearning how much I hated to be cold didn't help on my quest to figure things out.

The house sat on about five and a half acres of land, Early Creek running along the north and northwest edge. About a twenty-minute drive north of Fox River. Every mile I drove with Brandt Grace in pursuit, more and more doubts crept into my mind. Inviting him to stay in my spare room was a bad idea wrapped up in good intentions. I hadn't even made it clear if it was one night, however long it took him to find his own place, or indefinitely. By the time I parked behind the house on a patch of gravel, I had swung wildly between thinking I was brave and thinking I was stupid. Leaning heavily toward stupid.

Plus, I still wore the shoes that were trying to kill my feet.

"Where are we?" Brandt met me halfway from our cars to the house, his laugh tinged with nerves.

"I told you I lived by Early Creek."

"I forgot how far it is up here." His head swiveled as he tried to see in the dark around us. "And you live way off the main road."

"Sorry." I hesitated at the door, and Brandt stood a step away while I dug for my keys. I left the pile of dishes in the car and would have to go back for them, but it was worth it for free hands.

"You don't need to say sorry." He was hard to read when I couldn't see him. The darkness was more complete out here with no streetlights or businesses for miles in any direction. "I can't wait to see this place tomorrow."

"The light back here has been out for months. I've meant to replace it."

He made a noncommittal sound as I got the back door unlocked. We had reverted back to random snippets of talk without flow.

Awk-ward.

An old farmhouse, the surrounding land used to grow corn, but in years of neglect ran wild with saplings and vining ground cover. The Grace property, as well as my parents', were north and east of Fox River, well outside city limits like this, but without the creek. I'd definitely grown to love the far northwest of our area, and the land surrounding the house I called my own. Mr. Elderberry had already asked if I wanted to buy rather than rent, but I'd put him off signing a lease for another year, unable to make such a commitment.

I flicked the kitchen light on as soon as we made it through the door, fully illuminating us. Then I kicked my shoes off, sighing and stretching my poor pinched toes.

"You okay?" Brandt asked with a mix of concern and humor.

"Be thankful men don't feel the need to wear high heels." I bent and rubbed my tired feet.

"I did once," he said, and I lifted to look at him with bold interest. "There's a walk in Asheville every year to raise awareness about sexual violence, and the men wear heels. I did it last year."

"Wow."

If I'd been a cartoon, my jaw would have dropped open and flies would have flown into my mouth. He walked in heels? For a good cause?

"Yeah, well..." He shifted his weight and looked uncomfortable with me being in awe of him.

And I was in awe. Brandt Grace was a good guy. Despite it all. The way Asher yelled at him, saying he didn't trust him. The rumors that had followed him his whole life. The fact he'd been kicked out of his apartment. Despite all of it, this was a man willing to drive to a city and walk in heels to raise awareness for sexual violence. And to me, that made him unequivocally a good guy.

"I'll show you around," I offered as a distraction.

I led him through the kitchen, around to the living room of chairs, and then the dining room which housed my elliptical machine. I pointed out the utility room with washer, dryer, and oversize utility sink. He trudged along after me as I showed him up the stairs to the two bedrooms. I pointed out mine but didn't enter, instead taking him directly into the spare room.

"It's not much." And looked like less as I offered it up to him.

"This is by far the nicest place I've ever stayed," Brandt admitted softly.

"There isn't even a bed," I claimed, pointing out the obvious and no doubt uncomfortable floor in front of us.

He laughed, and I watched the way it moved his shoulders and stretched his face. I hadn't bothered to put a bed in the room because I never planned to have guests.

"I don't even have a sofa, or I'd offer that as a better solution." My house up to that point needed only to function for me. I liked my collection of squishy armchairs in the living room fine, but they didn't suffice as a bed.

"This is fine, Lola." I liked his face even more when it was severe. He had this way of looking at me that was penetrating. "It's one night."

"You can stay longer." I had no idea what I was saying. The words tumbled out of their own accord. Again. "If you need. Obviously, the room isn't being used, and it might take you a while, and it's... fine."

"Maybe until I can find another place," he said, still low, shaking his head like he knew he should say no.

I nodded and retreated so I stood just outside the doorway to his room. Brandt Grace had a room in my house. A room a dozen paces away from my own.

"There are towels in the bathroom, and spare toiletries too. Help yourself."

31

His eyes were soft and hard, blue and green, intense. I couldn't decide if he was amused or offended by my offer. I spun to leave him, to abandon him to the room with nothing but a desk and a stack of plastic storage bins, which I had offered up to him.

"Lola." I stopped and turned back. A wave of heat burned up from my toes and colored my pale skin. He saw, and I burned brighter. "I'll see you in the morning."

"Goodnight."

It wasn't late, barely after eight, but rather than put on a charade of entertaining Brandt, I escaped to my bedroom. I hadn't bothered with much furniture in the house overall. My room was sparse with an antique dresser, a platform bed, and a small bookcase. My portable record player was positioned on top of the bookcase, and my vinyl filled the shelves. I kept the volume low and cycled through my favorite depressing tunes, the ones that reminded me of what I had done and why I had to keep my distance from people.

Even when I couldn't see who I was, or couldn't explain even to myself who I wanted to be, my music knew. The lyrics of my favorite songs spoke of my soul. When I listened, all the complicated parts of me made more sense.

I fell asleep, unable to forget that Brandt Grace was in the room across the hall and that he had been sent here to break me. I had been alone just long enough to let my guard slip. Asking that unpredictable dark force to stay with me was a darn good way to remind me what I needed to do, how I needed to be, and to never let anyone in.

6

Brandt

The right answer was not following Lola home. Not chasing her taillights into the woods up by Early Creek. Not going in through her back door and shadowing her up the stairs to her guest room. There'd been something about her when she asked, the determination in her face, or the vulnerability in her voice. She wanted to help, and I could tell it meant something to her. Not to say I meant something to her - and I knew the difference - but I saw it there. I wanted to say yes to her, to give her this thing she asked for, even if I knew I should have stuck to my guns and left it at a firm no.

I nearly laughed out loud when I saw what she had to offer as a guest room - which was a floor and nothing more. A desk against one wall and some boxes of stuff left forgotten in a corner. But Lola felt bad about it, apologizing, and I couldn't make sense of that, when she was doing me the favor.

Her tour of the house had been brief, and she'd been shy, tucking her hair back and twisting her fingers. The house kicked ass - a hidden treasure, tucked way back off any main road and filled with charm. I could see why she chose it. Walking through had given me some insight into Lola, too, noting the sparse decorations touched with warmth and color. Simple, but cozy. Inviting, but only to her. And me, after I saw her sore feet pad across the old hardwood floors, and all I wanted was to watch her move.

I'd always loved Lola's simple grace. Her walk, the slight curve forward of her shoulders, the way she pulled her hair up off her neck all the time, the tilt of her head. I noticed people. Saw the lines of their bodies and movements. Studied the subtleties of facial expressions and nervous habits. It either made me an artist or a weirdo, and I chose to think the former.

My hands wanted to reach out to her, as she stood at the doorway of the final room, looking terrified of her own decisions, but brave too. Like this little action was her taking a stand. She'd said as much when I mentioned how angry Asher would be about this arrangement. When it came down to it, I only said yes because I found it impossible to say no to her. With her head lifted and her voice firm, I wanted to agree to her every demand.

Not that I planned to stay more than a few days. I could find a new apartment pretty quick, and I could stay in Fox River, or shorten my commute and move to Jesper. Hell, I didn't need roommates anymore, not since I'd been bringing in steady money. Took a few years for my work to improve and my reputation - the good one involving my tattoo skills rather than my personal one made of shit - to stick. Now I had a waitlist three months out to book a tattoo with me.

I wanted to call her back, to keep her there talking to me, but I had no good reason. Asking her to stay made no sense. Not in a way I could explain.

I spoke her name, knowing she'd look back at me, if only for a second. Her face flamed red beneath her pale freckles, and I got greedy knowing I had that effect on her. With a simple goodnight, I watched her scurry across the hall to her room.

She shut me out, and I couldn't blame her. It had been reckless of her to ask me to stay. Keeping her distance was the right answer.

Right. Wrong.

They had lost some of their meaning over the years, words worn soft from constant use and too much thought. I had too often done the wrong thing, knowing it, and unable to climb my way out. When I tried to do the right thing, it often turned out to be wrong, and I had lost all concept of which was which.

I waited until I didn't hear her changing the albums on her record player, then I made two trips to my truck and brought in all my stuff. Damn stairs creaked up and down, with nothing to do but wince as each noise echoed in the house.

Didn't go through her little desk in the guest room - though she left all her papers sitting on top. I was tempted to flip a few over, assuming she didn't want a stranger to have access, but I left well enough alone.

Needing a shower, and hoping it didn't wake Lola, I took refuge in her hallway bathroom. Not pink or girly, as I half expected, but minimalist. White towels. Toiletries hidden in the cabinet. Almost like she didn't use this bathroom and only kept it stocked for guests. All the guests she'd never had. It was a little weird stripping down knowing she was in the house, but the water stayed hot long enough, and the towels were soft, so you won't find me complaining.

I had a choice to make: get up early and get the hell out of her house before we had to make awkward conversation, or get up early and sit around her empty house soaking up all the charm before she came down. Either way, it would be awkward as all hell, but wanting to avoid anything to do with Black Friday, I stayed put at the house.

Least I could do was make myself useful. After a quick search of her pantry, I found muffin mix. Not one to bake on a regular basis, I read the directions carefully and multiple times. It reminded me of that day last year, when I'd helped Annabelle with the cake. Shit was already on my mind after the day we'd had.

Whole mess was my fault, after I'd scared Annabelle into dropping the birthday cake she'd made for Emily. Obviously, I wanted to help fix the situation: bought the supplies, and insisted on helping her bake the damn thing. Annabelle was jumpy as hell throughout the process and eventually admitted that Asher had banned her from ever being around me. Such a dick move, but unsurprising coming from Asher, with the first girl he ever cared about. I slipped out that night, before Asher showed up, and hadn't said a word. Never would.

I'd almost let myself believe things would get better with time. Asher would calm the fuck down. Annabelle would woman-up and tell Ash he couldn't dictate her life. My family would take a look at my life and see I maybe wasn't as bad as they thought, and they'd lighten up. But, no. Every interaction with my brothers was a goddamn fight.

Lola's house in the still of the early morning was peaceful in a way I'd never known. From the window over the kitchen sink, I could see the land that stretched out and away an indeterminable distance. The seclusion wasn't lonely, it was soothing. No wonder she lived out here and alone. It must have been a wonderful retreat for her, especially after spending days in an elementary school. I swung back around to thinking how wrong it was to be there, but also how right. I licked my lips and tried the words out in my mouth - right, wrong - as if I could feel and taste them and bring them to life.

I slid the muffins in the oven, made another pot of coffee, and tried to think of anything that wasn't my mess of a life.

7

Lola

S ome days, in that handful of minutes before I was fully awake, I forgot. My brain reverted back to what it had always known. The house I grew up in, filled with my mother, father, and two brothers. Lilac silk and ivory lace, like billowing clouds around me. Safety and security and my life going according to plan. A stable relationship with the best man I'd ever known.

It never took long for the truth to rush back in on me. Seconds that felt like minutes and strangled like hours.

I would wake to find myself in the small and ordinary room of the house I rented. Far away from my family and Vincent as I could get while staying in Fox River. My new home was just a house, not my own, but not theirs either. It was just me and my decisions, and I had grown accustomed to the silence.

Breaking the illusion of solitude that morning, I smelled something sweet and warm, and I heard muffled sounds from downstairs.

Brandt.

Brandt Grace. In my house. Baking something delicious. What was this life?

I considered hiding in my room. I didn't have work or plans for the day, with three more days off before school started back up. I had no idea if Brandt still worked at that tattoo shop, or if he'd have to work. We'd left things open-ended, and I didn't know what that meant for either of us. It could have easily taken me all day to debate with myself whether I should stay upstairs or go down and be sensible.

Smelled and sounded as if he was cooking something amazing, and that prospect was enough to pull me from the warmth of my bed, and the warring thoughts in my head.

I was nervous about going to my own kitchen, which irritated me. The fact I didn't know Brandt - not really - had grown overnight to meet me larger in the morning. He had music playing softly, Americana turned down low so that I only heard it when I came into the room.

"Good morning," I said as soon as I entered to alert him to my presence.

I watched him stand with his hip against the brown and orange retro laminate counter, his focus turned downward into the steamy mug he cradled in his large hands.

If I was picking a moment to last all day, it was this one, with Brandt an illusion brought to life in my kitchen. Domestic Brandt.

He slowly lifted his head, giving me time to look at him. Really look at him. His dark hair was a mess, sticking more up and out than it had the day before. The tattoos were expansive, covering all his exposed skin - colorful designs all fighting for my attention, no obvious correlation between one and another, and all beautiful. The colors were vibrant, the shading and shadows provided depth, curving colorful patterns intermixed with black and gray geometric lines, transforming him into walking art. He licked his lips, looked like he was preparing himself to face me, and I checked out the dark stubble across his jaw.

"Morning, Lola."

With a flash of worry written on his face, he finally brought his blue-green eyes to my face. God, his eyes were impossible. If they were a Crayola crayon, they'd be the color Peacock, which had always been my favorite. I'd use it down to a stub, then ask for a new box of crayons.

With an embarrassed smile, I fully entered the room, heading for the coffee he'd prepared.

I fixed my coffee and wracked my brain for something to say, silence stretching until it grew cumbersome. Brandt shifted out of my way, careful that he wasn't near enough for me to accidentally touch him.

"I hope you don't mind I made myself at home down here." He actually sounded concerned, which surprised me.

He kept surprising me. Number one takeaway from the brief time we'd spent together: he wasn't who I thought. Not at all. I loved every time he did the unexpected, and I wanted to stay close and not miss the next thing.

"Not at all." I blew across the top of my mug and spun around to mirror his stance, with my hip against the hard edge of the counter. "What are you making?"

"Blueberry muffins." He shrugged, and his face stayed guarded.

"That's really…" I took a sip of coffee and willed my brain to connect with my tongue and start making sense. "You didn't have to do that."

"Cooking is the least I can do after you let me stay."

"Yeah, well, it's no trouble," I said, realizing I meant the words. "Plus cooking is definitely the best payment. I'd trade just about anything for food."

He scoffed, and I caught his eye long enough to see the worry brewing there. He knew he was trouble, or that he'd cause me trouble. It wasn't a worry so much as an absolute for him. Before I could open my mouth to say anything, he busied himself checking the muffins and asking me if the music was okay.

He changed the subject, and I let him.

The room was warm and full, which was the opposite of how it had ever been before. Brandt filled the space, not only with his imposing size but with his generous baking and his unmistakable attempts at being courteous with me. I had a sharp desire rise within me to yell at him, to make him leave and take his pleasantness away with him. It went against all my efforts at penance to have the warm rush of gratefulness flooding me.

Mouths full of muffins made talking a non-issue. I caught myself watching Brandt chew and swallow one too many times, drawn in by the strength of his jaw and the fluidity of his every movement. Then, with effort, I looked everywhere but at him, to the point it became awkward. More awkward.

"I have to work today." Brandt stood at the sink, prepared to wash dishes, and dropped the information. "I expect it will be slow, so I can take off early and see if I can find a place to rent."

"It's Black Friday," I reminded him.

"Gypsy's is open." He dropped the name of the tattoo shop just outside of town.

"I meant apartments or wherever you were going to look to rent," I rambled. Just a little. Trying not to let old habits run wild. "It's a holiday weekend, and..."

He nodded, running hot water into the sink basin. I wondered how many people had seen him be domestic. He didn't strike me as the type to bake and wash up after, yet there he stood.

It occurred to me again, I didn't know him at all. I wondered if anyone did. Maybe we'd all made up our own stories about him to fill in the blanks - and maybe we were all absurdly wrong.

I knew of the Grace brothers. Obviously. Hard to grow up in Fox River without knowing most everybody, and especially knowing the notorious MacKenna brothers and the even more infamous Grace brothers. Asher and Hudson were both older than me and Brandt my age. I remembered seeing him around the hallways at school, but we never ran in the same circles. He was friends with the likes of Danny Albright and Jason Wakefield, both of which were known drug connections and losers. But I had stopped listening to gossip years ago and didn't know what had happened with any of them as adults.

I was barely hanging on to my own life, much less able to keep up with anyone else.

"Just put all that in the dishwasher." I joined him near the sink and gently toed the dishwasher with my striped wool sock-covered foot.

"Right." He shook his head and shifted gears.

I helped him, and he was jumpy every time I came near him. It proved to make me want him more rather than less. I should have thanked my lucky stars this guy was intent on not crossing any lines with me. I expended plenty enough energy in my life not getting involved with anyone, and his actions should have made it simpler. Instead, I couldn't figure out why he was so scared of me. My fingers tingled, and I knew they'd only stop after learning the texture of his skin.

"So, you still work at Gypsy's?" I wrapped my hands around my lukewarm coffee mug, keeping them occupied with a poor substitution for physical contact.

"Yep."

"Is that what you always wanted to do?" He definitely fit the image, but if I'd learned anything about Brandt in the last twenty-four hours, it was not to assume.

"Yeah." He dried his hands on my yellow gingham towel and cocked his head as he thought back over whatever led him to tattoos. "Hud started getting tattoos at sixteen years old. I was only eleven then, but I fell in love with the art. I used to draw all the time anyway, and I started trying all the old traditional designs, then putting my own spin on them. I was lucky Colin liked my work well enough to put up with all the trouble I caused."

My throat went bone dry, and my heart beat frantically at the mention of him.

"Colin?" I could barely get the name out, and my mind scrambled to push away errant thoughts, as well as find any connection between Colin and tattoos.

"Colin Littleton. He owns Gypsy's."

Different Colin. Different Colin. My breath returned and my heart slowed. My panic began to subside. I swallowed and almost choked, and I pushed my way past the murky memories my mind dredged up.

Tattoos. Gypsy's. Brandt. Focus.

I wanted to ask him what sort of trouble he caused that he was so thankful this Colin guy stood by him through it all. I wanted to ask him if he'd show me his drawings. I wanted to go to the shop and see him work. In all my life, I had never stepped foot in Gypsy's.

My stomach clenched as all the trouble I'd caused flooded my mind and reminded me I couldn't get to know Brandt. I didn't get to ask anything of him. I was capable of trouble myself, of breaking hearts and promises, of tearing apart lives. No matter what Brandt had done to make him think he

41

was trouble, I knew I was no better.

It happened again, as I knew it would, the memories I worked to bury resurfaced. The mention of Colin did me in. A slide-show of images, all blurry at the edges from alcohol, and all distinctly framed in disgust. I didn't remember following him to his car, or making the ride to his place. There were blank places in my head as I tried to recall going to his bedroom or removing my clothes. Had I done it? Or had he? Then the things I did remember, all vivid despite the slight blur, slid into place. His mouth, hot and smelling of beer, on mine. His hands, rough and unfamiliar, gripping and holding me. His face, leering and giddy, as he came into me. My revulsion and the hot tears that fell from my eyes, as I laid there and let him have his way. The word *no* dead inside me, never making an appearance.

Bile came up my throat and I swallowed hard, trying to drown it with the dregs of my coffee.

What were we talking about? Gypsy's. Yes, Brandt learning to tattoo and loving the art.

"Cool," I said a throwaway word, unsettled by my memories, and by our exchange for no real reason.

Back and forth. Up and down. I was bruised and battered from the waves of my memories, and my efforts to suppress them.

I went back to staring at the floor. Brandt's feet moved into my frame of view, his sock-covered toes near to mine. It was the closest he'd gotten to me on purpose, and like a fool, I loved it. I wanted to draw a picture of our feet like that, toe to toe, framed by ancient tiles, and tuck it into my heart.

"Why do you do that?" he asked, his soft voice going straight inside to the deepest, darkest parts of me.

"Do what?" I swallowed, unable to move the lump in my throat.

"Pull away."

Perceptive. Brandt noticed little things, picked up on moods, and I would do well to remember that about him. Another good reason to keep my distance.

I didn't want to explain about the flock of birds in my abdomen every time I shared space with him. Didn't want to get into a lifelong history of looking

42

down either, a move to keep people from being stuck looking me in my odd eyes. Folks couldn't seem to pick which eye to look at, or they went back and forth between them, and I'd stopped making it an option as a young child. I never talked about what I did, and I wouldn't start by sharing with Brandt. So many reasons to look away from him.

"Have a good day." I pulled away, moved far enough away that Brandt wasn't in so much as my peripheral. "I'll leave the door unlocked for you."

Finding the spare key took the number one - and only - spot on my to-do list for the day.

He let me get around the corner and halfway up the stairs before calling out to me. I paused there, unable to catch my breath as if I was actually running as I sought to escape him.

"Don't leave it unlocked, Lola. It isn't safe."

I nodded and disappeared into my room. I put on my own music to drown out the sound of him moving through my house, showering, and preparing to leave. Then I blasted music to drown out the lack of noise in his absence.

It was a mistake to invite him in, not because I believed he would hurt me which was the answer his brother Asher would have provided, but because it rubbed salt in my wounds that had yet to heal.

If you'd asked me if I was getting over what had happened, I would have given a resolute no. I was sure that the pain and my subsequent masochism was fresh - because I kept it that way. It wasn't until Brandt walked into my house - and my life - that I saw how I had let the past drop away. I kept myself apart from people, knowing I couldn't be trusted with them, and I stood proud in my loneliness. But I had found a measure of peace too, my heart no longer aching for the man I left hurt, and my life no longer reaching backward for the familiarity of old comforts.

I liked living in this old house on the creek, and I loved my job at Fox River Elementary, and I liked Annabelle Dare pulling me into her messy life. I liked stupid Brandt Grace with his tattoos and floppy hair, his careful and kind treatment of me, and the way he saw right through my walls.

Pulling away now, knowing that I had accidentally let my guard down, was harder. The pain raw, with an urgency that pounded against my ribs and spiked in my veins. I was a horrible person, and could only hurt people, and could never be trusted with love.

No matter what.

No matter who.

8

Brandt

She was hiding something. Lola Donovan had secrets and shame, and she didn't care for anyone knowing what they were. The memories hurt her, causing her to flinch, and I was struck with a physical need to comfort her. Wrap her in my arms and hold her close. Soothe the panic from her face and replace it with trust.

But trust in what? Me? Yeah, right.

Dylan: Dude, Ed is out. He showed up drunk off his ass and admitted he took your money.

I glanced at the text but didn't grab my phone. Fucking Dylan. Good dude, through and through, with a zero-tolerance for drama. I couldn't even blame him. But what did he expect rooming with two losers? Ed Tanner might have had a better reputation than me - based on his clothing choices, far as I could tell, and the lack of tattoos - but he would steal your shit without blinking. Then try to sell it back to you for a profit. I knew it, and still fell into his trap.

Trust is a fickle bitch. Not one I intended to flirt with again.

Funny how I thought of wanting Lola to trust me, then seconds later laughed at the idea of trusting anyone else. I could trust her. Even with her secrets, Lola was an open book, her emotions right there on her face. I didn't need reasons; I knew I could trust her. But could she trust me?

I pushed thoughts of Lola out of my head. Damn, she'd taken up residence awful quick, and I needed to break that habit fast.

"How you holding up?" I asked my client, without taking my eyes off the lines I inked into his forearm. "Need a smoke break?"

"Hell yeah," he grumbled with a slice of his pain slipping through into his words.

I didn't usually offer a break on a quick tattoo, but Gary had been coming in for years, and he'd booked this one special with me. I knew him well enough to know when he needed to walk away for a few minutes.

Dylan: I thought you'd be back by now. But you took your shit and got out fast. Where you staying?

Snapping my gloves off and throwing 'em in the trash, I shook my head at my ex-roommate. After washing my hands, I picked up my phone to respond.

Me: You told me to get out. I got out.

I turned the phone off and tossed it back where I kept it out of range of ink and blood splatter. Far as I was concerned, he didn't need any further explanation from me. He'd apologize. Probably invite me back to his apartment. I'd say no, if I bothered responding at all. Dylan and I weren't friends, and I didn't owe him anything. Not if he got my damn money back from Tanner. I didn't deal in second chances.

My mind turned to Lola as I finished up Gary's black and gray lantern. It was funny how I could concentrate so fully on both - part of my mind watching the shading I added to the tattoo design, but a bigger part remembering the curve of Lola's lips when she smiled. I usually worked with more singular focus, but Lola had swept away a good portion of my rational brain it seemed and taken up residency.

Guess that shit was already a habit. Too bad I didn't really want to break it, either.

My memories of her as a little girl were full of smiles. Teenage Lola had seemed happy, too, laughing with her friends and never hiding away. But this Lola, *my Lola*, rarely expressed her feelings. She wore a mask, sometimes one with a fake smile, and sometimes one with what could pass as a normal relaxed expression if you weren't looking closely. A handful of times, I'd seen her slip up and reward me with a genuine smile - the kind that lifted her cheeks and changed her eyes, the kind that made me want to do anything it took to make her smile again.

Maybe that's why I fixed the light.

She'd pointed out the light at the back door being out, saying it had been months. Every day when it got dark out, as days passed with me still in her house, I thought about that damn light and Lola home alone. She didn't have a tall enough ladder, not that I bothered to look too hard.

Hudson wasn't home when I went by to get his ladder. The shed out back of his house was where all the tools lived. Until Asher got his own house and took part of the haul to his place.

I'd intended to finish the job before Lola got home from work. With the house to myself in the mornings, while I tried not to think about what it meant that I hadn't left yet, I kept busy by fixing little things. A leak under the bathroom sink. A clogged shower drain. Loose cabinet knobs. Whatever I noticed and knew I could set right for her, I did. If she'd realized, she hadn't said anything.

She'd given me a key and didn't push for me to go. I'd looked at a couple apartments, and had one contender in mind, but it wasn't available yet. Walked through a rental house too, thinking about Asher's house, and what it might be like to feel a sense of home. Had I ever felt *home* before? Certainly not as a kid - I couldn't wait to get out, and my brothers couldn't wait to see me go. Hopping from couches to cheap rooms ever since had seemed like a good plan. Attachments weren't for me, and I didn't need a lot of square footage.

Then I'd put an air mattress in Lola Donovan's guest room, and I'd been struck with a need to stay. The revolting urge to settle down in one place, with another person, and to have a place we'd call home.

So I climbed up the borrowed ladder, and I put in new motion detector lights. Because what else could I do?

9

Lola

What the hell had I been thinking?

No, obviously I hadn't thought at all. Seemed to be my new personality; a personality disorder growing from having severed all logic from my brain and denying my heart all love.

If you asked another person, even folks close enough to be my friends, if Lola Donovan were impulsive, the answer would be a resounding no.

Giggles too much? Yep.

Likes old board games? Absolutely.

Collects vintage vinyl? Darn tootin'.

Cheats on her boyfriend? Nope. No. Nada.

Invites a near stranger to live in her house? Uh, no way.

Not even in the realm of possibility.

I came from a good family. Do-gooders and helpers. Known nice folk. I had been one of them.

Until I wasn't.

Time ticked by awkwardly as those vacation days passed. Nothing could be the same with Brandt in the house. Even when he wasn't there, I knew he'd be back, or that he had just been there. And the house smelled different - like strong coffee and man-soap and something animal that made my stomach get tight.

Whatever I thought I knew about Brandt Grace meant nothing.

He made for a considerate and cautious roommate.

Not that we were roommates. The arrangement stretched into a few days, not eternity. A week at most, probably.

Then he fixed the light.

Out of nowhere, I came home to find him up a ladder putting new bulbs in the motion detector lights by the back door. The one I'd been meaning to fix for months, but kept putting off, because I didn't like asking for help. Not while I was trying to be Miss Independent, living on my own and needing no-one. Besides, who would I ask? I'd distanced myself from near 'bout everyone.

"Where'd you get the ladder?" I called up to him, staring at him in shock, but also with undeniable longing.

I didn't ask about the lights because my heart beat in triplet at his gesture and bringing attention to it would make things worse. I didn't have a ladder, leaving me an opening to a more suitable topic.

Brandt's shoulders stretched his t-shirt tight, jacket dropped to the walkway at the foot of the ladder, and he looked like an apparition. A dream I didn't expect to have but never wanted to wake from.

"Hudson," he called down to me, not turning to look, which left me gazing up at him.

I may or may not have stared too long at his butt - hugged by his jeans, high and curved and making me envious as well as hot. Yep, it had turned awful hot despite the fact of near-Winter.

"Well... thank you." I swayed side to side, unsure what to do or say. "I should've asked my brothers, I guess. Or the homeowner. Sorry."

"Don't apologize." He stepped down the ladder, each foot sure, each movement graceful and gliding. Once he reached the bottom, he turned to face me, killing me with his eyes. "I didn't want you out here without a light. It's not safe."

"Right." I nodded. Too much. Until I made my head stop moving and forced a smile to cover the constant fumbling of this conversation. "How was work?"

Brandt's eyes stayed on mine another minute. I counted the seconds, wondering if it was a challenge to see if I'd look away, or if he didn't know it was odd to stare so long. Then he folded up the ladder, making it look easy, tucking its length under one arm.

"I haven't been yet." He laughed - just a little - barely a sound. Laughter like that makes you want to grab hold of it and keep it. Makes you want to hear again. "Working tonight."

"Cool." With nothing left to say, my lips pursed, twisting, and I moved for the door. "Maybe I'll come by one night."

Cool? Ugh, I needed to erase the useless word from my vocabulary. Sweet and awesome were just as overused. I should start saying boss or lit or whatever. Maybe I'd bring back neat or swell.

Yes, swell, that would be my new word.

The rest? Why did I say I might stop by? I didn't mean to say those words out loud!! Curiosity about Gypsy's, and about Brandt's job there put the idea in my head. It was meant to stay put in my head.

"Come by?" He almost laughed again. A hint of a smile curved his lips as he pinned me in place with his eyes once more. "Anytime, Lola. Anytime."

I swear I saw his shoulders shake with laughter as he walked away from me. Damn it!

"Yeah, uh, huh," I called back nonsense and let myself into my house.

My house. Not his. My sanctuary. The place I could sit by myself and not worry about hurting other people. Or myself. Or whatever.

I couldn't remember why I wanted all that space to begin with anymore. Vincent had taken out some girl from Jesper a few times and talk around town said they were getting serious fast. He was over it - over me - and how long did I really need to torture myself over him? Not that it was about him so much as my epic failure as a decent person.

Maybe that put Gypsy's on my mind, too. If I drove out of Fox River, heading southeast, I'd reach Gypsy's just before reaching the nothing town of Jesper. Small like my town, but without the charm, filled with mobile homes, closed storefronts, and logging trucks. A place made for leaving if you asked my mama.

Gypsy's.

Brandt.

Vincent.

Jesper.

Such a mess.

I poured myself water, adding lemon and lime both, because it was that sort of afternoon, and I had stopped drinking alcohol. When I got ice from my freezer, I looked at the bottle of vodka I kept stashed there. I eyed it, considered whether I craved it, and found I didn't. My gut-check in the form of constant temptation. The last day I woke up with a hangover, I held that bottle in my hands for hours, until I was sure I didn't want it. Then I packed it up with me and brought it to the house I rented out along Early Creek, and I kept it nearby as a reminder. As proof of my choice not to drink. Because I had made my choice.

One decision I'd made in the last year my family might be proud of. One tiny thing in a heaping pile of stupidity.

My phone pinged, and I dug it free from my purse to see Annabelle's name attached to a text.

Annabelle: jam tonight?

Friday in Fox River was for bluegrass jamming. I sat down heavily on the built-in bench seat of the breakfast nook. I could stay home alone, with Brandt at work. Or I could get off my lonely butt and go to the jam with my friend.

My tart water did nothing to satisfy my sour mood. Brandt hadn't driven away yet but hadn't come in the house again either. I resisted peeking out the curtains to check on his whereabouts. My mind did enough to conjure images of him securing the ladder in his truck, muscles moving in delicious ways. No, I didn't even need to see him to build up my infatuation with him. Best not to sit around daydreaming.

Me: yep, I'll meet you there

Annabelle: yay!! See you later, Lola Gal.

I rolled my eyes at my sweet nick-name prone friend. Then downed the remainder of my water, wiping my mouth on my arm afterward. My head stayed fuzzy. Unsure and anxious. My heart kept beating too fast, like a dumb song sped up and on repeat, singing "The Book of Love" by the Magnetic Fields.

Why that song? My obsession with nineties alternative rock went too far. I couldn't even think of a traditional song, like something by Elvis or the Beatles, or whatever sappy love songs were meant to sound like.

Dragging my body up the stairs to my room, I tossed my purse on my bed and pulled out the album I'd picked up at a thrift shop at least ten years ago.

"The book of love is long and boring..." The lead singer's voice slithered across the room deep and slow, the opposite of the version of the song in my head and heart.

I laid down on the floor, pressing my spine into the hardwood, and feeling the vibrations of the song throughout me. My heart slowed its beating. My head only knew the song as it played, filling me with angst.

Ah, yes, there it was, back again. The old familiar feeling of guilt and doubt and self-hatred.

I swear I loved this music before I'd so epically screwed up. I'd been a perky angelic schoolteacher, listening to Nirvana behind closed doors, knowing only they could speak of my soul.

Annabelle thinks it's because I grew up playing bluegrass, with a family highly involved in the weekly jams. She poured herself into the bluegrass scene, hoping for acceptance, which she never found in her family. If sweet Lola Donovan rebelled in any way, of course it was listening to electric guitars, and falling for rock gods with greasy hair. I'd laughed so hard when she said it, I snorted Sprite out my nose.

She wasn't wrong.

I waited in my car, watching the parking lot at the Fox River Community Center fill up, until I saw Asher pull in driving Annabelle's new car. As much as she loved Asher's motorcycle, it didn't make sense on so many occasions, including ones with instruments in tow. We all walked in together, and I allowed myself to be sucked into Annabelle's crowd, while resolutely ignoring anyone else in the old gym.

Hudson was there with Emily, setting up chairs, and offering me drinks and snacks from his cooler. Asher's old roommate Nate was there with his girlfriend Kendra, laughing loudly over something funny only to them. Kendra's older sister Kensie was there too, sitting on a quilt, knitting a Gryffindor scarf, and looking out of place.

I knelt down to hear Emily better as she rattled on about the book I'd sent home with her, and how she'd already read it through once, even though she had all weekend. I listened to her and asked the right questions, but at least thirty percent of my hearing switched over to Hudson complaining about ladder theft.

"Which do you like more, Junie B. Jones or Judy Moody?" I asked Emily, smiling, and already sure of her answer.

"The ladder's not in the shed, and yes I'm sure that's where I left it," Hudson grumbled to Asher and Annabelle.

"That's a stupid thing to steal, though." Asher laughed, but I could tell he was curious and wanted to get to the bottom of it.

"Junie B. Jones. But... I really prefer Amelia Bedelia. Not the new ones, but the old ones we found at the library."

Emily surprised me with her answer, and my heart melted into a puddle of goo.

"I looooove Amelia Bedelia!" We squealed and gushed, and I made a mental note to track down copies of the books for my classroom. The books were all way above kindergarten grade level, but Emily was an exceptional reader, and I didn't want her bored.

"No sign of a break-in, and far as I can tell it's the only thing missing." Hudson was shaking his head when I looked up at him.

"I think I can explain." I stood up, feeling extraordinarily small before the giant men. Seriously, my five foot two had never been so tiny. "Brandt borrowed the ladder."

"Borrowed?" Hudson repeated the word like he was testing it first and finding it unbelievable.

"How would you know that?" Asher caught on to the unspoken part of my statement and nailed me with it, his eyes shining and fierce.

"Oh, well, he's staying with me. Not like staying, but like living with me, maybe. I had an extra room, and he needed a room." I rambled with no chance of landing on the right words to smooth this over. I opened my mouth, trying to explain the ladder, and inadvertently outed us. "Brandt noticed the light at my back door was out. Or I told him? Anyway, he was fixing it when I got home today, and I asked about the ladder, because I don't have one, and he said he borrowed it from Hudson."

I stood there, the entire room a silent vacuum, as they stared down at me with absolute incredulity. Confusion marred both their handsome faces as they took me in, digesting my monologue of an explanation, and figuring out how to respond.

Their first action was a silent conversation over my head, spoken through looks and expressed entirely with eyes, silent mouths, and head tips. I'd had those with my brothers and was knocked sideways with a pang of longing for those days.

"It's not a big deal," I said the wrong thing and Asher actually gasped. "I just wanted you to know the ladder wasn't stolen. Brandt had to work tonight, but I'm sure he'll return it. You know?"

"Brandt is living with you?" Asher ground his teeth together and held in a tight breath, his chest expanding.

Hudson's eyes flicked to Emily at my side, and he blinked too many times like he could erase the truth with the motion. I know he wouldn't lose his cool, not with his daughter there. But I could tell, too, he was on edge about what he'd learned.

"Uncle Brandt? Cool." Emily's smile spread wide and showed off her missing lower front teeth as well as her pure joy.

I nodded but kept my mouth shut. I'd said enough.

"I noticed you're always in the audience, Em. Which instrument do you think would be the best to learn?" I tried desperately to change the subject.

They let me, the intimidating Grace brothers, they kept stiff shoulders and sideways glances, but they smiled and focused on Emily.

"Violin!" She jumped up and down. "I mean, fiddle!"

We all laughed and pretended nothing was amiss. Annabelle got quickly roped into teaching Emily fiddle, as she was an excellent musician, and close to Emily already. She took Em over to meet Denver McKenna, the best fiddler in town, and if his accolades meant anything, the whole southeast. I insisted I needed to tune before the jam started and moved away from the two older Grace brothers. All the while knowing their eyes stayed on me, and their words would surely be about me.

I worried endlessly about Brandt's reaction when he found out I'd gotten him in trouble with his brothers. Would he be angry? Would he want to move out? Oddly, I found that I cared about the answers, and hoped we could resolve this without issue.

10

Lola

Saturday. We were both home, quietly buzzing around rooms, bouncing into walls, and figuring where we fit. Could we do this?

The words, *I have to tell you something,* bubbled into my throat every four minutes. But I never spoke them, my nerve failing me each time.

An absurdly loud knock on the front door brought both Brandt and me to the sparse living room. Neither of us ever used the front door. Neither of us was expecting company.

"I'll get it," he offered, moving cautiously toward the door.

Brandt had this way about him, like a panther in a field, always either hunting or being hunted. I'm not sure what might kill a panther, but he was vigilantly aware of his surroundings and ready to be attacked, as if he weren't the predator.

"I should get it," I offered, moving close behind him.

"Open the door," a loud voice bellowed, and I flinched back instinctively. "I know you're in there!"

I jumped, and Brandt immediately shifted to block me from the door and the man yelling from the other side.

After a strained inhale, Brandt closed his eyes. Only for a second. Then he turned to me with a softer face. "Don't be scared, it's just Asher."

"Oh," I sort of squeaked, and took a stumbling step back, letting Brandt get the door.

I knew Asher Grace. Yet, I didn't. He'd always kept himself closed off, and I'd never been pulled all the way into his inner circle. I'd known him forever as a citizen of Fox River, but I'd also been hanging out with him the last couple years through Annabelle and Kendra. Typically, he was off to one side, friend to no-one outside of Nate, unusually quiet. I'd heard stories, about him and all the Grace brothers, losing tempers and being stupid.

But this? He was at my front door, yelling, and even though my brain told me it wasn't frightening, my body quaked and wanted to hide behind Brandt.

Brandt, who despite it all, equaled safety.

"What the fuck, man?" Asher barreled into the room as soon as Brandt had thrown the lock open.

Brandt met him with a hand firmly to his chest, stopping Asher's momentum. Their intense energy bled into every inch of the room altering the air and temperature, leaving me even less steady.

On Thanksgiving, Brandt had let Asher yell at him, and hadn't fought back. Not really. Now, as Asher pushed his way in and spilled his venom into my house, Brandt stood firm. He stood up to Asher and took control.

"Calm down or take it outside." Brandt was the calm one, the leader just then, the one I wanted to cling to.

I'd be a little monkey hanging on his back, and he'd carry me around keeping me safe. My crazy thoughts led me to think about wrapping my arms around his shoulders and burying my nose in his hair. I shivered for a whole different reason and told my brain to focus on the matter at hand.

Hudson eased in, and his always calm presence diffused some of the tension between the brothers.

"Hey, Lola," Hudson said so pointedly, I was stabbed by it, though I knew he meant to stick Brandt. Or maybe Asher as a measure to calm him down.

"Hi." I chirped and leaned around to see them more clearly, deciding I was overly skittish. "Want some coffee? Or tea? Sprite?"

"No thanks," Hudson chewed the words out, staring at Asher, who still directed his anger and attention at Brandt.

"Have a seat?" I gestured to the smattering of chairs in the room, phrasing my statement as a question.

"We won't be here long." Asher spoke up, a rough grit to his words, "We've come to collect our brother and take him out of your hair."

"What?" I squeaked again, then cleared my throat.

Brandt's sigh was long, exhaling from his toes, and when I looked at his eyes, they were pure fire.

"What is wrong with the two of you?" He said it like he was bone-tired, like he was sick of this shit and wanted - no, needed - a break from it. It didn't diminish the fire in him, the spark which could quickly spread if given the slightest chance.

He was the spark, and his brothers were the dry kindling.

Me? I was the forest at risk of burning down around them.

"Are you kidding?" Asher raised his voice. "You can not live here."

"Go take a walk, Ash." Hudson shook his head, something he did too often when wrangling his brothers and their insanity. "B, get your stuff. You'll stay with me."

"You?" Brandt laughed, and it wasn't the least bit amusing. Or believable. He vibrated with energy and indignation and whatever it was that fueled him. "Hud, no. I'm good. And this is temporary, so don't worry."

Don't worry, it seemed too little too late.

The word temporary became the most real thing in the room. The only important part of the whole messed up conversation. Me, my house, we were temporary. Hadn't I known that already? Hearing Brandt say it sent a heavy wash of loneliness over me. I wanted him to stay. I may not have been sure until that moment, but then I knew: I wanted Brandt to stay.

Asher stomped around my front porch - not precisely taking a walk, but close enough. The front door still thrown open, and the cold December air chilling the already chronically cold house.

"I'm sorry about this, Lola." Hudson directed his worried gaze at me, apologizing for his brother, or for them being there. I wasn't sure which.

"I think this is my fault." I stepped up, placing myself between Brandt and Hudson, and noting the stillness outside. Asher listening intently. "See, I invited Brandt to stay with me. Had to twist his arm actually. Then last night, with the whole ladder thing, I let the cat out of the bag. But we're good."

59

I looked at Brandt, sure he'd be angry this all came down to me opening my big fat mouth. He was still, but vibrating in that way of his, like he could yet pounce. Luckily, I wasn't his prey.

"We're good, right?" I check in with Brandt, hoping he'd agree with me.

Turned out I liked him, and I loved him being there. More than that, I didn't like the bully thing his brothers were pulling, showing up to drag him away. I became protective of Brandt and wanted to make this okay for him.

"If you say we're good, then yeah, we're good." His face softened again. Only for me.

Something inside me softened, too. Pieces of me turning squishy and longing to be molded into something lovely.

Then he faced Hudson, and Asher snuck back in through the still-open door, and Brandt was a riot inside a body.

It occurred to me he probably hadn't been saved by anyone before. His brothers thought they were doing it, saving me, or saving him, from some unforeseen lousy thing. But they made the mess themselves, and now I wanted to save Brandt, and the gentleness I saw on his face made me think he'd never had that before. Someone willing to stand up for him.

I'm standing up for Brandt Grace. Totally normal, everyday thing to do. Yep.

"You guys should go," I said it, but it came out too quiet, and they weren't paying attention to me.

I sucked in a breath to say it again, louder and more forceful. But didn't get the chance.

"Ladder thief can be added to your list of wrongdoings," Asher said with too much snark, not as heated as before.

"I borrowed the ladder. I'm returning it today. Ladder thief?" Brandt shook his head, looking like his eldest brother.

"B, you can't stay here," Hudson pleaded with him. It was pathetic, the way they wanted to tear him away from this house. From me.

"I know." Brandt nodded then, accepting their words, and giving another of those sighs coming from down below his feet.

"What? You just... and I just... ugh!" I laughed at my lack of intelligible words and faced Brandt fully. My eyes tried to say, *don't let them bully you,* and *please stay*, but I couldn't tell if he could read them.

"This was never permanent, Lo." He had the decency to look disappointed as he let me down easy. "Ash. Hud. Thanks for stopping by, but where I live is of no concern to you. But for your peace of mind," his dark chuckle told them what he thought of their interference, "rest assured I'm looking for another place. Until then, you'll have to trust me."

He brimmed with fury; I could see it pulsing in his veins and turning his tendons to rocks. Those Grace boys were all the same, descendants of anger and abuse, and so used to swallowing violence it became part of their body and soul.

"You'll leave here now!" Asher roared, stepping toward his little brother. "Because we can't trust you."

I skittered backward, startled by Asher's outburst, and bumped into Buzz, my wooden bear carving I bought from a man with a chain saw on the side of the road.

Their heads all swiveled, like on the same dial, to watch me scamper and bump and then yelp from hitting my knee.

"This. This is why you can't stay!" Asher seethed, and he'd gone low and growly. My heart had moved all the way up into my throat until I couldn't breathe. "You're scaring her!"

"Me?" Brandt didn't raise his voice. He shifted to put himself between his brothers and me. I could just see Hudson shaking his head again, looking at the floor, and flushed with shame. "I'm not the one barging in and yelling, Asher. That's you."

He corralled them both to the door, using his calm logic and his panther eyes to steer them. They let him, knowing they'd crossed a line, and throwing me glances filled with concern.

"Lola isn't afraid of me, brother." He stood at the door, blocking the space, as his brothers fell over themselves onto the porch.

They called out apologies, but I couldn't hear them for the pounding in my ears. I collapsed onto the nearest chair - the teal one with the big arms and softest cushions. I curled up with my legs tucked beneath me, my fingers tangling, and my head reverberating with the echo of my pulse.

61

"Shit, I'm sorry." Brandt closed the door and sagged against it. When he looked at me it was with kindness and sympathy.

I couldn't speak because I worked to keep my chin from wobbling. To keep him from seeing how close I was to crying. I hated crying and especially hated crying in front of people.

Brandt slid down the door. I wondered if he would sit there in a heap. But he moved across the floor slowly until he reached me. I couldn't look away from his hands, one in front of the other as he crawled to me, until they were at the base of my chair. Then I couldn't look away from his face, at eye level, and so open.

"They mean well." His voice was raw, explaining his brothers to me. "All that was them being nice, as odd as it seems. Trying to protect you."

"From what?" My voice caught, coming out husky and rough like his.

I knew the answer. I wanted to hear Brandt say it. To have him tell me he was the big bad wolf in this scenario. That his brothers were right and I should be happy they showed up to protect me. I wouldn't believe it until he convinced me.

"From me." Brandt's eyes fluttered down like he couldn't face me when he admitted it, and I got caught in the web of his long dark lashes.

"I know. That part was easy to figure out." I reached out my hands and put them on him, touching his skin like forbidden fruit, sure it would poison me, but willing to take the risk. "Why?"

I need to know if they were right - if I should be afraid of him. If I should kick him out rather than beg him to stay.

"Things tend to go... bad when I'm around." He leaned in, closer and closer to me, and looked like he wanted to absorb my touch. "They're afraid I'll break you."

"I'm unbreakable," I whispered the words, my body completely responding to Brandt's physical proximity, my mind sufficiently silenced for the moment. *Unbreakable.*

Because I'd already been broken.

"That's what they all say, Lo." He whispered too, his words a breath on my hands as they clung to him. Then he pulled himself free of me, rose to his impressive height, and gave me a sad, knowing smile.

Unbreakable.

Because I was putty in his hands.

I'd spent a year avoiding everyone and everything, forcing myself into a life of solitude and torture. One week of Brandt Grace in my life, and I was a metal shaving to his magnetism.

11

Brandt

Upstairs, unwilling to leave the house, but unsure if I should stay, I seethed with residual anger. My hands worked at ripping my hair from my head, as I paced the floor over Lola's head. She was the only thing keeping me from chasing down my fool brothers and knocking their heads together.

Her face as she moved backward away from Asher's anger was forever stamped across my vision.

But also her face as she looked at me with absolute trust in her eyes, her little hands trying to hold me in place. Lola wanted me to stay. The truth of it warmed my chest, making my heart too loud in my ears. I savored it, the gift she so easily handed over to me.

Unbreakable. She said she was unbreakable, as if she knew what that meant.

Me: WTF?

I send the same short message to both Asher and Hudson. Because, what the actual fuck had they been thinking?

Me: I borrowed the ladder. I can't borrow shit from the shed?

They didn't trust me. They hadn't trusted me since we were kids, and back then I couldn't blame them. I'd been wrapped up in Dad's shit with no way out, and I lied to their faces about everything. There'd been no other choice, not with a belt whipped off at light speed and wielded as a weapon if I stepped out of line. Not with all the threats and secrets he used to control me.

I didn't lie anymore. Not to them. Not to myself. I wouldn't tolerate lies. But my word meant nothing to them.

Blinking away the flood of shitty memories, I walked to the bedroom door, on my way back downstairs to Lola.

But, no, she didn't need me down there making things worse.

Lola with all her chairs and that rough-hewn bear. I'd heard her call him Buzz, talking to the bear like he was her pet. Chairs. No loveseat, no sofa, nothing that was made to be shared. Like she didn't want to be physically close to anyone.

Me: Shitheads, you show up here and scare Lola, I should...

Should what? I didn't want to fight with them, not really. What I wanted was for the both of them to back the hell off. To not barge in yelling like idiots, scaring the only... only what? *Stop, man, stop thinking those thoughts.*

Hud would apologize. He would legitimately feel bad for freaking out Lola - especially with her being Emily's teacher. Violence wasn't his thing the last six years or so, since he'd taken on the role of single dad. Nah, he'd end up saying sorry to Lola for sure. Maybe even me.

Asher would rather I run him over with my truck than admit he'd done something wrong. Especially when it came to me, his little brother, the only person he'd been able to boss around for too many years. It had been a long time since those days, and the only thing that kept us from ripping throats out was our niece.

We all thanked God every day for the gift of Emily in our lives; or at least, I did. She remained the light of all our lives and the only source of mutual love. The unspoken vow to show up with white flags waving no matter what was the glue that held our family together.

Although, once this incident got back to Annabelle, and it certainly would,

Asher might be moved to make peace. She was his soft spot and his call to reason. More importantly, she was Lola's friend, and no way would she stand for this shit. Fiercely protective, that one. A quality we shared.

As such, I made myself scarce as days passed, tiptoeing in at night, hours after I could've been home from work. Gypsy's closed at nine, and I didn't come in until midnight, giving Lola time to fall asleep. I laid on my inflated bed in the mornings, wishing I had the guts to go down and make her muffins and coffee, until she left early each morning. Then I had too many hours to fill before showing back up at work, and I spent them dusting wood banisters, and bleaching porcelain sinks and tubs; anything to keep my hands and my mind busy.

My latest sketchbook pages were filled with Lola. Her smooth hands. Her captivating eyes. Her wild hair. The lines of her ear, jaw, collarbone, breasts, knee, foot, you-name-it. I'd stopped myself from being with her, but I had allowed my interest in her to snowball. Until I could no longer resist the pull.

Her expression when she'd said the word *unbreakable* to me, and the feel of her skin beneath my hands, it haunted me and called me into action. Begged me for more. I wanted to know what made her so strong. Or what made her think she could trust me. Or the exact meaning behind the word that left me reeling since it passed her lips.

I'd promised myself I wouldn't get close to her until I'd resolved the brother issue. Not hers - mine. Starting with Hudson.

Note to self: her brothers are less likely to approve than mine, which can and will lead to problems.

A knock on Hud's door and a six-pack of his favorite IPA later, we were fine. I didn't drink one but stuck the bottles in his fridge.

"It won't happen again, B," Hud said with a crease between his brow giving away his discomfort. "I've already apologized to Miss Donovan. Uh, Lola."

"Good," I spit out, half-amused that he referred to her as Miss Donovan. "You two really freaked her out."

"Tell me you aren't really staying long term." His concern came out in a harsh exhale.

"I can't tell you anything." I sat down in his cramped kitchen and didn't give him a real answer.

I didn't have a real answer. The right thing would be to leave before all shit broke loose. *Shit* being me succumbing to my desires and kissing her, then taking her as far as she was willing to go. *Shit* being me eventually screwing up and hurting her. I couldn't let any of those things happen.

"She's a real sweet girl, and—"

"And you're not telling me anything I don't know, Hud." I shook my head at him, then let my face fall into my hands.

"You like her."

"I do."

"Well, damn. Little Lola Donovan after all these years." Hudson chuckled, and it plucked me from my thoughts.

"What are you talking about?" Suspicion colored my voice and shot up my spine. My body reacted, set on edge, and looked for something to fight.

"You had a crush on her when you were a kid." Hud said it like it was obvious. Common knowledge. "We all saw the way you watched her."

"I did not have a crush on her!" I growled at him in a low voice. "And I didn't watch her."

He made it sound like I was a stalker, some sort of creep keeping tabs on her. I didn't watch her so much as notice her.

"It's her eyes, huh?" Hud's lips curved into a knowing smile, and I wanted to claw it from his face.

I stood, stuffing my hands in my pockets, and looking in the corners for my demons to jump out and attack.

"It's not her eyes," I said with too much force. "It's not anything. I don't have a crush on her."

"Okay, my bad, B." He looked apologetic, but not like he didn't believe his assessment.

Shit.

"So, you're staying?" he confirmed.

"She asked me to stay." I threw out the truth of it, knowing my reasons went far deeper than what I said. "She lives out there all alone, and there's something… going on. I don't know. But for now, I'm staying."

"She trusts you, man." Hudson's voice turned low then; a warning.

"I know." I nodded, needing to hear it said out loud. "I know."

Lola - gorgeous, sweet, scared of something, Lola, trusted me. The weight of it kept me grounded and kept me in her house. I craved it. The trouble inside her, and the trust I saw in her eyes when she looked at me. Sometimes looking at her was like seeing myself in a mirror - and I could almost see why she hid behind her mask, why she held herself apart, why she looked away from me. It flickered and I could nearly make it out, then she shut herself down. The demons she kept under lock and key beckoned to me.

It was her strength that killed me. The conviction I heard in her voice when she insisted I couldn't break her was the nail in my coffin.

12

Lola

I worked days, bright and approachable to a classroom of innocents. Slipping into the role I knew well, finding comfort in teaching, and in my students.

Brandt worked afternoons and evenings and into the night, dark and brooding, inking skin. A mystery to me, as I craved to know him, rarely letting me catch sight of him.

He drew all the time. On napkins. In his mind, invisible ink from his finger tracing sure lines on the table, on the knee of his jeans, on nothing. It took everything in me not to hover over him to see the images he created from his brain. Once, I was sure I saw a doodle of mismatched eyes and spent every subsequent hour wondering if he had drawn me, and what he thought when he saw me.

What must it be like to see the world in lines and color? I imagined a mix of vibrancy and shadows, but couldn't fathom translating objects or people or ideas into art.

We were, as they say, ships in the night, passing without notice.

He hadn't been up to make coffee - or muffins - instead, remaining shut up in his room while I tiptoed around the house each morning.

Even when I dropped a pan, or clanged dishes, or accidentally on purpose tried to rouse his attention, he didn't come out.

When I arrived home from work, tired and touched with glitter and glue,

Brandt was nowhere to be found. Already left for work. Or avoiding me. His scent lingered in the house, a constant reminder of his presence.

An entire week passed before I saw him again. I'd grown hungry for the sight of him, my eyes were starving and mad to see if I remembered him accurately. Likely, I'd mixed up his tattoos, exaggerated his eyes, and forgotten the exact length of his eyelashes.

I came home Friday night, after a stop at the grocery store, ready for a night of cooking and nothing. Over the year, I'd learned to enjoy nothing.

Silence.

Leggings.

Food piled onto a plate, balanced on my lap, enjoyed wherever I wanted.

I could read, or watch a movie, or lie on my floor listening to albums. There were no rules to my nothing. It was mine.

Growing up, *nothing* had been a sin. Idle hands, and all that; time meant to be spent productively. Turns out, adult me found sitting around with no plans relaxing and even necessary.

Tote bags of food hanging from my hands, I went to unlock the back door and found it already opened.

Brandt.

He was home on a Friday night, and it sent a thrill up my body, like electricity. My fingers tingled with the urge to touch him again, and I longed to lay eyes on him and see him in the flesh. Heat washed over me as I thought of his skin, colorful as sin, and what it would be like to see all of him.

I sucked in a sharp breath, briefly wondered how awful my hair looked, then entered with a pounding in my chest.

He stood on a chair, an old wooden thing that came with the house, arms stretched high over his head, hands fiddling with light bulbs.

Soft laughter shook my chest, to see him once again putting in new light bulbs.

Surely, he heard the door, but he didn't turn, and I didn't announce myself. Instead, I stood there, bags weighing down my hands, and I stared at him. Unabashed in my need to absorb him.

He lost the cat-like ready-to-pounce aura in this position, seeming nearly vulnerable. A slice of his stomach exposed as his shirt stretched up with his arms, tattoos a smattering of color with no menace, bare feet with toes bent to grip the chair.

Finally, forcing myself to break the spell, I plunked all the bags onto the counter, shaking my hands in their freedom.

"I haven't seen you in a while." I found my voice, and it came out in stupid, so naturally I kept going. "Not that I expected to see you. Or whatever. Now you're changing light bulbs. Again."

"Two of these have been out since I moved in." If he looked down at me, I didn't know, because I kept my vision solely on the groceries I unpacked.

"Even on a chair, they're too high for me to reach." I shrugged and didn't mention how I'd tried to do the job myself.

"I'd need the ladder for the ones in the living room." His voice sounded tight, and it pulled at me until I turned and looked up at him. "Didn't seem worth the trouble."

I laughed as he lowered his arms and stood there towering over me, serious about the ladder.

"What is it with you and my lights?" Remnants of my laughter colored my voice, and I watched how he heard it. How he listened for it. "I keep coming home to find you replacing lights around here."

"Coincidence." He stepped down from the chair, making it look easy when it would have been more of a climb for me, with me holding on so I didn't fall. "I balanced the ceiling fan in the guest room, tightened the cabinet knobs throughout the house, and scrubbed the bathroom. You happen to walk in when I'm doing the lights."

Brandt's lips almost smiled, and I almost didn't stare at them.

"You don't—" I started, but didn't finish.

He was right, I hadn't noticed any of those things, and I stood there shocked at his revelation.

"I know I don't," he said simply, his face dropping back to serious. "I have a check for you too, for rent."

"We didn't talk about a price. And it's only been a couple weeks." My voice came out strangled because it sounded like he was leaving.

This was a moving-out conversation, and I choked on it, unable to swallow the truth.

"I found a place, but it isn't available until the first of the year." He was so, so matter of fact. "You know Travis Bell? He has a house in town he rents out, and I can move in next month."

Obviously, he didn't care at all and didn't want to stay here with me. Why would he? Living with a kooky girl? Having such a long commute? No, his staying made no sense.

Still, pain spiked in my chest, and I found it challenging to hide, to keep my face wiped clean.

"Oh, right, yeah, okay." I nodded, letting the string of words pour out.

Travis Bell, the oldest of the Bell kids, had joined the Coast Guard and moved away years ago, but kept a house in town. I figured he planned to come back one day but rented it in the meantime.

"Anyway." Brandt looked around us like he just realized we stood close in the kitchen, and that our voices had dropped down low between us. He cleared his throat and diverted his attention to the food I'd carried in. "Cooking tonight?"

"Lasagna." I breathed and watched him slide his hands neatly into his pockets as he moved a step back, positioning himself at a more appropriate distance from me.

"Mind if I help?" He sounded unsure of his offer, or of my answer.

"I'd love help." I sounded airy, and like I might float up to the ceiling.

Breathe. I sucked in a lungful of fresh air and tried to nail my feet to the floor.

I bumped into the chair in the center of the kitchen, and Brandt moved it away with a million apologies and a careful examination of my knee. His fingers firm yet gentle as he looked at my barely bruised skin.

He didn't take the lead with our meal prep, instead waiting for instructions and watching for cues, while we cooked. Working - having something to occupy our hands our minds - allowed us to find the comfort we'd had together on other occasions. Those brief times we'd fallen into something like friendship and easiness.

While the lasagna baked, we made a salad, prepping and chopping, and bumping elbows.

We stopped apologizing. I think because we both did it on purpose. Any excuse for my skin to have contact with his.

Contact. Touch. How I longed for it, my body called out for it and made it happen.

It had been a year since I'd been touched, really purposefully touched.

The old familiar memory flashed in my mind - hands on my skin, the wrong hands. It had felt wrong, and I'd hated it, but I did nothing to stop it from escalating. No, I let him touch me, run his hands all over my body, and I ruined everything. With every replay of the event, came the sickening truth that I let it happen.

"What's wrong, Lo?" Brandt immediately asked after I shivered, trying to shake off the memories. His fingers lingered on my shoulder as if he could offer solace.

"Oh, nothing, just..." I smiled at him, forcing my lips into the shape. "A shiver." I shook him off, not allowing his touch to continue.

I lied.

Because I had become a liar. Untrustworthy.

My feet carried me across the room, into the corner made by the kitchen counters, and I pressed myself into the sharp space. My brain thought, *wine would be nice right now,* then reminded itself, *there's a reason you don't drink, you lying whore.*

Positive self-talk would be a hurdle I attempted in the future.

"Lola, you're pale." Brandt approached, moving with caution like I might startle. "Here, sit down."

He took my hand and pulled me gently to the chair he'd moved to the other side of the room. I sat where his feet had been an hour before, and imagined the wood held his warmth. He looked me right in the eye, with no reaction to my freakish unmatched eyes, only concern and curiosity. I looked into his eyes as he looked into mine, and I fell, plummeting a thousand feet down making my stomach swoop and my head float. I kept getting swept away by

Brandt, and I knew it couldn't amount to anything good. But with him there, showing kindness in spades, I couldn't remember why it was such a bad idea.

"You okay?" He kneeled down, like he did the weekend before, after his brothers' visit.

I couldn't tell him the truth. He'd hate me. *Oh, yeah, that's why it would go to hell in a handbasket. Me.*

Brandt would hate me like Vincent hated me. Like I hated myself. I couldn't blame him, but I also couldn't tell him. He didn't need to know the ugly parts of me. Not with him moving out in less than a month. I only had to live with him for a few more weeks, and then he'd be gone, and things could go back to normal.

"Okay? Yeah. Yes." I shook my head, then changed it to a nod. "Low blood sugar, or something."

"Let's eat salad." He hopped up and grabbed our bowls, shoving one into my hands and watching me like I might faint.

"Did you sell heroin back in the day?" I held the bowl with my fingers, so tight it might crack apart, and I said the worst possible thing I could think of.

I ruined the moment on purpose. Self-sabotage had evidently become my thing. Of all the old rumors, I'd picked the most vicious one and wielded it as a weapon. Something to keep Brandt from being nice to me.

"Wow." Brandt lowered heavily into the bench seat at the breakfast nook, a couple paces from where I sat in the lonely chair. "Low blood sugar, huh?"

I could hear the distrust in his voice, mingled with the shock. Maybe something like pain, which was the intent. I wished I could take it back, but like all my bad decisions, it was too late.

"I never used or sold heroin." The words came out clipped, and when I looked, I could see the tension in his jaw muscles.

Masseter muscles. Tom Cruise jaw muscles. The ones that bulge at the hinge of the jaw. Making Brandt look handsome and fierce at the same time.

"I shouldn't have asked."

"No, you shouldn't have." He stuffed his mouth with salad, and I watched his stupid handsome jaw muscles as he chewed.

"I... I'm not... I mean," I stumbled over the truth because Brandt was not so bad, and I was not so good, and once I admitted it, everything would be a mess. "Never mind."

We ate in silence until the oven chimed. The room hung with the scent of tomatoes and herbs and tension. I took my plate of lasagna up to my room and ignored the way Brandt's eyes followed me. I pretended I didn't see the smidge of hurt in his expression as I walked away from him.

13

Lola

He left me a note. An honest-to-goodness handwritten note, waiting for me to find by the coffeepot.

Heart palpitations were a real issue as I held the paper with my fingers. Like with the chair, I tried to feel his hands on the paper, to imagine it had residual Brandt suffused in it.

Basically, I'd become a nut-case in a relatively short amount of time. The physical attraction to Brandt made all sorts of sense, but this other thing, it defied all logic. Falling for a man I barely knew and spending time fantasizing about him, it made zero sense for a girl who valued the get-to-know-each-other part of a relationship. I blamed my year of solitude - spending so much time cooped up alone - for making me feel things that I had no right feeling.

Lola,

I'm sorry you were so freaked out - and that it's because of me. I knew moving in was a bad idea, but I did it anyway. I could blame it on desperation. I could, but I won't.

There was something in your face that day, outside of A & A's place. I'm like a moth to a flame when I sense complications, and I should've stayed away from you. You're holding secrets and pain close, and I want to dig in and get dirty from them. Guess that's what's wrong with me, and why I always end up causing trouble.

If you want me gone, I'll go crash with Hud until the new year.

76

~~Lo, I~~ B

He'd marked out something at the end, and desperation to know what else he had to say clawed at me.

I traced the lone B at the end with my fingertip.

This, these words, was the most honest anyone had ever been with me. I'd never known anyone who could admit such deep internal thoughts, to put words to their own mess while exposing they craved it in someone else.

Brandt Grace continued to be a mystery, despite spilling truth as ink on this scrap of paper. Sketch paper, torn along the top.

If he craved my secrecy and pain - I craved his too. I could see the way he wore it like a badge, a sharp pin stabbed through his chest, directly over his heart.

I flipped the note over, seeing barely-there lines showing through from the back, to find a drawing. A quick and loose sketch of an umbrella over a teacup, with a storm brewing in the cup and underneath the umbrella. There was something backward about it, the umbrella sheltering the storm itself, rather than sheltering someone from the storm. A little paper boat floated on the waves in the cup, and raindrops splashed everywhere.

It looked like me, how he must see me, such a mess, all stuffed into something neat and tidy.

Saturday passed slow as molasses until after lunch when I threw myself into my car, and I drove to Gypsy's.

The trip took half a second; not nearly long enough for me to gather my thoughts or the proper courage. The miles eaten up then forgotten as I hurtled toward Brandt.

Then I parked outside, and through the ceiling-high windows, I saw Brandt leaning onto a glass counter talking with another man. I saw him, always a little taut and little lax at the same time, and I found I didn't need courage.

My heart pulled me from the car and through the door.

Bells rang, and heads swiveled to look at the arrival in the shop, but I only saw one set of eyes.

Blue-green eyes, round with surprise and lined with dark, dark lashes.

"Lo?" He barely got the word out, his name for me, as I crossed the space between us.

I held his note out in front of me. Maybe it led the way, not my heart. I couldn't tell the difference.

"I am a mess." I said the words with my hands still between us. "Like you said: a mess of pain and secrets and… you can't trust me."

"Looks personal, B. Take your girl to the back," a man said in a raised voice from behind Brandt.

I paid him no second mind, but I did note how he said *your girl* to Brandt. And that neither of us corrected him.

Brandt took my hand, the way he did the night before, and led me through the shop. His hand was sturdy, like an anchor that could keep me from drowning if only I'd never let go.

Buzzing resumed after we passed, skin forever changed in our wake. I didn't look at the people, only at Brandt, and in a blink, we were in a back room. Angled desks with tracing paper, stacked boxes of supplies, cups of pencils and pens, open bags of chips, and empty soda cans. And us.

He pushed a heavy door closed behind me.

"I do trust you, Lola. I didn't say I didn't, and—" Brandt still held my hand in his, squeezing a little.

"I know. I'm telling you. Because I want to be honest with you." I admitted my truth to him without telling him anything. "What does this mean?"

I shoved the note at him, flipping the paper, so his drawing faced upward. I watched his eyes as he looked at his art in my hand. I studied the lines of his nose, cheeks, and chin, to better memorize him. No longer holding hands, a feeling of disconnect reclaimed the air between us, and I gasped to catch my breath.

"It's just a sketch." He shook his head, and reclaimed his focus on me, stooping to look into my face. "A storm in a teacup, and an umbrella, I don't know, it seemed right for you."

"It is. It's so me, but I don't know why." I nodded at him, clutching the paper too tight in my free hand.

A storm in a teacup. I replayed the words in my head, catching hold of the meaning and the feel of them, knowing they were right for me.

"An umbrella is a symbol of protection, but in this case, it's sheltering the storm." The words came out sounding automatic. "It's reversed, but—"

"Don't move out," I cut him off. Again. Desperation pounding in my chest, the driving force to my words and actions, the reason behind my crazy.

"Okay." He readily agreed. Without seeming to care one way or the other.

It was too easy. Probably he felt sorry for me or was scared I'd cry or something. But I didn't care, as long as he'd stay.

"I like it. Having you there. I don't know why, but I like it, and I want you to stay." Once I started talking, it all came out. Everything except the things that would make him want to run.

It went against my life-code to beg for something I wanted. I'd spent a year denying myself, and for a good reason, then I stood in front of Brandt, and I asked him to stay. For me.

"You like having functional lights in every room," he joked, and I got all snagged in that half-smirk on his lips.

"Not every room." I allowed myself to stop obsessing, and to laugh instead. "The living room is too high for even you."

I made a motion with my hand, his note fluttering, at his height. A foot taller than me, at least.

"I'll risk my life and borrow the ladder again." I got a full flash of his smile, and it made my spine tingle. "I might even ask this time."

We laughed, and my ears fell in love with the combined sound.

I backed up a step, reality catching up to me, and my current whereabouts closing in around me.

Holy shit, I'd driven to the tattoo shop and confronted Brandt. What. The. Hell?

"You are a mess." His voice warbled in my ears, in time with my heartbeat pounding.

He moved in closer. The more I began to figuratively flail, the more he was drawn to me. Anything between us would be a nightmare, a big heart-shattering, no-holds-barred, no-one-left-standing disaster.

And like a fool, I leaned in.

"I'll walk you out." He took his note from me, folded and tucked it into my back pocket, before opening the door.

That's when I saw them all, the guys and one gal leaned over clients sprawled in somewhat awkward positions on cushioned black chair-table things. The buzzing bounced around my brain like bees swarming, and I walked with quick steps through them to escape.

Brandt walked me all the way outside and to my car. He lingered, waiting outside as I drove away. I couldn't remember why I'd gone to him that way, other than his note burning a hole in my pocket.

I only knew I'd asked him to stay, and he'd said yes.

14

Lola

Insane.

I paced my bedroom, contemplating the fact I might be legitimately insane.

It all started last year, and I wasn't keen on reliving it. But the truth remained that I had cheated on my boyfriend. My amazing, generous, kind, wonderful-guy boyfriend. Cheated. Before the very moment the cheating occurred, I would have called it an impossibility. There had been no indication I would be capable of such treachery.

Then I'd moved out of my parents' house - not crazy on its own - to live in punishment. I wanted to spend all my time and energy on not allowing myself happiness. Self-flagellation seemed the appropriate response to my terrible actions toward Vincent. It had worked too, turning me into someone I didn't recognize. The only time I even sort of knew myself was in the classroom, teaching my students. Each morning started with a fake smile, but I could never wholly hide my joy with the kids. And they deserved a whole person, so it wasn't about me in those hours, enabling me to let go of the hatred harboring in my heart.

I'd asked Brandt, a near stranger, to my house. To stay the night. To live. To be part of my life. Also, utterly uncharacteristic of the old Lola. I had been a sweet, loyal, friendly-but-not-an-extrovert type of girl, and definitely not the invite-Brandt-freaking-Grace-to-your-house type. Even after a year

81

of living alone, my decision made no sense. No matter how I dissected the offer, it still looked insane.

The driving to Gypsy's and begging him to stay?

Off the charts! I'd completely lost my mind.

I paced, my feet carrying me back and forth across the width of my bedroom.

Maybe I should go home. I could show up, and they'd love to have me there. I knew it, no matter what, I could always go back to my family.

Did I want to go back?

No. I'd grown used to having my own space. Without a hovering, although well-meaning mother. Without two boisterous brothers with no boundaries. My dad, he wouldn't have been in the way, with his quiet demeanor, but I'd always known his watchful eyes were on me. No, thank you, I'd not be going back.

Should I take it back and tell Brandt to move out?

Speaking of having my own space - it wouldn't be mine if he lived with me. Obviously, the whole living alone argument would be voided by insisting a guy move in and share the house with me.

See? Certifiably insane.

A soft knock at my bedroom door pulled me out of my circular thinking.

"Lola, you up?" Brandt's soft voice barely reached through the closed door to my ears.

"Yes." I swung the door open, stupidly eager to see him.

"I saw your light under the door." He shifted his weight on his feet, almost like he was nervous. "Tell me if I'm bothering you."

My lips curled up into a smile. A real one. Without permission. With a sting of guilt that I didn't deserve to have a drop-dead-gorgeous guy bring me to smiling.

"I was pacing," I admitted the truth because I hated lying to him. "So, you're not bothering me at all."

I sighed, my body sagging as I let go of the conversation I'd been having with myself. No use overthinking things, especially things like whether or not I was completely crazy.

Brandt opened his mouth, clearly about to say something, then closed it again.

Standing there, not running away from how I'd behaved when going to see him at his place of work, and his looking tired, my heart tugged toward him.

"Want to listen to music?" I took a step back, allowing him space to enter, and gestured to my record player and collection of vinyl.

"Yes." He nodded as he answered, and I loved the surety of the word. It did something to me to hear his resolute, *yes*.

Leaving the door wide open, I dropped to the floor in front of the bookcase that housed my music collection. I always listened on the floor, loving the connection it gave me to the music, the way I could feel the vibrations in my body. The sound of Brandt's amused exhale reminded me it was probably weird. Heat snaked up my spine and to my face, but I didn't react otherwise. No use hiding my oddities, right?

I patted the floor, and Brandt dropped in a fluid motion to sit near me. He took up so much more room than I did and crowded my music space in a way that made it feel more full. More alive.

He picked up one of my PJ Harvey albums, flipping it over to look at the images and words, attention caught and held.

"Here." I held out a hand, then pulled the record free and placed it on the player, carefully lowering the needle.

Brandt leaned against the wall, feet stretched out in front of him and closed his eyes. I latched onto the opportunity to stare at him without getting caught. To let my gaze linger on the marbled green stones which stretched his earlobes, and to examine the shape of his lips as he relaxed. There was so much to see, to take in when looking at him. He covered himself with art, not to hide behind it, but to show his inside on the outside. Or that's how it felt looking at him.

"I've lain with the devil, Cursed God above," her deep voice warbled to us, overtaking the room and our souls, while she sang. *"Forsaken heaven, To bring you my love."*

We listened to the whole A-side without moving or speaking. Only listening. And for me, watching. Brandt's head rested back, tipping his chin up, and leaving his throat exposed. His chest lifted and lowered with each breath, and I couldn't tear my eyes away from him - even the simple notion of him breathing enthralled me. I wanted to crawl to him, climb into his lap, and match my breath to his. To fit my body into his, torso to torso, with our limbs tangled. I could imagine the heat of his skin, and it warmed me.

"You're beautiful, Lo." Brandt's eyes fluttered open, and the words slipped out low and a little gruff. Like it hurt him to say it. "Cheeks flushed, and desire painted all over your body. You are so beautiful."

I gulped in air, shocked by his words, and rather than retreat, I inched closer to him. Drawn to him, body and words, pulled to him by some force of magic.

"I could look at your eyes forever. They're the most beautiful thing I've ever seen." Brandt's voice stayed low, like he uttered secrets, and I wanted to bury myself in them. "I've been fascinated since we were kids."

The album finished, the needle returning to its place, and leaving us in silence. The soundtrack shifted instead to be our mingled breaths, and the floor creaking below my knees as I moved ever closer.

"Come here." Brandt opened his arms, opening his chest and body and lap to me, and I clamored like a clumsy puppy to him.

Rather than take me into a lover's embrace, Brandt pulled me to him in something softer and sweeter. I ended up with my head resting on his thighs while he ran his fingers through my hair. And I'd never experienced such a blissful moment of total trust and relaxation.

But he didn't know what I could do, the ways I could hurt him. I did. I knew. The truth flapped bat wings in my chest, reminding me Brandt's trust in me was unfounded. He might think I looked beautiful in my dim room, in the middle of the night, with intoxicating music playing. He would change his mind in the light of day when I told him the truth, and he decided I wasn't worth the risk.

Tears slid noiselessly to Brandt's jean-clad leg beneath my cheek.

15

Brandt

The word that came to mind to describe Lola was erratic. Her moods shifted quickly, and her mouth spouted words she didn't seem to approve of beforehand. One minute sweet and soft, the next lashing out and putting on her armor. She kept surprising me, too. Like showing up at Gypsy's - a completely unexpected move. Then crying silently as she laid her head on my lap. I couldn't tell which way was up with her, and I loved it.

I loved her.

Fuck me sideways, I was in love with Lola Donovan.

The shock of it rattled me, setting me off balance. But it also steadied me, giving me a rock-solid core.

Somewhere between her telling me I couldn't break her, listening to her ask me if I sold drugs as an obvious ploy to push me away, then coming scrambling back to pleading with me to stay - somewhere in the middle of it all, I'd fallen in love with her.

Just like that. Huh.

My hands treasured the feel of her as she fell asleep with her body draped over my legs. She'd cried, for reasons I still didn't know, and wouldn't ask. Hudson was right: Lola trusted me. I didn't need her to tell me her secrets to know she trusted me. All it took was letting me stay in her house. It was clear by how she relaxed when she moved close to me. For whatever reason, Lola wanted me there.

As long as she wanted me, I'd stay.

16

Lola

Brandt helped me to bed, being infuriatingly careful with his touch. Unaware, of course, how I longed for his skin to graze mine. He didn't mention my crying. Or the way I'd wrapped around him like he was my anchor in a turbulent sea. No, he simply tucked me into my bed and slipped silently from my room.

How could I face him now, in the light of the morning?

Pretend it never happened. The chances of Brandt mentioning my clinging and crying were slim. Right?

The chances of his even being down there were slim. I rarely saw him at the house. The night before being a weird exception. *Probably because you stalked him at his place of work, Looney Lola.* Whatever, I'd go about my business like any other day.

Pulling on modest yoga pants and my favorite t-shirt, I trudged downstairs determined to live my normal life.

Brandt, as expected, was nowhere to be seen. After releasing the breath I hadn't realized I'd been holding, I checked out the window for his little truck. Gone.

House to myself. See? Nothing to worry about.

Coffee. Cleaning while I played obnoxiously loud Pearl Jam.

Groceries. Cooking too much and packing it to last the week.

Plain ol' regular Sunday.

But with jumpiness and curiosity coursing through my system. I couldn't shake it off, continually checking if Brandt was back home, wondering where he might be, and hoping a week didn't pass before I saw him again.

By early evening, I'd admitted defeat, and gave up on the busy-work. Flopped on my current favorite chair - the dusty rose damask one with the softest pillows - I put on a favorite movie and let it steal my mind.

Until my phone rang. Then after I ignored it, it proceeded to ring again. *Geez.*

My mom.

Taking a deep breath and steeling myself, I paused my movie.

"Hello?"

"We miss you at family dinners." She didn't utter a greeting, rather whispering her words into the phone. Pain zinged right into my chest, burning hot, and going by the name of Shame.

"I know. I'm sorry."

I couldn't be annoyed with her for missing me. Not when I knew it caused her such pain for me to stay away from our family.

"Don't be sorry, Dolores. Come home once in a while." Her sigh reverberated through me, settling deep.

She'd given up on asking me to move back home. On inviting me to every little event. Sunday dinners were a tradition going back well before I was born, stretching across generations. I knew each week, when I didn't show up, it pained her. Not only her but each member of my family.

When was the right time to go back?

How long was long enough to punish my family for my transgressions?

Did they know about Vincent? No, surely not. Seemingly Vincent never told anyone why we broke up. He let folks believe whatever reasons they came up with, not getting a single clue from either of us. After a year, it was old news, and no one cared. Except me. I knew the truth. I wasn't sure I could lie to my family if I sat there face to face with them. I wasn't sure what they'd think if they knew the truth either.

I'd started this campaign of solitude as a punishment to myself, but also to protect people from me.

A vivid memory of Asher and Hudson showing up at my house popped into my head. How much they cared for Brandt, no matter what they said, or how they behaved. It obviously came from a place of brotherly love. They were a tight-knit family. The way mine used to be.

I'd been the one to break our bonds. Out of my selfishness. Maybe the time had come to stop hurting them.

"Okay," I whispered back, the word shaky on my tongue. "I'll come next week."

She gasped, while my fingers held the phone in a death grip.

"Next week?" Her breath crackled over the connection. "Next week. Yes, that will be... perfect, Lola. I'll tell your father."

"Thanks, Mom." The ever-present *I'm sorry* wanted to come out, but I held it back, knowing she'd grown sick of my apologies.

"I'll, um, be at the jam on Friday, too." I squeezed my eyes shut, my pulse racing to near panic. Maybe this was too much too soon.

"Wonderful!" I could hear the excitement blooming and outweighing the shock and ever-present sadness. "We'll see you then. I... we love you, Lola Bean."

"Love you, too."

Inviting Annabelle and her crew to the jam became my next objective. I'd need friends there as a buffer. Which made me an awful daughter.

"Who have I become?!" I yelled the words at my ceiling, yanking on my hair, then collapsing back into my chair.

"I'm not sure the answer you're looking for..." Brandt's voice startled me as he came through the kitchen door behind where I sat. "... but mature, kind, and strong all come to mind."

"Oh, my heart!" I clutched my chest, breath coming hard and fast. "You scared me!"

"Sorry, Lo." He came around the furniture and fell into a chair adjacent to mine, a little smile on his lips. "Who were you talking to?"

"No one." I laughed through my answer, hands still tugging at my unquestionably terrible hair. "Myself."

"Hmm." His eyes glittered, but he didn't say anything else about my outburst. "Have a good day?"

"Yep." I nodded. Too much. *Stop nodding, Lola.* "I cooked. For the week. I mean, that's what I usually do on Sunday. I have extra if you need like lunch food or whatever."

I waved a hand toward the kitchen, then forced myself to stop talking.

The way Brandt looked at me rocked my world. As silly as that may sound, even to me, it couldn't be more accurate. His eyes saw everything, more than other people, and he didn't hide it. I felt seen, when Brandt's eyes were on me.

Terrifying, basically.

Also, incredibly boosting for my self-esteem.

Had anyone ever looked at me the way Brandt Grace did at this moment? This super casual sitting in the living room, nothing special, moment.

"You're wrong, you know." I didn't let him answer my food rambling, though he didn't seem inclined to speak up about it anyway. "I'm not all that kind or mature."

"No? Could've fooled me." He winked, crossed an ankle over the other knee, and watched me with his cat eyes.

"I've been fooling everyone, including myself, for years." The words spilled out, and I wanted to gobble them back up. I put a hand over my mouth, shocked at my confession. "I... should... go."

I stood, smoothing my hands over my soft clothes and looking for an excuse to leave. Other than my big mouth.

"Wait." Brandt snagged my hand as I moved to pass him, effectively stilling me. "What are you talking about, Lo?"

I stared at his blue-green eyes and saw curiosity and compassion there, an opening unlike I'd seen in him before. I wanted to tell him, to bare my soul and have him see the parts I kept hidden.

"I'm just not as sweet as everyone thinks, that's all." I shook my head, rattling my secrets around.

Brandt's lips curled up at the edges, giving away his amusement at my answer.

"You don't believe me." I managed to laugh, captured by his attention to me, and his smile that lit the room.

"Of course, I do." His head nodded solemnly, and he tried not to smile, tensing his cheeks. "You're a total badass."

I burst out laughing because although I wasn't the sweet girl everyone said, I also wasn't a badass. Far from it. Brandt watched me like he could absorb my laughter into himself. His hand squeezed mine and sent heat up my arm.

"I think you have our reputations confused." I kept laughing, but all I could focus on was his hand on mine, and the way my whole arm wanted to belong to him.

I'd cut it off and give it to him, if that weren't horrifying. Better yet, cut his off and keep it for myself, giving me the freedom to touch him whenever I wanted.

"What are we watching?" Brandt tipped his head to the movie paused on the screen and tugged on my hand.

Ten Things I Hate About You," I admitted, as my weight shifted into his pull, and I fell into his lap, where he adjusted us to sit tangled together in the chair.

Air no longer existed. Or other chairs. Or one of my favorite movies.

Only Brandt's thighs beneath mine. His chest against my side. And his hands on me.

"Now, Heath Ledger, he's a badass."

I mm-hmm'd, and started the movie back up from the beginning. Time became measured by Brandt's fingers tracing a pattern on my knee, then my arm, and in my hair. Night fell outside, and the movie played on, and I swiftly fell head over heels into something guaranteed to end in disaster.

17

Lola

Time slow-crawled until Friday finally arrived, bringing with it my reunion with my family. In public, at the jam, no less.

School days were counting down to the holiday break, each day filled with excitement and glittered art projects. Wednesday heralded my holiday break, and I faced two full weeks off before returning to school in the new year.

I'd picked a heck of a time to reunite with my family - if only for the jam and a dinner - being so close to Christmas. Without thinking, I'd set expectations that I'd go home and visit on the break. When my mother asked, I knew I would say yes. She'd cry, hug me tight, and I'd want to confess my sins.

I'd never been able to lie to my mother. It was the primary reason I avoided her so thoroughly. Otherwise I'd tell her everything, and I'd see the disappointment in her eyes, and I might never recover.

Hiding was more comfortable in many ways. But now that I'd put Sunday dinner on the plate, I found myself with a longing to be in my mother's kitchen. To be surrounded by my rowdy, albeit sweet, brothers. To see my father's solemn smile. My heart actually ached with longing for my family. They'd not done anything wrong, and my shunning them had caused fruitless pain.

Brandt and I went back to rarely seeing one another, as our schedules overlapped and didn't agree. I'd hear him come in shortly after I'd gone to bed, as he tried to be quiet but inevitably hit every squeaky floorboard on the stairs and whisper-cursed all the way up. If he heard me getting ready in the early mornings, he didn't react in any discernible way. Of course, I knew where to place my feet for a silent descent down the stairs.

My two weeks off for the holidays would be interesting when it came to my roommate. Suddenly we'd have more time together in the house. Time for plenty of accidentally-on-purpose run-ins. Yet, even when home for a few days, sleeping in and gliding around in my cutest PJs, I rarely saw him.

I made a mental note to pick up firewood. I'd never gotten the hang of keeping a good fire going, but I was determined to try again this winter. There was something so cozy about sitting in front of the fireplace, I couldn't resist.

Friday itself passed at warp-speed, hurtling me toward the weekly bluegrass jam. Before I got my bearings, I drove to the community center with my Dobro in tow and pretended my palms weren't sweating despite the cold of early December.

Wes and Seth had both texted me nonstop all week. Floodgates: opened. I adored my baby brothers, but they drove me nuts. Did not care they were technically adults with good reputations. To me, they were brats who made too many fart jokes and cut the hair off my Barbie dolls.

Heat pumped vigorously into the old high school gym, long since turned Fox River Community Center. It never ceased to stink of sweat and old sneakers, no matter how many years passed or how many pleasant-smelling events the building hosted. I stripped my coat off immediately and tilted off-balance with the heavy Dobro case in one hand.

"I'll get that." A husky - and achingly familiar - voice spoke at my side.

Finding myself without the weight of my instrument, I nearly toppled over the other way. Brandt used his free hand to steady me, sending heat searing through my thin sweater.

"Oh. Hi." I stared up at him, balance righted, but not moving away from his touch. "I didn't expect to see you. I mean…"

I gestured to the crowd of folks around us, and the environment I'd never once run into Brandt Grace. His brothers Asher and Hudson had started coming regularly. It started out as Ash being supportive of Annabelle and ended up being a fun family thing they all enjoyed. Even Asher's roommate, Nate, and his girlfriend, Kendra, came reasonably often. We used to spend most of our Friday nights at Asher and Nate's place. Back when I'd been with Vincent, and before my world imploded.

"You okay?" Brandt's voice sounded strangled, and it helped push the poison thoughts from my mind.

"Yes. Sorry, just spaced out." I shook my head, forcing myself to stay present.

"Emily mentioned seeing her favorite teacher at the jams, and how I had to come, and that it would be the most fun ever." His face lit up when he talked about his niece.

"Not sure it's the most fun ever," I said through laughter. "Especially if you're in the audience."

"Nope, I was promised fun." Brandt's eyes twinkled - I swear, it's true! - like an anime with literal twinkles in his pretty, pretty eyes. "And food. In fact, I heard your mother makes the best apple pie in the whole wide world."

I could have commented on Emily's penchant for exaggerating things. Instead, his statement, meant to be playful, stopped my heart for a second.

My mother.

How had I forgotten my nerves over my family? Gah. Darn Brandt Grace.

"Hey, what's up, Lo?" Brandt sat my case gently on the floor and bent over to see into my face. "You've got to stop worrying me."

"I'm um…" I shook my head again but found it more challenging to come out on top of my emotions. "My mother does make an excellent apple pie."

All the moisture had left my mouth. The thought of her pie made my stomach tense and hurt, which was not my usual reaction. Because: pie.

Plus, he was worried about me? Since when, and what did that mean?

Speaking of my mother, where was she?

"Lola Belle, you're here!" Kendra skipped up to me and threw her arms around my body.

Effectively breaking Brandt's physical contact with me and ending our awkward conversation.

"Yep," I spoke into her shoulder, my voice muffled by her hair and sweater. "Didn't Annabelle tell you?"

"Duh, but who knew if you'd actually show." She pulled back, looked me over with a friendly expression, then giving Brandt the side-eye. "This is awesome. How are you? Has Annabelle told you about our knitting group? You seriously have to come."

We worked at the same school, but Kendra taught fifth grade, and I taught kindergarten, and they were on opposite ends of the school, and we rarely interacted. Since I'd stopped hanging out with my friends - leaving them to Vincent, which seemed fair - I didn't see Kendra often. She was a breath of energy and joy, both of which I needed desperately. I'd kind of forgotten about Annabelle inviting me to the knitting group. But I had other things on my mind.

"I'm good." I smiled and started looking around for a member of my family. "Have you seen Wes or Seth?"

"No, but unlike you, they're always here." She giggled. I knew nothing she said was meant to be hurtful, yet her words stung.

"Right, of course, how about Annabelle?" I asked but allowed myself to be distracted by watching the front doors.

"She's around." Kendra shrugged and didn't elaborate.

"Lo." Brandt's use of his name for me grabbed my attention. I looked to see him giving me a significant glance, and if I read him correctly, he wanted to know where to walk my Dobro. Or he intended to save me from the conversation I was making awkward.

"This way," I spit out, then threw a, "See you, Kendra," behind me.

Get it together, girl!

Brandt stayed at my side, even after I picked a chair in the mostly empty jam circle and indicated he could leave my instrument there. But he lingered, taking my coat and hanging it over the back of the chair, and keeping a careful watch on me.

Things a boyfriend would do. Naturally I read too much into his actions, and my brain wanted to place a label on what was definitely not Brandt acting like my boyfriend. Still, he did hover in a sweet way, as if he wanted

95

to spend more time with me.

"Pie. We were talking about pie." He stuffed his hands in his pockets, looking down at me, and I wanted to laugh.

"No, we were talking about my mother." I allowed one sharp laugh. "I haven't seen much of my family, and they'll be here tonight. We used to be close, but then… we weren't."

"Ah." Brandt nodded his handsome head, and I took a moment to appreciate his pretty eyes. Even in the ugly lighting, the blue-green shone beautifully, and he had thick lashes creating a lovely frame. "My family is here too, and as you know, we're not always close either."

"Not true." I swatted playfully at him, and he caught my hand, giving it a squeeze before letting go. Talk about butterflies. Wow. "You guys are totally close."

"You remember my brothers barging in and demanding I move out of your house, right?" He pitched his voice low, and his words were spiked with sarcasm and maybe a little pain.

His dark hair fell over his eyes, and he didn't bother moving it away. His hair looked silky, and always stayed a little too long, and I especially loved the way it curled a little around his ears. My fingers itched with the need to run through his hair, so I copied him and put my hands in my pockets.

"Hard to forget the scene your brothers caused." I swallowed and tried not to swoon because we were having a real talk, and my head did not need to get caught up in silly things like holding hands for a nanosecond. "But you're still close to them, and I can't—"

"Dolores." My name said on the crest of an emotional wave.

"Mom." I automatically stood up taller when I faced her. Worn soft around the edges, my mother finally stood right in front of me.

"I don't mean to interrupt; I'll give you two a minute." She backed away a polite distance to wait for me.

Brandt leaned down, closer than ever until his lips neared my ear. Cheek to cheek, he stole my breath and bombarded me with heat.

"I'm sitting dead center, and you can't miss us. Come say hi to Em at the end, and I'll walk you out."

He wanted to walk me out. Definitely leaning toward boyfriend-ish.

His breath tickled my skin, and not hyper-ventilating became my new goal. I nodded my head and maybe leaned in a little so that my cheek pressed into his. When he sucked in a sharp breath, I knew he didn't miss my move and wasn't immune to my nearness. Glory be, I had fallen hard for this man.

Wishing I could spend the next couple hours dissecting the last few seconds, I turned to face my mom. She waited until Brandt loped away, then sidled up to me, folding me into a fierce hug.

Kendra had hugged me. Brandt had put a hand on my shoulder, squeezed my hand, and brushed his cheek along mine. My mother had pulled me in and held me until tears welled into the back of my eyes. It reminded me how touch-deprived I'd been up until Brandt moved in with me.

No wonder I'd become obsessed with having him around. He reached out for me, and I fell right into whatever he offered. Because I'd denied myself any physical contact for too long.

Opening my eyes and looking past my mother, I saw where Brandt sat with Emily climbing onto his back, absolute love and trust in her eyes. Seeing him there made falling for him inevitable.

Behind his group, I noticed none other than Vincent Berry walk into the Community Center.

"Oh, I've missed you!" My mom made a series of proclamations, and I held her hands, noting the feel of each bone and how familiar her grasp felt even to my adult hands. "You're too thin!"

I couldn't tear my eyes off Vincent, his friendly face, his long hair down and collar up against the cold, his tattoos all but hidden behind winter clothes. A walking, talking reminder of why I couldn't let people love me.

Sweetest guy, and incredible boyfriend. We got along well and saw a future spreading out before us. Until I threw it all away.

Flashes of an unwanted mouth on my skin, of lying perfectly still while I let someone touch me, of fear and guilt, it consumed me. My body was hijacked by my errant thoughts, stuck in the past.

I couldn't look at Vincent, even across the crowded room, and not be plunged into the drowning depths of my mistake. Taken right back to that moment when I didn't say no. I didn't fight or try to stop what happened. I had sex with another man, and I couldn't take it back.

The look on Vin's face when I told him would forever haunt me - the trust shattering pain I inflicted on him.

"I'm sorry, I have to go." I gave my mom a quick kiss on the cheek, ignored the slash of pain across her face, and hustled to grab my things.

She called after me, panic in her voice.

Brandt hopped up, gently setting Emily aside, and followed after me.

Vincent's eyes went wide as I rushed past him on my way out the door.

I threw my Dobro into the backseat, then threw myself into the driver's seat. Shivering, I realized I forgot my coat inside. I'd take freezing over going back in there.

What had I been thinking? Blinking back tears, I reversed then pulled out of the parking lot, leaving behind the mess I'd made.

No matter how I hated hurting my family, they were better off without me. No matter how much I craved touch and affection, I couldn't allow my needs to be a factor. Vincent wouldn't tell them what I'd done, and I wasn't worried about them ever finding out.

I knew what I did, what I was capable of doing, and that I should never again be trusted.

It didn't occur to me the headlights shining behind me were Brandt's until we turned north and left Fox River proper for the winding roads up along Early Creek.

He'd followed me, and I couldn't very well stop him when I'd begged him to stay at my house.

Like a moth to a flame.

Only I couldn't be sure which of us was the moth, and which was the flame.

18

Lola

I turned my phone off to block the onslaught of calls and texts from my family. My brothers blew up my phone and I couldn't handle their questions.

"What just happened?" Brandt hurried after me as I stormed into the house.

"Nothing," I threw out over my shoulder, determined to avoid my roommate. "I'm going to bed."

Think of him as your roommate, Lola. Nothing more.

You don't love him. He doesn't love you.

"It's not even eight o'clock," he said, confusion and frustration coloring his voice. "Something happened. What happened?"

I stood at the base of the stairs, hand gripping the banister until my knuckles went white. I didn't look at Brandt, because to see him would be to feel things for him.

Stupid feelings.

"Nothing happened. I changed my mind about the jam." I shook my head, my eyes staying toward the floor.

Still not looking at the gorgeous, mysterious, compelling guy. Nope.

His feet walked toward me, and my body went haywire. Stiff spine, wanting to stay strong and keep my distance. Loose arms, hands falling at my side, wanting to reach for him. Flapping heart, lurching in my chest, and making me ill.

"Don't tell me if you don't want to tell me. But don't lie to me." The edge to his voice spoke of his hatred of lies. His need for honesty. Something I couldn't give him, because at the core I was a liar.

"Seeing... my family, it was too much." I forced myself to move up the first step, then the next, putting distance between us. I told him a version of the truth. "I'm not ready."

"Ready for what?" Brandt's voice gentled, and he stopped with his toes at the foot of the stairs. Eye-level with me. "You can talk to me, Lo. Family drama is my specialty, as you well know."

Trying to mask his truth as a joke fell flat. But I still felt my lips quirk into an almost smile. He wasn't wrong - if anyone understood not fitting in with your family, or being the black sheep, it was Brandt Grace.

But to tell him my family problems, would be to tell him the truth. The whole truth. Everything about cheating on Vincent. It would dash every last hope of Brandt liking me. He'd never want to be with me, and I couldn't blame him.

A small, very selfish part of me wanted to hide in my room and never speak of this again. Keep him in the dark and never let him find out how capable I was of hurting people. But the part of me that lived for punishment and needed to strike out at myself, she wanted to tell him, if only to ensure it would ruin everything. I'd become addicted to hurting my own chances and getting only what I deserved. Which was nothing.

"Okay." I nodded, and descended down those two steps, forcing Brandt to move back and allow me through. "I'll tell you."

I curled up in my least favorite chair - the stiff wing back with nubby silk fabric - and swallowed my fear as the words began bubbling up in my throat. They fought it out, choking me. Brandt sat down, slowly, lithely, looking like he was ready to rise right back up at any given second. He never seemed too settled anywhere.

"It's why I live out here. Why I don't... get along with my family. Why I'm single. Why I don't have any friends. Other than Annabelle." Once I stopped fighting, the words came quickly, like they wanted to escape from where I'd trapped them inside me.

I didn't look at Brandt, but I could see him there. Sitting patiently, hanging on my every word. I could feel him there in the room with me, and I hated how much I loved it.

"I cheated on my boyfriend." I said the words out loud for maybe the first time, and they tasted as sour as I'd expected. "We'd been together for a long time, and we were really happy. And I cheated on him."

My confession made, I leaned back and exhaled. There, it was out, no taking it back. I finally lifted my eyes to look at Brandt and only saw concern and confusion in his expression.

"Oh-kay." He said it like he hadn't understood what I told him. He sat there waiting for more, so I gave it to him.

"Don't you get it? I broke his trust, and his heart, and I... I can never let that happen again," I screamed, filling the room with my agonized voice. "I can't be trusted. I can only hurt people!"

I watched him blink at me, seemingly not freaked out by my tantrum. He still looked confused with a crease between his brows, and his lips puckered slightly.

"Just say it, Brandt. Say that it makes me a horrible person and that you can't stand me now."

"That's not what I was thinking, Lo." His quiet voice changed the air in the room, and suddenly our conversation became intimate.

Just the two of us in the old house by the creek, surrounded by nothing but trees and water, and my ugly confession.

I shivered and wrapped my arms around myself. Brandt immediately stood, snagged a throw blanket and dropped it over me, tucking it in around my body. I sucked in air, smelling and tasting Brandt, and never wanted him to move away from me.

Please, please stay with me!

Gah, I couldn't have it both ways - wanting to push him away and wanting to drag him nearer. Why wasn't he mad at me?

"You aren't a bad person," he said the words in that quiet way of his as he slowly backed away from me.

"He trusted me, and I broke his trust. That's like the definition of a bad person." Tears welled up hot and heavy, the truth too much a burden to share without a flood.

Brandt lowered himself in front of me and placed his big strong hands on my thighs. He looked me in the eye, and I didn't see hatred or distrust there, only compassion.

Ask me ten years ago if I thought Brandt Grace would make a good confidant? No. And hell, no.

Ask me five years ago if Brandt Grace was kind and gentle? Um, no way. Not possible. I mean, have you met him?

Ask me three weeks ago if I'd be up close and personal with Brandt Grace, in real trouble of losing my heart? Not even a possibility!

Turns out I was wrong. We were all wrong! And knowing who Brandt was didn't mean I knew him. Clearly, my opinion of him based on rumors was ill-founded. Stupid people spreading stupid lies to other people stupid enough to believe the lies.

This guy, this incredibly patient and warm guy, he didn't turn away from my tears. He didn't hate me or think the worst even when confronted with my scars. He simply put himself at my feet, offered his strength, and gave his reassurance freely.

What, the what? I did not understand him.

"You told him?" he asked, and I nodded, tears flowing freely down my cheeks.

"You felt remorse?" he asked, and again I nodded, my lips trembling.

"That's all you can do." Brandt lifted a hand and swiped away the wetness on my face, then held my cheek in the cup of his hand. "You come clean. You learn from your mistakes. You move on and try not to make the same mistakes again."

I nodded, but I wasn't sure it was so simple.

"You left because of Vincent tonight. Not your family." He sussed out the truth I hadn't shared and presented it to me.

Vincent's name hadn't been shared, but he'd known. Small town or not, Brandt had paid enough attention to me a year ago to realize who I dated.

"Yes." I finally swallowed the lump in my throat and spoke.

"Okay." He stood up and looked down at me with sureness.

"Okay?" I didn't understand. My emotions still tangled in me, and my heart couldn't make up its mind about beating like a drum or stopping altogether.

"Yeah. Okay." He nodded at me and took a step back.

"But?" I struggled and wriggled to sit up, freeing my arms from the soft throw.

"But nothing, Lo. Don't lie to me. I won't lie to you." The edge came back to his voice, sharp and deadly, but not aimed my way entirely. More like he hated lies from another time and place, or the idea of them. "The past is the past. There's nothing we can do to change that stuff. Yeah?"

"Yeah," I agreed, knowing I'd need more time to mull over his proclamation before coming to any real conclusions. Suspicions arose that he spoke more about his past than mine, and his words held a warning.

"Ready for bed?" He dipped his head but held his eyes steady. "Or want to watch another horrible movie?"

"Hey!" I laughed and threw the nearest pillow at him. Which he caught with one hand, then held as he sat down. "You said you liked that movie."

"I liked watching it."

Ah, subtle difference, Brandt Grace. Subtle difference.

By the end of the movie, I had somehow moved to Brandt's chair and shared his space. Don't ask me how it happened - I'll never know how we kept coming together like magnets.

19

Brandt

She cheated on her boyfriend.

Love wasn't enough to keep her loyal to him.

What did that mean?

Fuck, I fell in love with a woman who admittedly cheated on her long-term boyfriend.

Of course, I did.

I told her it didn't matter, not so long as she knew it was wrong and had a guilty conscience. I wasn't even sure I wanted her to feel guilty, at least not to the extent that she did, beating herself up for so long. Plus, there was the fact that she wasn't with Vincent because of what happened - and whether Vin and I were old friends or not didn't change the fact I was damn happy Lola was single.

I'd mentioned the importance that she not ever lie to me, too - unable to stop myself. She probably thought I was a caveman. But I wouldn't lie to her either. I didn't lie. Not since I was a kid and knew my ass would be beat if I told the truth. Now I stood up to the truth, met it with force, and demanded it be told.

Clearly, she'd been beating herself up over the slip for a long time. Since whenever it happened, which was at least a year ago. That alone told me she wasn't likely to repeat the mistake. It also made her gun-shy in a big way.

I knew myself well enough to recognize my soft spot for broken people.

I'd known she had deep scars, and I wanted to get close to them. To draw her darkness out and meet it with my own. Part one fell into my lap after her freak out at the jam. Next step involved me divulging all my own dark secrets, and that had me throwing on the brakes hard.

I loved the truth. I told the truth. I demanded the goddamn truth.

Unless it involved me spilling it to the person I loved. Lola thought she knew me, and handed over trust like a gift. But there was so much she didn't know.

All the shit I did for my dad.

The drinking.

My sponsor dying and leaving me to start over finding someone to call when I needed help.

I'd been clean for four years, three months, and twenty-two days. I'd been talking to Talulah Summers for one year, ten months, and three days when she passed away. We met at a meeting and were both considering doing the online version of AA. It was nice having someone motherly to talk to, and she liked to talk, calling me on the phone at least once a week, and texting daily. She lived on the coast but had family in Jesper, and I'd tattooed her more than once. We clicked and found solace in our connection. Then she went into liver failure. Turned out she'd been drinking on the sly the last few months. My hatred of her lies warred with my grief at her passing. Suffice to say I hadn't been to a meeting in a while, and didn't have a backup sponsor, and had lost faith in the system as a whole.

Lola's ex, Vincent, was dating Talulah's daughter. Small world, and all that shit.

There was too much to tell Lola. My confessions dark and weighted, pulling me under.

I didn't remember making the choice to pour a drink.

I'd found a bottle of vodka in Lola's fridge. It hadn't shifted so much as an inch since I moved in. Not a sip had been taken from that bottle. Until I broke the seal and poured too much into the bottom of one of Lola's jam jar glasses.

Vodka wasn't my poison.

It worked well enough to send me out searching for a bottle of whiskey. The store near Asher's old apartment - not in the nicest part of town - where no-one cared if I fell off the wagon.

If I was going to fall off, I may as well burn the fucking wagon while I was at it.

***

My fist pounded on Asher's front door, cynical laughter scraping my throat as I waited.

"What are you doing here?" Asher asked as he pulled the door open, looking half annoyed and half bored.

"Need to tell you something." I nodded, gathering strength to keep talking. "A few things."

"You've been drinking." Ash stepped outside and closed the door behind him. "You need to sleep this off and we'll talk when you're sober."

"You inviting me in, brother?"

He rolled his eyes at my laughter but didn't budge.

"Didn't think so." I reached around him and knocked on the door again. Just to piss him off, knowing Annabelle would likely come check on us.

"Fuck." Asher shifted to block me. "I have a cot, and I'll set it up in the garage. Okay?"

"Nope. I need to talk to you." The words didn't slur, I was pretty sure, but they felt bulky coming out, like I had to work around them. "About Lola."

"Just let him in already." Annabelle opened the door, lips pursed and hands on hips. "Our place is better than anywhere else for him to go right now."

My brother must have agreed, because he ushered me in and led me to his sofa. It was Annabelle's - I remembered it from her old apartment.

"Talk." Asher stood, too tense to sit.

"I'm in love with her."

Damn, it felt good to say the words.

"Oh, wow!" Annabelle breathed and plopped down beside me. "That's awesome!"

"What? No, it is not awesome," Asher argued, and I sat back.

"Whatever, Ash." Annabelle turned to me, her eyes all wide and filled

106

with concern. "Lola hasn't been herself for... awhile. No one knows what happened with her and Vin, but she's been a mess since then. I'm really really happy you two are a thing!"

I knew what happened. I could still see Lola's lips moving as she insisted I think she was a bad person for cheating on Vincent.

Not my story to tell.

"We aren't a thing."

Not yet.

"Good. Then it's not too late." Asher moved into my space, ready to be an asshole as usual. "You move out of her house and you keep your distance."

"I'm not here asking permission." I stood, shoving Asher away from me. "I'm here to give you fair warning to leave her the fuck alone."

Annabelle gasped, but I didn't have the energy for her just then. Only Asher. My brother needed to understand that his time keeping folks away from me was over.

"You are way off base, coming in my house and talking to me like that." Asher got up in my space, and I didn't flinch or back down. "You think Lola is going to love you? She's too smart to fall for your bullshit!"

"Asher, stop!" Annabelle yelled at him.

"Do not go to her and get in the middle. Don't talk to her at all, Asher." My voice dropped low, and a growl came through, "I will take you out."

Goodbye wasn't necessary as I walked out their front door.

I took that bottle of whiskey to the old tobacco barn. The one that used to belong to us - used to sit on Grace land, before our dad had sold it to fund his sins. Seemed fitting I should go there to drown in my own sins.

I climbed to the top rafters, comfortable from a lifetime spent up there. Dad grew up working the tobacco fields, never blinking at climbing up to hang the tobacco to dry. Hudson, Asher, and I should've grown up the same. Instead, we made the climb for fun. Because we dared each other. Because we longed to know what it must have been like to see the farm a success. Because it was the best place to escape and think.

20

Lola

Brandt had convinced me to go home for Sunday dinner. Pointing out the obvious - Vincent wasn't likely to show up and throw me off course. Not that it changed my warring emotions between protecting my family and running into the loving shelter of them. He told me I had been too hard on myself, and unfair not only to my family but to me. I didn't entirely agree, but I did come around to the idea of bringing a smile to my mother's face.

I brought flowers, a broccoli casserole, and all my emotional baggage with me.

Then I stood at the front door, like a stranger at the house I once called home, and couldn't decide if I walked in or knocked first. I waited so long my hands went numb from the cold and the weight of all I brought with me. I waited so long, I nearly turned and left a thousand times.

"Are you coming in or what, Sis?" Wes swung the door open, laughed at me, and took the casserole from my hands.

He towered over me, tall like our father, but still lanky like he was growing into his frame. Daddy always said he didn't fill out until he was twenty-eight. The boys both looked forward to that golden age when they'd finally look like men. I always told them that day would never come, but I could see it happening already.

Wes had always called me Sis and only Sis. The name stuck from the moment I'd become an older sister, and hearing it brought back a flood of memories that felt like home.

"Obviously," I said, shoving my way past him, and pretending I hadn't been a freak standing at the door the last million minutes.

"Seth, you win!" Wes hollered across the small house while following me through to the kitchen.

The hub of our home. Where meals were made and shared. Where we sat together at least once a week. Until I'd stopped showing up. Where every important decision was made. Tears and smiles shared for a lifetime. Truly the heart of the home.

Nerves rippled across my skin, and I tried to keep my cool.

"Don't yell," my mother said simply, never raising her own voice, and continued stirring whatever she had on the stove. "I'm glad you came, Dolores."

"Ha. Told you!" Seth bounded into the room, barefoot and looking younger than his twenty years. Like a gangly teenager still. Just the way I left him. "Hey, Sis."

Seth wrapped me into a fierce hug, squeezing the breath from my lungs, and making it hard to keep hold of the flowers in my hand.

"Hey, Sethy."

Someone took the flowers from me, leaving my hands free to fold around my little brother. He'd always been the hugger of the family - the most sensitive and the most affectionate. He held me a long time, soaking me in like he might not get the chance again. My hands found his wing-like shoulder blades and held him tight, just as worried the moment would be fleeting.

When he let me go, I saw what looked like fear in his eyes. Wide brown eyes reflecting a well of feelings at me. I held his hand and tried to offer what comfort I could. A weak promise to not ignore him anymore.

He had our mother's brown eyes. Wes had our daddy's blue. Me, I had both. One of each, which my parents called a blessing, and brothers called freaky. Sometimes I forgot they didn't match.

"What did you win?" My chin wobbled as I asked, but we all ignored it.

"Wes bet you wouldn't show up." Seth shrugged like it didn't matter when we all knew it did.

Pain pressed hard into my chest and forced my heart to work at beating.

"It's a week of chores, nothing I can't handle." Wes laughed it off.

"Wes, get a vase for the flowers." Our mother stood still like if she moved, the spell would be broken, and I'd disappear. She held the bouquet in one hand and offered them to my brother.

"Yes, ma'am." He took them and set to work.

Silence fell heavy, as we all settled into this new reality. My being there became awkward, and I itched to run. Although part of me wanted nothing more than to fall to the floor and kiss the old hardwood I'd grown up on. The dichotomy of emotions tried to rip me apart.

"Where's Daddy?" I busied myself putting my casserole in the oven to warm and trying my darnedest to act normal.

"Fox got three chickens last night," Seth announced, bouncing on the balls of his feet and craning his head to look out the back window. "He's fixing the fence, or hunting the fox."

"He'll be in shortly," my mother offered in her soft southern drawl.

She grew up in a town smaller than Fox River, and her accent held slightly different tones and lilts than ours. It came out in a few of my words, passed down from her mouth to mine.

"Sure is good to have you here, Sis." Wes set the vase of flowers at the center of the old table, twisting them this way and that. "Why'd you run off on Friday?"

"Oh, I…" My departure from the jam flashed in my mind, making my palms sweat.

"Don't, you two," Mom softly scolded my brothers, waving off their questions.

"Okay, okay," Wes said, rolling his eyes behind her turned back, then giving me a silly grin. Twenty-three years old and the same as he ever was. "But is it true Brandt Grace is living with you?"

Our mother sucked in a breath but didn't respond otherwise. I couldn't tell if she reacted to the question or the possible answer.

"Um, yeah, that is true." I nodded and grabbed hold of the nearest chair-back for balance. "He needed a place to stay, and I have a spare room."

I smiled and played it off as no big deal. But the air in the room changed, and I could tell it would, in fact, be a big deal to my brothers.

"You can't be serious!" Wes wailed at me, half annoyed and half mad.

"Sis, he's like a drug dealer," Seth whisper-yelled at me.

"He is not! You two shouldn't listen to gossip. Geez." My turn to roll my eyes. I also cast them a pointed glare, silently begging them to drop the subject.

"Boys, leave your sister alone about this," Mom urged, her tone getting serious.

Then my daddy walked through the back door, lumbering in out of the cold, wearing the same old overalls as always, and giving us all a nod as greeting.

Michael Donovan was a quiet man. Large in stature, with a strong jawline and a penetrating gaze. I used to think he could see through to my soul and know all my deepest secrets. He didn't say much, and I loved that about him. The way he sat back and took everything in, rather than filling a space with unnecessary talk. He fixed cars and raised cows. He played upright bass and taught us all how to make music on any instrument we picked up. His lap was the safest place in the whole world - back when I used to fit there.

I watched as he toed his boots off, went to the sink to wash his hands, then leaned into my mother's space to kiss the top of her head. Their love was the compass by which I had navigated my life.

Until I veered so far off course, I knew I'd never find my way back.

Wes and Seth asked a hundred questions about the chickens and promised to hunt down the fox after supper. Which meant Wes would carry a gun, but not shoot it, and Seth would lobby for taking the fox in as a pet. They weren't hunters, either one of them, and left that part of our lives to Daddy.

"Boys, wash up, and set the table," Mom said, still avoiding looking directly at me.

"I'll set the table," I offered, and pushed my way to the sink first, snickering at my brothers as they glared at me.

Goody-goody, one of them whispered. They'd always told me I was a no-good suck-up and a goody-goody. They hadn't been wrong. I'd always wanted my parents to think the best of me, and always strived to earn it. You know, until I'd thrown it all away. Not that they knew what I'd done. But I knew, and it changed too much to ever be their good girl again.

The familiarity of pulling plates from the cabinets, utensils from the drawers, and napkins from the basket in the pantry, calmed my nerves.

You can do this, Lola.

As long as they didn't bring up Brandt. Again.

Or Vincent.

Or the epic failure of my personal life.

My phone chimed, and I ignored it, knowing the no-phones-at-the-table rule.

We held hands around the table, Daddy said a few words of grace and thanks, and I tumbled to a place of gratitude. Something I'd been missing the last year. A comforting sense of being thankful for family, home, and life.

I swiped tears from my eyes as we settled into eating. I listened to Wes's stories from being the Fox River sober ride, offering his services to anyone and everyone. Seth had gotten in on the business too, and together they'd built something. We might not have taxis or Uber in our town, but we had the Donovan brothers, and that was even better. The folks who'd made fun of Wes had begun to respect him as soon as they needed him.

They asked about my job, and we danced around the topic of Christmas.

Time trickled by, moving faster the more I tried to catch hold of it.

Until dinner came to an end, the dishes were washed by a set of unruly brothers, and my mother pulled me out to the porch to talk.

***

She might have said we were having a sip of brandy, but we both knew it was an excuse to talk. To have a few moments away from the others to see if we could bridge our lost connection.

I'd accepted the small splash of syrupy liquid in the ancient little glass passed down through generations. I held it and wondered if I should drink it to be polite, knowing that such a small amount wouldn't get me drunk. Also knowing the vow I'd made to stop drinking, out of concern for my body and mind, and knowing how quickly it could become a crutch for me. Something I'd use to erase my thoughts and feelings.

I lowered myself onto the worn slats of the front porch swing. It creaked softly, and my feet automatically pushed to sway me back and forth. I used to sit on that swing for hours at a time. Sitting, laying. Laughing, crying. Reading, writing. If the kitchen was the heart, the swing was a hand holding mine.

My mother looked thin but had strong muscles roping her bones. Her mostly gray hair hung thick and straight around her makeup free face. She had never encouraged nor discouraged me from makeup, simply said it wasn't for her and claimed she didn't have the time to devote to it. I could remember her face with fewer lines but loved the evidence of laughter and concern etched on her face.

"Tell me about this Grace boy," she stated with no pre-amble.

"Brandt. He's the youngest one," I said, and she nodded, already knowing that small fact. "He's not like everyone says."

I came to his defense automatically, as a reflex. Even if I didn't know him well - yet. And even if I didn't know if we were friends or becoming more, I couldn't bear having anyone judge him.

"I didn't say he was, Dolores." Her smile shone despite her eyes being unwavering and hard. "I simply want to know more about him and your living situation. I worry about you."

I explained about Thanksgiving - leaving out the more colorful parts of the story - and how Brandt ended up living in my house.

"It's been nice having him there," I tried to explain. "So I asked him to stay."

"Folks in town are talking." She lifted her brows at me.

"You taught me not to listen," I volleyed back at her.

"I did. Doesn't stop others from listening." She cocked her head to the side, swirled the tiny pour of brandy in her glass, and waited for me to catch her meaning.

"I'm not worried about my reputation, Mom." I shrugged because although I did care in some ways, it had nothing to do with Brandt Grace. I had much worse things to destroy my good name.

"And you're aware of his?" She leveled me with a look, then drained her glass.

I held my glass with the tiny pour of brandy, but I didn't take a single sip. My fingers clutched at that glass like a lifeline, like if I could only prove I didn't want the drink, I could also prove I was stronger than they thought. Than I thought.

And I didn't want it. I'd lost my taste for alcohol. For losing control.

"You always said to judge a person based on how they treat me. Brandt has been nothing but nice to me." Nice for lack of a better word.

Queue the blood rushing to my cheeks.

"You like him." My mother, quickly reading me, sat back in her chair, giving in to what she was learning in this conversation.

"I do." I set my glass on the porch floor, and picked at the sleeves of my thermal shirt, pulling them over my hands, and fighting my desire to run away.

"We used to talk about these things." Her voice lowered, sadness seeping through. "I don't want to press you or push you away. I just miss you, baby girl."

"I miss you, too." My voice wavered, and tears pressed hot behind my eyes. "And I like him. A lot. Even though I think I shouldn't."

She smiled as tears slipped from her eyes, and I gave up the fight and let mine fall too.

"Bring him to dinner next week. For Christmas, or the following Sunday. Let us meet him and form our own opinions." My mother's face showed a bit of a concern but mostly hope.

She said Sunday like sun-dee, in that way of hers, letting the Southern slip through.

I nodded without giving her a reply. Maybe I'd convince Brandt to come with me. Maybe I'd hide him away and keep him for myself. Maybe he'd move out, and my feelings for him would amount to nothing. Maybe he was the one, and we'd prove everyone wrong.

On my way to my car, I checked the missed texts on my phone.

Annabelle: Call me as soon as you can. Brandt showed up to confront Asher, and it got ugly. Then B took off, and I'm worried for him. I think he's been drinking. Did he go back to your place? A is pretending he doesn't care, but he's pacing and keeps calling. I still don't know all the Grace boy secrets, but I know Brandt came over here today to get Asher off his back about YOU.

Oh, wow, and double wow.

Too many feelings at once left me reeling.

I'd fallen asleep lying against Brandt, more than once, and could too clearly recall the smell and warmth of him. The way my heart bounced when I merely thought about him was a dead giveaway to how much I liked him. My brain couldn't even get on board to navigate my emotions, because it worked to make sense of the message from Annabelle.

He could be back at my house - our house - for sure. Or where else? I didn't know where Brandt went to cool off.

I read and re-read her text several times. It had been over an hour since she sent it, and I had two missed calls from her too.

No answers to offer, I went to respond anyway and explain my delay. Meanwhile, my mind churned through possible places I could find Brandt.

"Dolores." My father's voice startled me, and I shoved my phone in my back pocket. "A minute?"

"Of course, Daddy." I gave him my full attention, craning to look up at his face. More etched than Mom's, and with far more evidence of worry than laughter.

"You don't have to tell me what happened. It doesn't matter." He meant it, too, easily able to forgive me without knowing any details. "I will ask that you come 'round more often. Your mother cries over you, and I can't stand seeing her upset."

"Yes, sir." I nodded and swallowed the rise of emotion in my throat. "I'm sorry."

"You've said sorry near 'bout enough times now." He said the words quietly, and I got the message loud and clear.

Sorry wasn't enough. It didn't fix the pain I'd caused. Time to step up and make things right.

"I'll… try." The word try wasn't enough either. "I mean, I will. I'll come home more."

It was as good as a promise, and it soothed the frown off my father's face.

"Come here." He put out an arm and invited me into his chest.

Nothing compared to my father holding me in an embrace. My ear at his heart, I listened to the steady beat and remembered a lifetime of finding comfort from this strong man. He gave it to me freely, and I could've stayed forever.

Except for the gnawing worry that something terrible happened to Brandt. I didn't know the Grace boy secrets either, but I knew Brandt had darkness in him, and that his reputation for trouble came from somewhere, and that I cared deeply for him.

"I have to go, Daddy." I placed my hand on his chest as I leaned away, to soak up another couple beats of his heart. "But I'll be back soon."

He gave me a rare smile and tucked me into my car. I didn't bother texting Annabelle, instead rushing back to my house to start my search for Brandt.

21

Lola

I threw the door open, knowing I'd find the house abandoned. Brandt's truck wasn't in the drive, and I shouldn't have bothered going in, knowing I'd find nothing.

"Brandt!" I hollered without much hope and ran up the stairs to check his bedroom.

Nothing but an air mattress on the floor, covered by a tangle of sheets, and a few personal items. Jeans tossed over the chair beside the small desk I'd put in the room but rarely used. A stack of sketchbooks, a collection of pencils and erasers, and what looked like watercolor paints. Tempted to intrude and look through his things, I turned and left the room.

Where would he be?

I finally called Annabelle back.

"Hey, Lola. You okay?" She sounded breathless and worried.

"I'm fine, but Brandt isn't at the house." I rushed down the stairs and out the back door to my car. "Does Asher have any ideas where I can find him?"

"We know he's not with Hud, and not at Gypsy's." Annabelle kept her voice low, and I could hear Asher asking questions in the background. "Otherwise, I don't know."

"What's the deal with Asher and Brandt?" I started my car, then backed hastily around to face the driveway head-on. "If he's so worried, why isn't he out looking?"

I shouldn't have asked. No need for me to cause more trouble. Staying out of it would have been the smarter course. But worry obliterated reason.

Annabelle sighed. "I don't know. Honestly." A door closed on her end, and her boyfriend's voice no longer echoed in the background. "All I know is Ash has always warned me to stay away from Brandt. And that Brandt was over here telling us how much he... likes you. Warning Asher to back off."

"Whoa, that's... okay, I don't know what that is," I bellowed and turned onto the road toward town proper. "I want details on exactly what he said, but not right now. I'm too worried."

"Check Side Door," Annabelle said to me, then called out to Asher that she'd be out in a minute. "Remember when that creep Danny was there, and he said something about a past with Brandt. Or Asher said that. But either way, maybe that means something?"

"You are grasping at straws! But I'll be there in ten minutes." I let out a long sigh, balanced the phone and steering my car, and tried to tamp down the growing panic inside me. "I have a bad feeling, Annabelle."

"Me too, sweetie."

"I'll keep you posted." After ending the call, I tossed my phone to the passenger seat and pointed myself toward Side Door.

Danny. Yep, I remembered him. Creep defined him well, unfortunately. He'd come on strong to Annabelle, despite her blatant disinterest, and put us in an awkward position. Thankfully Asher had shown up and put an end to the situation before anything truly awful occurred.

A shiver ran down my spine as I remember the sneer on ol' Danny's face as he moved in closer and closer to Annabelle. I'd tried to distract him but couldn't figure out what else to do. I hated that sense of weakness that came from unwanted attention.

I threw my car into park and quickly hopped out of my car. My heart beat too fast and propelled me into Side Door.

Too bad I hadn't called Haley to join me. She worked at Side Door back in the day and knew the owner. But Haley and I hadn't talked in ages. Hardly at all in the last year since Vincent and I split up. Far as I knew she was still with her boyfriend Dylan, and they still hung out with Vin.

I shook loose the thoughts of my past and looked all around the dive bar. Barstools. Pool tables. Jukebox. No Brandt.

"Can I help you?"

"Maybe?" I turned to face the guy holding a tray of drinks. "I'm looking for... a friend."

I continued to scan the room, not finding Brandt in the thin crowd. Sunday evening wasn't a busy time at Side Door. Or anywhere in Fox River.

"Who might that be?" The man looked at me while still balancing his tray, and I didn't see a trace of flirtation there.

Thank goodness.

"Brandt Grace. Have you seen him?" I stared up at the waiter's face and saw the flash of surprise there.

"No, I haven't seen him. In fact" —the guy leaned down and lowered his voice— "he hasn't been in here since he stopped drinking. That was a few years back, darlin'."

Brandt didn't drink? I guess that made sense - it's not like I'd seen him have a drink. The news still came as a surprise. Annabelle's text had said he was drinking.

"Okay, cool." I searched for my phone, only to remember I left it in my car. "Thanks."

After sliding into the driver's seat, I pulled up Annabelle's message. It read: *I think he's been drinking.*

Thinks. Not knows.

Frustration joined with worry inside me, making my palms sweat, and obliterating any last bit of rational in me.

I pointed my car toward Prissy Polly's. Just in case. Then my phone rang the most annoying ring tone ever created. The one I assigned to my brother Wes.

"Hello?" I shoved the phone between my shoulder and my jaw, freeing up my hands to steer.

"Hey, Sis. Listen, I need to tell you something." Wes sounded nervous. The same strain in his voice as when he'd confess to breaking something of mine.

"What?" I only barely kept from screaming at him. I didn't have time for

Wes telling me I'd made Mom cry or whatever else.

"It's about Brandt." Wes cleared his throat. "He needs a ride. You know, from… me."

I pulled my car to the side of the road. Yanked it actually. My mind imploding at the turn this call had taken. Wes the town sober-ride only got requests for one reason.

"I'm sorry, what?" I sounded gruff and frantic. Same as I felt. It didn't occur to me to hide my cards before I gave them away altogether.

"His brother called me. Hudson. Said Brandt was… um, drinking, and needed a ride home. I thought you'd want to know." Wes felt guilty about relaying the information. I could tell.

"Where is he?" I already knew he wasn't with Hudson. Never mind the fact Brandt would never show up drunk around his niece, Emily. No way.

"Out at the old tobacco barn." He said it tuh-back-uh, the way we all did, his North Carolina roots showing through. "It's way back behind their house, falling over, and not even on their property."

I knew what he meant. The Grace's had owned hundreds of acres at one time before their father had sold it all off to fuel his habits. Some said liquor. Others said gambling. I didn't rightly know for sure. Only that Hudson owned the house and the one-acre surrounding, and not including any barns. Annabelle had said Brandt wasn't at Hudson, then it was Hudson who called Wes. What an epic mess.

"I'll go, Wes." I pulled back onto the road and re-routed myself back toward my parents' house and toward the old Grace land. "Thank you."

"Sis." Wes sighed, and I braced myself for what he might say next. "This isn't the first time, and he's… well, I think you should leave this to me."

"No." I shook my head, nearly dislodging my phone, and sped through town. "I've got this."

For the next ten miles, I convinced my brother to let me show up at the old tobacco barn. The only condition being that Wes would let Hudson know it would be me instead of him.

***

I took the rarely-used gravel path to the barn on the acreage behind

Hudson's house. Bumping over rocks, into potholes, and over the thick layer of fall leaves that had found their way to the low spot along the land. My tires in ruts as I steered through the valley, around the next hill, and to the flattest place around. The barn tilted precariously to the left, and I worried it would fall over with the next wind.

I parked to the right, just in case.

Fear bunched up in my stomach. I couldn't be sure what I would find, having never seen a drunk Brandt.

He has that reputation for a reason. I had heard enough times since inviting Brandt into my house. The words were easier to ignore when I wasn't walking into a dilapidated barn to confront a possibly drunk man.

"Brandt?" I called out as I pushed through the crooked door.

It smelled of hay and rot, and I heard a meow come from out of sight. That's good, a cat to catch the mice, meaning I didn't need to worry. Yep.

Night had fallen outside, plunging the landscape into darkness, but a small light caught my eye as soon as I entered the old barn. Way up high along the rafters where they used to hang the tobacco to dry.

The walls did a well enough job of blocking the wind, but I shivered in the cold of the night despite myself.

"Go home, Lo," came from above.

I shouldn't have been able to hear his low voice, but it carried to me and hit me smack in the chest.

"If you come with me," I called back up to him, squinting my eyes to see his position more clearly. His legs dangled from where he sat on a high beam.

"I can't." The sadness weighing his voice reached me and nearly pushed me down. "They were right."

"About what?" I moved toward the only ladder I saw - strips of wood nailed to the wall. They held Brandt, so they'll hold me, I told myself as I pressed my toes into the first narrow step.

"Me. You. Everything."

I focused on moving my hands and feet up the ladder, rather than trying to look at Brandt.

"No." Halfway to the first level of beams. "I don't believe that, Brandt."

"You don't know me." More volume in his words told how important he found that fact.

"Then let me know you." I kept climbing until I looked down and ended up clinging to the rough wood of the wall and the stupid non-steps. "I'm... I'm coming up."

Don't look down.

I looked over my shoulder and up to where Brandt sat beside a small flashlight pointed up to the ceiling. Dizziness swept over me, and my dinner pressed up into my throat. My fingers clenched as tight as they could to the old wood and laid my head against the wall to still the spinning.

Don't look up.

"Dammit, Lo." Brandt began to move, hauling himself to standing. "It's not safe up here."

"You're up there!" I yelled up at him, wishing fear hadn't stilled my movements and frozen me to the wall.

A light slur to his words indicated a certain level of intoxication. I couldn't tell how drunk he might be, and I wasn't asking.

"Shit." The flashlight tumbled to the dusty floor below us, dimming everything except the aged floor too far below. "This is what I'm talking about, Lola. I can only hurt you."

He moved steadily despite his words, working his way across the higher level beam toward the wall where I clung like a cat up a tree.

"I'm kind of freaking out right now," I admitted, fear causing a noticeable tremble to my words. "And I think there's a cat in here."

Way to be random, Lola.

"There are probably a few feral cats out here. But they won't bother us," he answered casually as if we weren't in this precarious position in a barn.

When I looked for him again, I saw the outline of him drop to the next level, the one nearest to me. One second he held the upper beam with his hands, the next he landed onto the one below his feet.

"Stop! You're going to kill yourself!" A new fear swelled in me, spreading out to my hands and feet, leaving my arms and legs shaking.

"I'm not worried about me." His voice moved closer until I could feel him at my back.

"You should be!" What did he mean? Was he worried about me? I couldn't fully concentrate on any such possibility, but it deserved thought. So much thought!

"Nah. I've been up here a thousand times." Then Brandt's words were a whiskey scented breath over the back of my neck. "You though, you, I worry about."

He moved until his body pressed behind me, sliding around and down, until he cocooned me, his hands at the step below my shoulders, and his feet somewhere lost below mine.

"Do you trust me?"

"Yes." His question held layers I couldn't dissect, but no matter which version he asked, my answer remained the same. "Yes, I trust you, Brandt."

"Move down a step."

I couldn't see how with his body all around mine. But I pried my fingers free - one hand at a time - and lowered them. Sucking in a breath, I began to move my feet.

Brandt moved with me, caging me in, and being a constant reminder I couldn't fall. Or if I did, I'd take him with me.

"I'd catch you," he murmured softly to my back.

Something about the roughness of his voice poured warmth down my spine and to my core.

Before I could get too worked up, Brandt's feet hit the floor, and his hands moved to my waist. He helped guide me to the floor with ease.

But I couldn't breathe, not with his hands on me, and not with his body so close to mine.

He turned me into his chest, then held me there. Calming me, probably, since I'd been scared. But my mind skipped over that part and instead noticed how my nipples hardened where they touched his firm chest. Desire for this man burned hot and low inside me and pushed me unflinchingly against him.

My hands wanted to gobble him up, to touch and smooth and keep every inch. Fear had driven me insane and I couldn't pry myself away from him.

"You're okay." His words sounded like they were meant for himself as much as me.

I nodded, the top of my head touching his chin. Clinging, I wrapped my arms around him and gripped his shirt in fistfuls.

Maybe I was more scared than I'd thought.

"Go home, Lo." Brandt's defeated voice rumbled in my ear but didn't sound like a demand so much as a rush of shame.

"No." I held him tighter, daring him to let me go.

"Why are you here?"

"To find you." I tipped my head back, trying to look at him, but not able to see well in the dimness. "I was so scared after Annabelle told me what happened."

"Shit." He stepped backward and pulled himself free from my frantic grasp. "I'm sorry. I'm so sorry."

He clutched at his hair, and I put myself right back in his space.

"For what?" I took his hands, holding them with my own, and staring at his dark features.

He sighed, his shoulders rounding. "For being a shitty person. I don't know, pick something, and I'm sorry."

"That doesn't even make sense." I tried to laugh, shaking his hands a little. "Let's start with the being drunk part."

"I'm—"

"No. Not you being sorry for it." I shook my head, and his eyes followed the movement. "Why you were drinking. Why you don't usually. All that part."

He sighed again and blinked his eyes too many times.

I knew that feeling. Trying to make sense of your thoughts when they swam in the alcohol.

Had I been afraid or caught up in the act when I let a stranger press me into the bed? When I cheated on the boyfriend I loved? The sick feeling in my stomach and the blurred vision of drunkenness kept my brain out of reach that night.

I pulled free from the tug of bad memories, of poor decisions, of the mistakes I had to live with, and focused on Brandt.

"Let's…" Brandt pulled free from me - again - and spun around, obviously looking for something. Then he picked up the flashlight and pointed it at an old table covered with dust, dirt, and years of disuse. "Let's sit."

Sitting side-by-side, our eyes adjusted to the addition of the flashlight shining near enough for us to make out facial features.

"I helped him." A deeper stickier darkness colored Brandt's voice. I wasn't sure who he talked about, but I stayed silent to hear him out. "My dad, when he sold off the property… And I used to hide the whiskey for him, so Hudson and Asher wouldn't find out he was drinking again. I carried his money to the dog track, too, where he'd lose it all. Everything we owned gone one parcel at a time, and I helped him."

He swallowed roughly, and I could see how the guilt of it all weighed on him. He held himself responsible for the bad decisions his dad made.

"He used to give me whiskey, too, telling me it was our little secret, and making it like a reward for doing all the shit he wanted." Brandt blew out a sigh tinted with fresh whiskey, and continued, "I hated it and got sick every time, but I didn't dare say no."

"How old were you?" In my mind, their dad died when the boys were pretty young. If I remembered correctly, it had been when we were in junior high. Meaning Brandt was far too young to take any blame.

"Thirteen when he died." He shifted his weight and clutched the edge of the table where we sat. "Don't say I was too young. It's bullshit. I knew better."

With lungs full of air, I had no response to his words. How could he believe that?

"Hudson had moved out, and Asher became Dad's punching bag. Thinking he was protecting me when all along, I was helping Dad."

"Why did you do it?" I moved my hands to the edge of the table too, pressing my pinky into his where our hands met between our bodies.

I formulated theories as to why he helped his dad, most of them having to do with fear, or a need to please.

"Because I'm not stupid." He spun his head to face me, defensive. "Asher thought the only way to save me was to let Dad hit him. But I'd figured out long before the best way to save my skin was to help the old man. I'm not stupid, but I am selfish."

How did I respond to that proclamation? Brandt clearly believed his own words. Thought he was selfish because as a young boy, he'd done what he had to do in order not to be beaten.

I knew - from Annabelle - that Hudson blamed himself. For taking off and leaving Asher and Brandt home with their jerk father. And that Asher blamed himself for not being able to do more to protect his little brother. Come to find out, Brandt had a hearty helping of self-blame too. When they all three should forgive each other and themselves, and place blame where it belonged. But I couldn't say any of that to Brandt. Not when I had no clue what it meant to grow up with fear the way they had.

Then Brandt's words to me - when I'd made my dark confession - found their way to my tongue.

"You come clean. You learn from your mistakes. You move on and try not to make the same mistakes again." I moved my hand to cover his and gave him a squeeze. "A smart guy I know told me that the other day."

Brandt managed to laugh, shaking his head at my advice. His own advice turned around on him.

"Smart, huh?"

"Smart, and not the least bit selfish. This guy, he's pretty wonderful in fact." My cheeks flamed with my admission, but he wouldn't see it in the weak flashlight aura.

"How can you think that of me when I just told you otherwise?" The tone of concern in his voice made me sad.

"Because you were a kid. And because I did worse things as an adult." I shrugged and swiveled to face Brandt. "Maybe forgiveness of our pasts can be our thing."

He nodded, a slight movement, then he tucked me under his arm, and held me to his side. I stayed there with him, sitting on that wobbly table in the old abandoned barn, and waited him out. Sometimes it took a long time to get right with yourself.

"We're trespassing," I whispered into Brandt's chest. "I've never broken the law before."

"Told you they were right." He almost laughed, his chest moving against me.

"Well, I forgive you." I laughed too and poked him in the ribs.

"Thanks, Lo," he said as he leaned down to kiss the top of my head.

With a sigh, I tipped my head back into the cradle of his shoulder and wished with all my heart for Brandt to really kiss me.

22

Brandt

I shoved everything into the back of my truck and I drove to Jesper. To the address Talulah Summers had once given me in case of emergency. My head ached, and I drank water in hopes it would ease the pain.

Small, tidy, and obviously cared for, the house of her sister Dorothy. The place Talulah stayed when she came to Jesper. The only connection I had to the woman who had kept my head on straight, all while killing herself.

"Hi. Can I help you?" A woman who looked eerily similar to Talulah answered the door.

"You're Dorothy?" I asked, sure but unsure, and kicking myself for showing up.

"Yes. And you are?" Her fake smile meant I put her on edge.

"Brandt Grace. I shouldn't have shown up like this, but…" I pulled in a deep breath, and watched her face change as she recognized my name. "I needed someone to talk to. Which doesn't make sense to you. Talulah was my sponsor, and then she, she drank herself to death and left me alone. Shit, sorry for rambling. And for cursing."

I turned to go. *Such a bad idea to show up! What the hell was I thinking?*

"Brandt," She called me back. "I'm angry too. Positively pissed off at my sister. If you're looking for Cricket, she's here, but to be honest she's not doing too well. You can talk to me."

Truth was, I had been looking for Cricket more than Dorothy. As Talulah's daughter, she seemed like the best connection. And I was grasping for straws.

"I should just go to a meeting. Or hop online. I just..." I didn't know what I wanted exactly, but it had led me to Dorothy's front door. "I'm real messed up right now."

Talulah Summers and I had stopped caring about the rules and dropped the pretense of anonymity over the course of the years. I knew who she was, and that her daughter started dating my friend. She knew me, all my old dark stories, and all my hopes for the future too.

"Come in, sweetheart."

I chuckled sadly as she invited me into her house. It was dim and smelled like wood fire and tea leaves. Cozy.

"This house stays so cold. Best place is here in front of the fire. Would you like some tea?" Dorothy tucked her hair behind her ears and floored me with her kindness.

We talked. For hours. Draining three brews of tea. I helped with new logs in the fireplace, keeping the fire going.

This woman, so like, and so very unlike her sister, sat with me until I relaxed. Until the poison of shame had drained from my system.

"I would make a terrible sponsor, Brandt." She sighed and looked sad. "I drink and have never had a problem with drinking. I don't understand the addiction personally."

"What I got from Talulah was more than a sponsor. She was just always there for me." It hit me - hard - that I wasn't angry with her for drinking. Only sad. "Guess what I need is someone to be there. That's too much to ask of a stranger."

Talulah drank to forget. She killed herself slowly over the years, all so she didn't have to remember all the things which haunted her. I didn't think it worked - she never truly forgot - and I hated that her sadness pulled her so deeply under.

"I have a daughter who moved away and never comes around. I rarely ever talk with her. But my niece Cricket? She's always been around, and she's honestly the only family I have, despite having another sister and a mother out there in the world. Cricket's best friend, Amelia, she's more like family than most of my own family. Brandt, honey, you are allowed to make your own family. Some of us aren't born into the love and support we need."

My brothers.

Emily.

Lola.

They were mine. All I had and all I wanted.

I needed to be strong for them. Clean and healthy.

Dorothy Summers showed me to her guest room - complete with four-poster bed and fluffy duvet - and allowed me to stay a few days.

Until I made my peace with Talulah's death.

Until I talked through all the anger I carried with me from my childhood.

Until Cricket and Vincent showed up, had me smiling and laughing, and assured me they had always trusted me.

How much of my life had been a lie I'd told myself?

All the fights with my brothers? Did I start them, or did they?

The rumors of selling drugs - stemming from being friends with a few of the wrong people at the wrong time - how often had I let them spread? Why didn't I protest the lies?

Even allowing myself to believe that Asher took the brunt of the physical abuse, to keep Dad away from me? Was that even true? It was just as likely our dad would have beat him no matter what.

I'd run off with no word to Lola, and I desperately wanted to get back to her.

First, I needed to make things right with my family. The one I'd been born into.

Dorothy gave me her number, promised to call and text until I was sick of her. Knowing I had someone strong at my back, gave me the confidence I needed to move forward.

I called a family meeting.

Demanded one.

They'd let go of our past, and see me for the man I'd become, or they wouldn't. But I needed to know. I couldn't keep living up to their poor views of me. They needed to rise up and take into account my behavior the last three years.

My sobriety started over with a clean slate.

My reputation needed to do the same.

23

Lola

He left.

His room scrubbed clean of his existence and returned to a barren guest room in my house.

I sank to the floor and allowed my memories of the previous night to overwhelm me. Those of Brandt's body pressed close behind me as he escorted me down the ladder. The ones of our hands together as he spoke his sins in a husky voice. Also, the sounds of him moving his things out, his feet up and down the stairs while I pretended to sleep and not notice.

Because I knew he'd leave, right? Brandt had opened up about his childhood and the things that continued to cause him shame, but he'd also been drowning in a fresh wave of guilt at having been drunk.

Tucked his tail and ran home, as they'd say.

Maybe not home precisely, but wherever damaged men go to lick their wounds.

I could stay there, on that floor, mourning the loss of what might have been with Brandt.

Or I could get myself up off the floor, woman-up, and face the mess I'd made of my life.

No school for another week and a half, and not much planning to be done during those days before we went back. Crap. I hadn't planned for having time off by myself. My new-norm had become uncomfortable, and I longed for... something.

Connection.

Truth.

The ache in my heart to subside.

How could I feel like something was missing, when I'd never had it to begin with? Brandt had been a flicker of starlight in the otherwise black night and had no right to blind me.

Sheesh, Lola, go make coffee and quit the romantic overture thoughts. *A flicker of starlight?* Get over yourself.

I knew what I needed to do. Holding tight to my coffee mug and settling deep into my favorite chair, I made the call.

Plans made to spend Christmas Eve, and consequently morning, at my parents' house, I set to work getting ready. Shopping, finding recipes, and figuring out how - and when - I'd go about telling them the truth.

"You come clean. You learn from your mistakes. You move on and try not to make the same mistakes again."

With Brandt's words circling my head, I knew I could face it. Stop handing out unexplained apologies, and give reasons and assurances instead.

Me: I miss you. Already. Pathetic, right?

Me: I'm going home for Christmas. All thanks to you - I'm braver because of you.

I didn't know if Brandt would bother responding to my messages. Annabelle said she wasn't sure the whole story, but hoped Brandt would show up on Hudson's doorstep for Christmas and join the family, like in years past.

Me: I'm coming clean. With my family, I mean. Telling them what I did and why Vin and I broke up. I can already feel the weight lifting. The truth shall set you free, and all that.

Me: That's also thanks to you.

I kept sending messages. Because he'd taught me to tell my truth. To face it head-on, and I hoped he could do the same. When no responses came, I didn't let it deter me. He needed time, and I could give it to him. Mostly. But I held on hope that he'd be back around.

Me: Call me. Or better yet, just show up.
Me: My parents want to meet you. Just saying.

But there was one last thing I needed to do. One last truth I needed to face and handle like the grown-ass mature woman I knew I could be.

Pulling up in front of the Berry house, doubt crept in. Big time. I should have at least given Vincent a warning.

Swallowing all the reservations, so they sat like a stone in my belly, I walked up the front path to the door.

Someone had planted pansies along the walk. Probably his little sister Louisa, but perhaps his mother. They both had a strong appreciation for colors and beauty and liked to surround themselves with it. I missed them. Their warmth, and my part inside the close-knit family, and the feeling I'd be welcome when I showed up. I couldn't be too sure these days.

Still, my hand reached out to press the doorbell, and my teeth clenched in near panic as I waited.

Vincent opened the door with a smile on his face. A smile that quickly fell and gave way to surprise.

"Lola." He said my name, but not how he used to, the new way filled with hesitation. "Hi. Um, what are you …?"

"Hi. Can we talk?" My voice came out too high, too bright, and I cursed my tendency to get extra girly when nervous. "Just for a minute."

"Sure." Vincent said the word, but he looked behind him into the house. "Out here."

He pulled the door closed, shutting off whatever lay inside. Probably his new girlfriend. I hoped she loved the Berrys as much as I once had and felt as welcomed into the fold. I hoped she treated Vin well. Meaning: better than I had.

"I'm sorry." The old familiar words fell out. "That's not what I'm here to say. It is, because I am, but that's not all."

"Okay." His lips almost smiled. He'd always said my rambling tendencies were sweet.

"I'm sorry that it happened." The words wanted to come up and out, but facing Vin in his cute sweater with his hands stuffed deep in his pockets, it was harder to say than I thought. "Obviously. But I'm sorry, too, that I let it happen. I was drinking."

I didn't say it as an excuse.

"So, I was right." He nodded, a sadness shaping his eyes and lips.

Not like, *I told you so*, but like, *oh, you really did have a problem.* Something we'd discussed, and I'd denied. Something I hadn't admitted to even myself - at least not in so many words.

Vincent moved to the old swing at the far edge of the porch, the wood and chains creaking as he sat. Then I joined him, noticing that his earthy scent was familiar but not enticing.

"Yes." I nodded and let myself feel the shame as it crawled over me. "I don't drink now. I had a couple drinks here and there in the beginning - you know, after - thinking I could handle just one. And I could. I did." My voice had a pleading tone, needing him to believe me. "Then I gave it up altogether. It's easier that way."

I didn't think of myself as an alcoholic, not in the traditional sense. Maybe it was a form of denial. But I knew I felt better when I didn't drink, so I didn't drink. I liked being in control of myself and my decisions, so I didn't drink. I wanted to be proud of the woman I was becoming, so I didn't drink. It became a choice I made every day until the temptation all but left me.

"I'm glad you're okay, Lola." His posture wasn't relaxed, and I got the feeling I was keeping him. But being a sweetheart and a gentleman, he stayed there with me, looking me in the eye and giving me what I needed.

"Do you want to know what happened that night? Or no? I... I don't know if it will help or whatever. I don't know how to... how to... not *fix it*, because we've moved on and all, but you know."

"Do you need me to know? Will that help you feel better?"

"How about the short version?" I offered.

All I'd told him a year ago was that I'd slept with another man. I couldn't wrap my own brain around my actions, and I'd offered no further explanation. There had been plenty of tears and a plethora of apologies. Vincent had consoled me - me! And he'd never divulged to anyone why we broke up, even though people assumed he'd broken my heart and not the other way around.

He nodded, and I sucked in a deep breath.

I told him how I'd been out with Kendra and Haley, and that we'd been drinking. Normal. Then they'd left, and I'd stayed behind, planning to call Wes at the end of the night. I'd danced with a few different guys, and had too many drinks, and lost myself. Less normal.

"I didn't say no."

Those words sat there between us, an echo of all the pain I'd caused.

"Going with him and letting him touch me." I shivered, and swallowed the bile in my throat, "It implied a yes. And I... I never said no."

Vincent didn't like my story. I could tell by the stiff set to his shoulders, and the way he blinked too many times.

"Lola." Vin's gruff voice pulled my full attention to him. "What are you telling me? Did he... force you?"

I could hear where he stumbled over the r-word, unable to say rape. Unable to probably think it. Because a man like Vincent Berry, he'd never do any such thing.

"No." I shook my head, and that's when the tears stung my eyes, burning hot. "I didn't want to, and I didn't like it, and I cried, but I never fought him. I never said no!"

"Oh, honey." He pulled me into his arms and held me. I fit there, the way I used to, but it was like hugging my brother or a friend. Comforting and familiar.

Vincent held me and let me soak the shoulder of his sweater with my tears.

"I'm going to tell you something because I think you need to hear it." He pulled back and looked at me with a grim expression, while I swiped at the wetness on my face. "But I'm also going to tell you that things are serious with Cricket."

"Cricket?"

"My girlfriend. Cricket Summers. She's from Jesper." He said the words as if I should have already known them.

"Right." I nodded and pictured the pretty girl I'd seen with Vincent. What sort of name was Cricket Summers?

No worse than the name Dolores Donovan. Parents can bestow strange names on their children. I chastised myself for mocking the girl's name.

"We can talk about her later if you want." The immediate happiness and assurance on his face were sweet. He loved her. "But I want you to know that what happened wasn't fair, Lola. If you were that uncomfortable, and especially with you crying, he should've noticed and stopped."

"I shouldn't have gotten myself in that situation in the first place!"

Vincent had pointed out how much I'd been drinking, and how far gone I'd get, to the point of not remembering some nights. It's the only thing we'd ever fought about, with me claiming it was typical for a woman of my age to indulge on the weekends. It wasn't like I drank every day.

"Maybe not. And, look, I wasn't there, so I don't know how far gone… he… was." Vincent swallowed, obviously uncomfortable with our line of talk, but continuing on. "Maybe he didn't realize, and maybe he's spent a year regretting what he did to you. But then again, maybe not."

I had thought about it. A million times. Million-trillion times.

"I don't know. I don't think I want to know." Because if as I suspected, he took pleasure from holding my thighs open, and from pushing his tongue into my mouth, it told a different story. "I've learned a lot, about who I am, and who I want to be, and I'm good with that."

It was enough.

"Good, Lola." He nodded and took my hand for a second.

"I'll let you get back inside to your family holiday stuff." I stood and smoothed my jacket down over my hips. "You must be freezing."

Vincent had come out in his sweater, jeans, and thin socks. No hat, coat, or shoes. He shrugged, evidently not caring.

I walked him to his front door, grateful we'd had this talk.

Closure.

"You and Brandt Grace, huh?" Vincent asked with his hand on the doorknob. His lips curled into a smile, and I liked seeing it there on his face.

"We'll see." I shrugged then, unsure what would come of Brandt and me if anything. "I hope."

"Just, be honest with him, Lola." Vin's voice dropped, and I knew what he meant. "If you'd told me then what you've told me now, things might've been different."

I nodded, understanding how my truth changed things. But also knowing we were both living our best lives separately.

It didn't do to dwell on what-ifs or trying to second guess the past.

24

Lola

When I turned back, walking toward my car, I noticed him.

Brandt Grace.

Standing beside his old truck, which he'd parked right behind my car. Tall, dark, and with an aura of danger. Standing there, with his gaze trained on me, and with a sense that he'd been waiting, and was now ready to pounce.

It made no sense, although I saw it with my own eyes, for him to be there.

Had he come for me? How had he known where I'd be? If I expected to see him at all - and I didn't - I figured it would be at my parents' house. Or back at our house after the holiday, when things settled down a little.

He moved in that graceful way of his and met me on the sidewalk that ran along the road.

My body ached to lurch forward into him, but I stood firmly in place.

"What are you doing here?" I asked, gesturing to the Berry house behind me.

It smelled like snow, and I could feel the heavy clouds press around us.

"Me?" Brandt's voice rumbled in a way that could've been a purr if I didn't know it was a low growl. "What are you doing here, Lo?"

I wanted to laugh and struggled to keep it tamped down. Not that I found humor in the situation, but because it was so absolutely absurd. Like Alice when they told her they were all mad in Wonderland, and she must be too, else she wouldn't have come.

"Closure." I nodded, hoping the word suitably summed up what had happened, and that it truly put an end to that chapter of my life.

I wanted to ask Brandt if he was there for me, but I'd gotten the sense I'd be wrong in assuming. I couldn't work through his connection to Vincent outside of me, not with my heart galloping the way it did. Had Vin ever mentioned Brandt to me, and I never noticed?

"Hmm." His intense blue-green eyes studied me like he could see too much and not enough. If there were fingerprints on my body, he'd see them, I knew it. "And did you get it? Closure?"

"Yes." I smiled through the word.

"Good." He nodded and took a step, closing the gap between us, but leaving enough space for the Holy Ghost. "I didn't expect to find you here, in Vin's arms no less."

A flash of guilt debilitated me for a moment. Numbed my tongue and stung my heart. He'd seen me crying into Vincent's chest, but I had no doubt it looked different from outside. Was Brandt angry? Jealous? I couldn't tell.

I opened my mouth, but no words came.

"I've never been jealous before," he admitted with a small smile tipping the edges of his lips upward. I got lost in the light of his enchanting eyes. "Because I've never cared enough."

"I'd say it was nothing, but it wasn't nothing. In the sense of you and me" —I moved my hand between our bodies, letting my fingers brush Brandt's chest— "it meant nothing. For Vin and me, it was a better goodbye. I needed to explain a few things, and Vin was kind enough to let me. He has a girlfriend, so you don't have to worry about anything. Not that you're worried. You're jealous?"

"Maybe. A little." He moved marginally closer, still not touching, but obliterating anything outside the two of us. Things like neighborhoods, families, sidewalks, it all went away, leaving only Brandt and Lola in a bubble. "Turns out I didn't like seeing you with him."

"Understandable," I said with a quiver in my voice, because we were very close to speaking some big truths. "If you liked me, or whatever."

His hands came to my head, framing my face, and infusing me with his warmth and strength, but also stealing away my breath.

"I like you, or whatever, Lola." His breath became mine, his lips melded to mine, and we were one.

Kissing was my favorite.

I'd almost forgotten how much I loved kissing, what with living in denial for over a year. Almost, but not entirely, because I'd secretly longed to fall into a life-altering kiss and never return.

The sensory overload of scent, touch, taste, everything. The way the whole world falls away, and the only thing holding me up is my lip-to-lip attachment to another person. I could kiss forever probably, symbiotic with another person, using someone else's air to breathe, their mouth and tongue to fill you up, and their body to support you.

Kissing Brandt became my new personal life objective. To feel his hands around my head, fingers tangled into my hair, and to have his scent completely envelop me. I could've eaten his lips, nibbling away at them like an insane little chipmunk intent on survival.

"Don't stop," I murmured as he took a breath, and I pulled him back to my mouth.

We kissed until I forgot we stood outside Vincent Berry's house until all I knew was Brandt liked me, or whatever.

When we finally stopped, hands still clinging and touching, we were panting like we'd run a marathon. Maybe a sprint - we'd try for a marathon some other time.

"Vin and I are old friends, Lo," Brandt said with honey and heat in his voice. "I'll be here a while, then I'll come to your parents' place."

I nodded, unwilling to relinquish him yet.

"Don't worry, darling." He leaned in, kissing below my ear and whispering something like a secret, "You'll never be rid of me now."

"Promise?" I giggled, because of the tickling kisses and because of my silly request.

"Promise."

Driving to my parents' house, my heart pounded the whole way, and I never stopped smiling. Not once. I'd go in looking like a lunatic with cheeks sore from all the happiness I wore on my face.

25

Lola

What was the best way to tell your family - on Christmas Eve, no less - about your traitorous past? Facing them should have been easy after talking to Vincent. Yet, a good time to bring up the topic had not presented itself.

My plan: do it before Brandt showed up. Which narrowed the window and forced my hand.

"Brandt's going to come over," I announced to the overly festive living room where we all strung cranberries on string, preparing to leave the fruit as an offering outside.

"Shit."

"Language, Seth," our mother admonished quickly.

Of the three of us, only Seth ever slipped up and cussed out loud in front of our parents. He, of course, told them he'd learned all the words from Wes, who then immediately threw me under the bus as having taught him. *Brothers.*

"We'll set another place at the table," she said, and I could tell from her face she mentally went over her preparation and including another person. "We can't wait to meet him. Officially."

"I have to tell you something. First." I stared at the needle in my right hand and the cranberry in my left. "Before he gets here."

"You're pregnant!" Wes yelled, dropping his portion of garland.

"No!" I stopped working too, staring at my brother. "Geez."

"Engaged?" asked Seth, looking too excited.

"No." I shook my head at their antics.

"Let her speak," our father intoned, effectively silencing everyone.

"It's not about Brandt," I said, looking at their eager and worried faces. I wished they'd go back to focusing on the task at hand. "I just want to talk about it before he gets here. It's about… before, with Vincent and me."

How many times had I been asked what happened? How many times had I refused to speak of it? I had their full attention, and I still had no idea how to explain.

To tell them I cheated, meant to tell them of my troubles with drinking, too. Dealing with their concern and judgment in the aftermath, and possibly forever.

They cried.

First, my mother furiously blinked back her tears, then she let them fall. She kept wringing her hands and stayed mostly quiet as I spoke, letting her body language speak for her. Then, Seth, moving to sit closer to me and shamelessly wiping the tears from his face. Later, Wes, shaking his head and saying too often how they forgave me. *They,* like he could proclaim it for all of them as a whole. Finally, my father, with a sheen in his eyes and tightness to his lips as he prayed for me.

I told them ninety-nine percent, leaving out the gory details, and taking full blame.

"You've been punishing yourself long enough, Dolores." My mother used her stern voice, making her point clear.

I nodded, getting choked up myself. Of course, they all loved me, and immediately said we could put it behind us and didn't want to dwell on it.

"To think I poured you that glass of brandy last week!"

"It's okay Mom." I didn't want her to worry. "I didn't drink it."

"I noticed." The look she shared with Seth meant she'd considered I might be pregnant when I hadn't taken a sip of the drink. "It won't happen again; don't you worry about that. In fact, we don't need any alcohol in this house."

With that, she got up and strode to the kitchen with purpose. *Perfect, they'd never let this go.*

"Thanks, Sis." Seth rolled his eyes and laughed.

"Shut up, you aren't even legal yet," I pointed out quickly.

"You know how I feel." Wes shrugged and sat back like he'd been right all along, and drinking led to no good. 'Bout time we all figured it out as far as he was concerned.

"Yeah, yeah, all of Fox River knows how you feel." I stuck my tongue out, playful, and we all laughed.

It was good to laugh together.

A loud knocking on the door led to all of us going to the front door in a group. Like maybe we usually moved in a pack to answer the door.

"You guys!" I whisper-shouted, hoping they'd all back off.

"We want to meet him," Seth said with a distinct tone of *duh* in his voice.

"Do not embarrass me!" I uttered before pulling the door open and slapping a smile on my face.

Looking every bit like a guy meeting-the-family, Brandt stood there with a potted poinsettia in his hands.

"He brought a plant!" Seth yelled over his shoulder to our parents lurking in the background, but still able to see for themselves.

"Shut. Up," I bit out to my baby brother. "Come in, Brandt."

He could plainly see the way I wore my nerves on my sleeve, same as he did, in this new situation. But he came in as if he were unafraid.

Pleasantries behind us, we moved back to the mess we'd made of the living room, hastily saying our garlands were done and forcing Seth out the door to hang them along the fence and porch railings. He yelled at us not to do or say anything important until he came back in.

"It's for the birds. Or the reindeer. Or something." I tried to explain the cranberries to Brandt.

"Cool."

My mom put the poinsettia at the hearth and said something about them being poisonous to cats, but thankfully we didn't have any cats.

"Can I get you a drink, Brandt?" My mother brushed her hands together and obviously needed something to do. "Not a drink-drink, as we don't drink in our house. Not that we admonish drinking per se, only with Lola's... you know." She paused, looked contrite and flustered, "Can I get you something?"

"Ha. Mom. Wow." I gave her my best death stare. Way to play it cool there, Mom. To Brandt, I tried to change the subject. "You see where I get my rambling, huh?"

Laugh. Har, har. Please focus on the genetic rambling and not the drinking thing.

"Water," Brandt said in a monotone voice as he looked at me with that way of his as if he could pull my secrets right out of me. "Will you show me to the bathroom, Lo?"

I sighed, and led the way, happy only that Brandt took my hand. I could take that as a good sign at least.

Was I seriously going to have to explain the drinking thing again? To Brandt?

"Did you tell them I don't drink?" Curiosity colored his voice, nothing more, although it hinted at something darker.

Given the way I'd found him the other night, and his subsequent embarrassment, and the fact we had yet to talk about it, I could see why he had concerns.

"No. It's me who doesn't drink. I told them... that." Among other things, but could we please not get into that right this minute?

"Because of me?" His gruff voice hinted maybe at embarrassment.

"No! No. Seriously, no." I doth protest too much, but really no.

"Then what's going on, Lo?" Only concern remained in his voice at that point. "Don't lie to me, I won't lie to you, right?"

"Yes, but it's nothing. I just don't drink." I swallowed the half-lies and knew I needed to tell him more. "Come in here."

I dragged him into the bathroom so we weren't standing in the hallway and locked the door. My parents could think whatever they wanted at this point.

The story came out one more time. I think it was all the re-tellings I had left in me for the foreseeable future. Except maybe for Annabelle, but that could wait until after New Year's at least. I told him the unabridged version

146

because I wouldn't lie to him.

His anger grew until it became palpable. A vibration in the room, swelling until it threatened to burst.

"I'm sorry." I ended my tale how I always did, with one last apology, as if it could be enough.

"Why the fuck didn't you tell me this before?" His fists clenched, and his eyes blazed, but it wasn't for me. Well, it was for me, but not at me. "His name. Right now."

"No, B." Ah, the guy. But I had no intention of giving up his name. "I've never told anyone, not even Vin."

"*Not even Vin?* Don't with me right now. Tell me." His insistence created a wave in the vibrations and crested ready to drown us both.

"Dinner is ready!" My brother Wes' voice came through the door. "Just saying."

"Let this go. Please," I begged of Brandt as he stood tall and brooding a scant few inches from me in the duck-themed guest bathroom. "I'm putting it behind me, finally, and I need you to do that too."

With a stiff nod which did nothing to convince me he'd let it go, Brandt opened the bathroom door and held it wide for me.

Dinner seated around our table passed in awkward starts and stops, as uncomfortable as I'd feared. But Brandt's knee pressed firmly against mine kept me grounded and gave me all the assurance I needed that everything would work out.

26

Brandt

I'd never struggled with anger - with my temper - the way my brother Asher did. I never ran away from a fight, but I also didn't need to start one over nothing. Last Thanksgiving, for instance, I'd instigated the verbal fight, but Asher had made it physical. My brothers were always hitting first and asking questions later - if ever. Being younger than them, I typically flew under their radar. Or they were too caught up in protecting me from Dad to bother with punching me themselves.

I didn't mind living my adult life without violence.

Sitting through dinner with the Donovans, I grimaced more than smiled, and could barely see through the red haze of anger clouding my vision.

Lola took the blame on herself. Punished herself for a damn long time over sleeping with some shit who didn't know enough to stop when a girl clearly didn't want his dick inside her.

I needed his name.

To put a face to the picture she painted of his hands all over her, while she laid there crying.

To put an end to whatever pleasure he derived from fucking a girl too drunk to give consent.

Violence had never looked so good as when I imagined tearing him apart.

Asking during family dinner was clearly not an option. So, I placed food in my mouth, somehow managed to swallow, and meanwhile made a terrible impression on her family.

When Lola walked me out, both of us still silent, I meant to ask her to Hudson's house. We'd made plans for Christmas Day, and I wanted my girl there with me. Show them who we were together.

But when I opened my mouth, the other thing came out. The thing I couldn't push from my mind not once in the last couple hours.

"You've gotta give me his name, babe. It's killing me." I spun and took both her hands in mine. I held them securely, hoping she could feel my love for her.

"Fox River is stupid small. If I tell you... everything changes," she explained, her eyes pleading up at me.

Her damn beautiful eyes. I pulled her in and wrapped my arms around her.

She didn't want to tell me because I knew him. Damn small town meant I knew the fucker. And if she thought it changed anything between us, it meant I more than knew him. Had to be a friend of mine. I thought back to a year ago, tried to remember anyone talking shit about getting laid with some drunk girl.

How many times had I heard a story like that? How many variations of the story had I heard over the years? Suddenly, it made me sick. I wanted to stand watch in every bar in town, not letting douchebags walk girls out, not when they were too drunk to stand on their own. Too drunk to choose what they wanted.

"What if I promise not to kill him?" I asked of her head, my mouth moving in her soft hair. My hands curved around her hips, feeling at home there, and wanting to pull her in rather than push her away.

Her body shook with laughter.

"Brandt."

"Lola." I ran my hands up her arms and pulled her back just enough I could look down into her face. "Please, trust me with this."

"Colin Felty." She sighed and then tipped her head down.

Her body immediately changed as she pulled back from me, leaving my embrace. Lola went stiff and when I bent to see her face, it was flushed red.

149

I'd been living with his brother Dylan up until last month. I'd seen Colin around, but we weren't friends.

Do not lose your shit, Grace.

I mentally overrode the instinct to hunt down Colin Felty and beat his face to a pulp.

He had been in our class in school. Preppy. Cocky. Dumb. Girls had always fawned all over him, but based on Lola's track record, he didn't seem her type. Too showy. Too pushy.

"I'm surprised he kept his mouth shut," I mentioned, knowing Colin well enough to know he bragged about his conquests.

"Yeah, well, I don't think he considered me big news." She laughed again but also blinked her wet eyes too many times. "Plus, I'm not sure how much he even remembers."

"You talked to him since?" I wanted to know if she'd asked him about what happened, and if he knew he'd taken advantage.

It came out sounding like I was a jealous prick and didn't trust her. Like I thought she might still be talking to him.

"No!" She looked offended. "Thank goodness, no."

"Sorry." I pulled her back to me, my hands smoothing her shaking limbs. "Don't worry about him, okay? You have me. No matter what."

I knew she knew what I meant when I said those words. Not giving her permission to cheat - giving her permission to tell me the truth.

I'd gone to Vin's house early to thank him for helping out when I'd been plummeting toward rock bottom. He didn't tell me Lola's secrets, but he did hint that things would've been different if she'd told him back then what she'd told him as her closure.

I for one was damn happy Vin had gotten his heart broken, and that he'd moved on to find Cricket, and that he was not the least bit hung up on Lola.

If Lola came to me with what happened to her, I'd forgive her. Help her through it all. The drinking. The nightmares. The pain and guilt. All of it.

"I love you, Lo." I whispered the words to her, and she squeezed me so tight I could hardly breathe.

"I love you, too, Brandt." Her words were watery, finally giving over to tears.

"For what it's worth, I think you are newsworthy. I'm going to tell every person in this whole damn town I love you."

When she laughed that time, it was full of humor and light. A sound worth fighting for.

I breathed her in and eventually pried myself away to leave her for the night.

If I went out searching for a certain vile man, I didn't let on to Lola.

27

Lola

I stayed the night in my childhood bedroom, as agreed upon, in order to wake up and be with my family for Christmas morning, reliving old traditions.

Saying goodbye to Brandt had torn me apart. I didn't want him to go; or I wanted to go with him. I stood on the front steps and watched him drive away, feeling every unresolved issue between us.

Would he move back in with me? Would we date? Or were we too far past that? All the possibilities still tangled there between us, and I clung to the knots, sure of them, but unable to smooth them out.

Hearing Brandt say he loved me seemed more like a dream than a reality. One I blissfully lived over and over again all night.

I woke to my brothers singing off-key carols. Standing at the foot of my bed.

"Stop!" I laughed and turned away. "You can both sing well. Why are you torturing me?"

"Get up already, Sis!"

"Yeah, see what Santa left us!" Seth shook the twin size bed to rattle me awake.

"Grow up, you two!" I moaned, but I threw the covers back and had to admit to wanting to get up and spend this morning together.

Instead of cocoa, we had coffee. Mom baked fresh bread in the oven after letting it rise all night, the same as she had always done. We dumped our stockings and tore into gifts like greedy children. Then slathered butter on the bread to replenish our energy.

By the third cup of coffee - the bread long since finished off - we had calmed down enough to sit in a loose circle and say thank you for each and every gift. To look at each other and feel the connection that had always been there, wounds I'd made healing up already.

Only at noon did we break away and take moments alone. Seth focused so hard on his phone, with a smile pulling at his lips, I suspected he texted with a girl. I didn't feel I could ask. Not yet. Hopefully he'd want to share the news with me soon. Wes went outside with our dad to catch up on feeding animals and doing everyday chores. I retreated to my room, ready to pack up and head home.

Brandt: Come to Hud's this afternoon?
Brandt: I'd love to see you. I'd love them to see us. You know?

Me: Yes. I'll be there in about an hour.

"What has you so excited?" Seth stood in my doorway, watching me smile at my phone.

"I suspect the same thing that had you so happy looking at your phone." I wore jeans and a sweater, and it would have to do unless I went home for a change.

"It's this girl. We've been talking," Seth admitted, and his cheeks went pink.

"How long have you two been *talking?*" I looked at my brother, his face full of hope and longing. "You don't have to tell me. I understand if you don't want to talk to me."

"Of course, I want to talk to you!" he gushed and fully entered my room. He lingered, looking around. "Mom would come in here like every day, and she's kept up with dusting and washing your sheets and all that."

"I'm not coming back, Sethy." I sat on the bed; lilac bedspread soft beneath me. "I like my house on Early Creek. In fact, you should come over. You could bring this girl."

"I'd like that." He nodded and looked like he wanted to say more.

I refused to apologize again. It wouldn't help, and everyone was sick to death of hearing it.

"It's not serious." Seth raised his eyebrows and went pink again. "Not yet. She's... I think you'll like her."

"I'm sure I will!" I hugged him and tried to send him sisterly-vibes to let him know I'd be there for him.

Six years between us was just enough I didn't know most of the kids his age. I could pick out a few, from seeing them over the years, but didn't know anyone well. I tried to remember girls his age who he might like, but drew a blank.

"I'm going to Hudson Grace's house. Wish me luck!" I spun to face the mirror above the vanity and took in my disheveled appearance.

"Hudson seems cool." Seth shrugged, and the way he said it sounded like he knew him.

"You know Hudson?" I asked, trying not to act like I was chomping at the bit for info.

"Sure. He helped with the rebuild of the barn." He seemed to think I should know that, but it was new to me. "Decent guy, if you ask me. Good to his men, too. Real fair, you know?"

"Right. Yeah." I nodded and forced a smile. "Sounds like Hud."

Only I didn't know Hudson Grace at all. Not beyond the ladder thief incident, and before that, Thanksgiving. If I looked any further back through my memories, it all came up as rumors and small town gossip - not to be trusted.

"Have fun, and I'm holding you to that invite to your house." Seth gave my shoulder a pat before leaving the room.

Throwing my hair in a messy bun, I decided I looked good enough. It was Christmas after all, and shouldn't we all look like we'd been sitting around?

***

Nerves ate at my stomach, making me sick and squeamish, and leaving me a wreck as I arrived at Hudson Grace's house.

I could just see the tobacco barn, if I craned around the house, and knew which hills to look between. I pushed those memories from my head, as I knocked on the front door.

"Well, isn't this a surprise," Hudson bellowed too loudly to his house at large. He gave me a wink before continuing, "Lola Donovan, at my front door."

He didn't seem the least bit surprised.

"Hi."

"Miss Donovan!" Emily pushed in front of Brandt as he moved toward the door, then past her father who held the door open for me and threw herself into my body.

"Hey, Em." I knelt to hug her, and she nearly knocked us both to the ground.

"I missed you!" She breathed her candy cane breath on me and kept hugging me.

"It's only been a week!" I laughed and pulled back to get a good look at her sweet and sticky face. "One more to go, then you'll see me practically every day."

"Let her in the house before it snows, Em," Hudson said, sighing, and giving me a non-verbal apology for her behavior.

I shook my head, because I didn't mind a bit.

"Her eyes are extra magical today," Emily said with no further explanation, then flitted across the room to jump on Asher.

"Sorry about that," Hudson stammered, a flush of embarrassment crawling up his face.

"It's okay, really," I assured him as I fully entered the warm house. "The kids think they can predict my mood based on how shiny my eyes are, and they have quite a few theories as to their mismatched colors. I haven't explained genetics, because it would ruin the fun."

Brandt stood there, in the middle of the impossibly small living room, waiting for me to stop babbling about my eyes. Once my gaze landed on him, it wouldn't veer away. A swell moved all the way from my core to my fingertips and drew me to him.

Hudson said something in reply to my explanation about Emily and my magical eyes, but I accidentally ignored him in favor of sinking deeper into Brandt's gravitational pull.

Brandt put one hand out, and I reached out to accept, knowing there had never been an alternative. Nothing in my life made sense outside of Brandt and me, our hands together, and our lives linked.

"Good to see you again, Lola," Asher said, but I didn't turn to see him, because I still couldn't look away from Brandt.

I nodded as Brandt pulled my body to his, securing our physical connection.

"Yeah, Lola Gal, good to see you," Annabelle said, and when I looked her way, she was poking Asher in the ribs.

Emily passed out candy canes, and Hudson took the rest to put away, which I suspected meant hide from his sugar-high daughter. She held up each of her gifts, giving us a long explanation of its origin, use, and allowing us each to marvel. Being a generous soul, she insisted that everyone else do the same, sharing her spotlight.

Not too old to nap on Christmas, Emily slept for an hour while the rest of us filled up the small house. Annabelle sat on a chair from the kitchen, with Asher on the floor with his back to her knees. Hudson also brought in a kitchen chair, sitting alone, and making me wonder if he ever dated. Brandt and I got the small sofa, sitting so that our knees bumped, and our hands brushed.

I spent a second holiday with the Grace family.

The first had been uncomfortable, with Asher yelling at Brandt, but ended with me inviting a near stranger into my home.

Little had I known a month later, we'd be holding hands and counting the minutes until we could be alone.

Christmas Day spent with Brandt's family was welcoming, if not also fragile. Old tensions lay beneath the surface, unable to dissipate completely. Questions loomed around us, with no answers yet. Judgment still lingered between the brothers, something I knew Annabelle sensed too, but we all ignored it in pursuit of having a good day.

It must always be that way for them, especially on holidays and when Emily was there, the way they skated over the issues. I knew it would be foolish to think I'd seen the last of Asher cussing at Brandt, or of Hudson showing up at my doorstep to give me a warning.

"Should I follow you home, Lo?" Brandt asked at the door to my car after we said our goodbyes to his family.

"Please," I said, unashamed to beg of him.

He placed a warm kiss against my lips, like a promise of more to come. I licked the sugar cookie taste of him off and could hardly wait for more.

A different sort of nerves skated along my skin as I drove home. Anticipation tickled until I thought it might drive me mad.

We barely made it through the door, as I pretended to show him around for the first time, and as he carried me up the last three stairs to my door.

"Yes?" he asked with a pause in his momentum.

I nodded, and he pushed into my room.

Everything had changed so quickly. I hadn't caught up yet. I didn't need to think about it; I knew. Every fiber of me knew Brandt and wanted to unite with him.

Looking into my eyes, he slowly lowered himself over me. Excruciating was the pain of how slowly he moved as I pulled at him and begged him to give in.

Then he kissed me, and we tumbled together into an infinite place made only for us.

"Kissing is my favorite," I whispered when he moved his mouth to my neck.

"We'll see about that," he breathed across my collarbone, savoring each taste of my skin as he went.

"You're my favorite," I amended, and pressed myself up into him, eager for everything at once.

"You're mine too, Lola."

We slept all tangled up together, our bodies spent, and our lips still longing to connect.

We woke up to a new day and a new life.

One we could build together from our broken pieces.

28

Lola

Brandt didn't move out of my room. Together we slipped into something more serious than I could have anticipated.

We talked about everything in our lives. Including but not limited to alcohol, sex, work, siblings, and the future.

Not going to a bar on New Year's made sense, so we went to the midnight showing of *While You Were Sleeping* at the theatre in Jesper .

Yes, that Jesper . Southeast of Fox River. Home of Cricket Whomever, girlfriend to my ex, Vincent Berry.

They might not have much in their town, and their population might be smaller than ours, but they had a theatre. One of the old ones with velvet seats and swirling architecture. It had been a number of years since I last visited the place, and I felt a pang of homesickness at seeing it, flooded with memories of going with my brothers and with friends.

"*Ghostbusters Two*, or *While You Were Sleeping*?" Brandt asked while looking at our options.

"Both classic New Year movies." I nodded, pretending to consider. "Obviously, *While You Were Sleeping*. Sandra Bullock pretending to be engaged to Peter Gallagher while falling in love with Bill Pullman? Classic, Brandt, it's a classic."

"I'd argue that *Ghostbusters* is also a classic, but meanwhile you've ruined the whole movie for me!"

"What? You've never seen it?" I stopped us in our tracks, shivering outside the marquis. "You can't be serious!"

"How and why would I have ever seen that movie?" He laughed, and his breath came out in steam clouds.

"Shoot, I'm sorry I ruined it. Forget what I said!" I laughed too, and he took my gloved hand. "You're going to love it though!"

"You have magic eyes right now." Brandt's hands framed my face, and his eyes held mine, his proclamation completely serious.

"Magic?" I giggled at his use of his niece's word.

"Yes, magic. You must be very happy." He leaned in slowly, closer and closer as he spoke.

Was I happy? Oh, yes, very much the definition of happy. Despite my best efforts, it seemed my time of self-punishment had come to an end. Rather than feeling terrible, I knew I was stronger than ever. It took me a while - maybe longer than it should have - but I learned my weaknesses and came through on the other side armed to fight for myself. For my body, mind, soul, and most importantly, my heart.

"Happy." I nodded while Brandt's hands covered my ears.

After a soft kiss to warm me to my toes, Brandt pulled back with a smile on his lips. A gentle smile, the one he wore just for me. He was happy too.

"Hey, Lola. Brandt."

We turned to see Vincent Berry. With a pretty - supremely pretty - strawberry blonde girl. She took my breath away, but there was something off-putting about her, too. An untouchable vibe that came off her.

"Hey. Hi." I tried to get my bearings. "What are you guys... never mind, you're seeing a movie. Obviously. Us too."

"Obviously," Vin said with a crooked smile.

"Good to see you, man." Brandt gave Vin a nod, and we all stood there, and it wasn't awful.

"This is Cricket Summers," Vincent said, proud and happy of the young woman at his side.

She paled. "Nice to meet you, Lola."

Shy. She must be painfully shy. Vincent would be a good fit for her, because he was sweet and low-key friendly. Protective too, which seemed like something she needed.

"You too," I said, unsure what else to offer.

"Have you seen Louisa and—" Vincent started to ask when another younger couple approached us.

"Hey, Sis," Seth said in a shaky voice.

All I could see was Seth's hand on the one and only Louisa Berry.

Seth. My brother.

Louisa. Vincent's sister. My ex-boyfriend's sister.

Whoa.

"We're doubling," Vincent said, then gave us all a wink, like he was doing them a favor, or like he knew it was adorable of him.

My brain slowly caught up, and acceptance was near, but I hadn't figured out what I felt yet. Some sort of crawling sick feeling, like I'd been lied to, or like I was about to learn something I didn't like. I couldn't focus on any of that just then and smiled at my brother.

"That's... great," I said, unsure of the word, and still reeling from all the crazy I observed on the movie theatre sidewalk. "It's cold."

"We'll see y'all, later," Brandt said, and tucked me to his side, turning us away from everyone else.

"So, you're freaking out, huh?" Brandt kept walking us straight to the right theatre for the silly movie I'd picked.

"A little bit," I admitted to him, still figuring out what it meant. If anything. "My brother. And his sister. It's weird."

"They're cute." He nudged me but didn't say anything else.

"They are. Like, super cute." I nodded, and we shimmied down the middle row to the best seats in the nearly empty theatre.

They almost looked too much alike, with brown hair and brown eyes, and soft features. Vin and I had been the same way.

I liked Brandt's hardness and the way we contrasted each other.

"You'll like Cricket, if you ever get to know her," Brandt said as we took our seats. "Her mom just passed away, so she's a little... off, lately. I did a tattoo for her not long ago."

"Right. Talulah's daughter." It made sense and didn't bother me, but the pieces were falling into place as I remember his fond words about Cricket's mother.

Pieces from all the information I didn't have before our countdown to the new year. My brother dating Louisa Berry. Brandt knowing Vin's girlfriend. Our circles were linked. Loops like the Olympic Rings, all intertwined. We were all connected. Made the world seem small - and our towns microscopic.

"Maybe we should triple date one day," I half-heartedly suggested, deciding I could be cool with Seth and Louisa.

I knew Louisa well and thought highly of her. Seth was an absolute sweetheart, and I'd always thought he would get his heart broken by the first girl he loved. But maybe that didn't have to be his story.

"Looks like tonight is the night," Vincent called out in a timely response to my words.

I turned to see him come down the aisle with Cricket, and our siblings shortly behind. The four of them moved slowly, as if giving us a chance to say no. Or maybe hoping for our approval. Without any qualms - well, without too many - we waved them in and gestured to the seats nearest us.

"She talks through movies," Seth said, pointing at me.

"I know," Vincent and Brandt answered at the same time.

Before I could panic about ensuing awkwardness, they both cracked up laughing.

We had the theatre to ourselves, and I couldn't have picked a better way to herald in a new year. Reconnected with my family, and learning how to be friends with my past, all while throwing myself into the arms of my future.

29

Lola

When I called Annabelle to tell her I was too tired to learn how to knit and would have to join her group next week, she was having none of it.

"You are not bailing on your New Year's Resolution!" she wailed at me on the phone.

"I don't know how." Never mind the conversation I had in mind needed privacy, not a group.

Annabelle was the last person I intended to share all my secrets with. She'd stuck by me through it all, even not knowing what I'd done. In so many ways, she had gotten me through my rough patch with her kindness and inclusion.

"Doesn't matter if you know how," Annabelle said so convincingly I wondered what else happened at knitting group. "I started going a few months ago with Kendra, and neither of us knew how to knit."

"I was thinking something just the two of us." I swallowed any residual worry at having to share the story one more time. "I have to tell you something."

"Figured." She smiled when she said it; I could hear the smile in her voice. "That's sort of the whole thing with knitting group: best girl talk I've ever had."

"But I don't knit."

She insisted I show up to Darlene's Coffee Shop, after hours, on Wednesday night. She texted me a list of supplies to buy beforehand, which required a trip to the yarn store an hour away. And somehow, I found myself excited to be spending the cold night with my hands tangled in yarn.

My mother could knit and crochet and embroider and whatever else one could do with yarn and thread. I had never shown any interest and had never learned. The memories in my head were cozy, and I found myself wanting to do this old-fashioned thing. To make something useful.

I could talk to Annabelle some other time, so I entered with no plans to spill my guts to the group I found circled up in Darlene's. The chairs were pushed into a loose circle shape, all facing the center, and every seat but one was filled.

"You came!" Annabelle hopped up immediately to grab me and led me to the vacant chair.

I was surprised to see I knew every face as I looked around the ladies. No, there was one man present, Beau MacKenna. Smiles met me, even from Matilda and Louisa Berry - Vincent's mother and younger sister. I expected old ladies whose names I'd mix up, not the relatively young gathering I found, full of friendly faces.

Louisa looked away, seeming shyer than I'd ever seen her. Had to be about my brother Seth. What a mess!

Definitely not talking about *the thing* with Vin's family in the room. No, thank you, I'd rather jab the knitting needles in my eyes.

"You know Kensie," Kendra said, with a head tipped toward her older sister. "She's the one who roped us in."

Kensie Lawson paled as I looked at her, uncomfortable with the spotlight, but she smiled and nodded in agreement.

I sat and held my bag of supplies like a shield in front of me, feeling as shy as Kensie.

"They've put you beside me, because I've been volunteered to teach you," a pretty young blonde said from the chair to my left. "I'm Penny."

My face must have given away my own discomfort, because her smile became kind and understanding. If I remembered correctly Penny moved to town last winter and was dating Dominic MacKenna.

"It's okay, Lola, she taught most of us." Kendra laughed and held up her striped length of work, what would clearly become a scarf with another foot added.

"True story," Magnolia Porter chimed in, surprising me, as she rarely spoke up. "Penny convinced me to come, and taught me, and this is... this group is ..."

If I wasn't mistaken, Maggie got choked up as she spoke. I looked around the circle again, taking in all the open and supportive faces.

Best girl talk.

"This is my sanctuary," Maggie finished her thought with wide eyes and a solemn nod.

Maggie was with Cotton MacKenna. Dots started connecting themselves between the ladies here.

Hugs and gushing professions of love poured into the circle, and I gave Annabelle a look. She just shrugged and silently laughed at my misgivings.

That's when I noticed each lady - and man - had a steaming mug near them.

"Ooh, can I get a coffee? Are they still serving?" I automatically looked to Natasha as I asked, since she worked at Darlene's and was likely the reason we were let in after hours.

"Sure thing, baby girl. Coffee in the pot is fresh." She lifted her own mug toward her mouth. "But this is Beau's special recipe, and it's spiked to high heaven."

"You like it, Natasha." Beau laughed and waved her off. "It's called a Nose Warmer, it's delicious, and you're welcome to have some."

"No thank you," I mumbled, then started pulling my new knitting needles and soft yarn from my tote bag.

A collective pause echoed in my head, then Olivia Hamilton started asking Beau about his recipe and if it was appropriate to serve at an upcoming winter party her parents were throwing. Mrs. Berry jumped in and I relaxed finding no-one cared what I drank or didn't drink.

Penny showed me how to do the knit stitch, and I practiced it, saying the silly chant along with it, until it almost felt easy. I dropped a few stitches.

164

My square was decidedly not square-shaped.

"It will make a good washcloth," Penny said with praise in her words.

"I guess."

She had finished it for me, binding off, and telling me she'd show me how on the next one. I held it gently in my fingers, oddly proud of the little wannabe washcloth. I'd made it - taken yarn from a ball and transformed it into something useful. Like magic.

Everyone talked the whole time, sharing real things. Not gossip. Not rumors. Personal stories and their thoughts. Guts spilled with ease, and ideas discussed with care. Natasha seemed happy to talk about race, and the reality of living in a small southern town. Similarly, Beau didn't hesitate talking about his sexuality. They were both met with sincerity and frankly, it was shocking. I'd never thought about how Natasha's dark skin affected her life in Fox River and the world. But my head had been buried so far beneath the sand the last year, I hadn't thought about anyone other than myself.

I listened, seeing why Annabelle called it the best girl talk she'd ever had and quickly understanding why Maggie found this group her sanctuary. I found I couldn't wait to meet up with the knitting group again. I felt more welcomed in an hour with these women, then I had in my whole life of friendships. My self-imposed solitude came to a crashing halt, and I found the idea of returning to it repugnant.

Going home to Brandt – and the feeling that it was indeed our home – was the final missing piece in putting myself back together.

30

Brandt

I bought a loveseat.

Impulse buy as I walked by a store with furniture in the window and saw it sitting there. Roomy enough for two. Cozy enough to ensure touching. Floral pattern Lola would love.

I rescheduled my clients for the evening, explaining I had a family emergency, and I loaded that loveseat into the back of my truck. Careful not to stain or tear the fabric.

Hudson came over with his ladder and fixed the living room lights. He helped me rearrange the furniture too. My oldest brother had clapped me on the back, told me he was happy for me, and that he trusted me.

Just like that he accepted all the truths I dumped on him. Said it took a lot of guts and maturity to be a man, and I made him proud. We bonded over the simple fact neither of us had turned out like our dad.

Asher wasn't quite ready to accept my peaceful life with Lola in that old farmhouse. Said he had reservations. He'd come around eventually. Especially since Lola and Annabelle were so close.

I made grilled cheese and tomato soup. I bought bottles of sparkling water, with lemon and lime as garnish. And I waited for my girl to come home from her new knitting group.

"I'm so happy to see you!" She pushed through the door, excited in a way that would never stop thrilling me. "Why aren't you at work though?

Everything okay?"

She looked at me closely, then spun around to take in her surroundings. Before I could explain, she gasped.

"That is the ugliest loveseat ever created!" She jumped up and I caught her. "I love it!"

Her lips brushed over my cheek, then to my lips, then around to the other cheek. Food all but forgotten, I held Lola up and kissed her right back.

Loveseat for the win.

Mmm, she smelled like coffee. I licked her lips and then deep into her mouth, savoring the taste of her. My greedy, greedy hands cupped her butt, and she took the invitation to wrap her legs around my waist.

I liked her there in my hands, little body wrapped all around me. Total and absolute trust in me to hold her and carry her. Giving herself over to me.

My brain kicking somewhat back into gear, I walked her over to the new loveseat and lowered us both down.

"What do you think?" I tipped my head to one side and reminded myself oxygen was necessary.

"I like sitting in your lap." She came up for a quick breath, then went right back to moving her lips over my skin.

I moaned when her tongue swiped below my ear. Was there anything she did I didn't find sexy? Gracious, I wanted her. Every inch of her.

Little vixen ground her hips against me, and my body responded exactly how she hoped. Flipping her onto her back - with not near enough room to lay down on the loveseat - I held myself over her.

"I made you dinner." My voice came out rough, giving away the height of my desire.

"That's sweet of you, Brandt." She tugged on my body and arched up to meet me. "I had something else in mind."

"We'll reheat it later."

I gave in, lowering myself until our bodies were close, close, closer. Until she squirmed beneath me, panting. I had been taking my time with her. To absorb every minute spent with her. To let her know I was in no rush. To make myself take my damn time.

Then I slid down her body and put myself on the floor. Positioning her hips at the edge, I pulled her pants down to her ankles.

Listening to Lola call my name, and having her beg me to never stop, made our cold soup worth it. I had no trouble putting her first. In fact, I'd grown to crave pleasing her.

I would listen to every record she owned, because the songs spoke of her soul.

Just like she loved to pour over my sketchbooks, telling me she could see inside of me in each drawing.

Happiness filled that old house as we learned more and more about each other. Taking our time, talking, playing, and exploring.

Growing up, as it turned out, kicked ass.

Not the trap I'd thought it would be. Not grueling or unforgiving.

Spent with the person you love, life could be a gift worth holding onto. A treasure. I needed a thesaurus to list all the way in which I loved my life. Our life.

31

Lola

I continued my venture into knitting. If by knitting I meant baring my soul to the group while tying haphazard knots in yarn. Penny had transitioned to teaching me how to crochet rather than knit, claiming it would be better suited to my natural talents. Penny was habitually encouraging and probably too kind for her own good. It was probably why we all loved her so dearly.

At peace with Brandt, having found a tight group of friends, and living my best life, I no longer dwelt on my past. At least the memories no longer popped up uninvited, and I didn't obsess. But I couldn't put the incident fully to rest no matter how many times I told myself I was over it. After several months of knitting, and learning each group members secrets, I was compelled to share mine.

Drinks emptied, knitting stowed away, we all remained in our circle, as usual, and talked.

"I have a question," I blurted in a small space between topics. "A sex question."

"Do tell, girl." Natasha sat back and stared at me with her dark eyes.

"I'm so excited!" Louisa squealed.

The group all shifted focus to me, watching and waiting on the edge of their seats for what I would ask.

Oddly enough, at this point, I craved a discussion. I wanted to hear what all these bright and lovely women thought about what happened. If I had been right in hating myself? Or if I was more right in forgiving myself?

I'd almost forgotten Louisa was there, tucked on the other side of her mother and mostly talking to Olivia. I pictured her with Seth, the way they looked at each other, and the way they held hands through the whole movie on New Year's Eve. She didn't need to hear my sex story.

I hesitated.

"Go on, dear," Mrs. Berry said, giving me a nod. "Don't worry about Louisa."

Was I seriously about to say all this out loud? To the group? To my ex-boyfriend's freaking mother?

Now or never.

"So, if you have sex, and you don't say yes, but you don't say no." I paused, pulling in a shaking breath. "I mean, if you haven't given consent, but you also haven't not given consent, then...?"

My throat closed up, and I could no longer push the words out. I simply stared back at all the faces surrounding me and wished for a hole to open up and swallow me. A nice little sinkhole beneath Darlene's would've been nice.

"Are you asking what I think you're asking?" Natasha sought clarification.

"It's not rape, at least not in my opinion," Kendra said in a normal voice. "It is unfortunate though. I've been there done that and wished I had said no."

I flipped my gaze to her, trying to read between the lines. No judgement. Only understanding.

"I don't know," Annabelle said next. "Did you give any clear signals one way or the other?"

We were talking about this. For real. And I found myself ready to answer her question, like it might actually help me get to the bottom of the emotional well.

"No. Well, maybe." I cleared my throat. "I was drunk, and I don't remember everything. I did kiss him back, at first. Then, I'm not sure, because the next thing I remember, I'm lying there wishing he'd stop. But I never asked him to stop. I did cry."

Tears burned hot behind my eyes, and I looked at my lap. Memories flooded my head, blurry and tired of being relived.

"I cry almost every time I have sex, so that's not a clear indication of no," Natasha said without flinching or holding back or anything.

I'd never had this sort of freedom in talking about sex.

"I'm a crier," Beau offered up.

I giggled, and couldn't stop.

"Really?" I looked around the circle but didn't see anyone else ready to agree with the happy crying. "I haven't. Not from regular sex."

"Who said anything about regular?" Beau asked and everyone laughed.

"I meant—"

"I know what you meant," he said, we all quieted down at his serious tone. "If you're looking for who to blame in this situation, it's not you, and it's not him either. We do stupid shit when we're drunk, sweetheart."

"I agree," Penny said in a very small voice. "I've only been with two guys, so I don't have a lot of experience or anything, but there were times with my ex when I did it even though I didn't want to. The whole time I'd be thinking about how I didn't want to be doing it. But I never said anything to him, which really isn't fair."

"I've done that, too." Mrs. Berry's voice surprised me most of all. "In my younger days, back before I was in a loving relationship, I found myself in that situation a few times. Waste of energy to blame yourself, if you ask me."

Time for the final shoe to drop.

"But I cheated on Vin." The tears finally snaked down my cheeks, burning hot like fire.

She nodded like she knew or suspected. "And I don't hate you. Neither does Vincent. This is just a thing that happened. One piece of your story."

"You cheated on Vin?" Kendra's raised voice made me jump. "Why didn't you just tell us this forever ago?"

"I thought you'd hate me!" I wanted to stand and yell, but I didn't. "I couldn't forgive myself, not until... well, until I met Brandt, and he taught me that I'm more than my mistakes."

"Aww." Annabelle held her hands together in front of her chest, oozing happiness that I was officially dating her boyfriend's brother.

"Now that's some sex-talk I want to hear," Beau said with a wicked smile. "I always thought Brandt was the cutest of the bunch."

Oh dear, I'd opened up the can and there was no stopping it now.

"Hudson," Natasha admitted, then licked her lips. "If we're picking a Grace boy."

"Asher," Louisa said in a small voice, unable to face Annabelle.

"I think the important question is: which MacKenna?" Kendra asked, batting her lashes.

Natasha smacked at Kendra playfully. "You better hope I don't tell my brother."

Kendra's long-term boyfriend Nate, younger brother to Natasha. *Small. Town.*

"Pshaw, Nate already knows who I'd pick." Kendra cackled.

"No, no, no, there are too many girlfriends here!" Annabelle said, spreading her arms wide and indicating half our group. "The brothers we need to discuss are the Bells. For me, it's Otis."

"Lewis," Penny piped up, then we watched her cheeks go pink. "I just met him, and he's... sweet."

"Puh-lease, you're dating the Sweetheart of Fox River already." Maggie laughed, and I loved the way her nose scrunched up.

"Otis," I admitted, remembering listening to him sing years ago, and thinking he could make anyone fall for him with his voice.

"What about you Olivia?" Penny asked with a sparkle in her eye.

Olivia simply shook her head no, then busied herself gathering all the dirty mugs. Oddest girl of the group for sure, and the one I knew the least. I'd always gotten the feeling she carried secrets and pain with her, hiding it behind all the perfect makeup and prissy clothes. But if I'd learned anything, it was that we all have hidden darkness.

I left Darlene's feeling different, like the steel bands had been released from my chest, and I could finally breathe properly. As I drove back to my house, knowing I'd wait up for Brandt to be home from work, I smiled at how things had worked out.

It may have taken me longer than it should have, but I'd found myself.

Twenty-five years, mistakes made, lessons learned, battles fought, and I'd become who I was meant to be all along: me. But me split wide open and stronger for it.

The Chapel

My next release is The Chapel, a fox river romance spin-off, centered around renovating an old church into a music hall. Look for this one to be out early 2020. Enjoy Chapter one ...

The thing about being in your late twenties is that you're supposed to have it all figured out. The career, the house, the long term relationship, the life plans sprawling out before you. You're expected to have your shit together.

I don't have a career. Not really. I'm still figuring out what I want to do with my life. I take photos and I'm good at it, but I don't enjoy wedding photography or infant photography or running wild toddler photography. I haven't found a way to make money doing nature or still life or anything else with my camera. I help run my Aunt Violet's vintage shop that barely brings in enough revenue to keep me on the payroll.

No house. Not one that's mine. Not one I want to live in for any length of time. The place I rent is small, smells bad, and the landlord is suspect. The neighbors are loud and disrespectful of my desire to sleep during the nighttime hours.

I have never had a long term relationship. I can't imagine one will crop up before I hit my thirties. The guys I've dated have been few and far between and never serious.

My life plans are vague at best. Dismal and depressing at worst.

The highlight of my week is meeting Tyler for a late lunch at our favorite Japanese place. It's a tiny closet of a building, where the heat from the kitchen permeates the four tables out front. I feel a bead of sweat roll down my back and hope I don't have noticeably wet pits.

"Why are you so nervous?" I can't help but ask.

Tyler is tapping his toe - a fairly normal habit of his - in overdrive. His eyes have darted around the place and to the door too many times. He's making me nervous.

"I'm not." He shakes his head at me, and it seems to put something in place. "I mean, I am. I have to tell you something."

"Okay."

That is never good. Never. The *we need to talk* and the *I have to tell you something* is always followed by news that you do not under any circumstances want to hear. Even from Tyler Covington, my cousin and best friend, I feel the rock-in-the-gut dread that accompanies those words.

"I'm heading out of town, Mallie Jo." His face is tight and etched with worry. Tyler watches me for cues as to what to say next. No, he watches to see if I'll cry or scream. Not yet. "Frank found a spot for me on a few albums, and I can't turn down the opportunity."

Frank lives in Nashville. He's worked as a session musician for years. An older guy with a real name around the town. He's been Tyler's mentor for practically his whole life; the one that taught him to play guitar.

"Oh, wow, that's really ... great."

It's so not great!

No, no, it is great for Tyler - just not great for me.

I smile and the muscles in my cheeks strain at the effort. They forget how to smile, how to pull my lips into place. It's not a rock in the gut, it's a punch in the gut.

I cannot survive without Ty. I moved in with him and Aunt Violet and Uncle Andy when I was four. I don't remember a life before them - a family that wasn't them. They took me in and have taken care of me ever since. Tyler and I became best friends and have remained close through the years. He's two years older than me - thirty to my twenty-eight.

"I'll meet a lot of great people. I'll get to play with a lot of great people." He emphasizes the word great each time he says it.

"When do you go?" My throat is closing up.

He shifts in his chair and looks down at his plate. His thin stainless steel fork scraps across the thinner ceramic of the plate. I know that whatever blow comes next, it will be worse.

"I'm driving over on Friday." He shifts again in his chair, but he looks up at me. He has this sad puppy-dog face as he waits. Waits for me to break down. Which is why I can't. "That way I'll have the weekend to get settled. I start on Monday."

"Friday is in two days." Two. As in barely more than one.

"I know."

"You're leaving." The words scratch on their way out, leaving wounds in my throat.

"Yeah." Tyler's face morphs into pleading. Not so worried and not so sad. Something worse. "Look, it will be fine. You will be fine without me."

"Ha." I can't help the sound that comes from me. The bitter scoff of a laugh. "When have I ever been fine without you?"

As pathetic as it sounds, Tyler has been my rock. My whole life, he's been the one to hold my hand, to have my back, to take care of me. I can't fathom a life that doesn't include him. What do I have without him? A pathetic job. A shitty rental house. No friends. No prospects.

"Mallie, you are a strong, smart, beautiful woman." He means it. He's always thought the best of me. "The best parts of your life are still to come."

"I sure hope so."

In some ways, the life I've lived thus far hasn't been great. It's not easy to spend a lifetime wondering about your parents, knowing you'll never have any answers. Throw in high school filled with awkward encounters that lead to unfortunate rumors, and you have a terrible few years.

"I know so." He sits back then, more relaxed and sure. His eyes glint with some morsel that he's yet to drop on me.

"What haven't you told me?" I go ahead and pry it from him, even as I'm not recovered from the initial bomb he's dropped.

"You know how I invested in O's project?" Tyler abandons eating, and his hands are active as he speaks, painting the invisible image of O's project.

I nod. Otis Bell. He's Ty's age and his closest friend. Where I wanted to stay home and hide from the high school drama, Tyler wanted to be front and center. Otis was right there with him. They ruled the school. The town.

Golden boys, the both of them. Otis has never liked me, and barely tolerates me. His typical response to my being in his presence is to thoroughly ignore me.

"I won't be around to help him like I thought. Obviously." Tyler tips his chair back onto its spindly back legs. He runs his fingers through his hair. He'd been blessed with a head full of thick wavy caramel colored hair. Lightened by hours in the sun. I will never stop being jealous I didn't have the genetic good fortune to get his hair. "He's got the music part down. O can handle booking bands, and hosting jams easily. Whatever. He's good with people."

It was true. People loved him. Women flocked to him and swooned over him. Men fell instantly into some sort of bromance with him. I had never met anyone who didn't love Otis Bell.

Good with people, except me.

Not that I cared.

Or mentioned it.

"That's cool. The location is great and the building is a gem. He'll be fine without you." I reassured Tyler, waiting for whatever else he was lobbing my way. I had no doubt that Otis could run a music venue without Tyler. He'd be fine.

Unlike me. I was working so hard at not losing it that I could barely get words past the lump in my throat. I was beyond being able to eat, leaving half my hibachi veggies on my plate.

"Not really. I mean, he has no clue about the other stuff. Running a business. He doesn't know how to set up, or that he should have concessions. Anything outside of the music, and he's clueless. I think if he does it right, the place can be a success."

Why were we talking about O and his old abandoned church-turned-music venue? I let a long sigh out through my nose. My mouth was dry and my eyes were too wet. My head was churning and my heart was aching.

Hold it together, Mallie.

"I want you to be his partner."

"Uh, no." My answer was automatic. I didn't need to think about it. Tyler's face was serious. He lowered his chair back to all four legs and leaned into the table, weight on his elbows. His eyes sparkled with anticipation. "Just no."

"Hear me out, Mallie Jo." He'd started calling me that when I had shown up on his doorstep at four years old. He'd said *Mallory Johansen is an old lady name, Mallie Jo is a good girl name.* To everyone else it was just Mallie. "You have exactly what it takes. You have style. I know you can go in there and work magic to make it funky and cool - but tasteful too."

"You are giving me way too much credit."

"Nope. I know you. I lived with you, remember? You could set up something for food. Good food. Drinks too. O can make deals with local wineries and breweries."

"You want me to renovate The Chapel?" I repeated it back to him, and still it made no sense.

"Yes. But not just that. I want you to help run it. There's so much more than just hiring a band and filling the pews. O can't think past the good acoustics in the building." Tyler's mouth moved into a half smile. A look that oozed with his fondness for his friend, including his shortcomings. "You can bring in all that local North Carolina stuff from mom's shop to sell. It would be a good spot for taking pictures too."

The old church was such a beautiful place, perched atop a hill, overlooking on one side historic downtown Fox River, and on the other side a working mill, with a wheel that churned in the river. The church was slated to be torn down, given a death sentence. No one had the money for upkeep and the city voted not to fund it any longer. Otis Bell threw his life savings into the place, and convinced Tyler to do the same. A fifty-fifty partnership.

O had visions of using it as a music hall.

I could see myself taking photos all over the meadow and the river bank, the mill, the view of our quaint town, even inside the church. Tyler was appealing to my interests with that last plea.

"That's why he wants you." Tyler nodded at me, gaining momentum. My face must have reflected my utter disbelief that Otis would want me for anything. "He wants you to shoot the bands. Also the jams. He has this idea that people will pay for prints of themselves playing. I think he's right. He'll be all over the fiddle conventions and festivals, and wants you to take photos there too. Same sort of thing. You capture the people while they're up on stage playing, or while they're sitting around jamming, then you offer prints for sale online."

"It's not a terrible idea." It could be fun. Shooting people without having to worry about family dynamics or setting. No one wanting certain poses that would never work. Very little, if any, interaction. Just finding the light and the angle and taking the shots. "But I can't work with Otis Bell."

Plus Fox River already had a photographer. The elusive Cotton MacKenna had been taking all the pictures in town for years. I wasn't sure how he'd feel about me treading in his territory. Not to mention he was already much more invested in the music scene than me.

"I told Otis you'd meet with him tomorrow morning. I also told him you'd have an open mind." Tyler gave me a pointed look.

I nodded, understanding exactly what he meant with the look

Oomph. This was so not a good idea.

I was not even close to accepting that Tyler would be gone in two days, much less able to wrap my mind around working with Otis. Ty told him I'd have an open mind. I wasn't sure I would be the problem.

"Will he?" I returned my own significant look.

It was a two way street. Our years of discomfort in the other's company wasn't one sided. He obviously hated me and didn't want to spend time with me. I couldn't say I hated him, but I did turn into a fumbling idiot whenever he was near. I tended to turn mute as well. If not instead into a babbling fool. Either way, nothing came out normal when I was in his presence.

"Of course. If nothing else, O is driven. He's a damn hard worker, and he has thrown himself into this business and wants it to be a success. He agrees that your eye and your talents will help him along."

"No. I mean …" How did I ask if it was possible for us to get along well enough to get a lick of work done? "All right. I'll meet with him."

"Good girl."

***

Tyler knew me well. He had me show up at The Chapel - what Otis named his historic little church on the hill - early in the morning. The sun had perfect golden fingers that reached down to the hilltop, setting everything alight with radiant warmth.

I walked around outside for too long, eyes glittering in the morning light, which was caught in the dew on each blade of grass, before forcing myself inside. The vestibule was dim with worn red carpet half pulled up from original hardwood floors. It was big enough to be a useful space, but it would take a lot of renovation.

Tyler knew I'd take one look at the place and fall in love. The wheels would start spinning and I'd have a thousand ideas. My heart thrummed with it, the desire to be in that space and make it beautiful. To transform it from a rotting heap into something both cozy and vibrant.

"I wasn't sure you'd come."

A large door squeaked on old hinges as Otis joined me.

"Neither was I." It wasn't hard to admit my reservations about this venture.

"What do you think?"

If that wasn't a loaded question.

What did I think of this insane partnering?

What did I think of the gorgeous building just waiting for a face lift?

What did I think of his army green t-shirt pulled taught across his muscled chest?

Stop thinking about his muscled chest!

"This place has a lot of potential, that's for sure." I managed the truth, without mentioning insanity or his muscles.

"Right?" His voice rose with the word, and he looked in awe of our surroundings.

I could see the pride and excitement in him. He was eager to turn this into something. Potential. Yes, there was a lot of potential.

My heart raced, sending blood storming through my body, because it was impossible to not have a physical reaction to our close quarters.

"I'm in." The words came out of their own accord. "I mean, if you'll have me."

His eyes skated down me and took their time coming back up to meet my gaze. My body was wound tight with tension. It had occurred to me at some point in our past that my tension with him veered dangerously toward sexual. Too bad he'd never see me that way.

Lingering eyes meant nothing. I'd seen him look at plenty of girls over the years.

Otis opened his mouth to respond, but before he could say anything, Tyler burst in through the big double doors.

"I'm late. Sorry not sorry. You two need to figure out how to be together without me." His laughter greeted us in a rush of warm air.

Tyler leaned down and kissed the top of my head. He did a man hug thing with Otis. It was very awkward as goodbye hung heavy between us all.

"We were figuring it out just fine, thank you very much." To my own surprise, I jumped in and defended us. Otis and I had worked well together. So far as saying hello went.

"Damn straight." Otis gave me a wink.

It was the first time I could remember him looking at me with a smile like that. Looking at me like I was on the inside. Looking at me like he didn't want me to disappear.

"Good. Thomas Aldridge will be here in a few minutes to make it all official."

The word official made my palms itch.

"Senior or Junior?" O asked casually, but I knew he cared which way it went, and more than that I knew he was anxious about moving forward with me as part of the team.

"Junior." Tyler assured him.

"Good. Ol' Aldridge Senior gets to talking and just about never shuts up."

We all laughed. Together. It was a moment.

We'd gone to school with Thomas Aldridge. Junior. He was older than Tyler and Otis by a year. I didn't know him well. Just enough to know his name and associate it with the law firm in town.

When he pushed through the doors and joined us in the too-dim, suddenly shabby entrance of the church, I wished we were anywhere else. Thomas wore a suit and tie. His black shoes were shiny, even in the low light.

"Tyler. Otis. Good to see you." He offered them each his hand. They shook hands like professionals. Like real grown ups. I skirted to the side. "You must be Mallory Johansen. I haven't had the pleasure."

Thomas turned his smile on me and I tried desperately to swallow my discomfort. I smiled back and I shook his hand. Not at all like a professional or like a grown-up that should be entering into a legal contract. More like a nervous bird, ready to take flight. His smile was such a show that it almost put me at ease. It took off the pressure of actually winning him over - or trying to - and just let us all coast on the surface.

"It's Mallie." I matched him smile for smile. "Nice to meet you."

The guys threw around names of folks from high school; Denver MacKenna, Elliot Davies, Natasha Mills. All folks I knew on sight, but none I called friends, as they were a little older than me and ran in different circles than me.

Otis directed us to an office tucked into the back corner of the church. It meant a trip through the main room and a glimpse at my future. It occurred to me I ought to have taken the grand tour before signing up. But it didn't disappoint. Morning sun filtered in through windows set high up along the walls, just beneath the roof. Stained glass scenes turned into fractured rainbows as sunlight poured through wavy glass windows surely as old as the building. Glorious.

The small office had dark wood built-in bookcases filled with dust-covered books. A large desk dominated the space, in the center of the room, facing toward the door. It was mostly clear of papers and dust, like Otis had cleaned it off recently.

Thomas got straight to work. We all signed our names or initials about a million times. He pointed and we put pen to paper. No one bothered to read any of the legal jargon, but Thomas gave us the condensed version as we proceeded. Basically Otis retained his fifty percent owner and revenue of The Chapel. Tyler didn't relinquish his hold completely, rather transferring thirty percent to me plus a salary, and keeping twenty percent and profit of his own. We all agreed to the terms. The whole thing was very amiable.

It seemed too easy.

My entire life had changed in the course of a day, and I had no idea what it entailed.

Hope you enjoyed your sneak peek of The Chapel! Look for this next installment in the fox river romance series early 2020.

About the Author

Jess B Moore is a writer of love stories. When she's not writing, she's busy mothering her talented children, reading obscene numbers of books, and knitting scarves she'll likely never finish.

Jess lives in small town North Carolina with her bluegrass obsessed family. She takes too many pictures of her cats, thinking the Internet loves them as much as she does. She is a firm believer of swapping stories over coffee or wine, and that there should always be dark chocolate involved.

All of Jess' novels combine her interests in family, music, and small towns into thoughtful tales of growing up and falling in love.

Please leave a review to tell other readers what you thought. Reviews are everything for writers!

You can connect with me on:
- 🌐 https://jessbmoore.com
- 🐦 https://twitter.com/authorjessb
- 🅵 https://www.facebook.com/authorjessb
- 🔗 https://www.instagram.com/authorjessb

Subscribe to my newsletter:
- ✉ https://mailchi.mp/26d3c6a08fb1/freebooksampler

Also by Jess B. Moore

All of my novels combine my interests in family, music, and small towns into thoughtful tales of growing up and falling in love. I promise to only write happy endings!

The Guilt of a Sparrow

Magnolia Porter has spent the entirety of her twenty-four years satisfying her mother's guilt. She was the good girl to her trouble making brother, Lucian – the one left behind to hold her mother together after he died. She is an invisible girl in a small town carrying the burden of her family's loss and pain. Maggie was nobody trying desperately to be somebody.

Cotton MacKenna is the one with the temper. Of the five MacKenna boys, he's the one most likely to throw the first punch. Never mind all those fights were a decade ago, all in an attempt to save a sweet girl from her bullying older brother. Now, Cotton has grown up, with his own photography business, yet as the fourth in the line of MacKennas, he would only ever be known for his past. Time for a change.

Maggie and Cotton are more than the labels placed on them, put there by their families, the town, and themselves.

Fierce Grace

A fierce connection…

Annabelle Dare is in a good place. She landed a sweet job, teaching at the quaint Fox River Elementary School. She has everything she needs: teaching music and sharing an apartment with her best friend. A simple life, she's convinced, is all she needs.

Asher Grace knows who he is and what he has to offer. Nothing. A poor boy from the wrong side of town, steel worker, with too much weight on his shoulders as he is trying to hold his family together. Best choice is avoiding too-sweet-for-her-own-good Annabelle at all costs.

Annabelle falls in love with the way she comes to life with Asher. He awakens a hunger for life and love in her that she didn't know she possessed.

Asher must learn his worth beyond his upbringing and his past. Annabelle must learn to stoke the fire of life as it burns within her and learn how close she can get before the flames lick her.

The Worth of a Penny

Sweetheart Penelope Davies is what her daddy calls gullible, right after he told her she was stupid and worthless. With her cheek red from being slapped by him, and her heart trampled by a worthless boyfriend, she packs up and follows her half-brother to Fox River, North Carolina, in need of a fresh start.

Dominic MacKenna is the youngest of five brothers, the friendly one with a killer smile and easy laugh. His brothers are all grown up, and one by one they're flying the nest, leaving him out of sorts and unsure of his place. Who is he if not the youngest MacKenna?

Penny falls in with the MacKenna brothers, welcomed in as family, and offered the kind of love and support she never knew existed. With a new job and a lot of determination, she is finding out what she's capable of. The last thing she needs now is to fall in love with the most notorious flirt in town.

Dominic falls for the sweet strong girl with a penchant for random facts and quirky homemade dresses. All he wants is to show Penny how wonderful she is, how smart and funny, and how desired and loved—even if he has to do it as her friend.

CPSIA information can be obtained
at www.ICGtesting.com
Printed in the USA
BVHW032210051119
562947BV00021B/71/P

CONTENTS

WORKING WITH THE MOON

- Gardening — 20
- Daily rhythms — 21
- Horticulture — 22
- Cultivating trees and shrubs — 23
- Harvesting — 25
- Plant-based decoctions — 27
- Fungicides and insecticides — 28
- Compost — 29
- Crop rotation — 30
- Agriculture — 31
- Hay — 32
- Cereal crops — 33
- Animal husbandry — 34
- Beekeeping — 36
- Winegrowing — 37
- Cider making/Beer making/Forestry — 38
- Miscellaneous — 40
- Plan of your garden — 109
- Companion planting — 110

PRACTICALITIES

- Understanding the calendar — 54
- Calculating world times — 80
- Index — 112
- How to use the calendar (tear out this page) — 113

UNDERSTANDING THE MOON

- The waxing and waning Moon — 2
- The ascending and descending Moon — 4
- The distance from the Earth to the Moon — 6
- Lunar nodes/Planetary nodes/Eclipses — 7
- Zodiac signs and constellations — 8
- The Moon in the zodiac signs — 9
- The Moon in the constellations — 10
- When signs and constellations are aligned — 10
- Planetary aspects — 11
- The Red Moon/Blackthorn Winter/Indian Summer — 15
- Tides — 16
- Chinese seasons — 18
- Geobiology — 19

LIVING WITH THE MOON

- Influence of the phases — 42
- Harvesting plants/For making infusions/ Medicinal plants — 43
- Hairdressing — 44
- Depilation — 45
- Skincare/Warts — 46
- Nails/Corns and callouses — 47
- Fasting/Detoxing/Treating worms — 47
- Eating — 48
- Treatments for the body/Teeth — 51
- Surgical procedures — 52
- The body and the zodiac — 53

LUNAR CALENDAR

- The calendar — 56
- Gardening notes — 81

UNDERSTANDING THE MOON

The waxing and waning Moon

This is one of the most familiar features of the Moon as viewed from the Earth. What we are seeing is the Moon's monthly orbit around the Earth (aka the synodic revolution), which starts with the New Moon and takes 29 days, 12 hours and 44 minutes. When new, the Moon is positioned exactly between the Earth and the Sun – thus, the illuminated area of its surface is not visible from Earth. This phase is represented on the diagram below by a black circle. As the Moon progresses on its orbit, it reflects a crescent of light that expands until it is seen from Earth as a luminous disc – the Full Moon. In this phase, the Moon is on the opposite side of the Earth to the Sun. From that point on, the illuminated area decreases until the Moon renews its orbit once more.

The waxing Moon

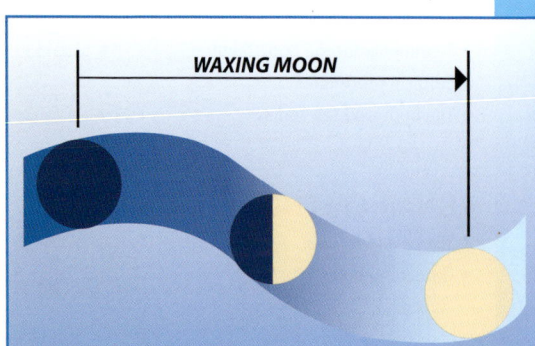

WAXING MOON

The Moon 'waxes' during the phase from New Moon to Full Moon – the illuminated area increases in size every day. On the calendar (pages 56-79), the colour of the blue band also becomes lighter as the Moon waxes.

In the night sky of the northern hemisphere, a quick glance will tell you if the Moon is waxing – the illuminated area is shaped like a crescent, which, if you were to add an imaginary line to the left of it, would resemble the letter 'p'. In the southern hemisphere, the illuminated area is also expanding but is seen the opposite way round, while in equatorial regions the crescent appears to be lying on its back.

This phase is indicated on the lunar calendar (pages 56-79) between the New Moon and the Full Moon.

Plants increase in vitality with moonlight and as the Full Moon approaches, their resistance to parasites and diseases increases. Fruits and vegetables harvested at this time store well and impart more vitality when eaten, while cut flowers last longer in a vase. Silage and mown hay are of better quality, compost is warmer and animals are less anxious when there are people around.

The waning Moon

The Moon 'wanes' during the phase between the Full Moon and the next New Moon. Every night the illuminated area becomes smaller. On the calendar (pages 56-79), the colour of the blue band darkens as the Moon wanes.

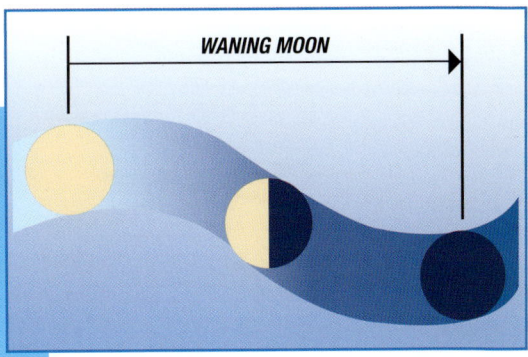

WANING MOON

In the sky of the northern hemisphere, the illuminated area of the waning Moon reverts to a crescent shape, but now if you were to add an imaginary line to the right of it, it would resemble the letter 'd'.

This phase lasts from the Full Moon to the next New Moon.

As the moonlight decreases, so does the vigour of plants, although their specific energy is increased – colours, scents and tastes are more perceptible during this phase, and nutritional and medicinal properties are more pronounced. However, it is more difficult to store harvested crops in their natural state and this phase is more suitable for preserving foods, making jams and bottling wine. Insecticides and fongicides are more effective.

The ascending and descending Moon

Many people think that an ascending Moon is the same as a waxing one when in fact they are totally different. The Moon can, for example, wax and descend at the same time. The path of the ascending and descending Moon is similar to the progress of the Sun during the course of the year. In the northern hemisphere, the Sun rises in the south-east and sets in the south-west at the winter solstice, toward the end of December. The arc that it describes in the sky is very short and at noon it is very low on the southern horizon. The closer we are to the summer solstice at the end of June, the nearer to the

north-east the Sun rises and the nearer to the north-west it sets. Its arc is much longer at this time and at noon the Sun is very close to its zenith. The sun is therefore ascending during the six months between the winter and summer solstices and descending during the six months between the summer and winter solstices. The Moon also ascends and descends, but over a period of 27 days, 7 hours and 43 minutes, known as the **periodic lunar cycle**. In the northern hemisphere, the Moon ascends in the sky and then descends again, while in the southern hemisphere the reverse takes place.

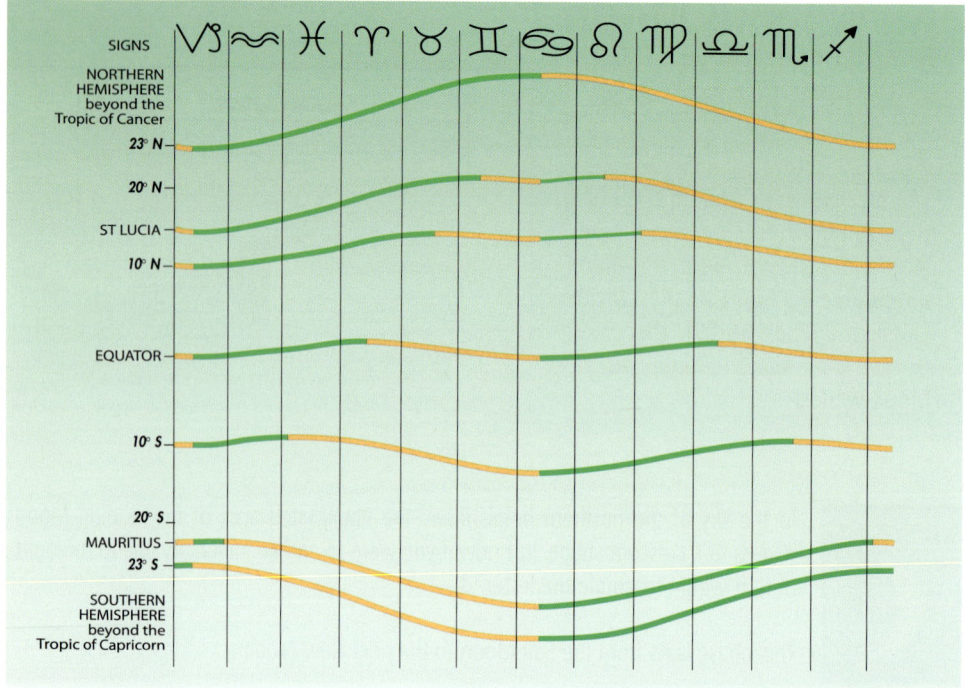

On the calendar on pages 56-79, the narrow coloured band beneath the date band shows the path of the ascending and descending Moon in the northern hemisphere as far as the Tropic of Cancer (to determine the path in the southern hemisphere, south of the Tropic of Capricorn, simply invert the colours). Between the two tropics, there is a regular pattern of inversion (see diagram above).

The influences of the ascending and descending Moon and Sun grow steadily weaker the nearer we get to the Equator. Beyond the tropics, the forces that result from such movements are linked with three factors: the ascending/descending Moon, the waxing/waning Moon and the tides (see page 16). Any of these factors can predominate – for example, in Europe, grafting is best done when the Moon is ascending. However, the nearer you are to the Equator, the more the influence of the ascending/descending Moon diminishes, while that of the two other factors increases. For instance, nearer the Equator it is more beneficial to graft plants when the Moon is waxing than when it is ascending.

In the northern and southern hemispheres, in regions beyond the tropics, the ascending/descending Moon has a very strong influence in certain areas of the lunar calendar. In equatorial regions, on the other hand, it is the waxing/waning Moon and the influences of the tide that have greater influence.

The Moon is ascending when, every night, its orbit is higher than the night before. Look at the Moon, ignoring the stars, for two consecutive nights to work out whether it is ascending or descending. On the first night, establish its position in the sky as accurately as possible. A little later on the following night, the Moon will pass through the same vertical once more. If it passes through at a greater height, you will know that it is ascending.

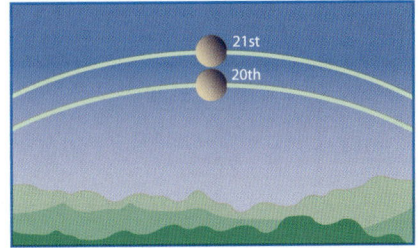

The ascending Moon

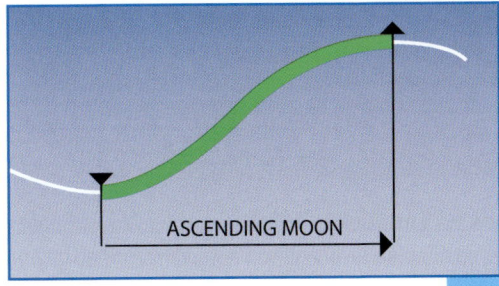

ASCENDING MOON

On the calendar (pages 56-79), the Moon is ascending when it travels from its lowest point (▼) to its highest (▲). This continual oscillation is shown in the illustration. When the curve rises, the Moon is ascending.

The fluids within plants rise and fall with the Moon. When the Moon is ascending, plants contain more sap so there is more activity in their aerial parts (those parts above ground). This is a good time, for example, to cut scions, to graft plants and to harvest fruit with a high juice content, as well as to collect sap from silver birches, etc. However, it is better to avoid pruning trees or cutting plants for drying at this time. Cutting lawns when the Moon is ascending tends to encourage plenty of growth; it is a good time to aerate them.

The descending Moon

On the calendar (pages 56-79), the Moon is descending when it travels from its highest point (▲) to its lowest (▼). When the curve falls, the Moon is descending.

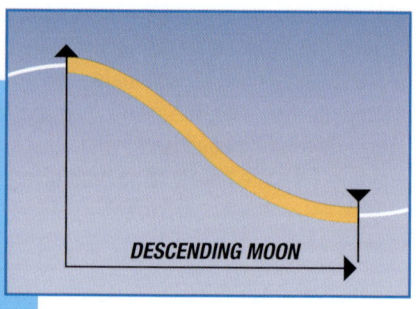

DESCENDING MOON

When the moon is descending, the flow of fluids in plants descends also and growth occurs mainly in the roots. This is a good time to **harvest root crops** or the aerial parts of a plant that you want to dry quickly, and also for **pruning, pricking out, re-potting, ploughing,** spreading **compost or manure** and **cutting wood.** The grass of lawns that are cut at this time forms stronger roots and anchors the soil better.

The distance from the Earth to the Moon

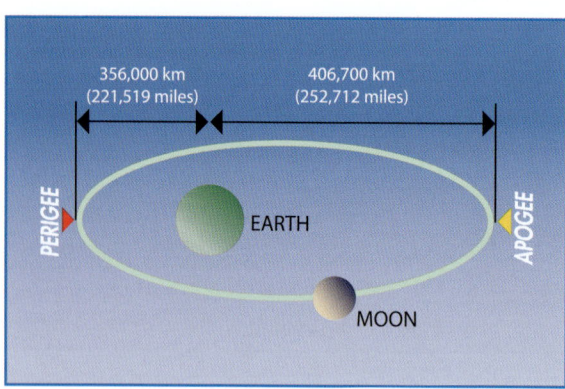

356,000 km
(221,519 miles)

406,700 km
(252,712 miles)

PERIGEE

EARTH

APOGEE

MOON

The Moon moves around an elliptical orbit, with the Earth as one of its foci. This means that the distance between the Earth and Moon is always changing. When the Moon is closest to the Earth, it is at its perigee, and when it is furthest away, it is at its apogee. The progress of the Moon from one perigee to the next is known as the **anomalistic lunar cycle** and takes 27 days, 13 hours and 18 minutes.

The Moon's effects on plants increases when it nears the Earth and its influence is, therefore, strongest around the time of the perigee. It is advisable to avoid all work involving soil and plants on the day of the perigee itself.

The Moon is closer to the Earth at the perigee; it looks larger at this time and, conversely, smaller at the apogee. In the calendar on pages 56-79, the Moon is shown at its largest near the perigee and at its smallest near the apogee, set in a band that is similarly widest at the perigee and narrowest at the apogee. The point of the perigee is indicated by the letter **P** and of the apogee by the letter **A**.

Lunar nodes

The Earth moves in an elliptical orbit, with the Sun as one of its foci. The plane of this ellipse is called the **ecliptic**. The Moon also moves around an elliptical orbit, with the Earth as a focus. The plane of this ellipse is at an angle of 5° 9' to the ecliptic. As it moves around the Earth, the Moon therefore crosses the ecliptic twice: once when descending – this is the **descending node** (☊), and once when ascending – which is the **ascending node** (☋). Experience has shown that disturbances occur when the Moon is at its perigee or its nodes and these are unfavourable times for cultivating the soil, sowing and harvesting.

On the calendar (pages 56-79), the times to be avoided are indicated in red. Obviously, the closer we are to the nodes and the perigee, the more harmful the influence. Since this influence develops gradually, we cannot indicate precisely when it begins and ends; to get an approximate idea of the hours to avoid, however, simply check the time that the red zone begins and ends.

Planetary nodes

The planets also have nodes, just like the Moon. We have taken them into account up to the present in the last band of the calendar on pages 56-79. This year we include them in the note pages (81–108) using the node symbols (☊ ☋) followed by the appropriate planet symbols (☿ ♀ ♂ ♃).

Eclipses

An eclipse takes place when the Moon is new or full, when it is aligned with the Sun and the Earth in the plane of the ecliptic (2): when the Moon is new it is an eclipse of the Sun and when the Moon is full it is an eclipse of the Moon. When the line of the lunar nodes intersects the Earth's

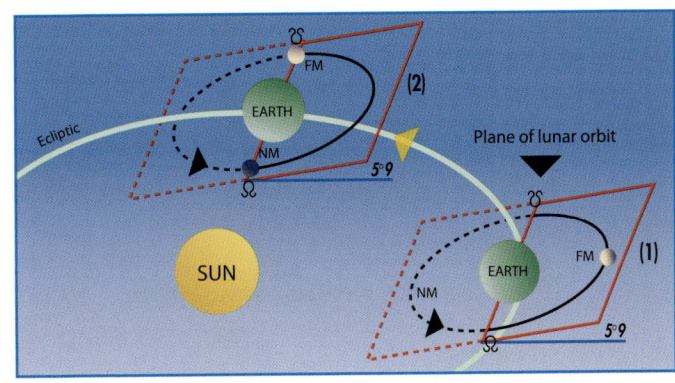

Planes of the EARTH-SUN and MOON-EARTH rotation.

plane of rotation around the Sun and the Moon's plane of rotation around the Earth (1), an eclipse will take place if the node coincides with the New Moon or the Full Moon.

For eclipses in 2009, see the following page.

Eclipses of the Moon in 2009:
- 9 February: total eclipse, reaching its maximum at 14:38 (GMT).
- 7 July: total eclipse, reaching its maximum at 10:38 (BST).
- 6 August: total eclipse, reaching its maximum at 01:39 (BST).
- 31 December: partial eclipse, reaching its maximum at 19:22 (GMT).

Eclipses of the Sun in 2009:
- 26 January: annular eclipse reaching its maximum at 07:58 (GMT), visible in the Indian Ocean, Borneo and Sumatra.
- 22 July: total eclipse reaching its maximum at 03:35 (BST), visible in India, Nepal, Tibet, China and around the Pacific Ocean.

Zodiac signs and constellations

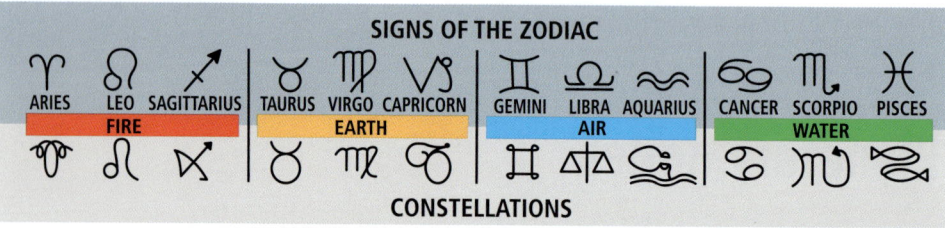

SIGNS OF THE ZODIAC

ARIES	LEO	SAGITTARIUS	TAURUS	VIRGO	CAPRICORN	GEMINI	LIBRA	AQUARIUS	CANCER	SCORPIO	PISCES
FIRE			EARTH			AIR			WATER		

CONSTELLATIONS

The constellations of the zodiac are groups of stars, named after their various shapes. These constellations are of different sizes. When the Moon passes in front of, or 'through', a constellation, it activates the influences belonging to it and transmits them to us. We owe our understanding of the laws concerning the Moon in the constellations to Rudolf Steiner, the father of anthroposophy. In 1924, he became the founder of biodynamic cultivation and his work has promoted the development of different systems of organic farming.

Centuries ago, the Chaldeans of Mesopotamia imposed a regular structure on the constellations, dividing them into 12 equal parts of 30° in order to mirror the length of their year. These divisions were called signs and the system will be familiar to followers of sun-sign astrology (dates when the sun changes sign and constellation are included, for information only,

on the calendar on pages 56-79). The zodiacal year begins with the sign of Aries in spring, at one of the two points in the year (vernal and autumnal) where the ecliptic crosses the celestial equator (imagine the plane of the terrestrial equator extending into space). In biodynamics (see page 19), the same regular structure is imposed on the lunar cycle. An astronomical phenomenon means that the natural rhythm of the constellations does not correspond exactly with the 'imposed' rhythm of the signs, and because the influences of constellations and signs are different (see below), both are used in biodynamics, sometimes in harmony (see page 10).

The influences of signs and constellations are not the same: the signs affect energy by influencing the fundamental qualities (hot, cold, dry, wet), while the influences of the constellations are more physical and directed towards specific zones, such as plant organs.

The Moon in the zodiac signs

The four fundamental qualities (hot, cold, dry, wet) act upon plants largely through the signs of the zodiac.

Hot tends to assist and accelerate plants' metabolism and helps in the exchange of fluids. Crop production is increased. However, if you actively increase heat, plants could dry out, particularly if there is already internal or external dryness. If there is already too much internal or external moisture, the risk of contracting parasitic or viral diseases increases. 'Hot' helps to counterbalance excessive external 'cold'.

Cold tends to slow down the development of the plant, hinder the exchange of fluids and limit metabolic changes. It also improves resistance to heat.

Dry tends to limit the amount of water in the tissues, concentrates the sap and helps to resist external moisture. Too much can cause the plant to mature too rapidly and wither.

Wet governs the amount of water in plants, which can reach more than 99% of plant mass. It stimulates active principles and nourishes the whole plant. Excess fluid can lead to decomposition and rotting.

- The expansive and vapourizing effects of 'wet' by 'hot' creates AIR. Air is therefore hot and wet.
- The condensation of 'wet' by 'cold' creates WATER. Water is therefore cold and wet.
- The concentration of 'cold' by 'dry' creates EARTH. Earth is therefore cold and dry.

It is not possible, therefore, to apply one quality in isolation. If you want to apply the quality 'dry', you must choose DRY and COLD (in other words, an EARTH sign) or DRY and HOT (a FIRE sign).

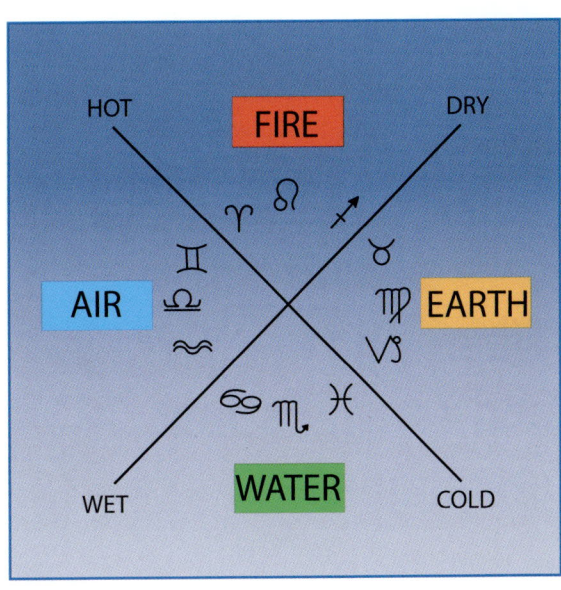

- These qualities cannot exist in isolation; they combine to create the four elements.
- The intensification and concentration of 'hot' by 'dry' creates FIRE. Fire is therefore dry and hot.

For example, if you want a specifically dry effect, work alternately when the Moon is in an Earth sign and when it is in a Fire sign; the alternate hot and cold qualities cancel each other out and the dry effect of your work will remain.

The Moon in the constellations

When the Moon is in a **Fire constellation** (Aries, Leo, Sagittarius), plant activity is concentrated mainly in the development of **fruits** and **seeds**. It is a good time for growing tomatoes, French beans, peas, apples and cereals of all kinds (and for maintenance and planting seeds, where appropriate).

When the Moon is in an **Air constellation** (Gemini, Libra, Aquarius), the **flowering** part of a plant grows well, so this is a positive phase for cultivating vegetables such as cauliflowers and artichokes, and ornamental flowers.

When the Moon is in a **Water constellation** (Cancer, Scorpio, Pisces), the **leaf** parts of plants grow well. Now is the time to work on salad vegetables, spinach, chard and so on.

When the Moon is in an **Earth constellation** (Taurus, Virgo, Capricorn), **bark** and **roots** develop well, making it an ideal time to concentrate on carrots, potatoes, asparagus, celery, parsnips and other root vegetables.

When signs and constellations are aligned

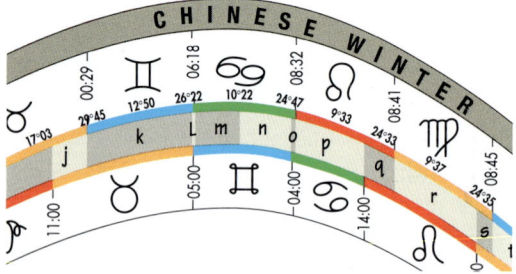

Better results are achieved when certain signs and constellations are aligned. We have concentrated on the effects of these alignments on food and wine crops, but further observations will allow us to focus and expand on the effects on other plants.

These alignments are represented in the bands on the calendar (pages 56-79) by letters of the alphabet. For example, 'p' indicates that the sign of Leo coincides with the constellation of Cancer. Varying shades of grey indicate periods corresponding to a letter and the times of changes are noted within the signs and constellations bands.

Planetary aspects

The planets revolve around the Sun at different distances and speeds. Viewed from the Earth, they move constantly across the sky. If we look at two planets at any given moment, they form an angle of which the Earth is the apex. If we see these two planets in alignment, the angle formed with the Earth is 0°. When this happens, they are in conjunction. When one planet sets and the other rises, it is known as an opposition (180°). When the position of a planet creates an angle of 60°, 90° or 120°, it is in aspect. Each aspect has been given its own colour in order to make location easier.

- An angle of 0° is a conjunction (♂), represented by ♂
- An angle of 60° is a sextile (✳), represented by ✳
- An angle of 90° is a square (□), represented by ▣
- An angle of 120° is a trine (△), represented by △
- An angle of 180° is an opposition (☍), represented by ☍

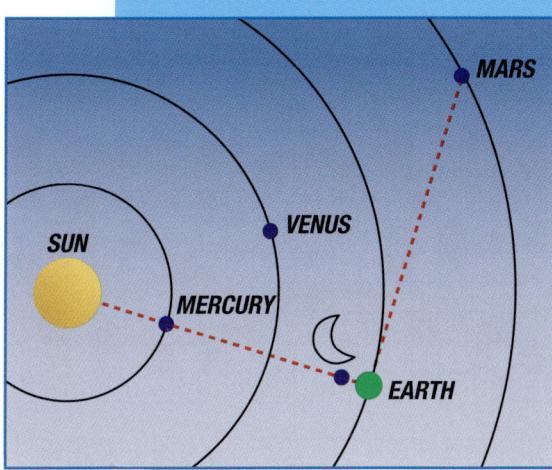

In the illustration, the Moon is in conjunction with Mercury and the Sun (☾ ♂ ☿ ☉) and also square to Mars (☾ ▣ ♂).

Some of these aspects can promote the harmonization of energy, leading to healthier growth. Others can disrupt the plant's energy, causing such problems as slow growth, excessive growth and disease.

In several chapters, we refer to planetary aspects - the days and times of these are indicated in the following pages.
We have observed that some aspects play a major role in various domains, during a time scale varying from a few hours to a whole day. You too can make your own observations and use planetary aspects in other ways than listed here.
For instance, checking in the tables that follow one of the moon's planetary aspects is: January 1 at 08:00 when the Moon is sextile to Mars (☾ ✳ ♂).

JANUARY	1	2	3	4	5	6	7	8	9	10	11	12	13	14	15	16	17	18	19	20	21	22	23	24	25	26	27	28	29	30	31
☉: SUN	✱23			12		△20					☍3				△15			3		✱19						☌8					✱13
☿: MERCURY			✱15			0		△5				☍6				△9		13		✱19					☌9					✱1	
♀: VENUS					✱20			2		△6				☍14					△15			9			✱3					☌9	
♂: MARS	✱8		20			△5				☍11				△18			3		✱17						☌3					✱8	
♃: JUPITER			✱9		16		△19				☍20					△3		12			✱1					☌5					✱3
♄: SATURN		☍18					△5		5		✱4				☌8					✱0		13			△1				☍23		
♅: URANUS		☌14					✱1		2		△1				☍4				△21			10		✱23					☌21		
♆: NEPTUNE					✱3		6		△7				☍7				△17			4		✱16					☌17				
♇: PLUTO	✱3		12		△18				☍21				△21			2		✱10					☌10					✱10		20	
	1	2	3	4	5	6	7	8	9	10	11	12	13	14	15	16	17	18	19	20	21	22	23	24	25	26	27	28	29	30	31

FEBRUARY	1	2	3	4	5	6	7	8	9	10	11	12	13	14	15	16	17	18	19	20	21	22	23	24	25	26	27	28			
☉: SUN		23			△6				☍15					△7		22			✱16						☌2						
☿: MERCURY	7		△13				☍19					△4		15			✱7					☌22						✱4			
♀: VENUS				✱4		8		△12				☍21					△22			13			✱4					☌0			
♂: MARS	18			△1				☍9				△20			6		✱21						☌7					✱7			
♃: JUPITER		10		△14				☍18					△0		9		✱21						☌1				✱20				
♄: SATURN			△10		13		✱13				☌16					✱5		17			△5					☍1					
♅: URANUS			✱10		13		△14				☍17					△8		20			✱9					☌6					
♆: NEPTUNE	✱11		15		△18				☍19					△4		13			✱2					☌2				✱18			
♇: PLUTO		△2				☍8				△10		13		✱20					☌19					✱19			3				
	1	2	3	4	5	6	7	8	9	10	11	12	13	14	15	16	17	18	19	20	21	22	23	24	25	26	27	28			

MARCH	1	2	3	4	5	6	7	8	9	10	11	12	13	14	15	16	17	18	19	20	21	22	23	24	25	26	27	28	29	30	31
☉: SUN		✱0		8		△14					☍3					△1		18			✱12					☌16					✱9
☿: MERCURY		16			△1				☍18					△19			15			✱14						☌7					✱9
♀: VENUS				✱10		13		△15				☍21					△11		22			✱7				☌19					✱0
♂: MARS		15		△22					☍8				△23			11			✱4					☌11					✱6		12
♃: JUPITER		2		△7				☍13				△22			6		✱18					☌21					✱14		19		△23
♄: SATURN		△13		16		✱18				☌22					✱10		20			△9					☍5				△16		19
♅: URANUS		✱18		22			△0				☍6				△19			7		✱20					☌17					✱4	
♆: NEPTUNE		23			△2				☍7				△15			0		✱12					☌12					✱2		7	
♇: PLUTO	△9				☍16				△21			0		✱6					☌4					✱3		11		△16			
	1	2	3	4	5	6	7	8	9	10	11	12	13	14	15	16	17	18	19	20	21	22	23	24	25	26	27	28	29	30	31

APRIL	1	2	3	4	5	6	7	8	9	10	11	12	13	14	15	16	17	18	19	20	21	22	23	24	25	26	27	28	29	30	
☉: SUN		16		△23					☍16					△20			15			✱8					☌4				✱15		
☿: MERCURY		21			△9					☍14						△8			6		✱23					☌17					
♀: VENUS		0		△2				☍6				△18			5		✱18					☌14				✱23			2		
♂: MARS		△18					☍7					△3		18			✱11					☌15					✱4		8		
♃: JUPITER					☍7				△17			2		✱13					☌16					✱8		11		△13			
♄: SATURN		✱22					☌4				✱16			2		△14					☍12				△22		23			✱1	
♅: URANUS	7		△10				☍18					△8		19			✱8					☌6				✱14		15		△18	
♆: NEPTUNE	△10				☍17					△3		11		✱22					☌23					✱13		16		△17			
♇: PLUTO	☍23					△6		10		✱16					☌13					✱13		21			△1				☍5		
	1	2	3	4	5	6	7	8	9	10	11	12	13	14	15	16	17	18	19	20	21	22	23	24	25	26	27	28	29	30	

MAY	1	2	3	4	5	6	7	8	9	10	11	12	13	14	15	16	17	18	19	20	21	22	23	24	25	26	27	28	29	30	31
☉: SUN	22			△6					☍5					△15			8		✶23					☌13				✶21			4
☿: MERCURY	✶2		7		△14					☍6					△2		12		✶19				☌23				✶22		23		
♀: VENUS	△6				☍19					△18			9			✶2					☌4				✶15		18		△23		
♂: MARS	△14					☍6					△7		23			✶16					☌16					✶1		4		△9	
♃: JUPITER		☍19					△8		17			✶5					☌7				✶23			1		△2				☍5	
♄: SATURN				☌8				✶22			8		△20					☍20					△7		8		✶8				☌14
♅: URANUS					☍3				△18			5		✶18					☌17					✶1		2		△2			
♆: NEPTUNE		☍23					△11		20			✶7					☌8					✶0		2		△2				☍5	
♇: PLUTO			△11		16		✶23					☌20					✶21			6		△10				☍12				△16	
	1	2	3	4	5	6	7	8	9	10	11	12	13	14	15	16	17	18	19	20	21	22	23	24	25	26	27	28	29	30	31

JUNE	1	2	3	4	5	6	7	8	9	10	11	12	13	14	15	16	17	18	19	20	21	22	23	24	25	26	27	28	29	30	31
☉: SUN		△14					☍19						△7		23			✶11				☌21					✶4		12		
☿: MERCURY	△4				☍22						△5		22			✶14					☌8				✶18			4		△18	
♀: VENUS			☍19						△2		21			✶15					☌14				✶22			2		△9			
♂: MARS				☍4					△10			3		✶19					☌15				✶21			0		△5			
♃: JUPITER			△18			3		✶15					☌17					✶10		13		△13				☍13				△23	
♄: SATURN					✶5		16			△4					☍5				△19		20		✶20				☌23				
♅: URANUS	☍10					△2		14			✶3					☌2				✶12		13		△12				☍16			
♆: NEPTUNE			△17			2		✶14					☌15					✶9		12		△12				☍13				△22	
♇: PLUTO	21			✶4					☌2					✶3		13		△19				☍21				△22			2		
	1	2	3	4	5	6	7	8	9	10	11	12	13	14	15	16	17	18	19	20	21	22	23	24	25	26	27	28	29	30	31

JULY	1	2	3	4	5	6	7	8	9	10	11	12	13	14	15	16	17	18	19	20	21	22	23	24	25	26	27	28	29	30	31
☉: SUN		△1					☍10					△22			11		✶20					☌4				✶13		23			△14
☿: MERCURY						☍15						△18			14			✶4				☌20					✶16			9	
♀: VENUS			☍11						△0		19			✶11					☌5				✶13		18			△4			
♂: MARS			☍3					△11			3		✶18					☌11				✶16		19			△0				
♃: JUPITER			8		✶20					☌21					✶16		20		△21				☍20					△1		10	
♄: SATURN		✶13			1		△14					☍15					△7		10		✶10				☌11					✶0	
♅: URANUS			△9		20			✶9					☌9				✶22		23		△23					☍0				△14	
♆: NEPTUNE			8		✶19					☌21					✶16		21		△22				☍21					△4		13	
♇: PLUTO	✶9					☌6					✶8		18			△2				☍7				△6		8		✶14			
	1	2	3	4	5	6	7	8	9	10	11	12	13	14	15	16	17	18	19	20	21	22	23	24	25	26	27	28	29	30	31

AUGUST	1	2	3	4	5	6	7	8	9	10	11	12	13	14	15	16	17	18	19	20	21	22	23	24	25	26	27	28	29	30	31
☉: SUN						☍2					△9		20			✶3				☌11					✶0		13			△6	
☿: MERCURY		△7						☍3					△10		20			✶2				☌11					✶7		22		
♀: VENUS		☍12						△3		19			✶8				☌22					✶7		16			△5				
♂: MARS	☍0					△9			0		✶13					☌4				✶9		13		△19					☍21		
♃: JUPITER	✶20					☌21					✶16		22			△1				☍1				△4		10		✶20			
♄: SATURN	12			△1					☍2				△19		23			✶1				☌2				✶13			1		△14
♅: URANUS		2		✶14					☌14					✶4		7		△8				☍9				△20			6		✶19
♆: NEPTUNE		✶0					☌1				✶21			3		△6				☍7				△11		18			✶5		
♇: PLUTO		☌11					✶13		23			△7				☍16				△16		17		✶22					☌17		
	1	2	3	4	5	6	7	8	9	10	11	12	13	14	15	16	17	18	19	20	21	22	23	24	25	26	27	28	29	30	31

SEPTEMBER	1	2	3	4	5	6	7	8	9	10	11	12	13	14	15	16	17	18	19	20	21	22	23	24	25	26	27	28	29	30	31
☉: SUN				☍17					△18			3		✶10				☌20					✶14			6			△0		
☿: MERCURY	△14					☍15					△3		5		✶4				☌1				✶3		10		△20				
♀: VENUS	☍19						△5		18			✶4				☌17					✶7		20			△14					
♂: MARS				△5		17			✶4				☌17					✶0		5		△12					☍15				
♃: JUPITER		☌20					✶15		22			△2				☍6				△9		14		✶23					☌23		
♄: SATURN					☍15					△7		12		✶15				☌18					✶5		15			△5			
♅: URANUS					☌18					✶8		13		△15				☍17					△2		12			✶0			
♆: NEPTUNE			☌6					✶1		7		△12				☍16				△20			2		✶12					☌13	
♇: PLUTO			✶18			5		△13				☍22					△2		4		✶7					☌1					
	1	2	3	4	5	6	7	8	9	10	11	12	13	14	15	16	17	18	19	20	21	22	23	24	25	26	27	28	29	30	31

OCTOBER	1	2	3	4	5	6	7	8	9	10	11	12	13	14	15	16	17	18	19	20	21	22	23	24	25	26	27	28	29	30	31
☉: SUN				☍7					△2		10		✶17					☌7					✶8			1		△19			
☿: MERCURY		☍20					△17			3		✶12					☌6					✶12			9			△7			
♀: VENUS		☍4					△6		15			✶0				☌15					✶13			7			△2				
♂: MARS		△21			7		✶15					☌2				✶11		17			△2					☍5					△7
♃: JUPITER				✶18			0		△5				☍11				△17		22			✶7					☌7				
♄: SATURN			☍4				△18		23			✶3				☌9				✶20			6		△18					☍18	
♅: URANUS		☌23					✶12		16		△19					☍1				△10		19			✶5					☌5	
♆: NEPTUNE					✶7		12		△16				☍22					△4		10		✶19					☌19				
♇: PLUTO	✶2		12		△19					☍4				△10		13		✶17					☌10					✶10		20	
	1	2	3	4	5	6	7	8	9	10	11	12	13	14	15	16	17	18	19	20	21	22	23	24	25	26	27	28	29	30	31

NOVEMBER	1	2	3	4	5	6	7	8	9	10	11	12	13	14	15	16	17	18	19	20	21	22	23	24	25	26	27	28	29	30	31
☉: SUN		☍19					△9		16		✶23					☌19						✶3		22			△14				
☿: MERCURY		☍16					△12		21			✶7					☌9						✶1		23			△15			
♀: VENUS	☍10					△4		11		✶20					☌16					✶23			20			△14					
♂: MARS		15		✶19					☌4				✶15		22			△8					☍11					△11		17	
♃: JUPITER	✶3		8		△12				☍18					△2		9		✶18					☌20					✶18		23	
♄: SATURN				△6		9		✶12				☌20					✶9		19			△8					☍8				
♅: URANUS			✶17		20		△22					☍5				△16			1		✶12					☌13					
♆: NEPTUNE	✶13		18		△21					☍3				△11		18			✶3					☌4					✶0		
♇: PLUTO		△3				☍10				△16		20			✶1				☌19					✶20			7		△14		
	1	2	3	4	5	6	7	8	9	10	11	12	13	14	15	16	17	18	19	20	21	22	23	24	25	26	27	28	29	30	31

DECEMBER	1	2	3	4	5	6	7	8	9	10	11	12	13	14	15	16	17	18	19	20	21	22	23	24	25	26	27	28	29	30	31
☉: SUN		☍8				△17			0		✶9					☌12						✶0		18			△7				☍19
☿: MERCURY			☍10					△1		11		✶23						☌8					✶18			5		△11			
♀: VENUS	☍14					△2		9		✶18					☌22						✶13			8		△23					☍15
♂: MARS		✶20					☌0				✶9		16			△2					☍3					△1		7		✶9	
♃: JUPITER			△2				☍5				△15		23			✶10					☌12					✶12		18		△21	
♄: SATURN	△20		21		✶23					☌5				✶20			6		△19					☍20					△9		10
♅: URANUS	✶2		4		△5				☍10				△23			8		✶20					☌22					✶13		16	
♆: NEPTUNE	4		△6				☍9				△18			1		✶11					☌12					✶10		16		△18	
♇: PLUTO			☍20				△23			3		✶9					☌4					✶6		18			△2				☍8
	1	2	3	4	5	6	7	8	9	10	11	12	13	14	15	16	17	18	19	20	21	22	23	24	25	26	27	28	29	30	31

The Red Moon

This period begins with the New Moon immediately after Easter and ends at the following New Moon. Since Easter is the Sunday following the first Full Moon of spring, **this year the Red Moon lasts from 25 April to 24 May**.

During this time, young shoots and buds can become damaged by the cold even when the air temperature is above zero. This phenomenon is probably due to the balancing of the temperature in the upper atmosphere with the soil temperature, rather than to the light of the Moon. In fact, when the sky is clear, the temperatures are balanced by radiation, which is greater at soil and plant level. As a result, while the temperature in the air may be just above zero, the temperature of the air surrounding plants can fall below zero, scorching young buds and leaves. This balancing occurs throughout the year but only produces this effect during the period of the Red Moon due to the combination of fragile buds and the low soil temperature.

Blackthorn Winter

A drop in temperature and the last of the spring frosts usually takes place during May; this normally occurs around **11, 12 and 13 May**.

Indian Summer

Around 11 November, six months after the Blackthorn Winter in May, the exact opposite takes place, and an un-seasonal rise in temperature occurs, known as an Indian Summer.

At both times, it appears as if the previous season is making one last effort to assert itself before the next season takes over.

Tides

You might think that the influence of the tides is restricted to the movement of water, but in fact tidal influence also affects the soil and most plants. Tides are caused by the gravitational attraction of astronomical bodies; their strength depends on the mass of the bodies and the distance between them. As far as the Earth is concerned, the two bodies with the most significant effect are the Moon and the Sun. The Moon's effect is, on average, 2.17 times stronger than that of the Sun. This attraction subtly alters the shape of the Earth, and this phenomenon is most apparent in the movements of the oceans. As centrifugal force counterbalances the strength of gravitational attraction, the Earth's ocean surface which is naturally shaped like an egg (1), is pulled into the shape of a rugby ball (2).

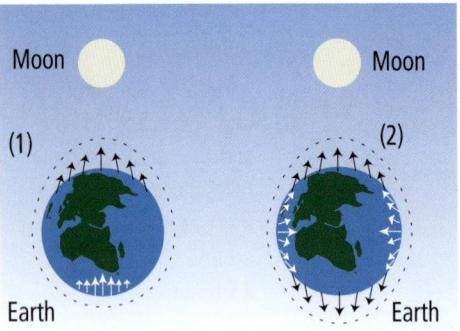

Since the attraction of the Moon is greater, its position determines the tides. The effect of the Sun is limited to reducing or increasing the Moon's gravitational attraction. When the Moon is new or full, the Sun, Moon and Earth are aligned, so the two gravitational pulls combine to cause the highest tides (spring tide). During the first and last quarters, on the other hand, the lunar and solar gravitational attractions oppose one another, so the tides are lower (neap tide).

Atmospheric pressure has a delaying effect on the natural rhythm of the tides, but without this influence the tide would always be at its lowest when the Moon is ascending. During the time the Moon takes to reach its highest point, or meridian (on average 6 hours and 12 minutes), the tide rises (incoming tide) before beginning to recede (ebb tide) until the Moon sets. The tide then rises again to reach the opposite meridian (+180°) before receding once more until the following evening. This double cycle of rising and receding tides takes 24 hours and 50 minutes, the time the Moon takes to return to the same meridian and a little longer than one rotation of the Earth (to compensate for the Moon's displacement during the Earth's rotation).

It is not only the seas that are affected – scientists have shown that the Earth's crust lifts 30 cm (12 in) or more during high tides and it is also known that the tides can affect living creatures. It seems obvious to us that tides have an influence on sap and on crops in general. Although we have not been able to gather together enough evidence to verify the following points, and despite the practical difficulties involved, we consider it useful to take them into account when carrying out certain tasks.

Choose a rising tide for the following:
- sowing, when the Moon is descending to balance energies
- grafting
- cultivating heavy soil
- spreading compost (avoid compacting the compost)
- harvesting, when the Moon is waning

Choose a receding tide for these tasks:
- sowing, when the Moon is ascending to balance energies
- pricking out
- cultivating light soil
- cutting wood
- harvesting, when the Moon is waxing

Tidal influences are not felt immediately, and with plants, the delay is estimated at about an hour. For example, the first effects of a rising tide will be felt about one hour after the Moon rises or sets; the effects will continue until one hour after it reaches the meridian. In the time (up to thirty minutes, in fact) that precedes or follows the change, the effect will be greatly reduced, so avoid these times if you want to get the maximum benefit from your work. The effects of a rising tide are stronger in the morning, while those of a receding tide are stronger in the afternoon. This pattern occurs near the New Moon and the Full Moon; tidal influences are weaker around the 'quarters'.

The times given in the notes pages (81–108) are for GMT standard time (26 October to 29 March) and British Summer Time (30 March to 25 October) – see page 80 for other countries.

The times given for the rising and setting of the Moon are for London. For the times for where you live, see the table, page 80.

On pages 81-108, to make the calculations easier, the time that a rising tide begins to affect plants is marked in green and the time that a receding tide begins to affect plants is marked in black. The times for London are valid for a good part of England. For greater precision, see the time differences marked on the map, right.

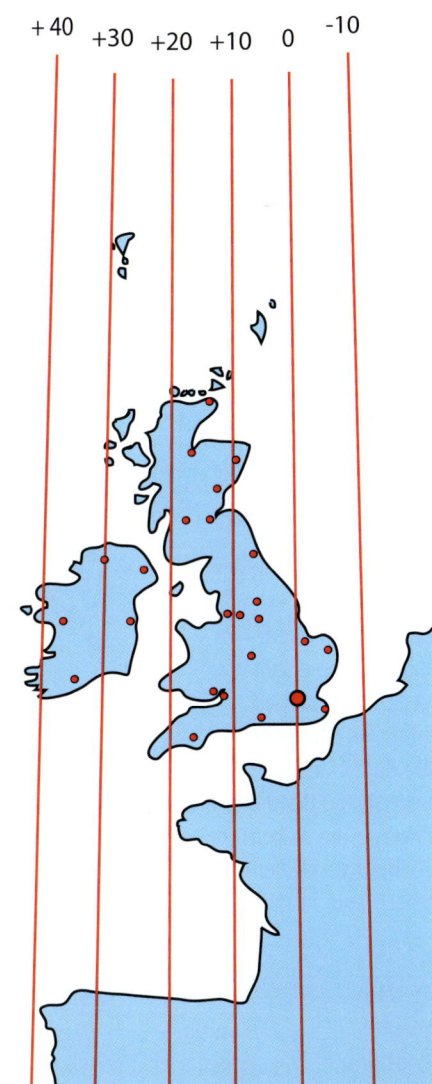

TIME DIFFERENCES FROM LONDON

For Ireland add 30 minutes to the times indicated. For example, if you want to carry out a crown graft on 25 April and benefit from the effect of the rising tide, do it between 06:15 and 14:15 if you are in the London area. If you are in Ireland, do it between 06:45 and 14:45.

Chinese seasons

The traditional Chinese year is made up of 12 lunar months (13 months in 7 years out of a 19-year cycle), each month beginning at the New Moon and lasting 29 or 30 days. The Chinese New Year takes place between 21 January and 20 February. Chinese springtime is determined by the Sun and begins halfway between the winter solstice and the vernal (spring) equinox. Between each season comes an 'inter-seasonal' period of 18 days that makes it easier to adapt to the change from one season to the next. According to traditional Chinese culture Qi (pronounced chi) is the energy or 'life force' that is present everywhere in the universe and that flows around us as part of that universe. The seasons influence the nature of the Qi. The five elements (wood, fire, earth, metal, water), and all that is linked to them, form the basis of Chinese culture and medicine (see the table below). The main focus of Chinese medicine is on the prevention of illness by taking into account the rhythm and flow of the Qi – treating the patient at the appropriate time enables treatment to work more effectively.

The method used in acupuncture is simple and effective – treatment is given during the inter-seasonal period before the season that governs the part of the body that is affected. For example, for problems involving the element 'water' (such as bladder, kidneys, fatigue and anxiety), treatment is carried out between autumn and winter. By taking into account the patient's Qi, the most effective days for treatment can be selected. As a result, knowledge of the Chinese seasons is extremely useful for practitioners whose work involves energy flow.

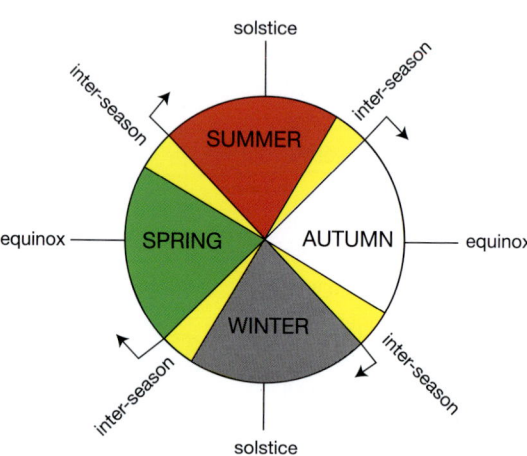

ELEMENT	WOOD	FIRE	EARTH	METAL	WATER
SEASON	Spring	Summer	Inter-season	Autumn	Winter
DIRECTION	East	South	Centre	West	North
ORGAN	Liver	Heart	Spleen	Lung	Kidneys
VISCERA	Gall bladder	Small intestine	Stomach	Large intestine	Bladder
TASTE	Acid	Bitter	Sweet	Pungent	Salty
COLOUR	Greeny blue	Red	Yellow	White	Black
ORGAN/SENSE	Eye/sight	Tongue/speech	Mouth/taste	Nose/smell	Ear/hearing
EMOTIONS	Anger	Joy	Thoughtfulness	Sadness	Intense fear
ENERGY	Wind	Heat	Wet	Dry	Cold

Geobiology

The Earth is an electromagnetic body, with its own electromagnetic grid pattern. This grid has an effect on all living things and includes telluric lines, underground streams, ley lines and geological fault lines.

For the past fifty years, physicists, doctors and dowsers have demonstrated how a specific location, or soil, can influence the growth or behaviour of plants, trees, animals and people. Dr Hartmann and Dr Curry are both well-known exponents of the theory, having highlighted the existence of electromagnetic fields.

This sickly tree has suffered as a result of being planted on an intersection of electromagnetic lines (causing the double trunk, canker, stunted appearance, smaller leaves and fruit).

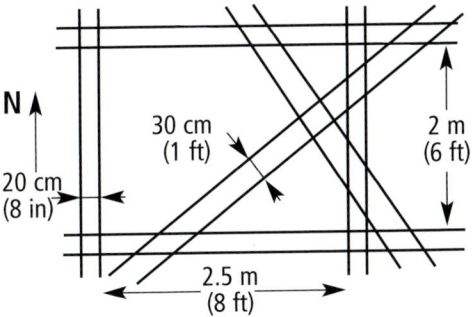

The **Hartmann** Grid consists of naturally occurring charged lines measuring 20 cm (8 in) in width and occurring at intervals of, on average, 2 m (6 ft) running from north to south and 2.5 m (8 ft) from east to west. The grid is like a large-meshed fishing net covering the Earth, and its influence can be felt even at the top of the highest buildings. The **Curry** lines measure 30–40 cm (12–16 in) in width and run diagonally to the Hartmann lines and at irregular intervals.

Many animals avoid the lines, including dogs, cattle, horses, pigs, deer, stags and wild boar. Others are drawn to them, such as cats, ants and swallows.

It is advisable not to spend too much time where the lines occur and to take great care over the positioning of furniture and equipment, including beds, workstations and the chair used regularly for watching television. It is important to remember that every living thing positioned directly above the intersection of these lines (the nodes) will be adversely affected at some stage. Pay particular attention to where you plant trees and shrubs and position beehives and animal hutches.

You may already have experienced the effects of electromagnetic fields. If not, it is relatively easy to locate the fields after a few lessons on using a divining rod, a dowsing pendulum, a Hartmann lobe or your own hands.

Hartmann lobe

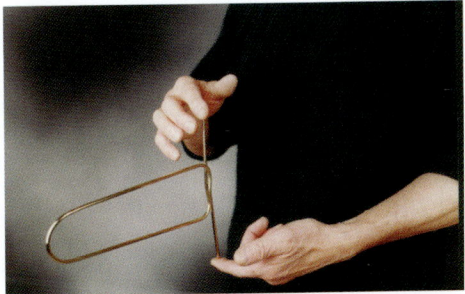

WORKING WITH THE MOON

Each time we cultivate the soil, we can modify or increase any influences. If you have sown a crop at an unfavourable time, you can reverse the effect to a certain degree by hoeing at a favourable time.

SOWING: always choose a constellation appropriate to the crop you are sowing (ie. favourable to fruit, root, flower or leaf plants) and preferably sow in the morning. If possible choose one with the maximum number of stars indicated in the lowest band (summarising lunar and planetary influences) on the calendar on pages 56-79.

PLANTING AND PRICKING OUT: choose days when the Moon is descending and also, if possible, when it is opposite a constellation appropriate to the crop that you are growing (ie. favourable to fruit, root, flower or leaf plants) and preferably in the afternoon.

HOEING: for eradicating weeds see page 31.
IN WET WEATHER: if possible, weed in the morning in a Fire or Air sign when the Moon is waning.
IN DRY WEATHER: weed in the evening, if possible, and in an Earth or Water sign when the Moon is waxing.

WATERING: to avoid plants developing shallow roots, instead of watering little and often, water them generously but less frequently. The ideal time is when the Moon is in the descendant and in the constellation of Virgo, Gemini or Libra. Avoid nodes and the superposition of the sign of Leo with the constellation of Leo.

MULCHING: mulch helps to fertilize and protect the soil, and limits the evaporation of moisture and weed germination.
A variety of materials can be used as mulch, such as straw, grass cuttings (a thin layer, fresh or dried), composted bark (very effective, a thickness of 2 or 3 cm/about 1 inch is enough).
It is best to mulch when the Moon is waxing and in an Earth or Air sign.
Aeration of the soil should ideally be carried out when the Moon is ascending; soil decomposes and breaks down more easily (via worms and micro-organisms) when the Moon is descending.

STRAWBERRIES: separate and plant out runners during the constellation of Leo ♌ preferably when the sign of Leo ♌ is in superposition with the constellation of Leo ♌ (q) for example, from 11:00 on 23 July until 05:24 on 24 July.

THE END PRODUCT: always bear in mind the kind of crop you are growing. Take endives as an example – sow and hoe them on dates favourable to 'root' plants in order to help the roots develop well, but, to ensure a good crop, harvest them on dates favourable to 'leaf' plants when the Moon is descending. Their growth should be forced on a good 'leaf' date when the Moon is ascending.

GREEN SALAD: until July, sow green salad in a Water constellation when the Moon is waning in order to prevent these plants from going to seed. During the autumn many forms of energy are in decline. To compensate, sow green salad in a Water constellation, but when the Moon is waxing.

POTATOES: plant potatoes on a day favourable to 'root' plants, but not too close to the perigee. To raise seed potatoes, plant when the Moon is in the sign of Taurus.

To avoid producing green potatoes, earth up when the Moon is in an Earth constellation and when it is waning and also, if possible, with a receding tide.

To remove the eyes (buds) from potatoes that have been lifted and stored so that they will keep longer, choose a time when the Moon is waning and descending, and prefer-ably when it is in the constellation of Virgo.

CROP ROTATION: see page 30.

Pleasing to the eye and beneficial for the plants, grown in the right combinations, plants can work well together (see pages 110-111).

Daily rhythms

The Earth's energy patterns vary according to the seasons. During spring, when the Sun is ascend-ing, the Earth 'breathes out', whereas in the autumn, the Sun descends and the Earth 'breathes in'. The same pattern is echoed by the Moon when it is ascending (sometimes called the lunar spring) and when it is descending (also known as the lunar autumn). And energies rise and fall through-out the day too, rising in the **morning** when the Earth 'breathes out' – a good time to **sow** (for example, carrots during the morning of a day favourable to 'root' plants), to **weed** in wet weather, and to **harvest aerial plant parts**. In the **afternoon**, the Earth 'breathes in' so it is a good time to **plant, prick out, plough, weed** in dry weather and **harvest root crops**. The inter-vening period, from 12:00 to 15:00, is a period of transition and is best avoided.

Horticulture

BULBS: plant bulbs when the Moon is in the constellation of Libra (♎).

REPOTTING: repot plants when the Moon is descending.
- Choose a date favourable to 'leaf' plants for those grown for their foliage (♋ or ♏).
- For flowering plants, choose a date favourable to 'flower' plants (♊ or ♎).

FERTILIZING: add fertilizer when the Moon is descending and if possible, when it is waxing, avoiding Fire signs.

GRAFTING ROSES: shield budding can be carried out during any month of the year on a date favourable to 'flower' plants when the Moon is ascending. Graft as low down the stem as possible towards the base to prevent suckers from forming.

PRUNING ROSES: choose a 'flower' date when the Moon is descending. All roses should be pruned when they are dormant or semi-dormant, ie. between autumn and when the buds are just beginning to break out in the spring, but avoiding frosty periods. Prune to an outward facing bud, removing dead, diseased and dying shoots and any crossing growth. Pruning will also help to prevent damage to tall stems caused by wind rock. Most modern roses flower on new or the current season's growth and so should normally be pruned fairly hard to stimulate new growth and to encourage flowering. Shrub and old garden roses should be pruned lightly.

- **Cluster-flowering bush roses (Floribunda):** cut back main stems to 30–40 cm (12–16 in) from the ground or, for taller cultivars, to about one third of their length.
- **Large-flowering bush roses (Hybrid Tea):** cut back to 20–25 cm (8–10 in) from the ground, or slightly less severely in very mild areas.
- **Climbing and rambling roses:** climbers should not normally be pruned in their first two years except to remove dead or diseased stems. In subsequent years shorten side shoots and leave main shoots unpruned unless they are too long. Shorten the side shoots of ramblers in the first two years to a vigorous shoot. In subsequent years cut back old or diseased stems to ground level to maintain a good framework and allow air to circulate freely.
- **Shrub and old garden roses:** prune only lightly – these flower on wood that is two or more years old.

PRUNING FLOWERING SHRUBS: remove dead or diseased stems and any suckers at the base of the plant, retaining the strongest stems. Prune above a lateral bud on a date favourable to 'flower' plants with a descending Moon.

- **flowering shrubs (old wood):** prune as soon as flowering is over (eg. forsythia).
- **flowering shrubs (new wood):** prune quite hard when the worst of the cold weather is over at the beginning of spring (eg. buddleia).

Cultivating trees and shrubs

PLANTING

The following rules are important for planting a tree:

Location: avoid very windy positions and see Geobiology information (page 19).

Soil: ensure it is well balanced — for instance, if it is too acidic, add lime-rich material such as spent mushroom compost, if the soil is too heavy, dig in some sharp sand.

Time of year: avoid heavy frosts. It is preferable to plant trees in the autumn, provided that the following winter is not likely to be too hard. You can also plant in spring but you will need to water the young tress more regularly during the following summer. Whichever season trees are planted in they need a lot of attention during their first few years before they become established (watering, aerating the soil, adding compost).

Planting: it is essential to avoid the lunar nodes (do not plant for two days after an eclipse) as well as times when the Moon is square to the Sun, Mars or Saturn (☾ ▣ ☉ ♂ ♄) – see pages 12–14.

- **Flowering and fruit-bearing trees and bushes:** plant when the Moon is descending, if possible when it is also waxing and when the tide is receding. If the Moon is waning, choose a time that corresponds with a rising tide.
- **Deciduous trees and shrubs:** mainly as for flowering and fruit-bearing trees above, except for trees that grow quickly and those that tend to 'rush' (poplars, maples), when it is better to plant with the Moon ascending and waning and with a receding tide. This configuration produces softer wood but it will encourage this type of tree to grow more quickly and with fewer knots.
- **Conifers:** plant when the Moon is in the descendant and if possible waning. This helps conifers such as firs to develop deeper roots.

PRUNING

As a general rule, prune when the Moon is descending, although an exception can be made when pruning a young tree since the ascending Moon will encourage new wood to grow more quickly. Avoid lunar nodes, when the Moon is square to the Sun, Mars or Saturn (☾ ▣ ☉ ♂ ♄) – see pages 12–14 – as well as the perigee, the equinox and periods of severe cold.

- **Fruit trees and bushes:** prune when the Moon is descending, and if possible when it is also waning and when there is a rising tide.

- **Flowering shrubs:** prune when the Moon is descending, and if possible when it is also waxing and when there is a receding tide.

- **Conifers, deciduous trees and hedges:** prune when the Moon is descending, if possible when it is waxing and with a rising tide. However, prune cypress trees, pyracanthas and trees and hedges that have reached their desired height when the Moon is waning rather than waxing.

GRAFTING

Choose an ascending Moon, on a date favourable to 'fruit' plants preferably or on a date favourable to 'flower' plants if this is not possible. Remove and heel in the grafts when the Moon is ascending (in December/January in the UK).

- **Crown graft:** this form of graft is preferable to cleft grafting, which often causes canker and fruit scab. Wait until the rootstock begins to flower so that there is plenty of sap rising and graft on a date favourable to 'fruit' plants when the Moon is ascending, for example 25 April.

- **Shield budding:** this should be carried out in August on a 'fruit' day with a rising moon when the sap is rising for the second time, for example 30 August. To ensure plenty of rising sap, water the rootstock during the fortnight before the grafting. Make the 'shield' from the thin bark of the rootstock, with just a little of the wood attached – by leaving a strip of wood, you prevent the grafted bud from falling out.

PROPAGATING WITH CUTTINGS

Ideally, cuttings should be taken just as the Moon is coming to the end of its ascension and should be planted as it begins to descend.

- **Cuttings from bushes:** (such as gooseberries, blackcurrants, etc.) in autumn, on the last day of the ascending Moon, take cuttings of around 10–15 cm (4–6 in) in length from the current year's growth. Gather the cuttings together in bunches of ten or so, and gently hold the stems together with a rubber band, place them in a plastic bag and leave them for a day in the refrigerator. When the Moon begins its descent, plant the cuttings out at an angle of about 45°, leaving a little less than half the cutting above ground. Planting at this angle helps promote their growth. In spring, as soon as the first leaves appear and when the Moon is descending, gently lift the cuttings and place each in a pot full of enriched peat. A few weeks later, when the roots have developed, plant them out or pot them on in soil-based compost. Propagating cuttings in bunches has been seen to increase hormonal activity, resulting in improved growth.

Harvesting

Various factors influence the quality and preservation of fruit and vegetables after harvest. As a general rule, choose an ascending Moon for harvesting plant parts that grow above ground and a descending Moon for parts that grow below ground, but avoid the perigee, lunar nodes and stormy weather. Fruit and vegetables that do not store well will last much longer if you avoid harvesting during Water signs and constellations (Cancer, Scorpio and Pisces). On the harvesting band on the calendar on pages 56-79, look for the days marked with stars – green stars for aerial parts and yellow for roots.

Other factors to take into account:

- Fruit picked when the Moon is ascending will stay juicy for longer and will have more energy-giving properties.
- The ascending Moon will also help plants to develop and ripen.
- The descending Moon promotes the preservation of certain properties in harvested crops.

As there are many different factors that need to be taken into account we have produced a quick-reference summary:

- Harvest fruit that should be allowed to ripen as slowly as possible (strawberries, raspberries, cherries, apricots, peaches, plums, etc.) when the Moon is waxing and descending (if need be, when it is ascending and waning) and if possible on days with one of the following planetary aspects: (☾ ☌ ✳ △ ♀ - ☾ ☌ ☿ - ☾ ☌ ☍ ♅) see pages 12–14.

- For squashes and varieties of pumpkin that do not keep well, choose a waxing (but not ascending) Moon during the following periods: a - b - i - j - k - L - q - r - s - t - z - (see the calendar on pages 56-79) and if possible pick them during one of the following aspects (☾ ☌ ✳ △ ♀ - ☾ △ ☉) see pages 12–14. For example, **AUGUST:** 21- 22am*- 22pm - 23 - 24 - 29pm - 30am*- 30pm - 31 - **SEPTEMBER:** 19 - 20 - 26am - 26pm*- 27 - 28am. (am = morning, pm = afternoon).

- When harvesting root crops, follow the guidelines on the calendar (pages 56-79) and try to combine the descending with the waning Moon, except in the case of garlic, onions and shallots, when you should choose the waxing Moon.

We believe that the tides also affect the harvest (see page 16). When the Moon is waxing choose a receding tide and when it is waning choose a rising tide. The best time to harvest crops is when these periods occur in the early morning with dew on the ground, as this gives positive and magnetic energy to the harvested crops.

Plants diseases

On the whole, diseases can be avoided or at least contained through a good soil balance and intense biological activity (microbes and roots). It is essential to stimulate and restructure the soil with the help of living matter. For instance, green fertilizer is one of the best way to obtain such a result. Using 'young' compost can also generate good results in the soil, except for vegetables which require a 'mature' compost.

In most cases, this intensification of soil life will give enough energy to the plants to avoid disease. Plant decoctions also act as a preventative against diseases (see next chapter). Some other products also have a healthy effect on the soil and help prevent diseases. Here are some of the ones we have begun testing with success against oidium and mildew [what are they?]. Perhaps you also have experiences you would like to share with us?

CHARCOAL

Charcoal reinforces the soil and has a purifying and cleansing effect that prevents cryptogamic diseases in a localized area. It is particularly efficient at preventing the dispersion of spores and seeds. It regulates the soil by assisting in the storage of nutrients. Use natural, pulverized, charcoal, mixed with the soil prior to sowing the seeds, 100 to 150 g/m2. Ideally this should happen during an ascending and waning moon.

SOOT

Soot resulting from burning wood also helps to prevent cryptogamic diseases as it protects the living organisms in the soil. However do not apply if you have already used charcoal, or if the soil is very acid!
Mix 200 to 300 g of dry (not wet) soot with 10 litres of water, ideally during a waxing moon (a, b, c, d, i, j, k, l periods), avoiding lunar nodes and Moon-Saturn squares (☽ □ ♄). Do not use metallic containers, as these can taint the mixture, instead use wood or sandstone. Let the mixture steep for several days stirring every evening; spray on the soil, renew monthly.

BIRCARBONATE OF SODA

Bicarbonate of Soda has the ability to stimulate and re-balance chalky soils, resulting in a decrease in diseases.
Spray onto the soil at dew time a few weeks before seeding, using between 20 to 50 g by litre of water. 5 to 10 g per litre can be used directly on plants in the same way as grapefruit seed extract (see below).

GRAPEFRUIT SEED EXTRACT
(available commercially)

Grapefruit seed extract reinforces and purifies plants, acting as a disinfectant and fungicide. Spray on plants at the dates shown in the Fungicide tables, using 35 to 40 drops per litre of water, or even 50 drops to avoid mildew. Renew every 10 to 15 days, and after rain.

Plant-based decoctions

A plant-based decoction used as a liquid fertilizer provides a natural way of feeding plants and preventing certain diseases. Those made from stinging nettle or comfrey are best known, but other plants can be used such as horsetail, camomile, marigold, achillea or dandelion, either individually or in combination.

Whichever plant you choose, the process for **making liquid fertilizer** remains the same. Cut up the fresh plants into small pieces and soak them in water (use 1 kg/2 lb of plants per 10 litres/15 pints of water) and leave it to steep for between one and four weeks – use a wooden or stoneware container, or even plastic if necessary, never use a metal container. Stir the liquid from time to time to help it ferment; then filter out the plant pulp. Use the resulting liquid fertilizer diluted in the proportion of 1:10–20, as appropriate.

WHEN TO MAKE A PLANT DECOCTION

• **To protect against fungal disease:** begin making the decoction when the Moon is waxing and, if possible, when it is also descending. The Moon in conjunction, sextile and trine with the Sun (☽ ☌ ✳ △ ☉) as well as superposition (q), will improve its effectiveness even more. Favourable dates are: MARCH: 6 - 9 - APRIL: 5 - 29 - MAY: 2 pm - 4 am - 30 am - JUNE: 2 - 26 - 27am - JULY: 1 pm - 23 pm - 26 - 31 - AUGUST: 20 - 24 pm - SEPTEMBER: 23 - OCTOBER: 18. If you also take into account the influence of the rising tide on these dates (see p16), the result will be even better (am = morning, pm = afternoon).

• **To use as a plant feed:** begin making the decoction when the Moon is waxing, and if possible when it is also ascending. The Moon in conjunction, sextile and trine with the Sun (☽ ☌ ✳ △ ☉) will strengthen its influence.

Stinging nettles

Very favourable dates are: MARCH: 26 - 31 - APRIL: 25 - MAY: 24 pm - AUGUST: 30 pm - OCTOBER: 23 - 28. (am = morning, pm = afternoon). Make the most of the receding tide on these dates to improve the result even more. Liquid fertilizer made from plants should preferably be used when the Moon is descending and, if possible, when it is also on the wane.

DECOCTION OF STINGING NETTLE

• To use as a fertilizer follow the instructions top left, leave the nettles to steep in water for three weeks and then dilute in the proportion of 1:10 if it is to be spread on the soil, but in at least 1:20 if it is to be sprayed on leaves.

• To prevent fungal diseases, let the mixture steep for a week and then dilute it in the proportion of 1:15–20. The fresh plant can also be used – for example, when potting up tomatoes, put a handful of nettles in the planting hole.

Comfrey

DECOCTION OF COMFREY

A decoction made from comfrey helps combat tomato whitefly, but comfrey really comes into its own as a fertilizer. Fresh leaves can be laid on the soil surface, wilted leaves can be dug into the soil, or it can be used in a liquid fertilizer. To make the liquid feed, soak the leaves in water (see top left this page) for two to four weeks and then dilute in the proportion of 1:10 if applying it directly to the soil or 1:20 if spraying it on leaves.

LIQUID FERTILIZER MADE FROM COMPOS

This is made by mixing one part well-rotted compost to ten parts water and leaving it to steep for one to two weeks. It is effective against cryptogamic (fungal) diseases when sprayed on the leaves of a plant and works on two fronts: it reinforces the plant's immune defences as well as destroying certain fungal spores.

Fungicides and insecticides

We recommend the use of natural products, both for the sake of the environment and to produce a better quality of crop. You can also use liquid fertilizers to prevent cryptogamic diseases such as those caused by fungi (see below and page 27).

A decoction of horsetail is very good for controlling fungal disease. Use about 50 g (2 oz) of horsetail per litre of water (1½ pints) and boil it for 20 minutes. Then dilute with water in the proportion of 1:5 and spray on the leaves or directly on the soil, several times between spring and autumn. If you use sulphur or Bordeaux mixture it is also possible to add horsetail decoction, or liquid fertilizer made from stinging nettles or compost in order to increase the efficiency and reduce the dosage.

Insecticides: a decoction of comfrey can be used to treat tomato whitefly and a decoction of many other plants can be used to produce natural insecticides, such as wormwood, pyrethrum, English ivy, etc. The table below indicates those dates that are the most favourable for applying insecticides and fungicides. The greater the number of stars (★) the more effective will be the application.

☐ favourable for insecticides
◼ favourable for fungicides

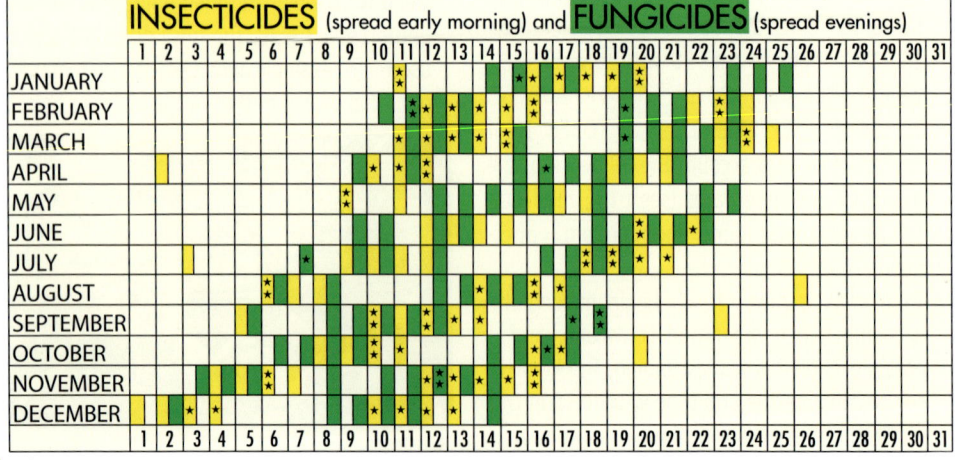

INSECTICIDES (spread early morning) and FUNGICIDES (spread evenings)

	1	2	3	4	5	6	7	8	9	10	11	12	13	14	15	16	17	18	19	20	21	22	23	24	25	26	27	28	29	30	31
JANUARY											★					★	★	★	★	★											
FEBRUARY											★	★	★	★	★	★			★				★								
MARCH												★	★	★	★			★					★								
APRIL										★	★	★						★													
MAY									★																						
JUNE																			★	★		★									
JULY									★									★	★	★	★	★									
AUGUST					★									★			★	★													
SEPTEMBER				★						★		★	★	★				★	★												
OCTOBER									★	★						★	★	★													
NOVEMBER				★								★	★	★	★	★		★	★												
DECEMBER			★	★						★	★	★	★																		
	1	2	3	4	5	6	7	8	9	10	11	12	13	14	15	16	17	18	19	20	21	22	23	24	25	26	27	28	29	30	31

Compost

Composting is the process by which animal or plant waste decomposes and breaks down into a substance that is both nourishing and easily assimilated by the soil's micro-organisms. A combination of plant waste and animal manure is normally required in order to ensure the constituents of the compost are in the correct proportions.

The composting process can normally be activated by adding stinging nettles (with their seeds heads removed) and comfrey, either as plants or in the form of a liquid. Good compost should be well oxygenated and loosely packed, not compacted. When it is ready to use, it should be light, rich and have a pleasant smell of humus, so it is important to make it at just the right moment. We have summarised all the different factors that will help you to produce good compost in the table below, including certain Moon/Pluto aspects.

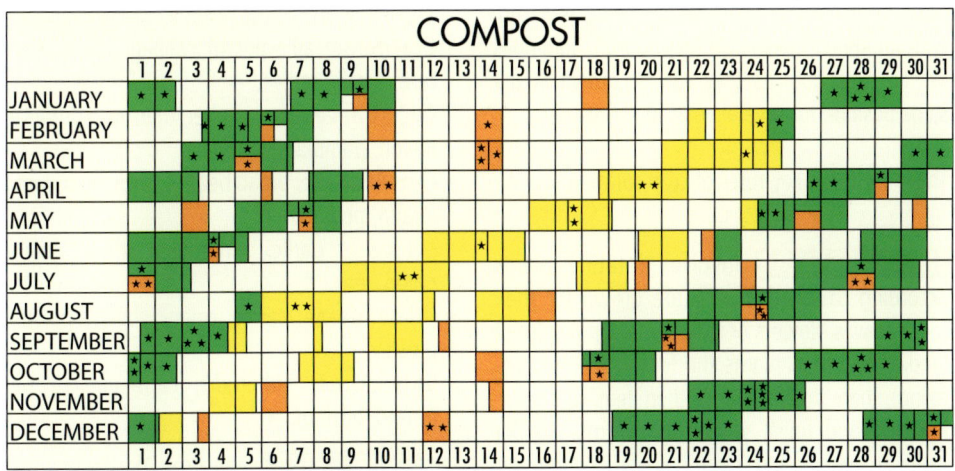

COMPOST

	1	2	3	4	5	6	7	8	9	10	11	12	13	14	15	16	17	18	19	20	21	22	23	24	25	26	27	28	29	30	31
JANUARY	★	★					★	★	★																		★	★★★	★		
FEBRUARY			★	★	★	★							★										★	★							
MARCH			★	★	★								★★	★									★							★	★
APRIL										★★								★★							★	★		★			
MAY							★							★	★									★★	★						
JUNE				★	★								★																		
JULY	★	★★								★★																	★★				
AUGUST				★		★★																		★	★★						
SEPTEMBER	★	★	★★	★																★★							★	★	★		
OCTOBER	★	★	★															★							★	★	★★	★			
NOVEMBER	★																					★	★	★★★	★			★	★	★	★
DECEMBER	★								★★												★★★	★							★		
	1	2	3	4	5	6	7	8	9	10	11	12	13	14	15	16	17	18	19	20	21	22	23	24	25	26	27	28	29	30	31

(★) the more stars, the more favourable the day

🟩 a good time to add to or turn compost heaps that generate a high internal temperature (the majority of compost heaps)

🟨 choose these dates for working on slower acting compost heaps that generate less heat (often preferred by farmers and gardeners who practise biodynamics)

🟧 recommended for surface composting with non-rotted manure (broken down by worms);

🟩⬜ a vertical line dividing a date box indicates morning (left) or afternoon (right)

🟩🟧 a date box divided by a horizontal line indicates it is favourable for a certain type of composting (green for high temperature compost and orange for surface composting)

MANURE: spread manure when the Moon is descending, if possible on days marked orange (see the table above).

Crop rotation

Each plant has its own nutritional needs and different plants draw nourishment from different layers of the soil. As a result, growing the same plant in the same place can lead to an imbalance of soil constituents and even the depletion of some, along with an increase in parasites, weeds and diseases. In most instances, it is a good idea to wait for three to five years before growing the same crop in the same place again. You can reduce this period, or even ignore it entirely, for vegetables such as spinach and lettuce, which have a short growth cycle. On the other hand, extend the period for crops such as strawberries and asparagus where the plant itself remains in the same position for several years before being replaced, with an annual harvest of just its fruit. Tomatoes are an exception, as they can be grown in the same position for several years in succession.

There are three key rules of crop rotation:

THE FIRST RULE involves rotating plants according to whether they are grown for their roots, leaves, flowers or fruits. On a single plot of land, grow 'fruit' plants the first year (nitrogen-fixing), then 'flower' plants, then 'leaf' (nitrogen-hungry), and finish with 'root' plants. So, for example, you could plant squash, courgettes, maize and French beans, followed by cauliflowers, broccoli or green manure (phacelia, lupins, clover) which would not be cut until the flowering stage; then cabbages, spinach, lettuces and leeks, and, finally, potatoes, celery, beetroots, onions and carrots. You could achieve several rotations in the same year – for instance, green manure could precede or follow a crop. In addition to the rotation of the different crops, it is also important to bear in mind which plants grow well together (see page 110).

THE SECOND RULE is not to grow two plants of the same botanical family one after the other. The main botanical families are as follows:

- **Chenopodiaceae:** beetroot, spinach, Swiss chard.
- **Compositae:** artichoke, cardoon, chicory, endive, lettuce, dandelion, black salsify, Jerusalem artichoke.
- **Cruciferae:** all types of cabbage, cress, mustard, turnip, radish.
- **Cucurbitaceae:** cucumber, marrow, courgette, melon, pumpkin.
- **Leguminosae:** broad bean, French bean, lentil, alfalfa, pea, clover.
- **Liliaceae:** garlic, asparagus, chive, shallot, onion, leek.
- **Umbelliferae:** carrot, celery, chervil, parsnip, parsley.
- **Solanaceae:** aubergine, capsicum, pepper, potato, tomato.

THE THIRD RULE concerns the amount of manure a crop needs. It is good practice to follow a crop that requires large amounts of manure with one that requires little or none.

- **Crops requiring large amounts of manure:** aubergine, celery, cabbage, spinach, fennel, maize, leek, pepper, potato, tomato.
- **Crops requiring little:** garlic, chervil, cress, shallot, broad bean, French bean, corn salad (lamb's lettuce), onion, radish, lettuce.

Other crops fall between the two extremes, requiring an average amount.

Agriculture

ERADICATING WEEDS

- Eradication will be most effective during the days following the full moon, or in the middle of the day – with the best results obtained by combining both together.
- Dig over the soil when the Moon is in the constellation of Leo, which favours germination (marked in in the following table). This will encourage the majority of any weed seeds present in the soil to germinate. Then dig over the soil again to remove them.
- It is possible to contain germination by digging over the soil when the moon is in the constellations of Virgo, Libra and Capricorn (marked in yellow in the following table).
- **Thistles:** remove thistles when the soil is dry to help prevent them from seeding too easily. They are difficult to eradicate, but for the best results, work in the middle of the day on the dates marked in purple or blue on the chart below. These dates are also the best for dealing with convolvulus.

CULTIVATING THE SOIL: the work of ploughing, planting, pricking out and spreading compost or manure is best carried out when the Moon is descending. If possible, combine the descending Moon with the waxing Moon when working on light, sandy soil, especially when the weather is dry. In the case of heavy clay soil, if possible, combine the descending Moon with the waning Moon, particularly during wet weather.

- **Dock weed:** dig up dock weed on dates marked in purple or orange.

Choose dates marked with stars (★).
If you have no option other than to dig the soil on dates when there are nodes, dig it over again a few days later to help reinstate positive influences.

If only a part of the day is favourable, the time is indicated by a vertical line (the left section for the morning, the right for the afternoon – see above and left for the key to the colours). On days that are divided horizontally, two favourable aspects are recommended, as indicated by the two colours. For example, the morning of 9 January after 09:00 is favourable for restricting germination and the afternoon for pulling up thistles.

WEEDS - THISTLES - DOCK WEED

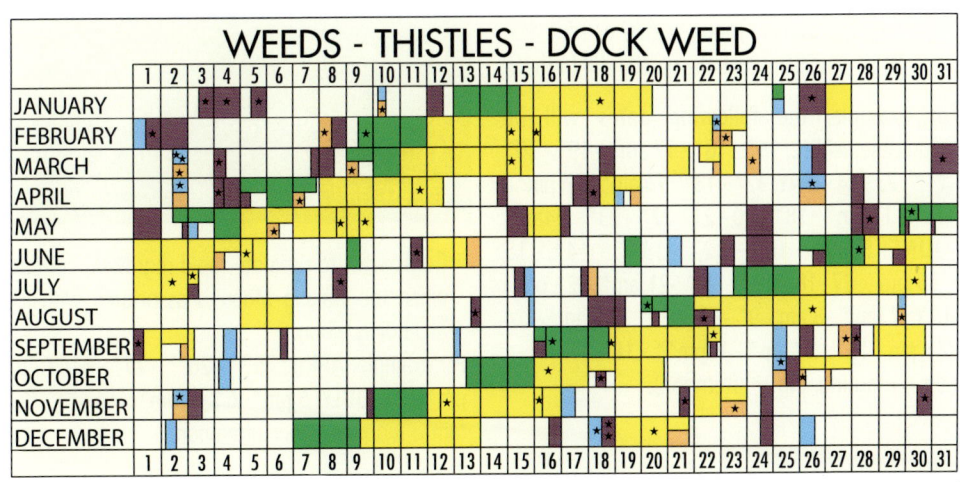

	1	2	3	4	5	6	7	8	9	10	11	12	13	14	15	16	17	18	19	20	21	22	23	24	25	26	27	28	29	30	31
JANUARY			★	★	★													★							★						
FEBRUARY	★									★		★				★	★							★							
MARCH		★★	★						★					★									★								
APRIL		★				★					★														★					★	
MAY						★		★	★																★			★			
JUNE				★	★							★														★					
JULY	★	★							★																				★		
AUGUST															★									★							
SEPTEMBER	★																★				★				★★						
OCTOBER																	★							★							
NOVEMBER		★										★				★						★								★	
DECEMBER								★								★★			★												
	1	2	3	4	5	6	7	8	9	10	11	12	13	14	15	16	17	18	19	20	21	22	23	24	25	26	27	28	29	30	31

W O R K I N G

CLEARING LAND: to clear land of plants such as thorns and brambles, dig them up or cut them down at the perigee and if possible when the waning Moon is close to becoming new (for instance: JUNE: 22 - 23 pm - JULY: 21** AUGUST: 19* - SEPTEMBRE : 16 (am = morning, pm = afternoon).

MANURE: manure is absorbed by the soil more effectively when the Moon is descending and, if possible, waxing, but avoid spreading manure during Fire signs.

- **Seaweed and natural phosphates (such as in bone meal):** see 'Manure' left.
- **Leaf mould (minerals):** spread leaf compost in the morning (but in the evening if the forecast is dry and hot), with an ascending and if possible a waning Moon. Avoid Fire signs.
- **Pig manure:** to avoid burning meadow grass, spread chicken manure when the Moon is ascending and, if possible, waxing. Water and Air signs are also preferable.
- **Cattle slurry:** spread cattle slurry when the Moon is waning and avoid Fire signs.

Hay

A permanent wild flower meadow

- **Quality:** hay will be of better quality if it is cut when the Moon is ascending and if possible also waning. The aspects Moon sextile or trine Sun (☽ ✳ △ ☉) will improve the quality still further.

For example, the following dates will be favourable: **APRIL:** 15* - 16* - 17 am* - 19* - 20* - 21* - 23 - 24 - **MAY:** 12* - 13* - 14 am* - 14 pm** - 16* - 17 pm* - 18* - 20 - 21 - 22* - 23* - 24am* - **JUNE:** 8 - 9* - 10* - 12* - 13** - 14* - 15 - 16 pm - 17 -18 - 19* - 20* -21 am* - 21 pm - **JULY:** 7 pm* - 8 am - 9* -10* - 11* - 12 am* - 14 - 15 pm - 16* - 17 am* - 17pm** - 18*.
(am = morning, pm = afternoon).

> When cutting hay, always avoid times that are close to lunar nodes, the perigee (including about 6 hours before and after) and the following aspects: Moon square Sun, Mars and Saturn (☽ ◻ ☉ ♂ ♄) (about 4 hours before and 2 hours after).

- **Regrowth:** to promote rapid regrowth, cut hay when the waxing Moon is associated with an ascending Moon.
For example: **APRIL:** 25** - 26** - 27* - **MAY:** 24 pm* - 25 - **JULY:** 5 pm*- 6* - 7 am*.
(am = morning, pm = afternoon).

Cereal crops

Sow cereal crops on a day favourable to 'fruit' plants, but if this is not possible, choose days favourable to 'flower' and if not 'root' plants. Days favourable to 'leaf' plants are the least beneficial. Also take the following information into consideration to improve results even further. It is organized according to the type of cereal crop.

OATS, WHEAT, BARLEY, RYE
- **Sow:** preferably when the Moon is ascending and if possible waning, with a receding tide.
- **Harvest:** on days favourable to 'root' or 'flower' plants with the Moon waxing and ascending (on dates favourable to 'fruit' plants there is more dust in the air and the risk of weevils is greater, on 'leaf' dates there is a greater risk of fermentation).

Examples of favourable dates are: **JUNE:** 12 - 13 - 14 - 15 before 16:00 - 20 - 21 - **JULY:** 9 - 10 - 11 - 12 - 18 - 19 - **AUGUST:** 5 - 6 - 7 - 8 - 14 - 15. (am = morning, pm = afternoon). Combine the influence of a rising tide with these dates.

The waxing and descending Moon can be suitable mainly when the soil is heavy.

MILLET
- **Sow:** when the Moon is ascending and if possible waxing.
- **Harvest:** when the Moon is waxing and if possible ascending, but avoid 'leaf' dates.

MAIZE, SUNFLOWERS
- **Sow:** preferably when the Moon is ascending and if possible waning, with a rising tide.
- **Harvest:** when the Moon is ascending, avoiding dates favourable to 'leaf' plants.

OILSEED RAPE
- **Sow:** preferably when the Moon is ascending and if possible also waning.
- **Harvest:** when the Moon is waning and ascending, avoiding 'leaf' dates.

Animal husbandry

COVERING: for cows and mares, the best time is between the first quarter and the Full Moon in Fire and Earth signs and, if possible, with the Moon in the descendent. For ewes, the period between the first quarter and the Full Moon during Earth and Air signs is best, with an ascendant Moon if possible. Avoid the perigee and the lunar nodes if possible.

TRIMMING THE FEET OF LIVESTOCK: carry out this task in the signs of Taurus, Leo, Virgo, Sagittarius or Capricorn when the weather is calm or wet and, if possible, when the Moon is waxing. Avoid stormy or icy periods.

SHOEING: choose the waning Moon, particularly when it is in Earth or Air signs.

WORMING: this should be done two or three days before the New Moon or, if this proves impossible, two or three days before the Full Moon.

CLEANING & DISINFECTING COWSHEDS: this will be most effective when the Moon is waxing and in a Fire or Earth sign.

MATING RABBITS: results will be best between the New Moon and the first quarter.

MALE OR FEMALE CHICKS: eggs collected around the time of the last quarter will produce mainly male chicks. For female chicks, eggs should be collected around the first quarter. For best results, incubate the eggs so that they hatch between the New Moon and the first quarter.

WHEN TO START OUTDOOR GRAZING: choose the following correlations of signs and constellations: a - b - c* - d* - k* - L* - m - n - s* - t* - x (see page 14). For example, MARCH: 3* after 08:00 - 4* - 5 am* - 5 pm - 6 - 11 pm - 12* - 13* - 16 pm - 17 - 19 - 20 - 21 - 22* - 23* - 31* - APRIL: 1* - 2 - 3 before 16:00 - 8* - 10 am* 13 - 14 am - 15 - 16 - 17 - 18 pm - 19* - 27* - 28 pm - 29 - 30 - MAY: 5* - 6* - 7* - 10 - 11 - 13 - 14 - 15 pm - 16* - 17* before 15:00 - 24* after 8:00 - 25* - 26 pm - 27. (am = morning, pm = afternoon).

MOVING CATTLE: move cattle between the day after the first quarter and the day before the last quarter, to reduce damage to grass.

BRINGING CATTLE IN: cowsheds will be dryer in winter if cattle are brought inside during autumn when the Moon is passing through the constellation of Leo.

TO AVOID: In addition to the above, avoid turning out, moving or bringing in animals on the following days: JANUARY: 10 - 11 - 12 - 15 am - 26 - FEBRUARY: 8 pm - 9 - 11pm - 22 pm - MARCH: 7 pm - 8 am - 10 pm - 11 am - APRIL: 4 am - 9 - 18 am - 21 - 28 am - MAY: 1 am - 8 pm - 9 - 15 am - 26 am - 28 - JUNE: 7 - 11 - 23 - 24 pm -JULY: 7 - 8 - 12 pm - 21 pm - 22 am - 25 am - AUGUST: 5 pm - 6 am - 18 pm - 19 am - SEPTEMBER: 1 am - 4 - 5 pm - 12 - 16 am - 28 am - OCTOBER: 4 - 13 - 16 am - 25 am - NOVEMBER: 2 - 7 - 21 - 27 am - DECEMBER: 2 - 4 pm - 18 pm - 24 pm - 31. (am = morning, pm = afternoon).

Beekeeping

BEES

For the best results, work with bees during the following constellations.

During Fire constellations to benefit the queens and increase the production of honey.

During Air constellations to benefit the queens and to encourage the development of young bees.

During Earth constellations to maximise the cell-building instinct. Honey collected during Earth constellations will set more quickly.

Avoid all work with bees during Water constellations – these periods have an adverse effect on the hives and honey.

Extract honey in a Fire or Air constellation.

As a general rule do most of your beekeeping when the Moon is in a Fire or Air constellation and avoid the perigee, lunar nodes and Water constellations.

Winegrowing

PRUNING GRAPE VINES

Prune grape vines when the Moon is both descending and, if possible, waxing, with a rising tide. Avoid the lunar nodes and when the Moon is squared with Saturn (☽ ▯ ♄).

DISBUDDING

Disbud when the Moon is waning and, if possible, descending, with a receding tide. Disbudding with the Moon sextile or trine Sun or Mars (☽ ✳ △ ☉ ♂) should reduce the growth of suckers (see pages 12–14).

POLLARDING AND CUTTING BACK

Carry out this work when the Moon is descending, with a receding tide and, if possible, with one of the planetary aspects mentioned above.

HARVESTING GRAPES

An ascending Moon will give a better yield but the wine produced will keep better when the Moon is descending. To improve the quality of the wine and reinforce its character, harvest the grapes according to the constellations. Choose dates favourable to 'fruit' plants for fruity wines, 'root' days for vines grown where the soil plays an important part in the flavour, and 'flower' days for more floral wines. Avoid lunar nodes: they can hinder the development of aromas.

Cider making

DECANT

Decant cider when the Moon is waxing and descending if possible, and with a rising tide. Choose days when the weather is calm, preferably early in the morning with dew on the ground.

BOTTLE

Bottle cider when the Moon is waning and descending, preferably in the constellations of Virgo (♍) or Leo (♌) and, if possible, with a rising tide. Avoid days when the Moon is squared with Mars, Jupiter, Saturn or the Sun (☽ ▣ ♂ ♃ ♄ ☉) – see pages 12–14. Also avoid stormy, windy and very cold weather.

Beer making

WHEN TO START

Make your beer when the Moon is descending and, if possible, waxing, with a rising tide. Moon–Venus aspects (☽ ☍ ♂ △ ✶ ♀), except square, are very favourable. Avoid lunar nodes, the perigee and dates when the Moon is squared with Mars, Jupiter, Saturn or the Sun (☽ ▣ ♂ ♃ ♄ ☉) – see pages 12–14. For the best results use hops picked when the Moon is ascending and with the influence of a rising tide.

BOTTLE

Bottle beer when the Moon is descending and, if possible, between the last and first quarters. Choose a time influenced by a rising tide to help with the development of aromas. Choose an Air sign if possible, and avoid stormy, windy and very cold weather.

Forestry

If possible, only cut down trees after they have lost their leaves, but while the Sun is still in the descendent (before the winter solstice).

TIMBER

Cut timber when the Moon is descending but avoid the last day of this phase. The wood will react differently according to the sign of the zodiac that the Moon is in.

The day on which wood is both cut and used is very important.

- To avoid **parasites** and **rotting**, cut wood in the following signs: Leo , Virgo , Scorpio or Sagittarius .

- To prevent wood from **warping and splintering**, cut it during Libra or, better still, in Scorpio .

- Cut wood to be used for **frameworks for buildings and other structures** in Leo , Virgo , Libra , Scorpio or Sagittarius .

- Wood for **tools** should be cut in Leo , Virgo or Libra .

- To prevent the softwood from coniferous trees from **flaking**, cut it in Scorpio or Sagittarius .

- **The superposition of the sign and constellation of Leo (q) is a good time for cutting wood**, for example from 01:00 to 20:07 on 7 December .

- When the sap is flowing, leave a felled tree for several weeks before removing the branches (the leaves draw out the sap).

Useful tip: to prevent wood from warping when you are using it (for frames, cladding, etc.), choose these dates , especially those marked with stars (★).

In the table below, the signs are represented by colours for easier reference:

Gemini: ■ Cancer: ■ Leo: ■ Virgo: □
Libra: ■ Scorpio: ■ Sagittarius: ■

Those planetary aspects that will improve the wood are shown by a star. Those that are harmful are coloured in red ■ .

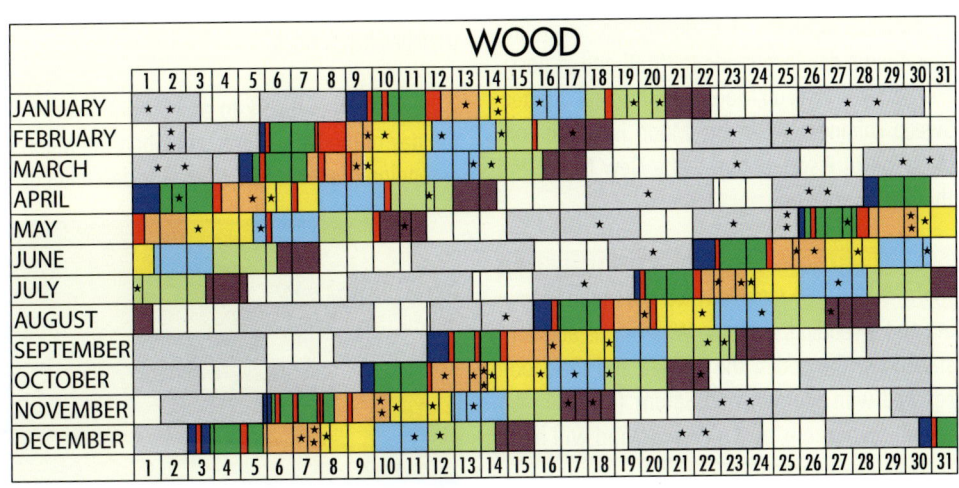

WOOD

	1	2	3	4	5	6	7	8	9	10	11	12	13	14	15	16	17	18	19	20	21	22	23	24	25	26	27	28	29	30	31
JANUARY	★	★												★	★	★				★	★						★	★			
FEBRUARY		★						★	★		★		★			★			★					★		★	★				
MARCH	★	★							★	★			★	★							★								★	★	
APRIL		★			★	★				★										★					★	★					
MAY				★			★					★								★			★						★	★	
JUNE																				★					★		★		★		
JULY	★																		★				★	★				★			
AUGUST													★							★		★									
SEPTEMBER																★			★			★	★								
OCTOBER									★		★	★	★		★		★		★			★									
NOVEMBER									★	★		★		★									★	★							
DECEMBER					★	★	★			★		★								★	★										
	1	2	3	4	5	6	7	8	9	10	11	12	13	14	15	16	17	18	19	20	21	22	23	24	25	26	27	28	29	30	31

FIREWOOD: cut firewood when the Moon is descending, avoiding days close to the New Moon. Stack firewood when the Moon is descending, if possible between the first and last quarter – it will dry better then.

CHRISTMAS TREES: cut Christmas trees when the Moon is ascending and waxing to stop them shedding their needles too quickly. The following aspects will strengthen this effect – Moon sextile, trine or square Sun or Venus (☽ ✳ △ ◻ ⊙ ♀) – see pages 12-14.

Miscellaneous

WORKING ON BOATS ON DRY LAND: carry out painting work when the Moon is in the descendant during periods (a, b, c, i, j, k). The following aspects can be beneficial: Moon sextile or trine Sun (☽ ✳ △ ⊙) and Moon conjunction Jupiter (☽ ☌ ♃). Avoid the nodes and Moon square Sun (☽ ◻ ⊙). Return boats to the water when the Moon is waning, if possible between the last quarter and the New Moon and when the Moon is in an Earth or Air sign.

CHIMNEYS: to improve the 'draw' of a chimney in autumn, light the fire during an ascending Moon, on a day favourable to 'fruit' and, if possible, between the Full Moon and the final quarter. Sweep chimneys when the Moon is in the constellation of Pisces between the New Moon and the first quarter.

MOSS ON TILES, SALT DEPOSITS ON BRICK-WORK, MOULD: remove when the Moon is waxing and ascending, avoiding Water signs and constellations. The nodes, the perigee and the Moon squared with the Sun and Saturn (☽ ◻ ⊙ ♄) are all favourable, and a drying wind will help.

DRAIN SOIL: when the Moon is ascending.

PATHS AND COURTYARDS: to work on paths and courtyards, choose (the best are marked *): **FEBRUARY:** 8 - 9 - **MARCH:** 8 - 9* before 16:00 - **APRIL:** 4 - 5* - **MAY:** 1 - 2 pm* - 28 - 30 am* - **JUNE:** 24 - 26* - **JULY:** 22 - 23 pm* - **AUGUST:** 20 pm. (am = morning, pm – afternoon).

TRENCHES: the sides of trenches dug or cleaned out when the Moon is ascending may erode more quickly, especially if the soil is light, but should not fall in completely. Trenches dug when the Moon is descending tend to erode and collapse. Choose a time close to the Full Moon to help trenches last longer.

SPRINGS: begin work to collect spring water on the day of the New Moon and when the Moon is ascending (water is lost when it is descending).

MUSHROOMS: usually emerge a few days after the New Moon and are more prolific when the Moon is waxing.

SILVER BIRCH SAP: collect silver birch sap when the Moon is ascending, avoiding the nodes and period (f).

PRESERVE FOOD: when the Moon is waning.

SAUERKRAUT: pick cabbages and make sauerkraut when the Moon is ascending, avoiding the same periods as for bread.

JAMS: jams with a low sugar content will keep better if made when the Moon is waning.

SOURDOUGH BREAD: this will rise well and be extra delicious when the Moon is ascending. If the Moon is descending when baking, ensure that it is also waxing. Avoid nodes, the perigee, the periods (f, o, w), Water signs and constellations, if possible, and the Moon squared with the Sun and Saturn (☾ ▣ ☉ ♄) – see pages 12-14.

CLEANING AND MAINTENANCE WORK: will be more effective when the Moon is waxing.

CLOTHES: put clothes away for storage when the Moon is in conjunction with Venus (☾ ☌ ♀) – see pages 12-14.

WOODEN POSTS: to make them last longer, cut them when the Moon is new (or just before) and insert them in the ground when the Moon is in the constellation of Leo. If they are made of softwood, you can also burn the point a little to make it harder.

LAWNS: sow lawns when the Moon is waning and descending on a day favourable to 'leaf' plants or, if necessary, a 'root' date. Aerate lawns when the Moon is ascending on a 'flower' date. To help slow down growth, cut lawns when the Moon is in the constellation of Gemini and Libra or, if necessary, in Virgo or Aquarius. To promote growth, cut lawns in Pisces or, if necessary, in Cancer or Scorpio.

LIVING WITH THE MOON

Do not use the information contained in this chapter as a substitute for medical advice. If you think you have a medical problem, consult your doctor.

Influence of the phases

NEW MOON

• The renewal of physical energy is at a minimum during this phase.

• This is a good time to start eliminating toxins or to tackle a bad habit.

WAXING MOON

• We express ourselves more easily and freely.

• The body makes the most effective use of the nutrients that it receives during this phase.

• If you tend to put on weight, this is a time to be particularly frugal..

• This is an ideal time to learn new skills or to start new projects.

FULL MOON

• Our physical energy levels are restored during this phase.

• When the nights are lighter sleep can be interrupted, and insomnia can be an issue.

• The extra energy and excitement caused by the Full Moon can be channelled into physical activities.

• Now is a good time to undertake a project.

• Some of the effects of the Full Moon and the New Moon can be felt for two or three days.

WANING MOON

• This is a good time for introspection, reflection and spirituality.

• Choose this phase to follow a detox programme; it promotes the elimination of toxins from the body.

Harvesting plants

Waxing Moon: plants harvested during the Full Moon period will have more vitality, but their medicinal properties are weaker than when the Moon is waning.

Waning Moon: plants tend to become dry but their fragrance heightens as the New Moon approaches. Plants picked during this phase will retain more of their medicinal properties.

FOR MAKING INFUSIONS

In the morning while the Moon is ascending: before midday, the Sun's influence is felt mainly on the aerial parts of a plant. It is the ideal time for harvesting leaves, flowers, fruits and seeds, and the effects are enhanced when the Moon is ascending.

In the evening while the Moon is descending: after 15:00 the Sun's influence stimulates activity in the lower parts of plants. This is the time to harvest roots. The effect is enhanced when the Moon is descending.

The following days are harmful: avoid harvesting plants when the Moon is passing through the lunar nodes when ascending or descending or when it is at its perigee (see red zones).

Colt's foot

MEDICINAL PLANTS

Harvesting flower heads (borage, St John's Wort, meadowsweet, etc.): when the Moon is waning and, if possible, also ascending, in an Air or Earth sign. Early morning is best. The following aspects are favourable: Moon conjunction, sextile or trine Sun, Venus and Mercury (☾ ♂ ☀ △ ☉ ♀ ☿) – see pages 12-14.

Borage

Harvesting roots (gentian, marsh mallow, dandelions, etc.): when the Moon is descending and, if possible, also waxing, in an Air or Earth sign. Late afternoon is best. The following aspects are favourable: Moon conjunction, sextile or trine Sun, Venus and Mercury (☾ ♂ ☀ △ ☉ ♀ ☿) – see pages 12-14.

Harvesting from trees (hawthorn, pine nuts, elderberries, etc.): when the Moon is ascending and, if possible, waxing, with the influence of a rising tide and in an Air or Earth sign. The following aspects are favourable: Moon conjunction, sextile or trine Sun, Venus and Mercury (☾ ♂ ☀ △ ☉ ♀ ☿) – see pages 12-14.

Lime blossom

Hairdressing

The table below summarizes for quick reference the best dates and times of day on which to cut hair.

■ a good day for cutting hair to **slow down hair loss**

□ a good day for cutting hair to make it **thicker and stronger**

(★) **the number of stars** indicates the strength of influence

■ **not advisable** in any circumstances. Also, to a lesser extent, it is not recommended on days marked with the sign (–)

▌ a vertical line indicates the importance of a particular part of the day. The example shows a morning favourable for reducing hair loss and a neutral afternoon

▬ days divided horizontally are favourable for the influences represented by the two colours

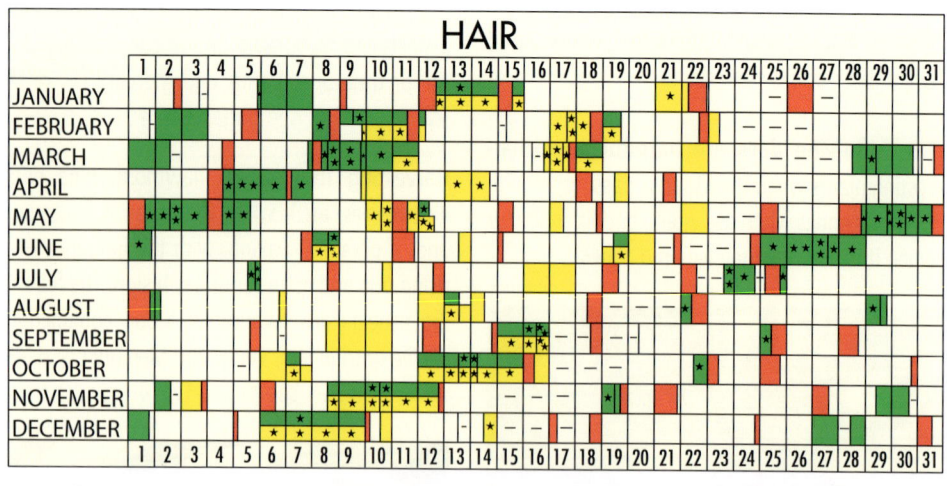

HAIR

The dates marked in this table (■, □), especially the starred ones, are highly favourable for hair. Take note of them, even if you have no particular hair problems.

- For more **manageable hair**, choose dates marked in green when the Moon is waxing.
- For a **perm**, choose the superpositions of sign and constellation ♉ ♉ (j) or ♍ ♍ (s) (see calendar pages 56-79), if possible with a waning Moon. It sets better when the Moon is waxing but the hair suffers more damage.
- Hair **coloured** when the Moon is ascending and waxing will achieve better results.
- To help hair **grow quickly**, cut it when the Moon is ascending and waxing.
- If you tend to have **split ends** and/or you want your hair to grow less quickly, we recommend that you have it cut on the following days:

am = morning   pm = afternoon

JANUARY: 11 - 12pm - 13 - 14 - 15 pm - 16 am* - 16 pm - 17 - 19 am - 19 pm* - 20 am - 20 pm* - 21 - **FEBRUARY:** 9 after 15:00 - 10 - 11 am - 12 - 13 - 14 - 15 pm - 16 am - 17 - 18 am - **MARCH:** 11 - 12 - 13 am - 13 pm* - 14 - 15 - 16 after 15:00 - 17 am* - **APRIL:** 9 after 16:00 - 10 - 11 -12 after 14:00 - 13 - 14 before 14:00 - **MAY:** 9 before 16:00 - 10 am - 10 pm* - 11 pm - **JULY:** 19 after 14:00 - 20 - **AUGUST:** 16 - 17 - 18 am - **SEPTEMBER:** 13 - 14 before 15:00 - 15 - 16 am - 16 pm*- **OCTOBER:** 10 - 11- 12* - 13 - 14 - 15 - 16 pm*- **NOVEMBER:** 6 pm - 7 - 8 - 9 - 10 - 11 - 12 before 16:00 - 13 - 14 - **DECEMBER:** 3 - 4 - 5 - 6 - 7 - 8 - 9 - 10 am - 10 pm* - 11 am - 11 pm* - 12 - 13 am - 14.

Depilation

The removal of unwanted hair is best performed when the Moon is descending; if combined with the waning Moon, regrowth will be slower. Slow down regrowth even more by choosing certain planetary aspects.

A summary indicating the best dates is shown in the table below. The dates are divided into four categories:

▢ fairly good days   ▢ good days   ▢ very good days   ★ excellent days

▮ a vertical line indicates a particular part of the day

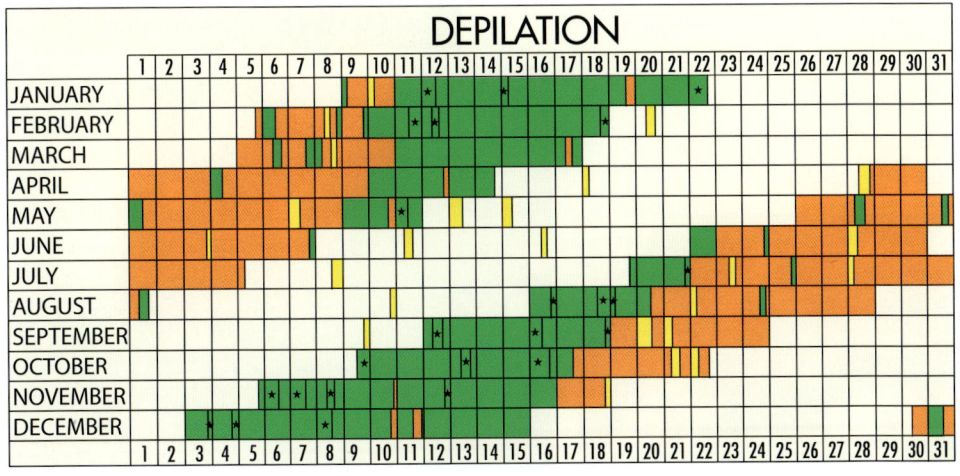

DEPILATION

Skincare

SKIN CLEANSING

(Blackheads, impurities, etc.) Treatment works best if carried out when the Moon is in the descendent and in an aspect with Venus (♂, ✳, ▢, △) – see pages 12-14.

NOURISHING THE SKIN

Moisten the skin with dew before applying any cream for best results. Walking barefoot in the dew is good for your general health.

- **Face packs,** moisturizing and revitalizing treatments: the right time depends on skin type.

- **Dry and combination skins:** treatments will be more effective when applied during a waxing Moon. Avoid the following signs: Aries, Cancer and Capricorn.
- **Greasy skin:** when the Moon is waning and trine and, especially, sextile with the Sun (☾ △ ✳ ☉) – see pages 12-14. The skin will absorb the products a little less well but the cleansing action will be more effective. Perform during a waning Moon to help prevent dilation of the pores, making the skin firmer and more attractive.

Warts

Marigold

> To remove warts with the sap from plants such as greater celandine, marigold and the fig tree…

Start when the Moon is descending, preferably during the last quarter, and when it is in the superposition of the following signs and constellations:

- Leo/Leo (♍),
- Gemini/Taurus (♉)
(see pages 56-79)

Celandine

Nails

For stronger nails, cut or file them when the Moon is waning and in an Earth or Air sign. Avoid the nodes.

Reduce the risk of in-growing nails by cutting them when the Moon is in the following signs: Leo, Virgo, Sagittarius, Capricorn and Aquarius, avoiding the lunar nodes.

Corns and callouses

Remove these when the Moon is waning and in the sign of Capricorn or Taurus. Another suitable time is when the Moon is waxing and in the sign of Virgo or Libra, though the effects are likely to be less successful.

Fasting

Fasting can be of great benefit to most people, but it is advisable to get permission from your doctor before embarking upon your first fast. Monitoring is essential for long fasts.

The New Moon is the best time to carry out a one-day fast, as your body will be cleansed more effectively. The New Moon is also a good time to begin fasts of up to a week. If you wish to fast for longer, begin when the Moon is descending and sextile with the Sun (☾ ✳ ☉) – see pages 12-14.

Detoxing

Start taking plants that help to detox your system through the liver when the Moon is in the sign of Virgo, and plants that work through the kidneys when it is in the sign of Libra. If possible, choose a time when the Moon is waning and sextile or trine with the Sun (☾ ✳ △ ☉) – see pages 12-14.

Treating worms

Carry out treatment to eradicate worms two or three days before the New Moon or, failing that, two or three days before the Full Moon.

Eating

This section is for those who have difficulty absorbing or digesting food and those wanting to derive the maximum benefit from their food.

Healthy eating involves two basic principles: moderation and intuition.

Moderation: do not overload your system by eating more than you need. Eat a varied diet made up of all the foods your body tolerates well.

Intuition: we need to learn to listen to our own body to discover what is right for it and what is not. There is no universal advice: what is right for one person is not necessarily right for another.

For example, people whose bodies tend to produce too much mucus find the condition eases if they reduce their intake of dairy products or eliminate them from their diet for a while. The problem could be a temporary one, due to tiredness or emotional stress, for example. In such instances the liver becomes overworked, and some foods, such as eggs, are less easily absorbed.

Some people have a lower tolerance to acid-producing foods. Do not confuse the acid taste of fruit such as lemons with the acidity that can upset digestion and disturb the acid-base balance (meat, cereals). Similarly, stress, oxygen debt and lack of sleep, all of which require immediate attention, increase levels of acidity. In this case, the best solution is to eat only vegetables, except for tomatoes and sorrel. Eat all other foods in moderation to avoid nutritional deficiencies, but eliminate acidic fruits from your diet.

The following principles apply to most people, but it is important to find your own 'truth'. If you are in any doubt bout a particular food, try giving it up for two or three weeks and monitor your bodies reactions.

- Meals should be eaten in a **calm, relaxed atmosphere**, so that you can appreciate the quality of the food and the energy it provides. It is also important for your food to appeal to your senses (sight, smell and taste).
- Try to **eat less in the evening** – at the end of the day nutriments are more likely to be stored in the form of fat than used as energy.
- Meals should be taken at **regular times. Chew well** and savour them to the full.
- Avoid snacks between meals to give your **digestion a rest**.

- **Avoid** food that is **too hot or cold**: the body has to use energy to restore and maintain body temperature.
- Choose fruit and vegetables either **grown organically** in your garden or from a recognised organic grower, these will be GM free and contain no chemical pesticides or herbicides. Their magnetic energy is greater if they are picked wet with dew. Choose **unrefined foods** (first cold-pressed oil, unrefined sugar, etc.).
- Eat fruit and vegetables **in season** and **grown locally** (their energy is best adapted to our bodies).
- Eat raw fruit **between meals**.
- Eat salad and raw vegetables at the **beginning of meals**; some people should avoid eating them in the evening.
- In winter in particular, eat **sprouting seeds** regularly; they are rich in vitamins and trace elements.

- **Seaweed** – rich in vitamins, trace elements and iodine – improves digestion when added to meals.
- **Avoid eating** meat, fish and animal by-products in the same meal.
- Some people should **avoid combining** starchy and protein foods in the same meal. Digesting them simultaneously makes conflicting demands on your stomach.

- Eat more **fibre**. Generally speaking, in affluent countries we eat too many animal products, particularly fatty foods, and insufficient fibre.
- Eat smoked products in moderation.
- Limit the amount of **preserved meats** you eat, especially if you suffer from high blood pressure, and during hot weather, when they are harder to digest.
- **Avoid** eating too many **soya beans** because of the amount of purines they contain. Leguminous plants require considerable energy to be digested.
- **Avoid oats**, which require a lot of energy to be metabolized and overheat the system. **Brown rice** is more digestible and more nourishing than white.
- If you have **kidney problems**, avoid asparagus, cress and sorrel.
- When **tired**, avoid eggs, lentils and raw pears.
- Cucumber and melon are very indigestible, especially when eaten ice-cold and with alcohol.

Vegetables are easier to digest and more nourishing if you cut them very thin and cook them for two or three minutes in a saucepan or wok with a little olive oil.

The Moon influences our metabolism. If you are not lucky enough to have a cast-iron stomach, digestion and absorption will improve if you pay attention to the times when the Moon is passing through the signs and constellations (indicated by letters on the calendar on pages 56-79). Foods not mentioned below should, as a rule, be easy to digest at any time.

Digestion of the following foods demands a good deal of energy, particularly during the periods indicated by the letters (see page 16 and the calendar on pages 56-79). **Avoid eating them at these times.**

This list is not exhaustive but it applies to most foods that take a lot of time to digest. Other factors can also play a role. Stormy weather, for example, tends to hinder digestion.

Meals and the Moon

- When the Moon is waxing, nutrients are absorbed more easily.
- When the Moon is waxing and ascending, digestion requires less energy.
- People who suffer from constipation should avoid foods that contain little water (such as cereals) during Fire signs and the lunar nodes.

Beef in sauce: c-f-g-o-u-w

Mutton in sauce: d-e-f-j-r-s-u

Pork in sauce: c-d-h-o-q-s-t

Poultry in sauce: b-i-j-q-r-s-u-v-w

Preserved meats: c-d-h-i-j-L-q-r-s-t-w-x-y

Oily fish: b-c-e-f-j-k-L-o-p-y

Smoked fish: a-b-c-d-h-i-j-k-L-o-p-q-u-v-y-z

Oysters and raw shellfish: h-m-n-r-u-v-y

Eggs: f-g-i-L-m-n-q-r-u-y

Dried beans: e-j-m-n-q-r-y

Lentils: b-c-e-m-n-q-s-y

Raw celeriac: i-j-k-l-q-w-y

Raw cabbages: c-d-i-j-m-n-v-w-x

Raw cauliflowers: e-f-g-h-m-n-o-q

Cucumbers, melons: b-c-d-f-s-t-u-v-w-y-z

Radishes: a-i-j-k-q-r-s-x

Salads (curly endive, escarole): e-i-j-k-L-m-n-r-s-y-z

Raw tomatoes: b-i-m-n-o-q-r-y

Body treatments

As the Moon passes through each sign of the zodiac, certain parts of the body are stimulated (see the table on page 53). If you treat the relevant part of the body during this period, with massage, medicine, etc., you will enjoy a greater therapeutic effect.

Teeth

The table below provides a summary of the favourable and unfavourable times for dental treatment. For example, avoid having any treatment, extraction or any other operation in the upper jaw when the Moon is passing through the sign of Aries.

Similarly, avoid treatment to the teeth of the lower jaw when the Moon is passing through the sign of Taurus.

Reading the table:

- favourable for extracting teeth and removing nerves
- suitable only for extracting teeth and removing nerves from teeth in the upper jaw
- favourable for implants and crowns
- (★) the number of stars indicates how favourable the influence is.
- **not advisable** under any circumstances; to a lesser extent, it is good to avoid days marked with the sign (–)
- a vertical line indicates if only a part of the day is affected – the example shows the morning as favourable for tooth extraction and the afternoon as neutral
- days divided horizontally are favourable for the two treatments represented by the colours

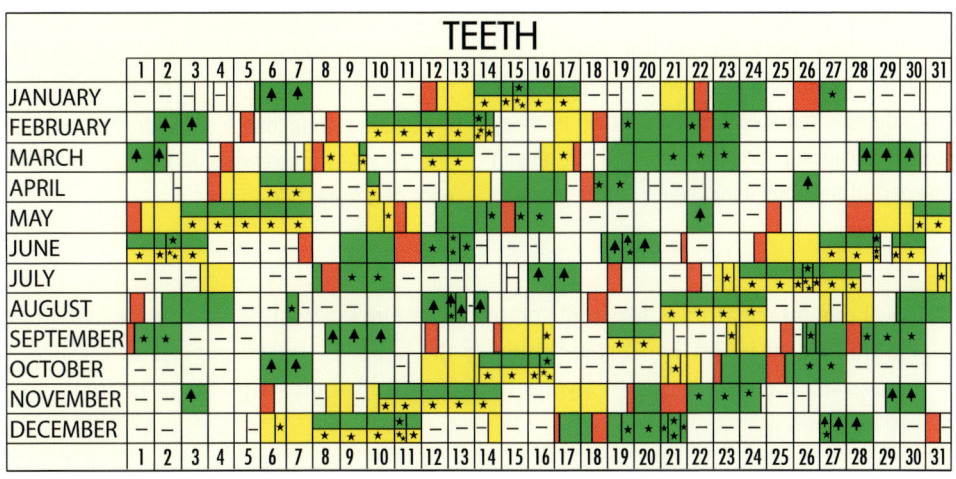

TEETH

Surgical procedures

The information below has not been validated by scientific experiment. However, it forms part of a long tradition that began with the Chaldeans and was adopted by the Egyptians, Greeks and finally, by traditional medicine in the West. It contains useful information, but it is also important to make it clear that levels of sensitivity to lunar influences vary from person to person. For example, some people suffer from sleep disturbance on nights when there is a Full Moon, while others sleep soundly. It seems that the same applies to surgical procedures and that not everyone will react in the same way.

The following information relates to operations scheduled in advance. It does not apply to emergency procedures.

As the Moon passes through the different signs of the zodiac, it stimulates different parts of the body (see the table on page 53). This makes certain treatments more effective (see page 51) but equally it can have a negative effect on surgical procedures – sometimes slowing down recovery and even causing complications, and not only in the part of the body immediately concerned.

Do not operate on any part of the body when the Moon is passing through the sign that corresponds to it exactly.

To improve the healing process and promote recovery choose a date with a waning and, if possible, an ascending Moon.

Generally, the following signs of the zodiac are favourable for surgery: Capricorn (a-b), Aquarius (c-d), Taurus (i-j), Gemini (k), Virgo (r-s) and Libra (t).

The following aspects are favourable (see pages 12-14): Moon sextile or trine Sun (☾ ✳ △ ☉), Moon conjunction, sextile or trine Venus (☾ ♂ ✳ △ ♀), Moon conjunction, sextile or trine Mercury (☾ ♂ ✳ △ ☿). Avoid the Full Moon, including the day before and the day after, as well as the New Moon and the three days following. Also avoid lunar nodes, the perigee and the Moon square with Saturn or the Sun. For successful surgery involving the skin (cosmetic surgery), see the recommendations for surgery (above) and also choose a descending Moon with the influence of a rising tide.

The above information is far from complete, its aim is simply to raise awareness of this traditional belief. For further study of the subject, consult experts in the field or specialist books. Be sure to always take any medical prescriptions or instructions into account.

The body and the zodiac

This table shows the correlation between the signs of the zodiac and different parts of the body.

ARIES	skull, brain, upper jaw, face, facial muscles, eyes
TAURUS	throat, neck, lips, palate, larynx, tonsils, tongue, ears, cerebellum, neck vertebrae, thyroid, lower jaw
GEMINI	upper limbs, hands, lungs, bronchial tubes, respiratory tracts, nervous system, capillaries
CANCER	oesophagus, stomach, ribs, breastbone, upper lobes of the liver, pancreas, breasts, diaphragm
LEO	heart, solar plexus, aorta, back vertebrae, spinal cord
VIRGO	abdominal region, duodenum, spleen, lower lobe of the liver, small intestine, large intestine
LIBRA	kidneys, adrenal glands, ureters, lumbar region, skin
SCORPIO	bladder, urethra, genital organs, prostate, descending colon, rectum, nose, pubis
SAGITTARIUS	hips, pelvis, coccyx, sacrum, thigh bones, ischium and iliac bone (hip), the sciatic nerve, femoral artery, saphena veins
CAPRICORN	knees, knee caps, cartilage, skin, nails, hair, bones in general
AQUARIUS	leg, tibia, fibula, ankle, Achilles' tendon
PISCES	feet, toes, lymphatic circulation

Understanding the calendar

On the calendar on pages 56-79, the phases of the Moon (New Moon ●, first quarter ◐, last quarter ◑, Full Moon ○) as well as its perigee **P** and its apogee **A**, are represented in the top band.

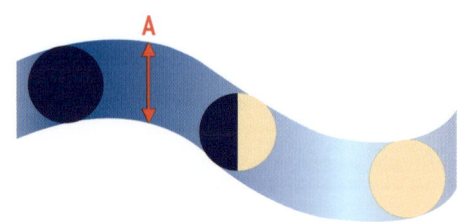

The band beneath shows the Chinese seasons and inter-seasonal periods. Beneath these are the bands indicating the signs and constellations of the zodiac, each of which is illustrated by a coloured strip that corresponds to the four elements:

FIRE	EARTH	AIR	WATER

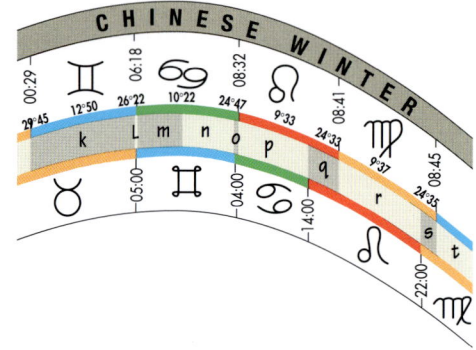

The letters between these bands indicate where signs and constellations can be used in conjunction (see page 10).

The curve of the coloured bands represents the Moon ascending and descending and the black triangles indicate when the change occurs. When the bands curve upwards, the Moon is ascending and vice versa. This movement is also reflected by the thin coloured bands beneath the wider blue band with the dates – green for the ascending Moon and yellow for the descending Moon.

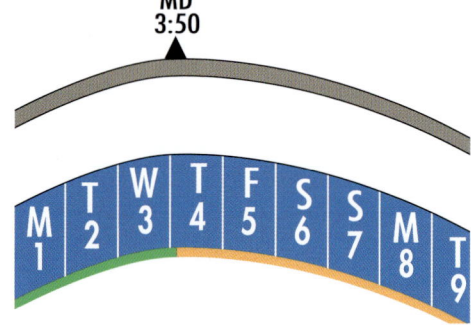

Cultivating the soil (particularly at depth), planting (for example, trees), planting out (especially plants with bare roots) and spreading compost or manure should be carried out when the Moon is descending, which is the best time for plants to take root.

The signs, letters and numbers in the white band are relevant to harvesting. The length of time is indicated by the vertical lines.

Ascending Moon:
harvest aerial parts of plant (green stars)
Descending Moon:
harvest parts of plant below ground (yellow stars)

The period for sowing different plants is indicated by the green band, which is in parallel with the constellations. The time when work should be carried out depends on why the plant is being grown (for its fruits, roots, flowers or leaves), avoiding the red zones. For example, choose a date favourable to 'leaf' plants for houseplants that do not flower and a 'flower' date for plants that do. Another example is to sow endives on 'root' dates and force their growth on 'leaf' dates.

The white band completes the information given in the green band. A summary of all the lunar and planetary effects on crops is given by indicating various zones ranging from 'harmful' (red band) to 'very favourable' (***) and also 'to be avoided' (—). Use these symbols in conjunction with the green band above for a clear and comprehensive understanding.

All the times mentioned are Greenwich Mean Time or British Summer Time, as appropriate.
For other countries, see page 80.
Cut out the detachable page giving instructions on how best to use the calendar and use it as a bookmark to remind you to use the calendar every month.

JANUARY

4 January: the Earth is at its closest to the Sun (the perihelion) – about 147 million km (92 million miles).

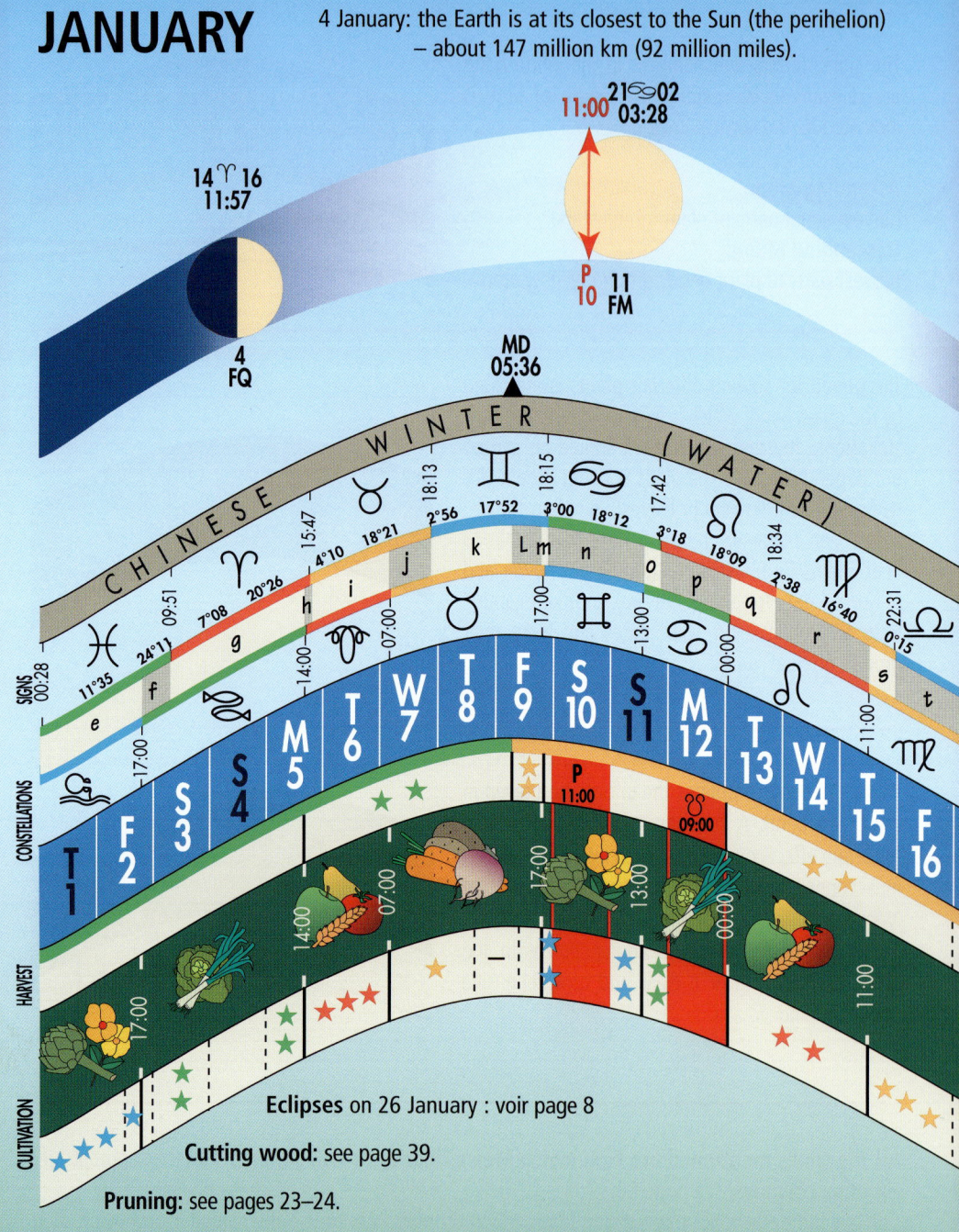

Eclipses on 26 January : voir page 8

Cutting wood: see page 39.

Pruning: see pages 23–24.

The colours of the stars relate to different types of plants (for example, red = fruit plants).

To help you make full use of the calendar, activities are suggested for each month.

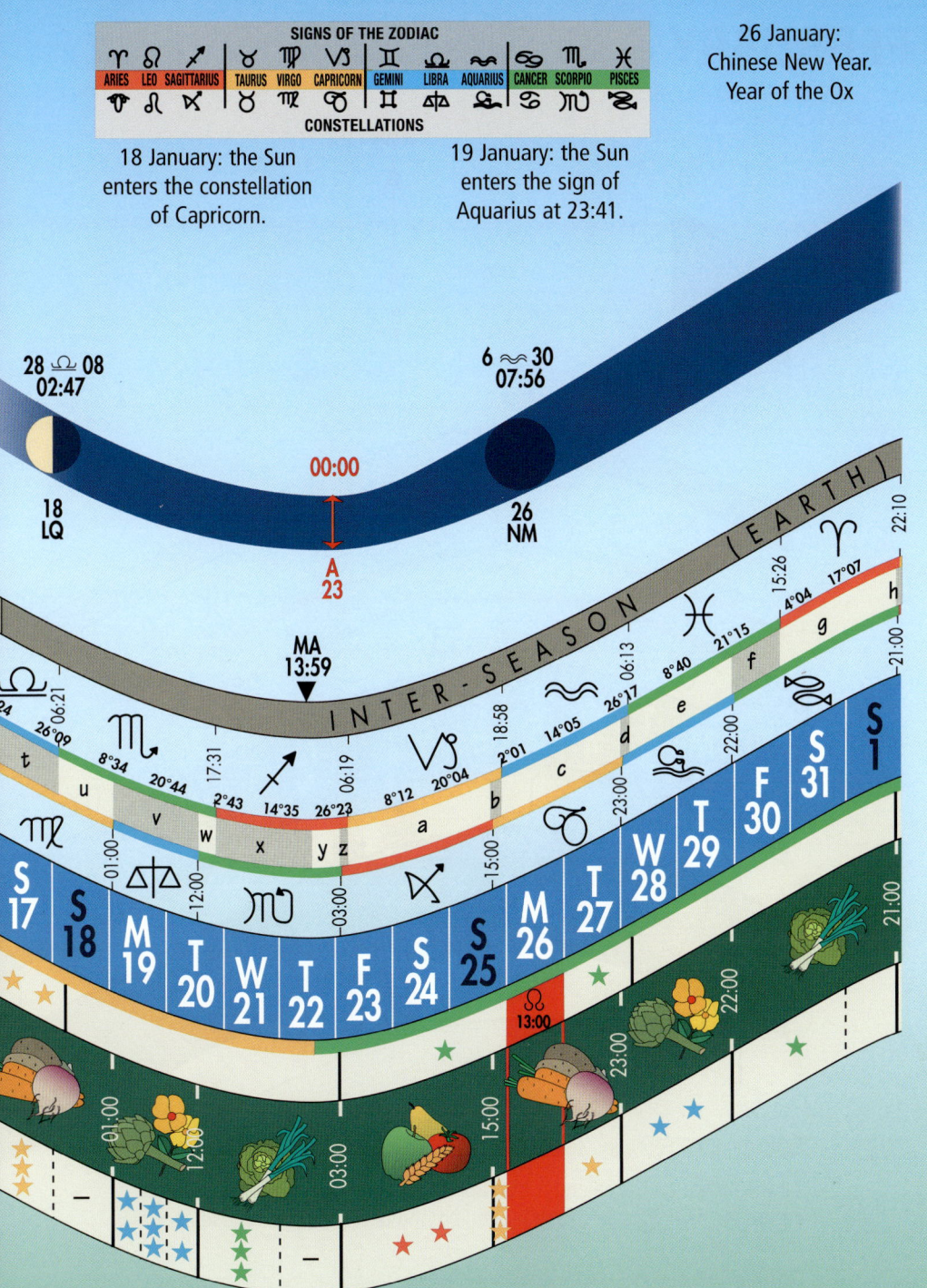

SIGNS OF THE ZODIAC

| ARIES | LEO | SAGITTARIUS | TAURUS | VIRGO | CAPRICORN | GEMINI | LIBRA | AQUARIUS | CANCER | SCORPIO | PISCES |

CONSTELLATIONS

18 January: the Sun enters the constellation of Capricorn.

19 January: the Sun enters the sign of Aquarius at 23:41.

26 January: Chinese New Year. Year of the Ox

28 ♎ 08
02:47

6 ♒ 30
07:56

00:00

18
LQ

26
NM

A
23

MA
13:59

INTER-SEASON (EARTH)

Note: all times given are in Greenwich Mean Time.

FEBRUARY

14 February: the Sun enters the constellation of Aquarius.

Eclipses on 9 February: see page 8.

All the advice on the calendar also applies to **the southern hemisphere**, except for the inversion of the ascending and descending Moon (see page 4).

Note: all times given are in Greenwich Mean Time.

SIGNS OF THE ZODIAC									
♈ ♌ ♐			♉ ♍ ♑			♊ ♎ ♒			♓
ARIES	LEO	SAGITTARIUS	TAURUS	VIRGO	CAPRICORN	GEMINI	LIBRA	AQUARIUS	CANCER	SCORPIO	PISCES
♈	♌	♐	♉	♍	♑	♊	♎	♒	♓
CONSTELLATIONS									

18 February: the Sun enters the sign of Pisces at 13:47.

6 ♓ 35
01:36

28 ♏ 21
21:38

17:00

25
NM

16
LQ

A
19

(W A T E R)

MA
21:07

W I N T E R

♈
03:34
27°25
i ♉

♓
9°51 21:25
17:55
14°02 g
h

5°13
13:01 f
e
d

2°07
22°44
10°30 c

28°26
16°31
4°42
22°53 b

13:26
11°01 a
z

00:54
29°02 y

1°18
16°49 ♏

u
v
w
x

02:00
♉

05:00

06:00

09:00

10:00

20:00

22:00

S
15

M
16

T
17

W
18

T
19

F
20

S
21

S
22

♌
20:00

M
23

T
24

W
25

T
26

F
27

S
28

S
1

02:00

20:00

05:00

06:00

22:00

09:00

10:00

20:00

Cereal crops: see page 33.

Hair care and depilation: see pages 44-45.

MARCH

13 ♊ 52
07:47

11 March: the Sun
enters the constellation
of Pisces.

15:00

4
FQ

20 ♍ 40
02:39

P
7

MD
21:36

11
FM

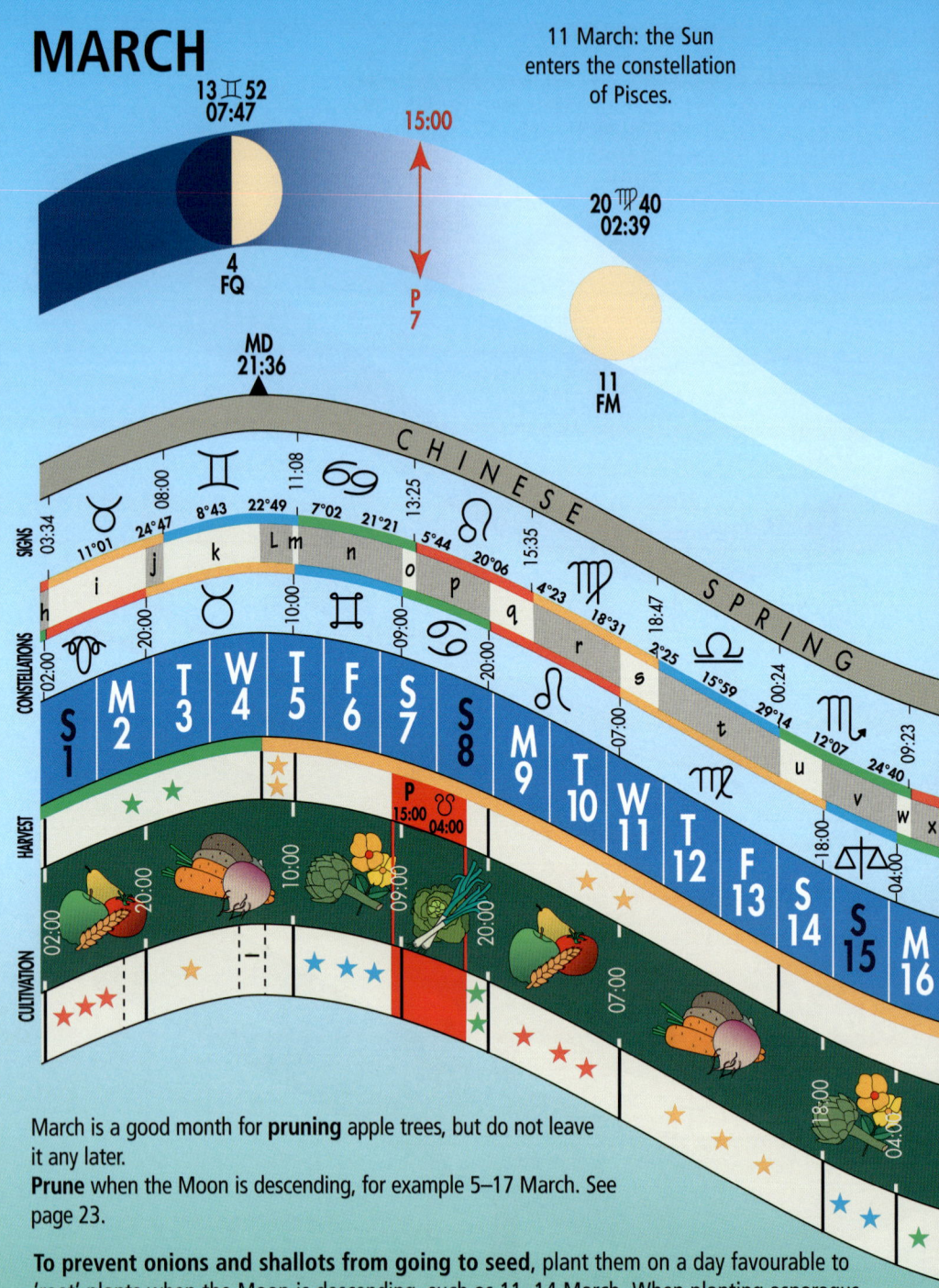

March is a good month for **pruning** apple trees, but do not leave
it any later.
Prune when the Moon is descending, for example 5–17 March. See
page 23.

To prevent onions and shallots from going to seed, plant them on a day favourable to
'root' plants when the Moon is descending, such as 11–14 March. When planting asparagus
crowns, wait for a 'leaf' date when the Moon is descending, such as 16–17 March.

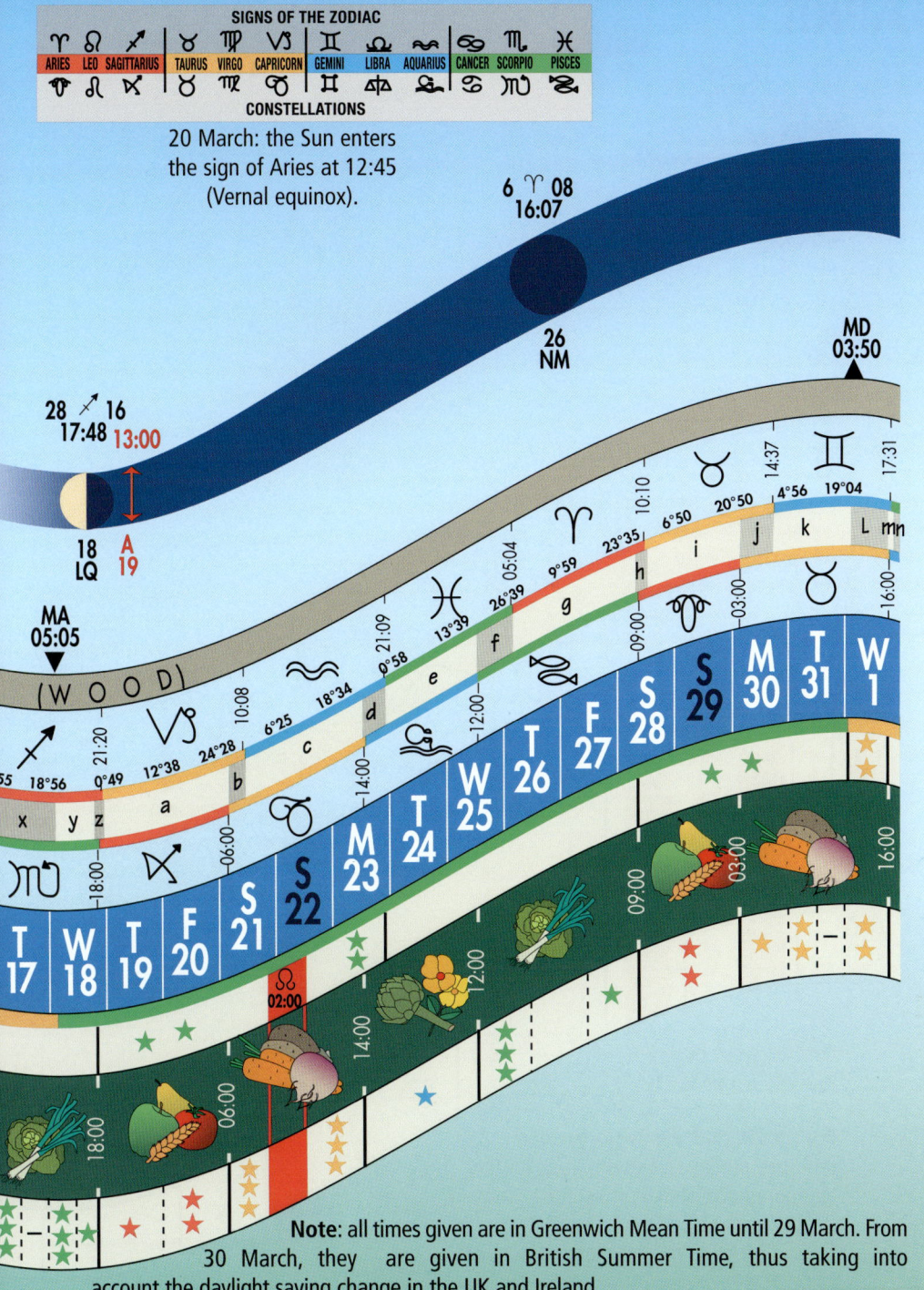

20 March: the Sun enters the sign of Aries at 12:45 (Vernal equinox).

Note: all times given are in Greenwich Mean Time until 29 March. From 30 March, they are given in British Summer Time, thus taking into account the daylight saving change in the UK and Ireland.

APRIL

SIGNS OF THE ZODIAC										
♈	♌	♐	♉	♍	♑	♊	♎	♒	♋	♏	♓
ARIES	LEO	SAGITTARIUS	TAURUS	VIRGO	CAPRICORN	GEMINI	LIBRA	AQUARIUS	CANCER	SCORPIO	PISCES
CONSTELLATIONS											

12 ♋ 59
15:35

03:00

P 2 2
2 FQ

19 ♎ 53
15:57

MD 03:50

9 FM

C H I N E S E S P R I N G W O O

SIGNS

♊ 17:31 3°13 17°21 20:34 ♌ 1°26 15°26 00:02 29°23 ♍ 13°14 04:23 26°56 ♎ 10°28 10:24 23°46 6°48 ♏ 19°34 19:02 2°02 ♐ 14°15 06:28 26°17

MA 14:00

CONSTELLATIONS

♉ 16:00 ♊ 16:00 ♋ 04:00

k L m n o p q r s t u v w x y z a

HARVEST

W 1 | T 2 | F 3 | S 4 | S 5 | M 6 | T 7 | W 8 | T 9 | F 10 | S 11 | S 12 | M 13 | T 14 | W 15

P 03:00

♉ 08:00

♍ 17:00

♎ 14:00

♍ 03:00

CULTIVATION

18:00 16:00 04:00 17:00 04:00 14:00 03:00

Grafting: see page 24.
Weeds: see page 31

For plants that easily go to seed
(lettuces, onions and so on), look for the
appropriate constellation with the Moon in
the descendent. For instance, 13–14 April for lettuces.
1 April is a good day for planting potatoes.

8-9-10 April are good days to plant potatoes.

19 April: the Sun enters the constellation of Aries.

20 April: the Sun enters the sign of Taurus at 00:45.

25 April: the beginning of the Red Moon.

07:00

5 ♉ 04
04:24

11 ♉ 36
21:45

P
28

25
NM

1
FQ

MD
09:50

27 ♑ 40
14:37

10:00

INTER-SEASON (EARTH)

♉ 22:03   ♊ 23:39   ♋ 01:57
16:07   15:05 29:36 14:00   28:15

17
LQ

A
16

0:34   k   L m   n   o p

♈ 19:47   j
17:56 1:53

15:10   i
4:21

♓ 21:10   h   ♉
g   18:00   11:00

25:55   f   ♊ 22:00
8:22

≈ 06:56   e   ♋ 21:00
13:16

♑ 19:20   d
1:49

c   ♉ 23:00

°10 19:58   b
a

♐ 16:00

S
1

F
1

T
30

W
29

T
28

M
27

S
26

S
25

F
24

T
23

W
22

T
21

M
20

S
19

S
18

F
17

T
16

P
07:00

♉
09:00

♋
06:00

Green manure: while waiting for the next food crop to grow, sow green manure to protect and enrich the soil (clover, phacelia, mustard, cereals with vetch or peas, buckwheat and spinach). Sow on a date favourable to 'leaf' plants to achieve abundant growth or, better still, a 'roots' date for maximum improvement to the structure of the soil.

63

MAY

13 May: the Sun enters the constellation of Taurus.

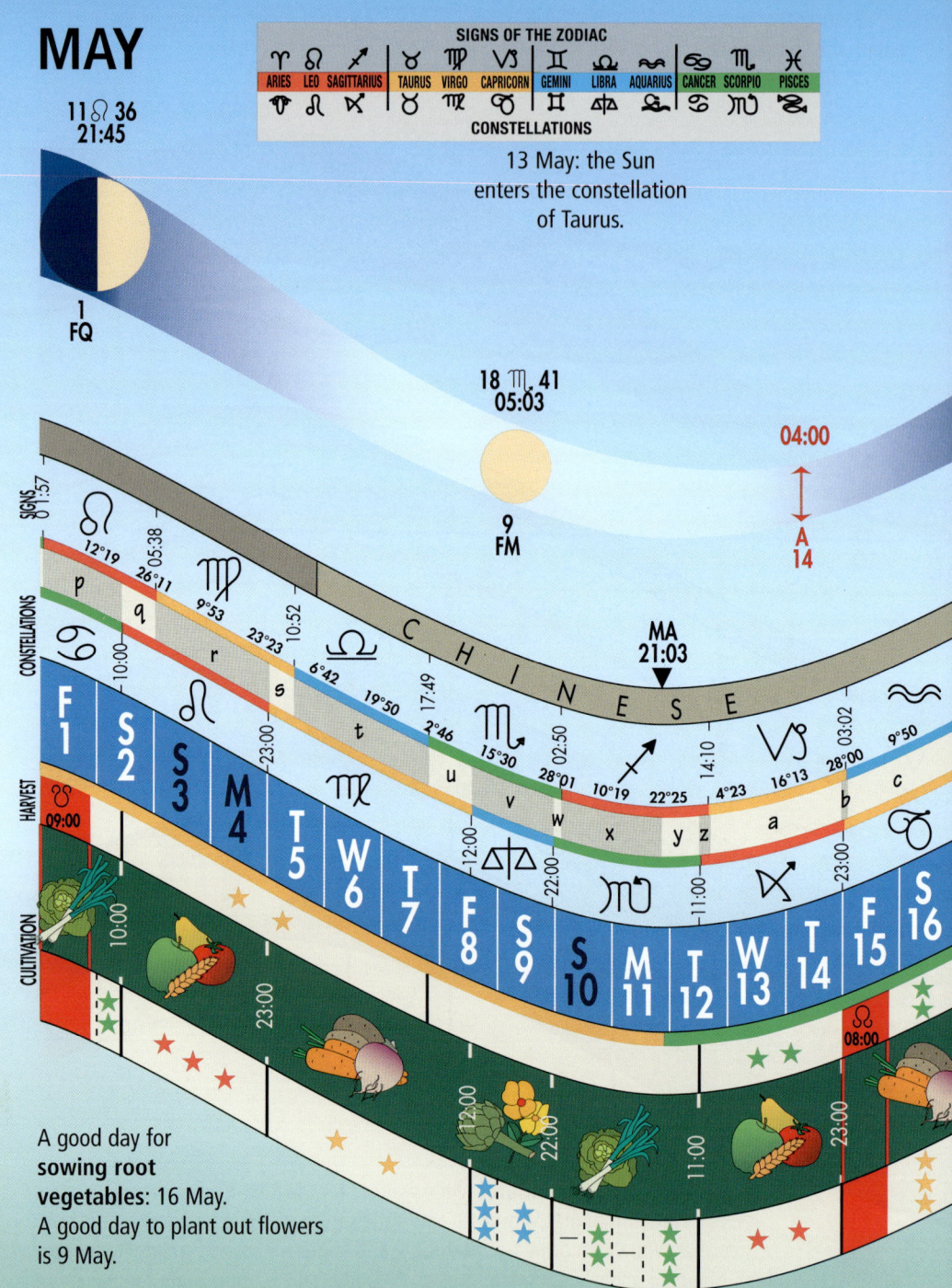

A good day for **sowing root vegetables**: 16 May.
A good day to plant out flowers is 9 May.

Note: all times given are in British Summer Time..

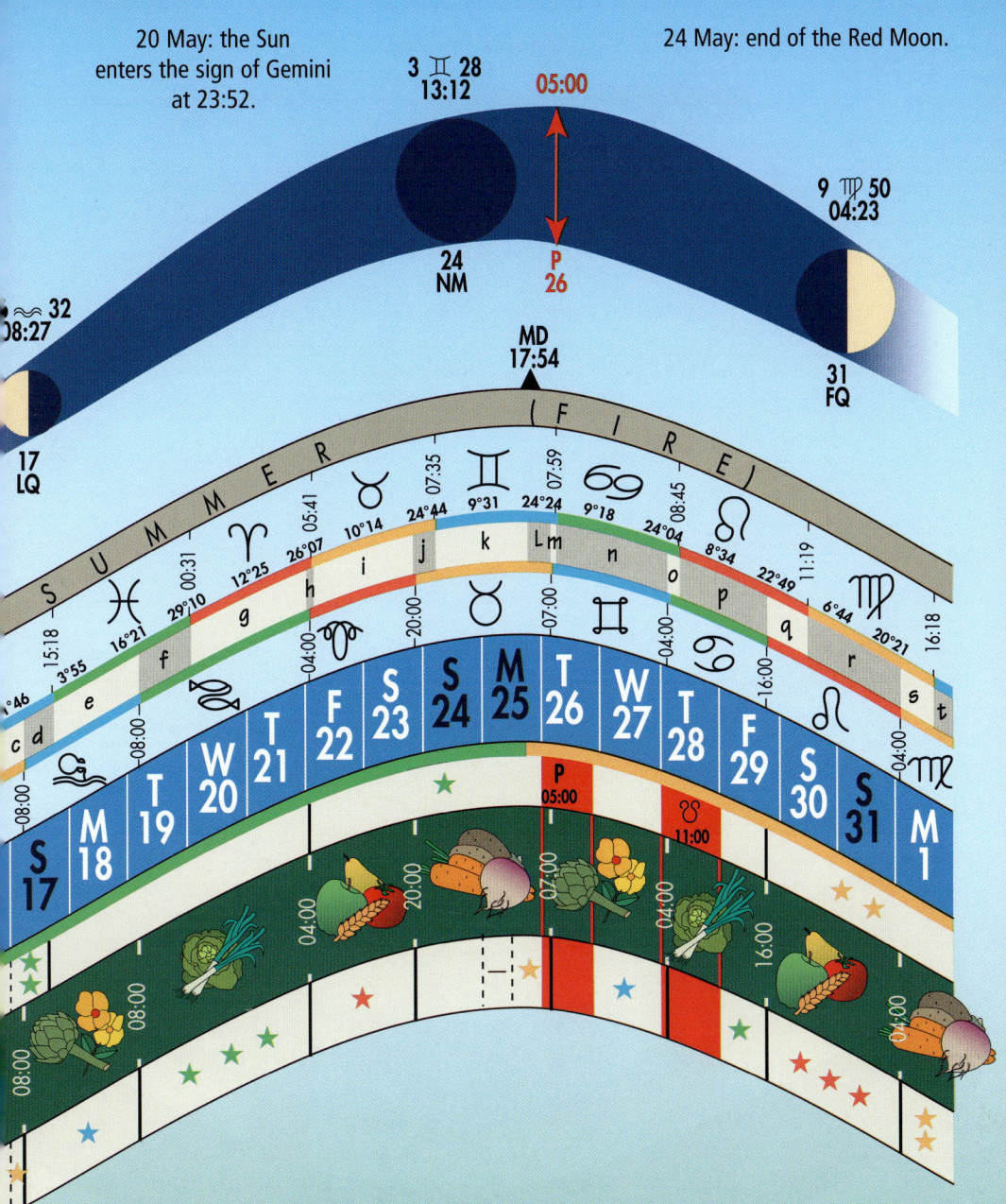

20 May: the Sun enters the sign of Gemini at 23:52.

24 May: end of the Red Moon.

3 ♊ 28
13:12

05:00

9 ♍ 50
04:23

24
NM

P
26

♒ 32
08:27

MD
17:54

31
FQ

17
LQ

When sowing, always choose the constellation that suits the type of plant, if possible when there is the maximum number of stars. For example, 20, 21 May for leeks, 9 May for flowers. Always avoid the red zones and, as far as possible, days marked with the sign (—).

JUNE

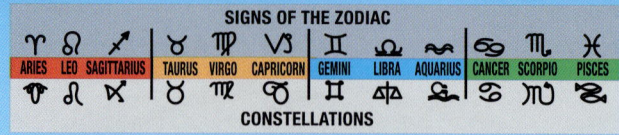

SIGNS OF THE ZODIAC

♈	♌	♐	♉	♍	♑	♊	♎	♒	♋	♏	♓
ARIES	LEO	SAGITTARIUS	TAURUS	VIRGO	CAPRICORN	GEMINI	LIBRA	AQUARIUS	CANCER	SCORPIO	PISCES

CONSTELLATIONS

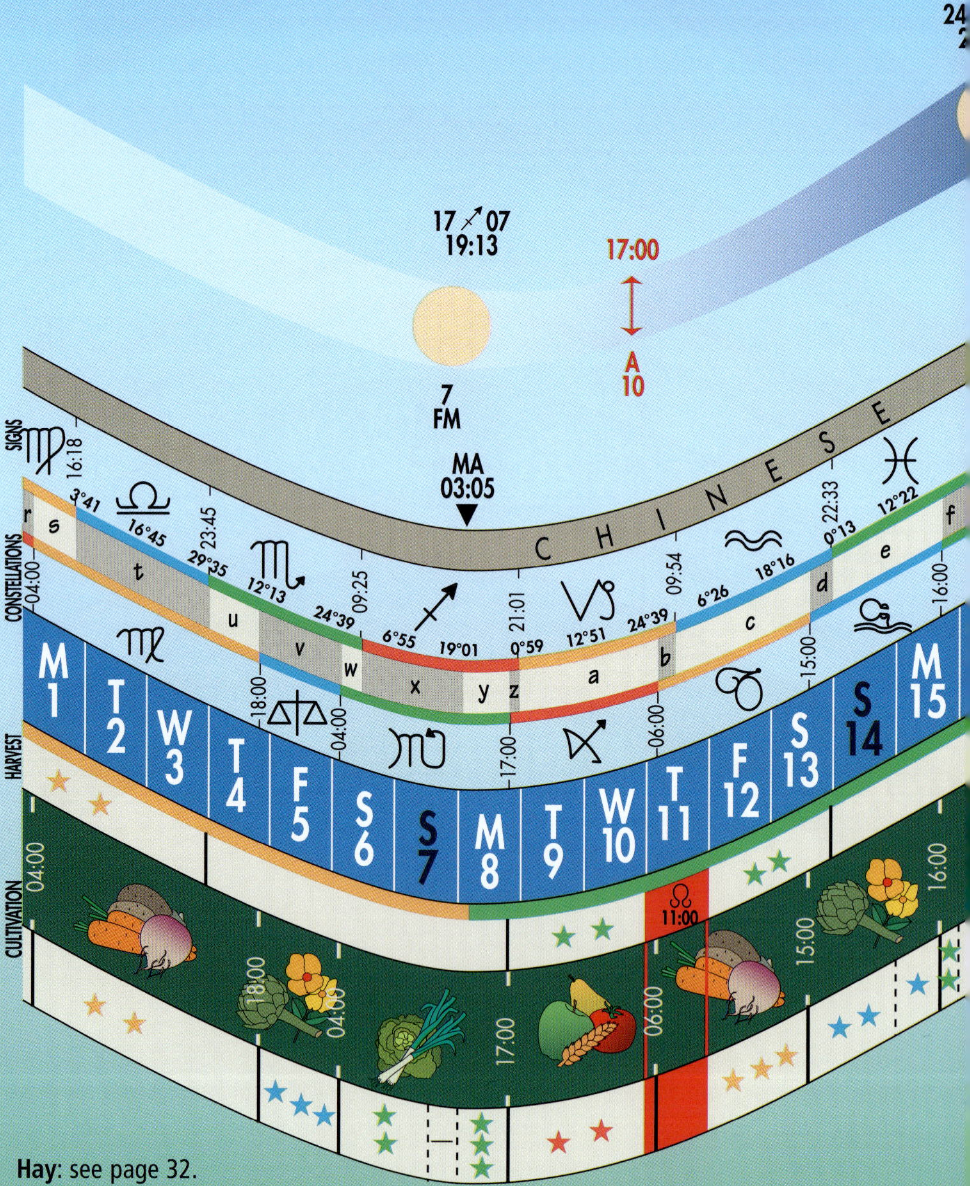

24

17 ♐ 07
19:13

17:00

↕
A
10

7
FM

MA
03:05
▼

SIGNS

♍
16:18

C H I N E S E

♓
12:22

CONSTELLATIONS

r s
3°41
♎
16:45
23:45
t
29°35
♏
12°13
u
24°39
v
09:25
w
6°55
x   y z
19:01
21:01
♑
12°51
24°39
a
09:54
b
6°26
c
18°16
d
0°13
e
22:33
f
16:00

0°59

04:00

18:00

04:00

17:00

06:00

15:00

16:00

M 1	T 2	W 3	T 4	F 5	S 6	S 7	M 8	T 9	W 10	T 11	F 12	S 13	S 14	M 15

HARVEST

♏

☊

♎

♐

♍

CULTIVATION

04:00

18:00

17:00

06:00

11:00

15:00

16:00

☊
11:00

★ ★

★

★

★★

★

★★

★★★

★★

★★★

★

★★★

★★

★ ★★★

★

★★

★★★

★★

Hay: see page 32.

66

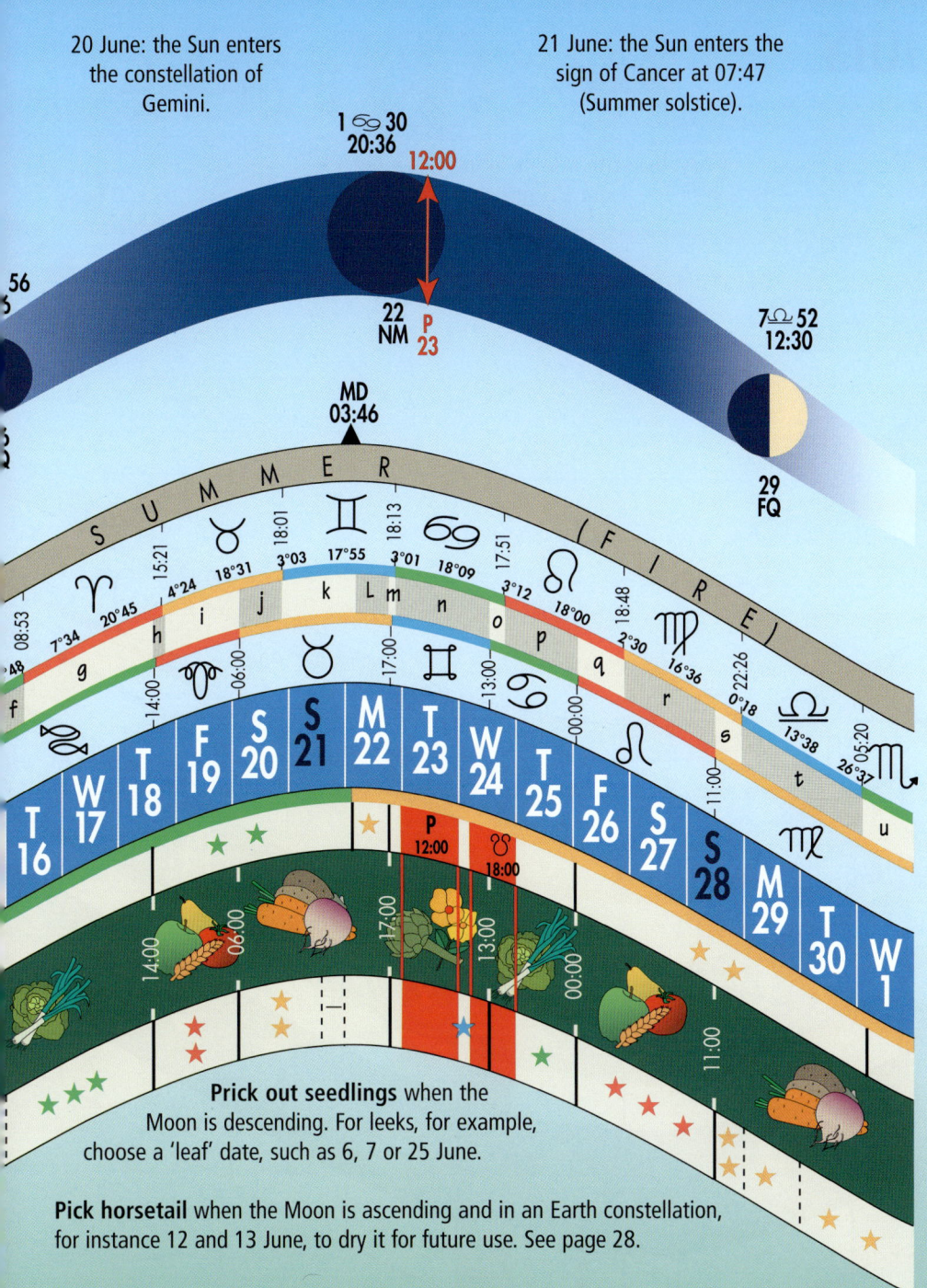

20 June: the Sun enters the constellation of Gemini.

21 June: the Sun enters the sign of Cancer at 07:47 (Summer solstice).

1 ♋ 30
20:36

12:00

22
NM

P
23

7 ♎ 52
12:30

MD
03:46

29
FQ

S U M M E R   (F I R E)

Prick out seedlings when the Moon is descending. For leeks, for example, choose a 'leaf' date, such as 6, 7 or 25 June.

Pick horsetail when the Moon is ascending and in an Earth constellation, for instance 12 and 13 June, to dry it for future use. See page 28.

To ensure grass grows back more slowly, cut it on a date favourable to 'flower' plants or, if that is not possible, when the Moon is descending, for instance 1, 2, 3, 4, 5, 23, 29, 30 June.

JULY

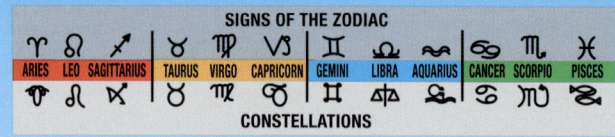

SIGNS OF THE ZODIAC

♈	♌	♐	♉	♍	♑	♊	♎	♒	♋	♏	♓
ARIES	LEO	SAGITTARIUS	TAURUS	VIRGO	CAPRICORN	GEMINI	LIBRA	AQUARIUS	CANCER	SCORPIO	PISCES

CONSTELLATIONS

4 July: the earth is at its furthest from the Sun
(its aphelion) – about 152 million km (95 million miles).

23 ♈ 03
10:54

15
LQ

15 ♑ 24
10:23 23:00

7   A
FM 8

MA
08:39

SIGNS
05:20

C H I N E S E S U M M E R (F I R E)

♏
9°18   21°43   15:12   ♐   03:09   ♑   16:04   ≈   15°14   27°07   ♓   21°23   ♈   3°49   16°36   29°43   ♉
                                      16°00   27°56   9°48   21°36   3°24   15:41   23:31
                                                                                                                  22:00

CONSTELLATIONS
t
u   v   w   x   y   z   a   b   c   d   e   f   g   h   i

♏   ♎   ♍   ♌   22:00
23:00   10:00   00:00   12:00   ♋   21:00   22:00

W 1	T 2	F 3	S 4	S 5	M 6	T 7	W 8	T 9	F 10	S 11	S 12	M 13	T 14	W 15	T 16

HARVEST

22:00

♊
16:00

CULTIVATION
2:00   10°   00:00   12:00   21:00   22:00

Note: all times given are in British Summer Time.

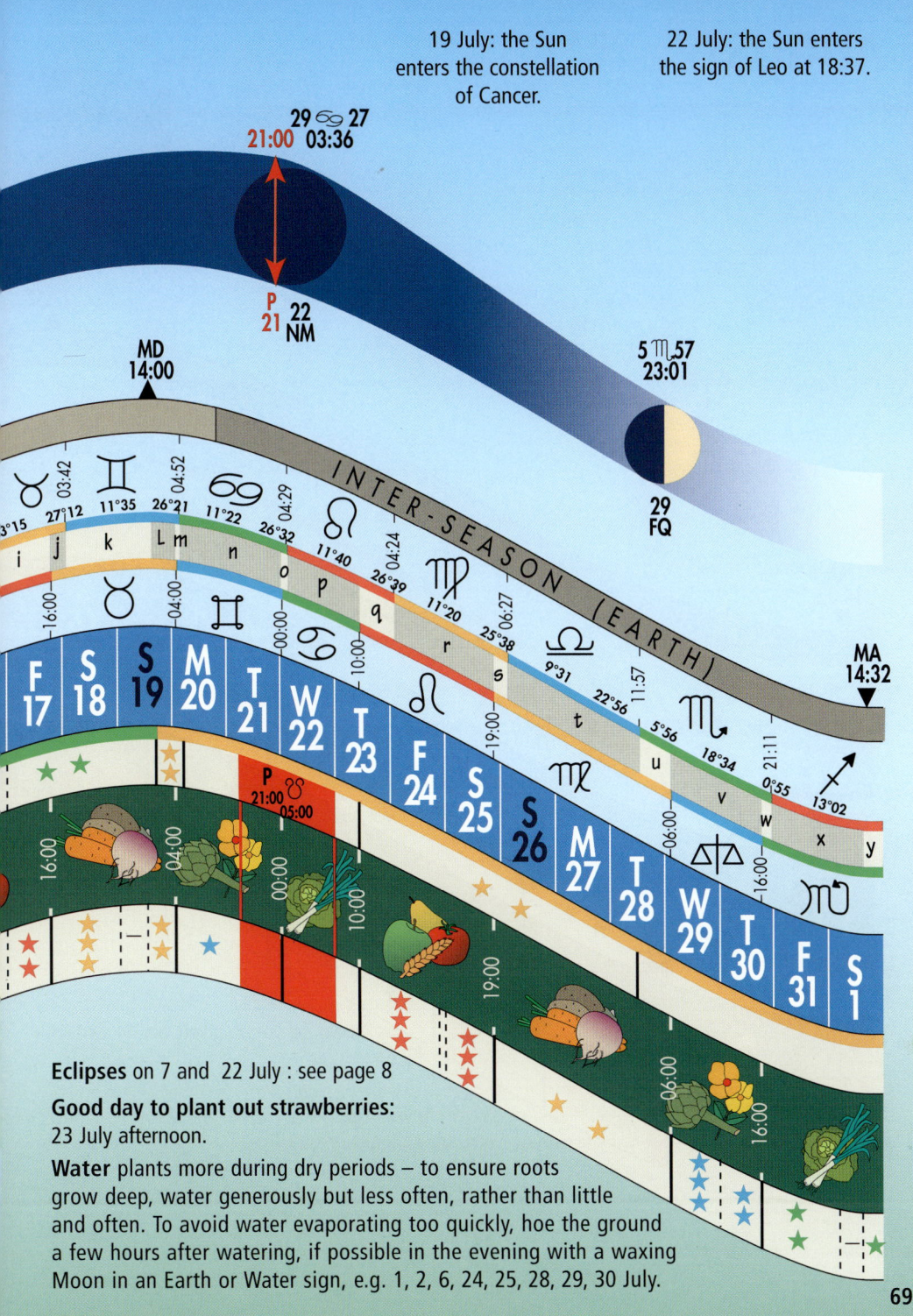

19 July: the Sun enters the constellation of Cancer.

22 July: the Sun enters the sign of Leo at 18:37.

29 ♋ 27
21:00 03:36

P
21 22
NM

MD
14:00

5 ♏ 57
23:01

INTER-SEASON (EARTH)

♉ 03:42
3°15 27°12 ♊ 04:52
11°35 26°21 ♋
11°22 26°32
04:29
n ♌
11°40
o
26°39 04:24
♍
11°20
25°38 06:27
♎
9°31
22°56 11:57
5°56
♏
18°34
21:11
0°55
13°02

29
FQ

MA
14:32

i j k L m n o p q r s t u v w x y

♉ 16:00
♊ 04:00
♋ 00:00
♌

F 17
S 18
S 19
M 20
T 21
W 22
T 23
F 24
S 25
S 26
M 27
T 28
W 29
T 30
F 31
S 1

P ♉
21:00
05:00

16:00
04:00
00:00
10:00
19:00
06:00
16:00

Eclipses on 7 and 22 July : see page 8

Good day to plant out strawberries:
23 July afternoon.

Water plants more during dry periods – to ensure roots
grow deep, water generously but less often, rather than little
and often. To avoid water evaporating too quickly, hoe the ground
a few hours after watering, if possible in the evening with a waxing
Moon in an Earth or Water sign, e.g. 1, 2, 6, 24, 25, 28, 29, 30 July.

AUGUST

10 August: the Sun enters the constellation of Leo.

21 ♉ 09
19:56

13
LQ

13 ♒ 43
01:56

02:00
↕
A
4

6
FM

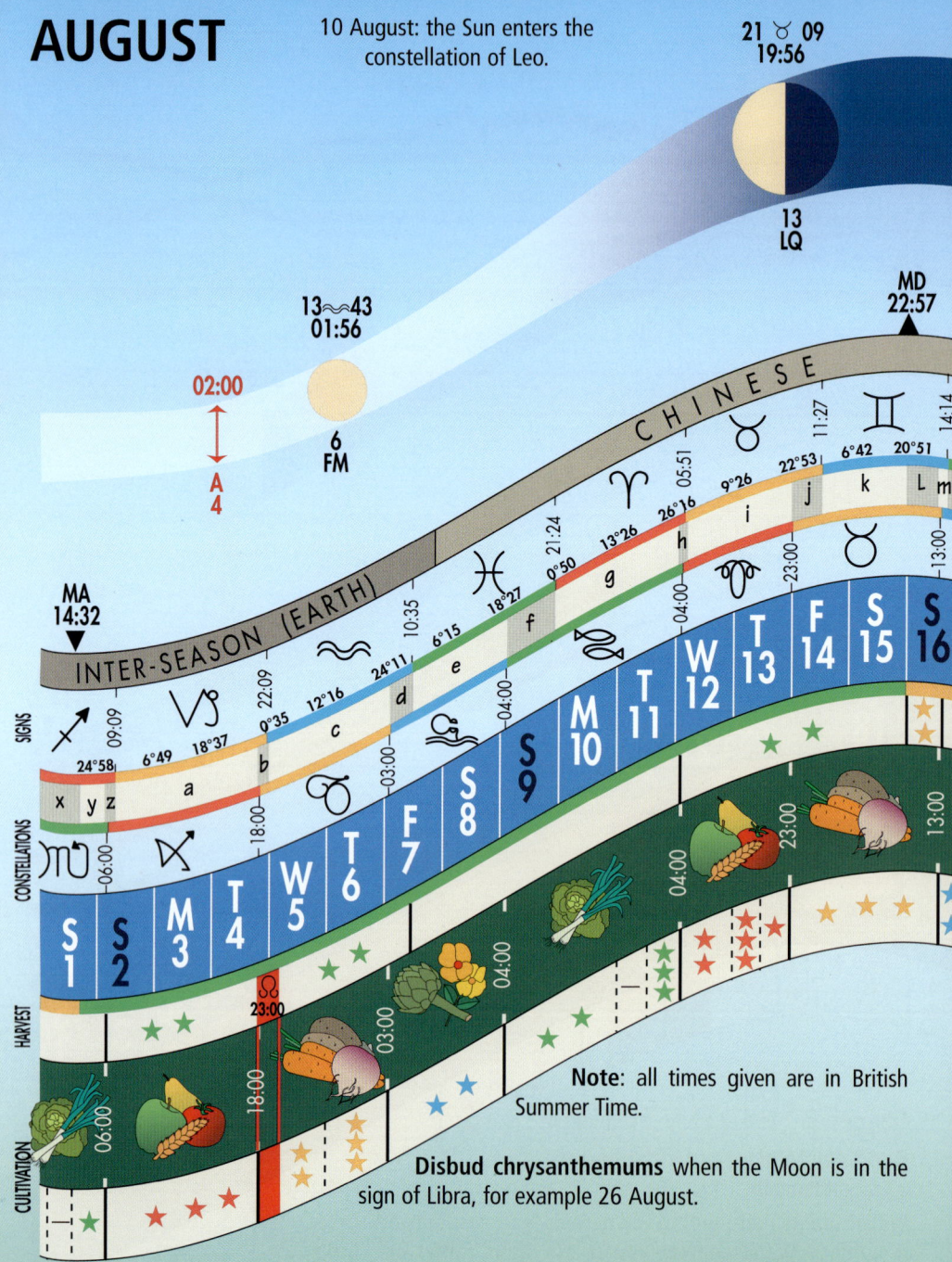

Note: all times given are in British Summer Time.

Disbud chrysanthemums when the Moon is in the sign of Libra, for example 26 August.

Eclipses on 6 August: see page 8.

Shield budding: see page 24.

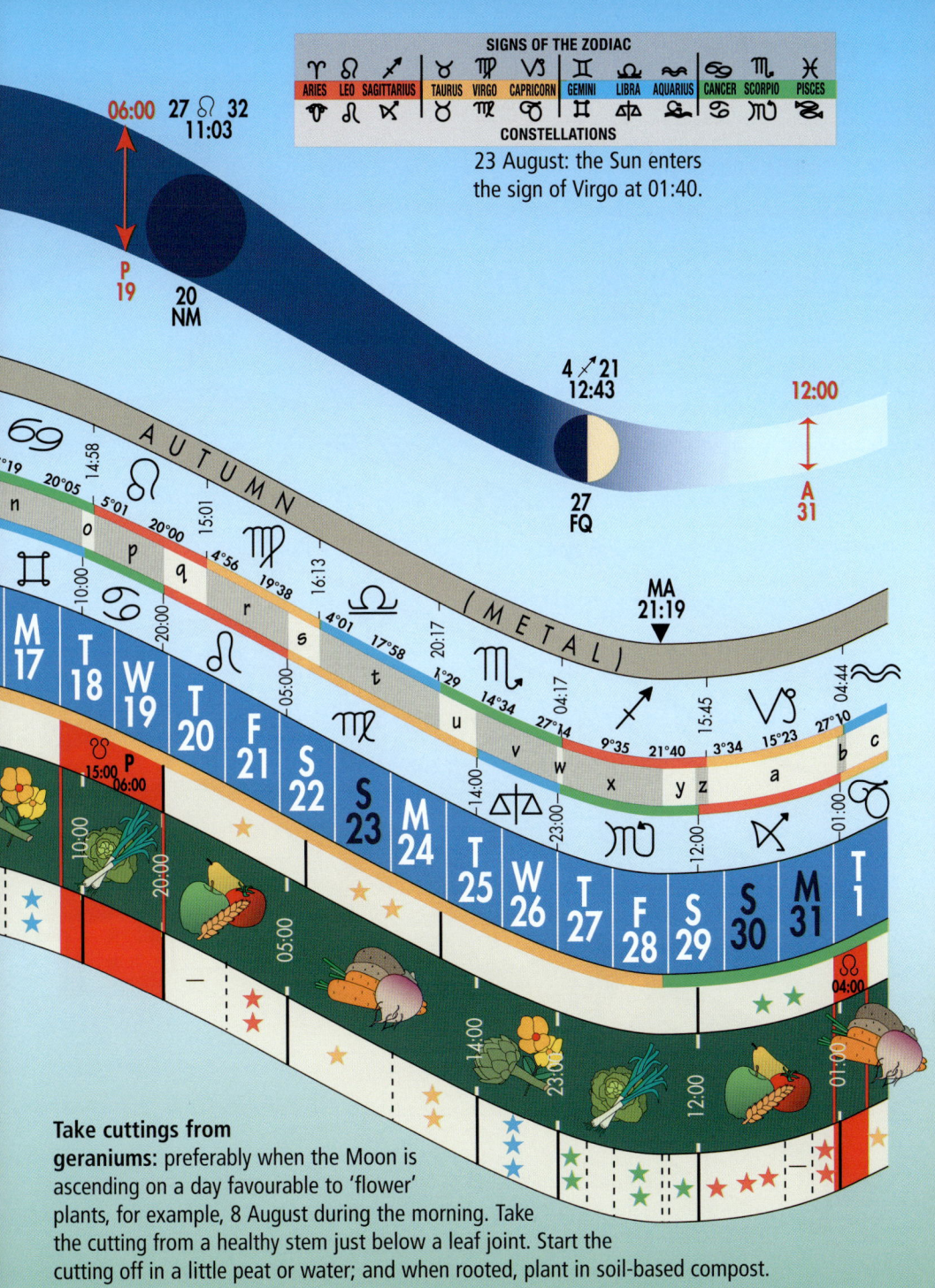

SIGNS OF THE ZODIAC

♈	♌	♐	♉	♍	♑	♊	♎	♒	♋	♏	♓
ARIES	LEO	SAGITTARIUS	TAURUS	VIRGO	CAPRICORN	GEMINI	LIBRA	AQUARIUS	CANCER	SCORPIO	PISCES

CONSTELLATIONS

23 August: the Sun enters
the sign of Virgo at 01:40.

06:00 27 ♌ 32
       11:03

P
19

20
NM

4 ♐ 21
12:43

27
FQ

12:00

A
31

MA
21:19 ▼

Take cuttings from
geraniums: preferably when the Moon is
ascending on a day favourable to 'flower'
plants, for example, 8 August during the morning. Take
the cutting from a healthy stem just below a leaf joint. Start the
cutting off in a little peat or water; and when rooted, plant in soil-based compost.

SEPTEMBER

15 September: the Sun enters the constellation of Virgo.

Compost: apply compost on one of the dates given on page 29.
Wait for the a descending Moon before applying.
For **spreading manure**: see page 29.

Cereal crops: see page 33.　　　　**Harvesting grapes**: see page 37.

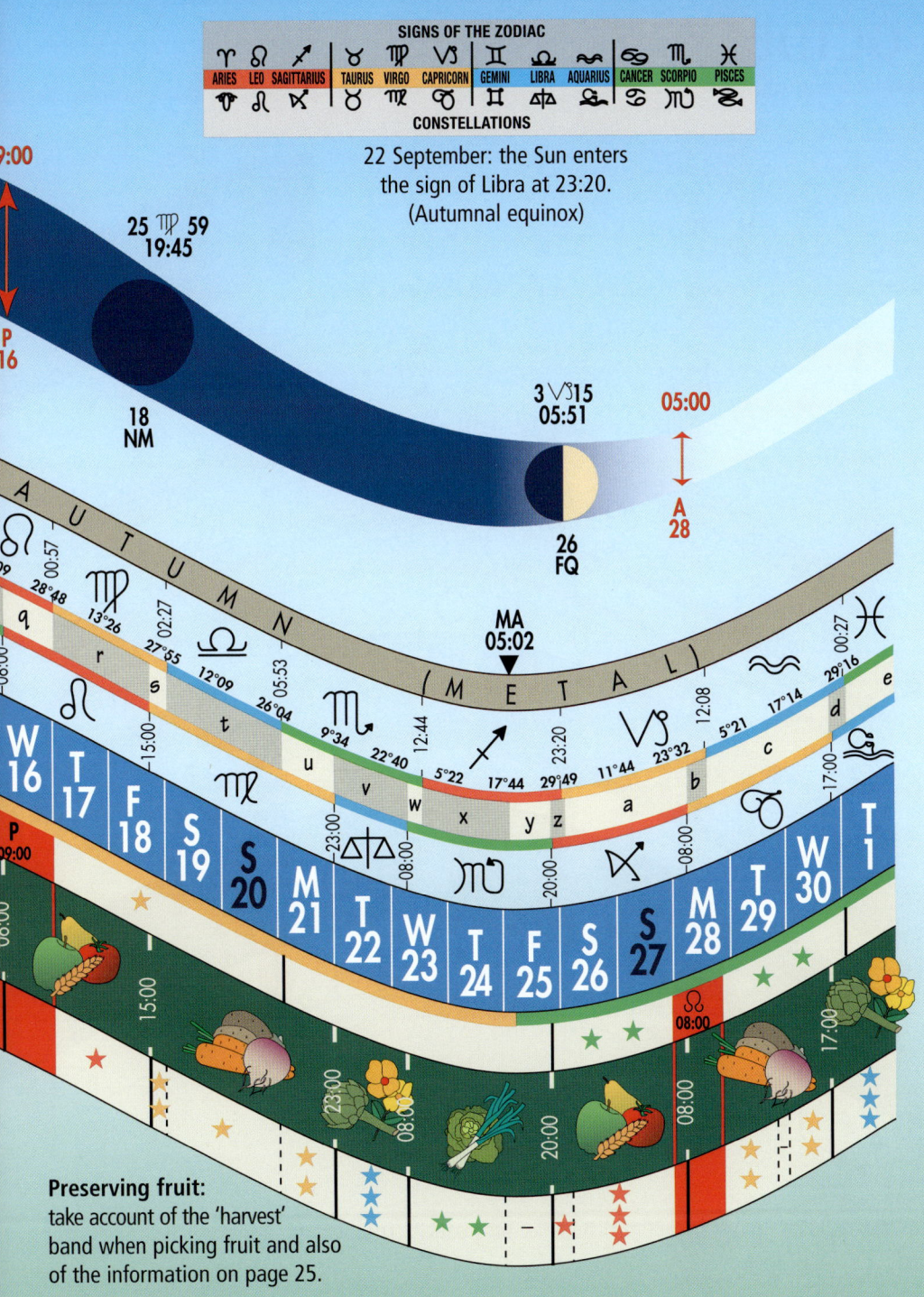

SIGNS OF THE ZODIAC

♈ ♌ ♐	♉ ♍ ♑	♊ ♎ ♒	♋ ♏ ♓
ARIES LEO SAGITTARIUS	TAURUS VIRGO CAPRICORN	GEMINI LIBRA AQUARIUS	CANCER SCORPIO PISCES

CONSTELLATIONS

22 September: the Sun enters
the sign of Libra at 23:20.
(Autumnal equinox)

9:00

25 ♍ 59
19:45

P
16

18
NM

3 ♑ 15
05:51

05:00

A
28

26
FQ

MA
05:02

Preserving fruit:
take account of the 'harvest'
band when picking fruit and also
of the information on page 25.

Note: all times given are in British Summer Time.

OCTOBER

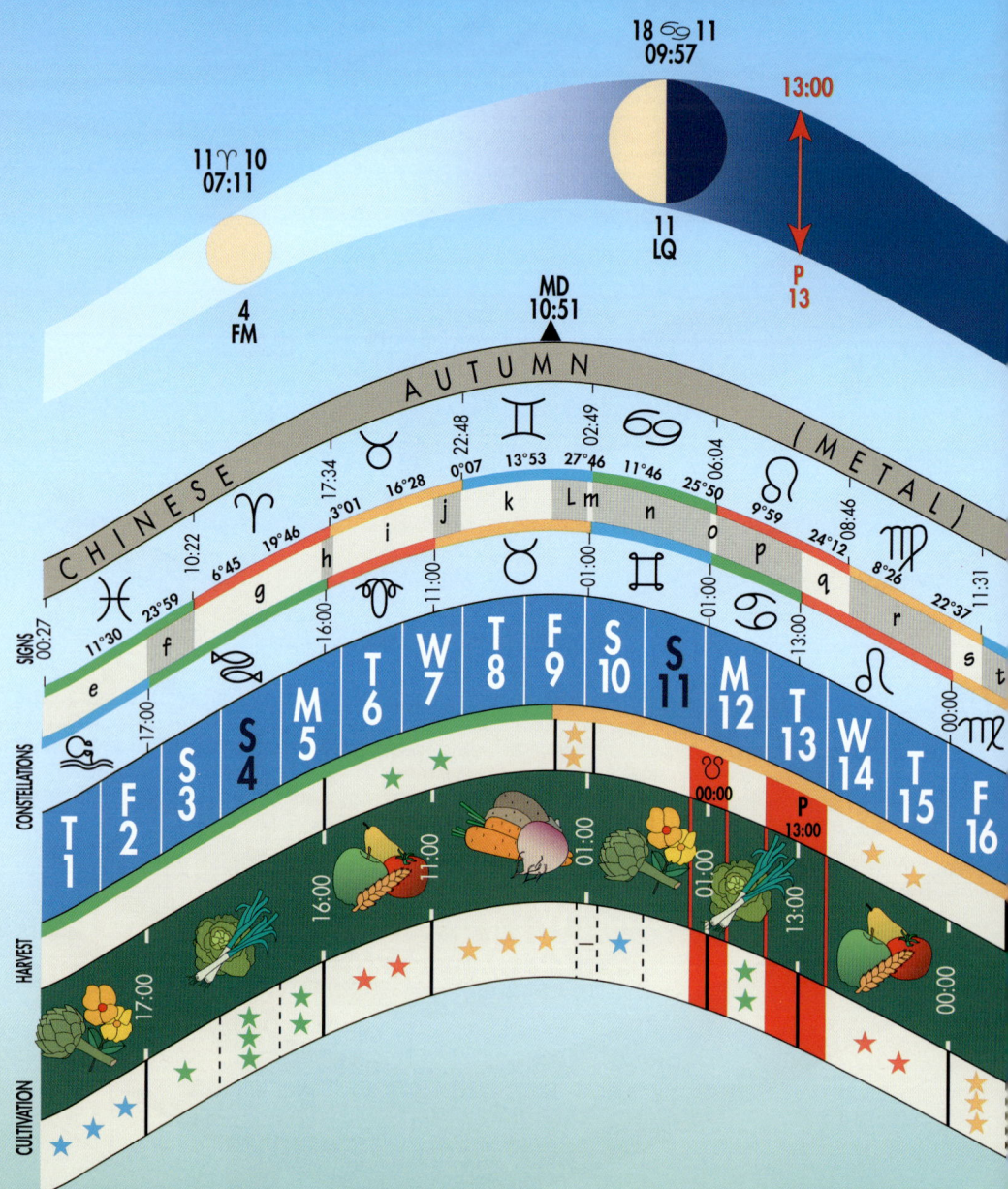

18 ♋ 11
09:57

13:00

11 ♈ 10
07:11

11
LQ

P
13

4
FM

MD
10:51

A U T U M N

(M E T A L)

C H I N E S E

SIGNS

CONSTELLATIONS

HARVEST

CULTIVATION

Note: all times given are in British Summer Time until 25 October and GMT from 26 October.

Cuttings: cut the morning of the 9th (end of the ascending moon) and plant during the afternoon of the 9th (beginning of the descending moon)

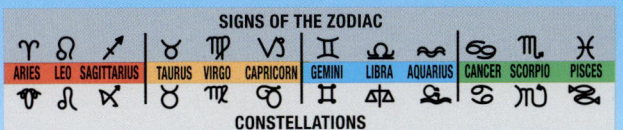

SIGNS OF THE ZODIAC

♈	♌	♐	♊	♍	♑	♊	♎	♒	♋	♏	♓
ARIES	LEO	SAGITTARIUS	TAURUS	VIRGO	CAPRICORN	GEMINI	LIBRA	AQUARIUS	CANCER	SCORPIO	PISCES

CONSTELLATIONS

23 October: the Sun enters
the sign of Scorpio at
08:45.

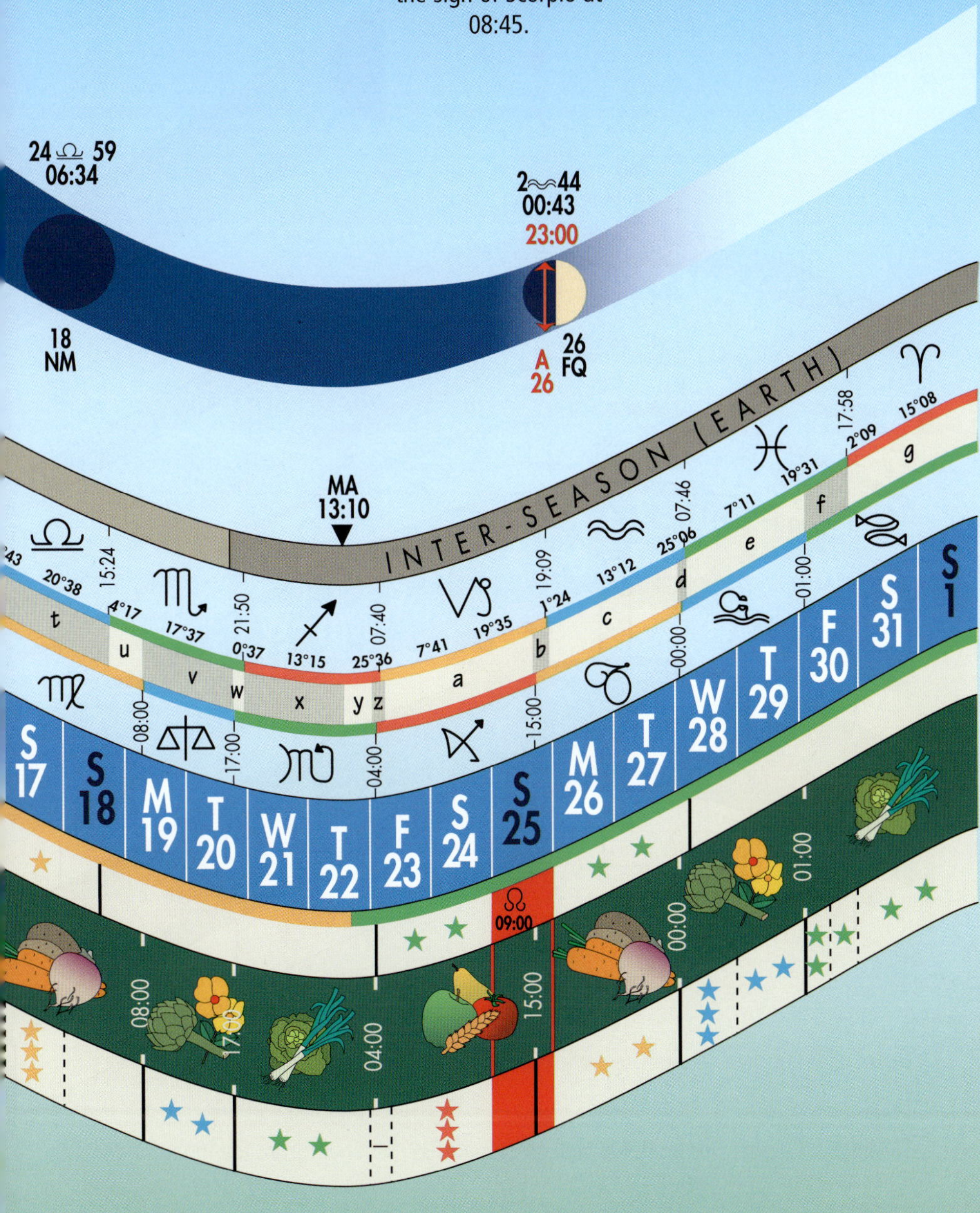

24 ♎ 59
06:34

2 ♒ 44
00:43
23:00

18
NM

A
26
26 FQ

MA
13:10

I N T E R - S E A S O N (E A R T H)

17:58
2°09
15:08
g

19:31
f
e
07:46
25°06
d
13:12
c
1°24
b
19:09
19:35
7°41
a
25°36
07:40
13°15
0°37
21:50
17:37
4°17
15:24
20°38
43
t
u
v
w
x
y z

♈

♓
♒
♑
♐

**S
1**

**S
31**

**F
30**

**T
29**

**W
28**

**T
27**

**M
26**

**S
25**

**S
24**

**F
23**

**T
22**

**W
21**

**T
20**

**M
19**

**S
18**

**S
17**

00:00
01:00
15:00
00:00
15:00
04:00
17:00
08:00

♉
09:00

NOVEMBER

1 November: the Sun enters the constellation of Libra.

Note: all times given are in Greenwich Mean Time.

Timber: cut timber on the dates marked on page 39 to benefit from the lunar influences, if possible during November and December to benefit from the descending Sun as well.

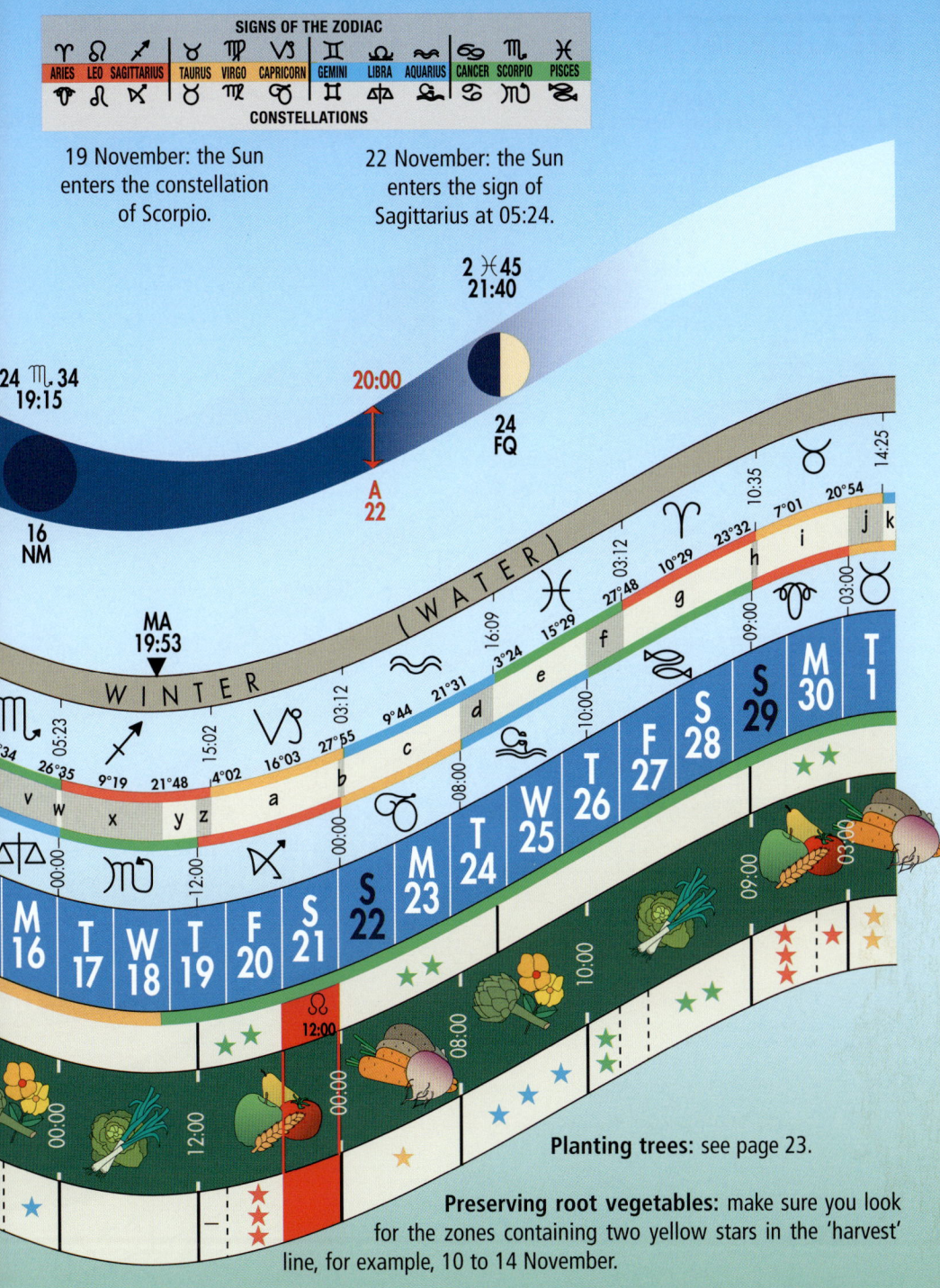

SIGNS OF THE ZODIAC

♈	♌	♐		♉	♍	♑		♊	♎	♒		♋	♏	♓
ARIES	LEO	SAGITTARIUS		TAURUS	VIRGO	CAPRICORN		GEMINI	LIBRA	AQUARIUS		CANCER	SCORPIO	PISCES

CONSTELLATIONS

19 November: the Sun
enters the constellation
of Scorpio.

22 November: the Sun
enters the sign of
Sagittarius at 05:24.

2 ♓ 45
21:40

24 ♏ 34
19:15

20:00

24
FQ

A
22

16
NM

MA
19:53

(W A T E R)

W I N T E R

Planting trees: see page 23.

Preserving root vegetables: make sure you look
for the zones containing two yellow stars in the 'harvest'
line, for example, 10 to 14 November.

DECEMBER

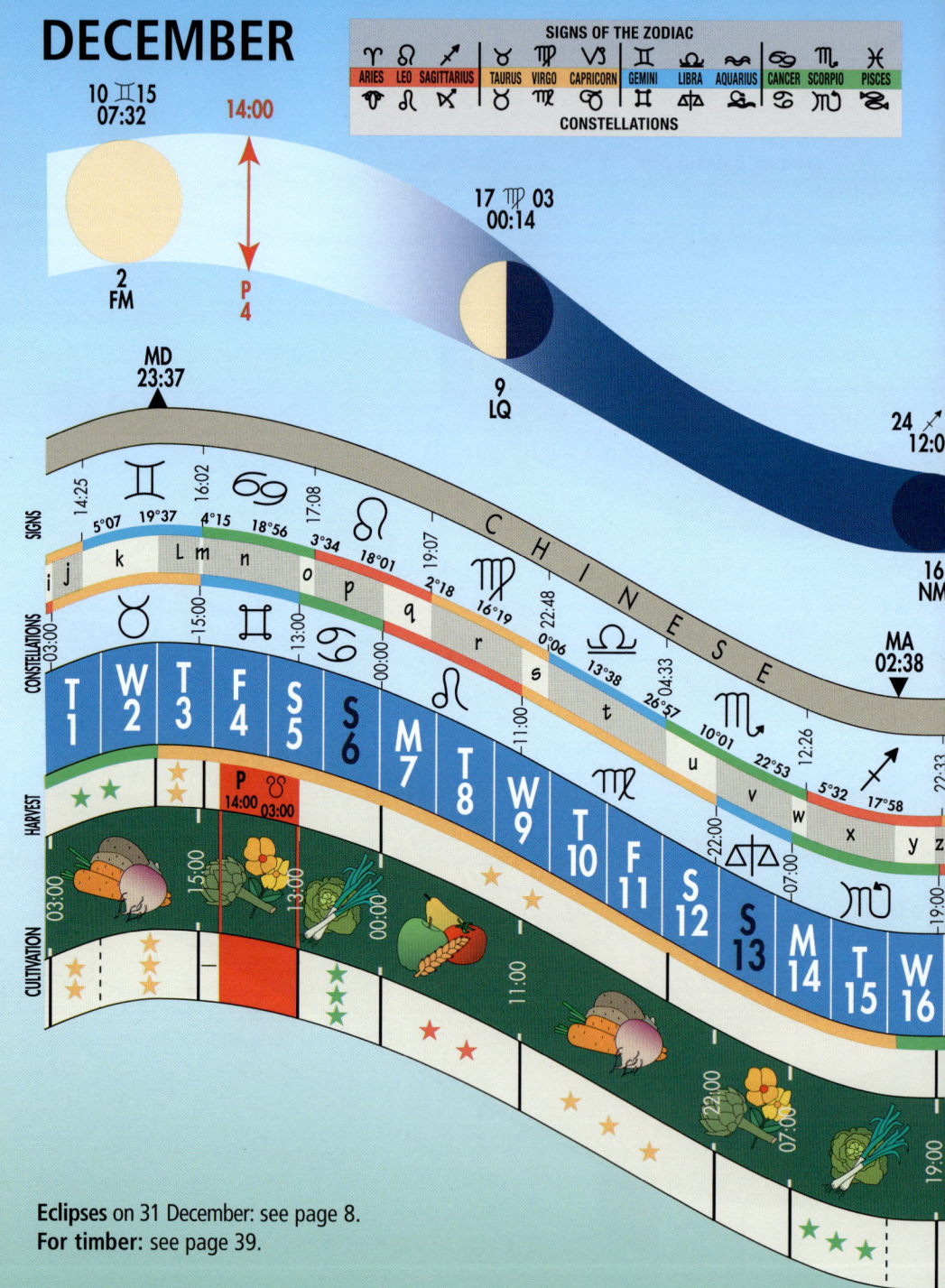

SIGNS OF THE ZODIAC

| ARIES | LEO | SAGITTARIUS | TAURUS | VIRGO | CAPRICORN | GEMINI | LIBRA | AQUARIUS | CANCER | SCORPIO | PISCES |

CONSTELLATIONS

10 ♊ 15
07:32

14:00

2
FM

P
4

17 ♍ 03
00:14

9
LQ

24 ♐
12:0

MD
23:37

16
NM

MA
02:38

SIGNS
CONSTELLATIONS
HARVEST
CULTIVATION

CHINESE

14:25 ♊ 16:02 ♋ 17:08 ♌

5°07 19°37 4°15 18°56 3°34 18°01 19°07

i j k L m n o p q ♍ 16°19 r 2°18 22°48

03:00 ♉ 15:00 ♊ 13:00 ♋ 00:00 ♌ 11:00 ♎ 13°38 s 0°06 ♏ 04:33 t 26°57 u 10°01 v 22°53 w 5°32 x 17°58 y z 22:33

T 1 W 2 T 3 F 4 S 5 S 6 M 7 T 8 W 9 T 10 F 11 S 12 S 13 M 14 T 15 W 16

P 14:00 ♉ 03:00

♍ ♎ 22:00 ♐ 07:00 ♑ 19:00

03:00 15:00 13:00 00:00 11:00 22:00 07:00 19:00

Eclipses on 31 December: see page 8.
For timber: see page 39.

Cut **firewood** when the Moon is descending from 3 to 15 December.

19 December: the Sun enters the constellation of Sagittarius.

21 December: the Sun enters the sign of Capricorn at 18:48.

The period between Christmas and Epiphany is a good time for people to **reflect and take stock**. You can also make use of this time to try and predict what the weather will be like during the next 12 months. Make a very precise note at fixed hours several times a day of what the weather is like between 24 December and 6 January.

In theory, the weather in January will correspond to the weather as it was on 24/25 December, the weather in February to the weather conditions on 25/26 December and so on. Keep 24/25 December as your starting point. Try it and see if it works.

Calculating world times

Times throughout the book are given in **Greenwich Mean Time** (26 October to 29 March) or **British Summer Time** (30 March to 25 October), as appropriate. **For those in the United Kingdom and Ireland, all times given, both summer and winter, are those shown on your watches.** The number of hours to take off or add on for other countries appear in the table below:

COUNTRY	From 1/1 to 29/3 From 26/10 to 31/12	From 30/3 to 25/10
USA (New York), Canada (Ottawa)*	- 5h*	- 5h
Iceland, Morocco	0h	- 1h
Canary Islands, Ireland, Portugal	0h	0h
Australia (Sydney)	+ 9h	+ 9h
Austria, Belgium, Czech Republic, Denmark, France, Germany, Holland, Hungary, Italy, Luxembourg, Norway, Poland, Slovakia, Spain, Sweden, Switzerland, Tunisia	+ 1h	+ 1h
South Africa	+ 2h	+ 1h
Bulgaria, Finland, Greece, Romania, Turkey	+ 2h	+ 2h
New Zealand**	+ 13h	+ 11h
Japan	+ 9h	+ 8h

* **USA (New York) and Canada (Ottawa)** from 9/3 to 29/3 and from 26/10 to 1/11: - 4h
** **New Zealand** from 30/3 to 6/4 and from 29/9 to 25/10: + 12h

Using the calendar made easy

This diagram provides a clearer, simpler version of the information contained in the tear-out section. This information is a summary of our interpretation of the various lunar and planetary influences.

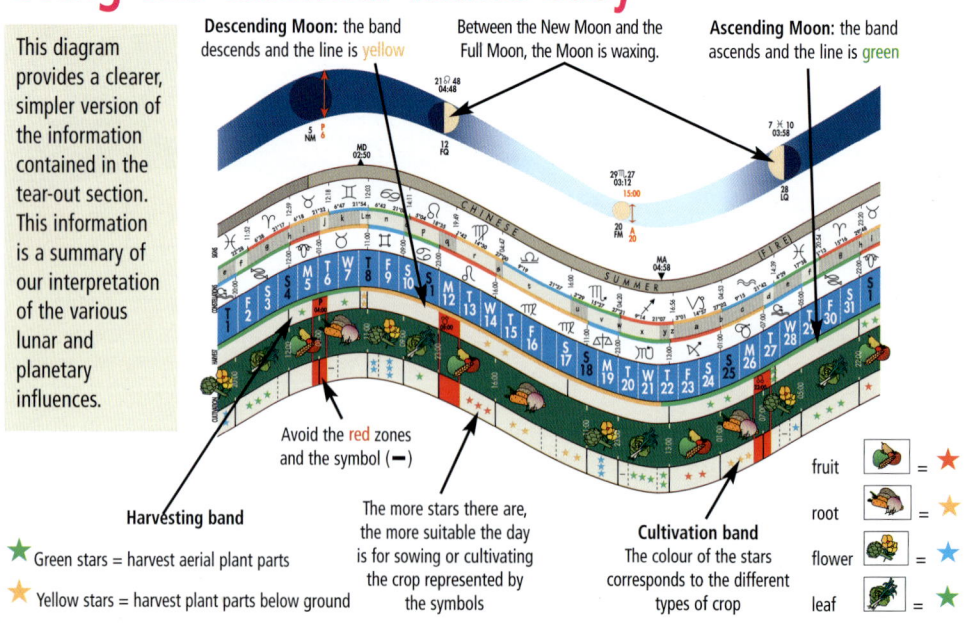

Descending Moon: the band descends and the line is yellow

Between the New Moon and the Full Moon, the Moon is waxing.

Ascending Moon: the band ascends and the line is green

Avoid the red zones and the symbol (—)

Harvesting band

The more stars there are, the more suitable the day is for sowing or cultivating the crop represented by the symbols

Cultivation band
The colour of the stars corresponds to the different types of crop

Green stars = harvest aerial plant parts

Yellow stars = harvest plant parts below ground

fruit =

root =

flower =

leaf =

The note pages

Many thanks for your feedback which helps us improve In Tune with the Moon each year. Your many remarks and suggestions have helped us rethink the 'planner' part, with three main objectives: (i) increase the space reserved for note-taking, (ii) giving a more attractive look to those pages, and (iii) above all, render these pages more 'independent' in order to avoid having to consult the monthly chart each single time. So we have repeated the synthesis (using stars) of the various tasks and have arranged for ascending/descending and waxing/waning moons to be seen simultaneously at a glance. Additionally, it is only in these note pages that the times of moonrise and moon-set are recorded, as well as the effects of the tides and planetary nodes (see p.7).

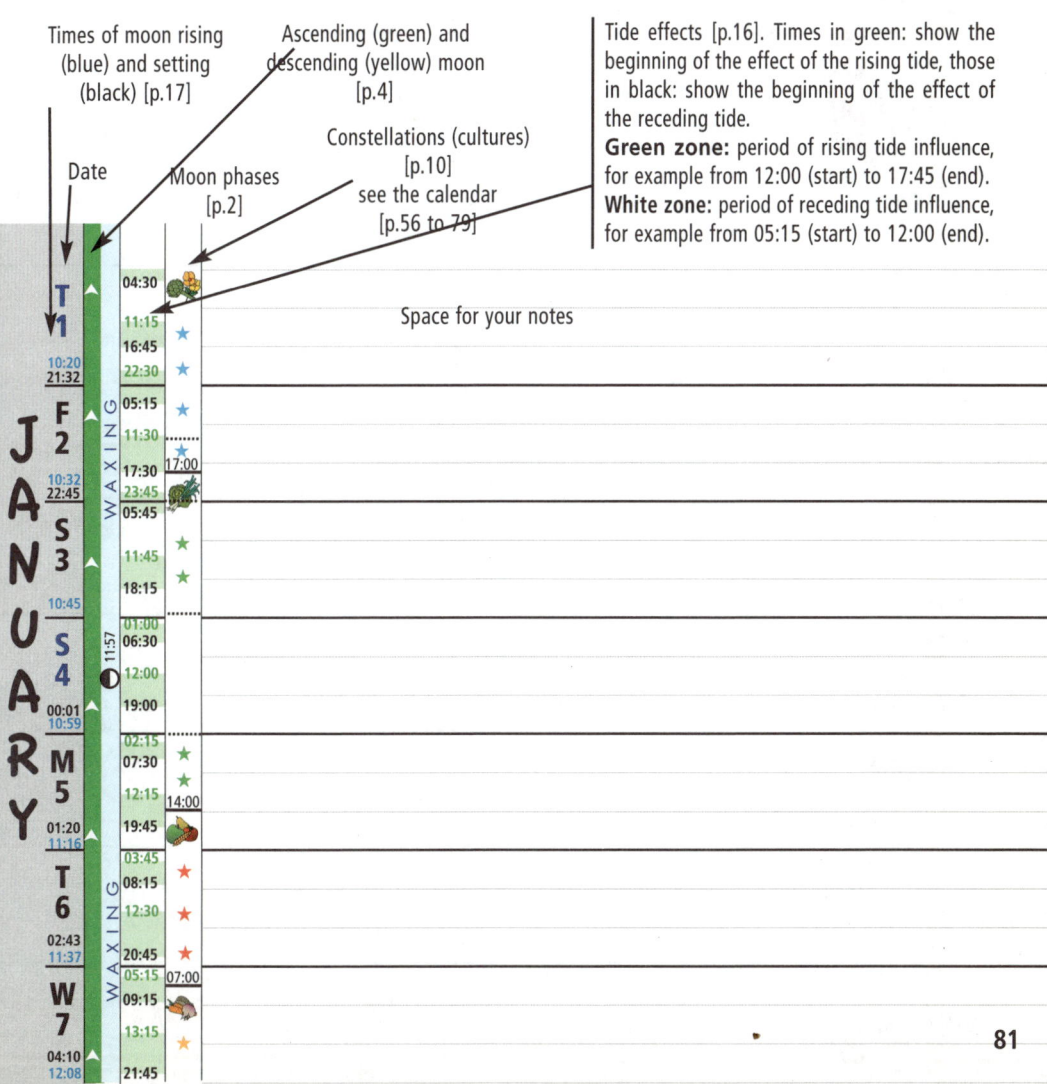

Times of moon rising (blue) and setting (black) [p.17]

Ascending (green) and descending (yellow) moon [p.4]

Date

Moon phases [p.2]

Constellations (cultures) [p.10] see the calendar [p.56 to 79]

Tide effects [p.16]. Times in green: show the beginning of the effect of the rising tide, those in black: show the beginning of the effect of the receding tide.
Green zone: period of rising tide influence, for example from 12:00 (start) to 17:45 (end).
White zone: period of receding tide influence, for example from 05:15 (start) to 12:00 (end).

Space for your notes

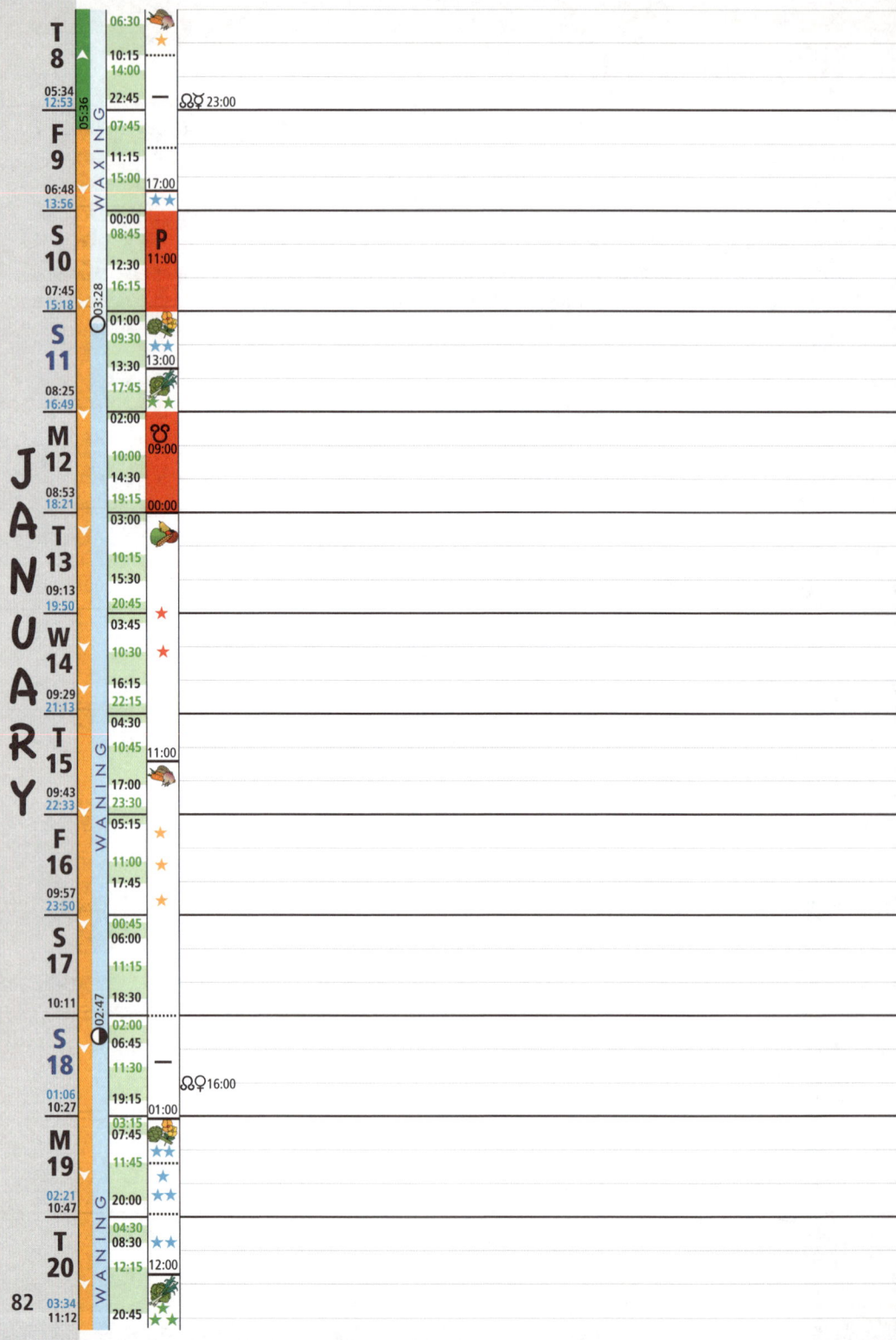

JANUARY

Day	Times	
W 21	05:45 / 09:15 / 12:45 / 21:45	
04:41 / 11:46		
T 22	06:45 / 10:00 / 13:30 / 22:30	— A
05:41 / 12:30	13:59	00:00
F 23	07:30 / 11:00 / 14:30 / 23:15	03:00
06:30 / 13:26	WANING	
S 24	08:15 / 11:45 / 15:30	
07:08 / 14:31		
S 25	00:15 / 08:30 / 12:30 / 16:45	15:00
07:36 / 15:42	07:56	
M 26	01:00 / 09:00 / 13:15 / 18:00	♋ 13:00
07:57 / 16:55		
T 27	01:45 / 09:15 / 14:00 / 19:15	23:00
08:14 / 18:09		
W 28	02:30 / 09:30 / 14:45 / 20:15	
08:28 / 19:22		
T 29	03:15 / 09:45 / 15:30 / 21:30	22:00
08:41 / 20:35	WAXING	
F 30	03:45 / 10:00 / 16:15 / 22:45	
08:53 / 21:50		
S 31	04:30 / 10:00 / 17:00	
09:07 / 23:07		
S 1	00:00 / 05:15 / 10:15 / 17:45	21:00
09:22		
M 2	01:30 / 06:15 / 10:45 / 18:30	
00:27 / 09:41		

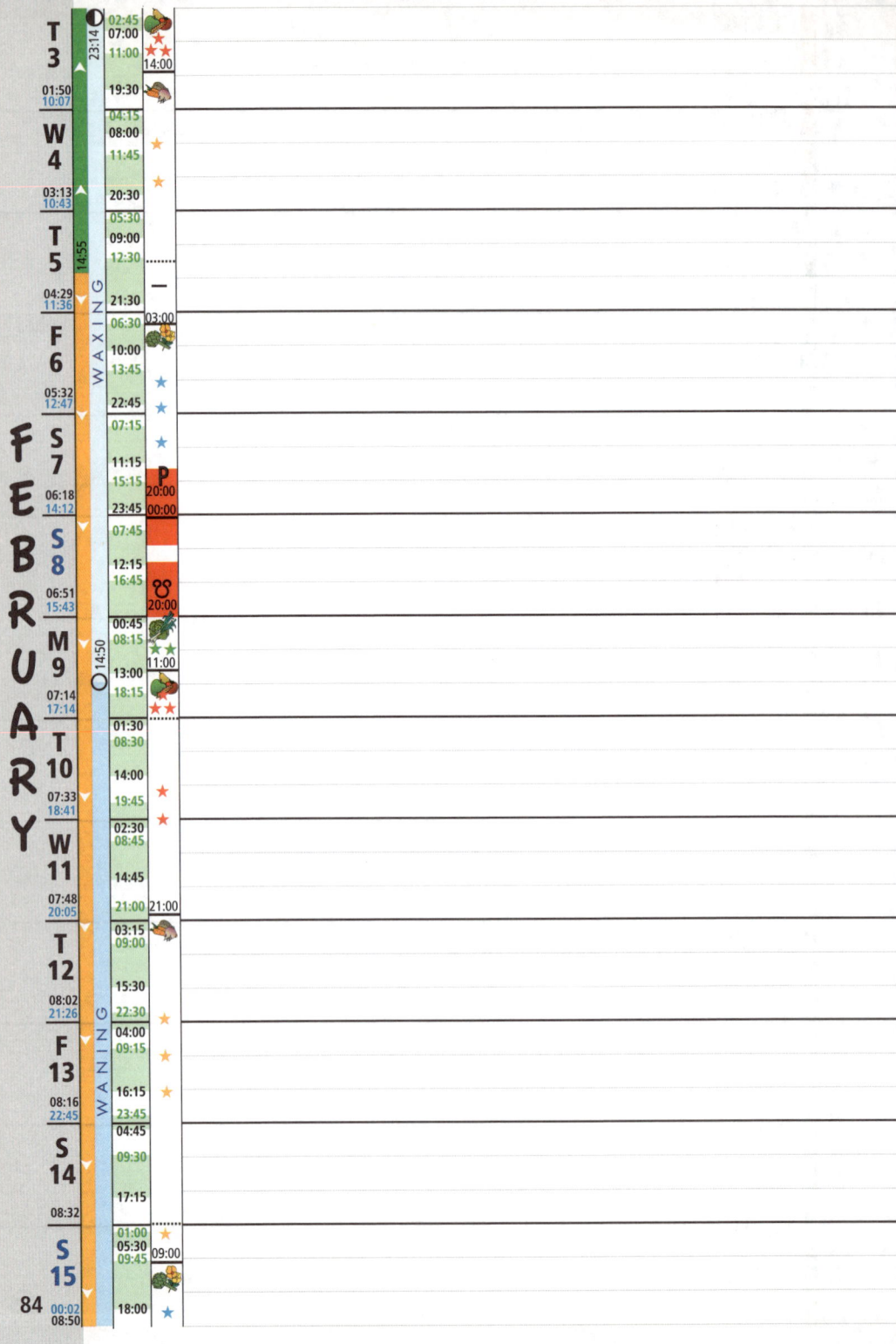

FEBRUARY

T 3	23:14	02:45 / 07:00 / 11:00 — 14:00
01:50 / 10:07		19:30
W 4		04:15 / 08:00 / 11:45
03:13 / 10:43	14:55	20:30
T 5	WAXING	05:30 / 09:00 / 12:30
04:29 / 11:36		21:30
F 6		06:30 — 03:00 / 10:00 / 13:45
05:32 / 12:47		22:45
S 7		07:15 / 11:15 / 15:15 — 20:00 / 23:45 — 00:00
06:18 / 14:12		
S 8		07:45 / 12:15 / 16:45 — 20:00
06:51 / 15:43		
M 9	14:50	00:45 / 08:15 — 11:00 / 13:00 / 18:15
07:14 / 17:14		
T 10		01:30 / 08:30 / 14:00 / 19:45
07:33 / 18:41		
W 11		02:30 / 08:45 / 14:45 / 21:00 — 21:00
07:48 / 20:05		
T 12		03:15 — 09:00 / 15:30 / 22:30
08:02 / 21:26	WANING	
F 13		04:00 / 09:15 / 16:15 / 23:45
08:16 / 22:45		
S 14		04:45 / 09:30 / 17:15
08:32		
S 15		01:00 / 05:30 / 09:45 — 09:00 / 18:00
84	00:02 / 08:50	

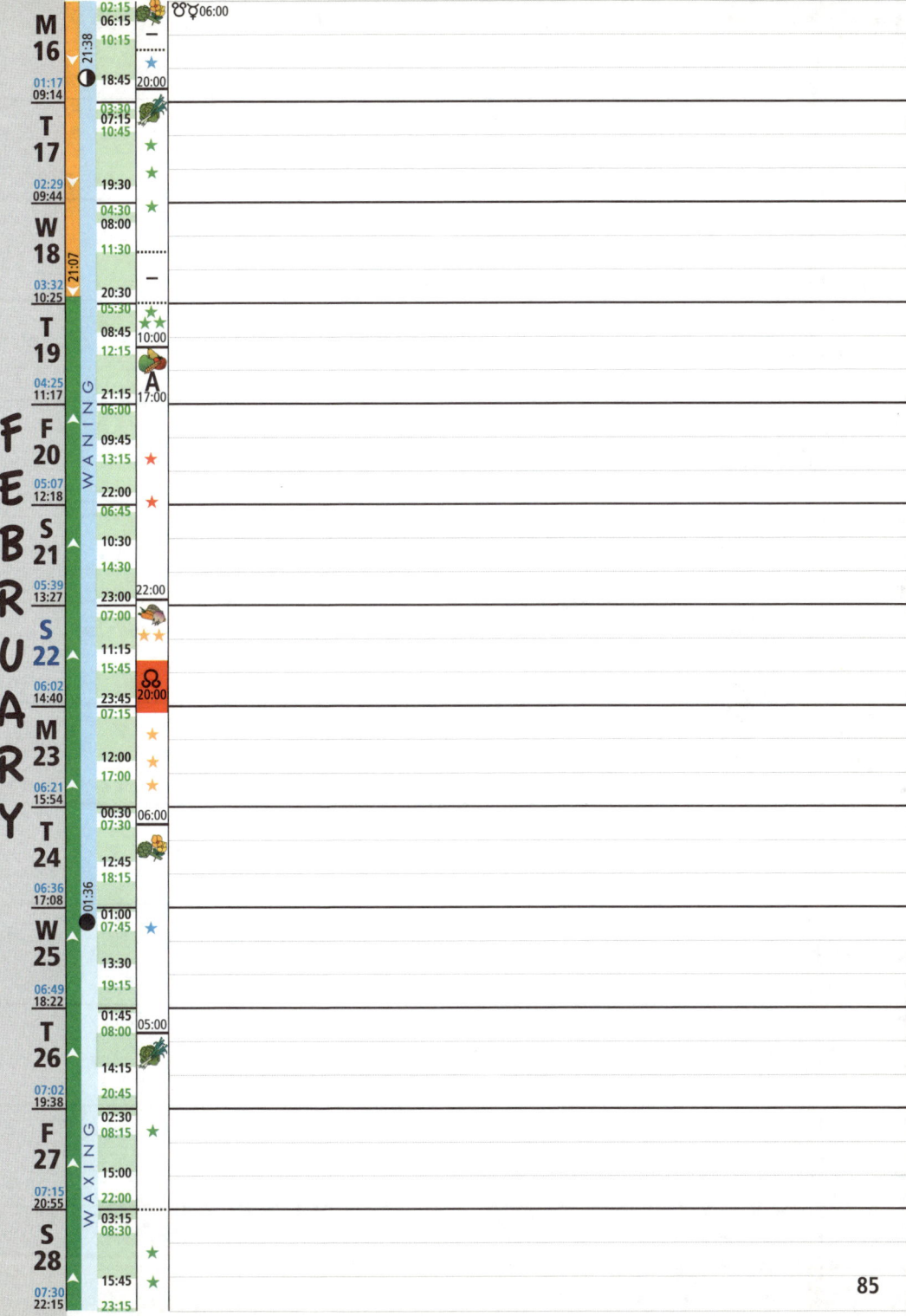

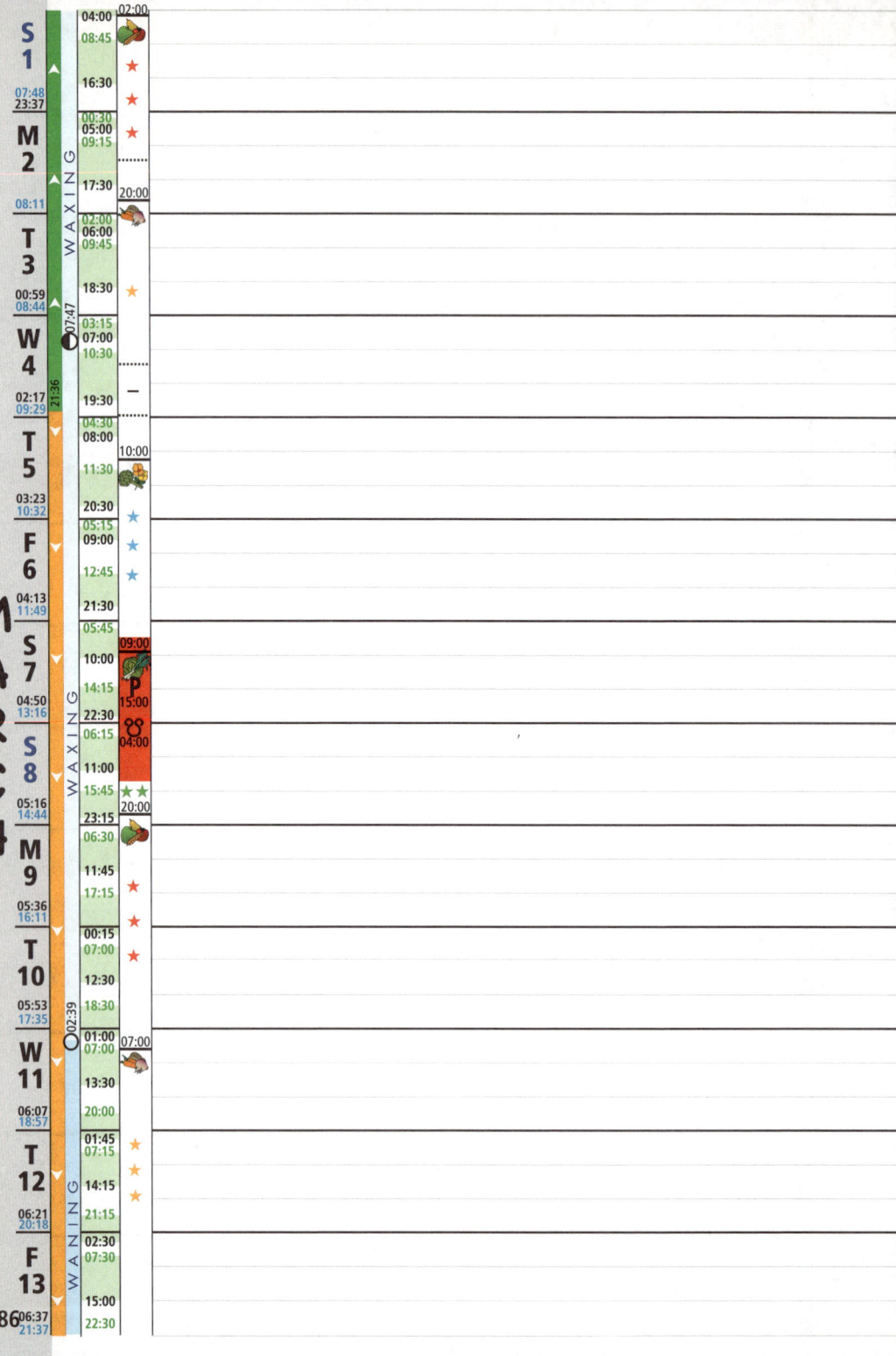

MARCH

S 1	WAXING	04:00 08:45 16:30	02:00 ★ ★
07:48 23:37			
M 2		00:30 05:00 09:15 17:30	★ 20:00
08:11			
T 3	07:47	02:00 06:00 09:45 18:30	★
00:59 08:44			
W 4	21:36	03:15 07:00 10:30 19:30	—
02:17 09:29			
T 5	WAXING	04:30 08:00 11:30 20:30	10:00 ★
03:23 10:32			
F 6		05:15 09:00 12:45 21:30	★ ★
04:13 11:49			
S 7		05:45 10:00 14:15 22:30	09:00 P 15:00
04:50 13:16			
S 8	WAXING	06:15 11:00 15:45 23:15	04:00 ★ ★ 20:00
05:16 14:44			
M 9		06:30 11:45 17:15	★
05:36 16:11			
T 10	02:39	00:15 07:00 12:30 18:30	★
05:53 17:35			
W 11		01:00 07:00 13:30 20:00	07:00
06:07 18:57			
T 12	WANING	01:45 07:15 14:15 21:15	★ ★ ★
06:21 20:18			
F 13		02:30 07:30 15:00 22:30	
86 06:37 21:37			

MARCH

Day	Times	Other
S 14	03:15 / 08:00 / 15:45	18:00 ★★★ 🥬
06:54 / 22:55		
S 15	00:00 / 04:15 / 08:15 / 16:30	★ ★
07:16	WANING	
M 16	01:15 / 05:00 / 08:45 / 17:30	04:00 🥦 ★
00:10 / 07:44		
T 17	02:15 / 05:45 / 09:15 / 18:15	★ ★★ —
01:18 / 08:20	05:05	
W 18	03:15 / 06:45 / 10:15 / 19:00	★ ★★ 18:00 🥬
02:16 / 09:08	17:48	
T 19	04:00 / 07:30 / 11:00 / 20:00	★ A 13:00
03:03 / 10:06		
F 20	04:45 / 08:15 / 12:15 / 20:45	★ ★
03:38 / 11:12		
S 21	05:00 / 09:15 / 13:30 / 21:30	06:00 🐟 ★ ★★
04:05 / 12:23		
S 22	05:30 / 10:00 / 14:30 / 22:15	☿ 02:00 ★ ★
04:25 / 13:36	WANING	
M 23	05:45 / 10:45 / 15:45 / 23:00	★ 14:00 🥦
04:42 / 14:50		
T 24	06:00 / 11:30 / 17:00 / 23:45	★
04:56 / 16:04		
W 25	06:15 / 12:00 / 18:15 / 00:30	12:00 🥬 ★
05:09 / 17:20		
T 26	06:15 / 12:45 / 19:30	★ ★
05:22 / 18:37	16:07	●

87

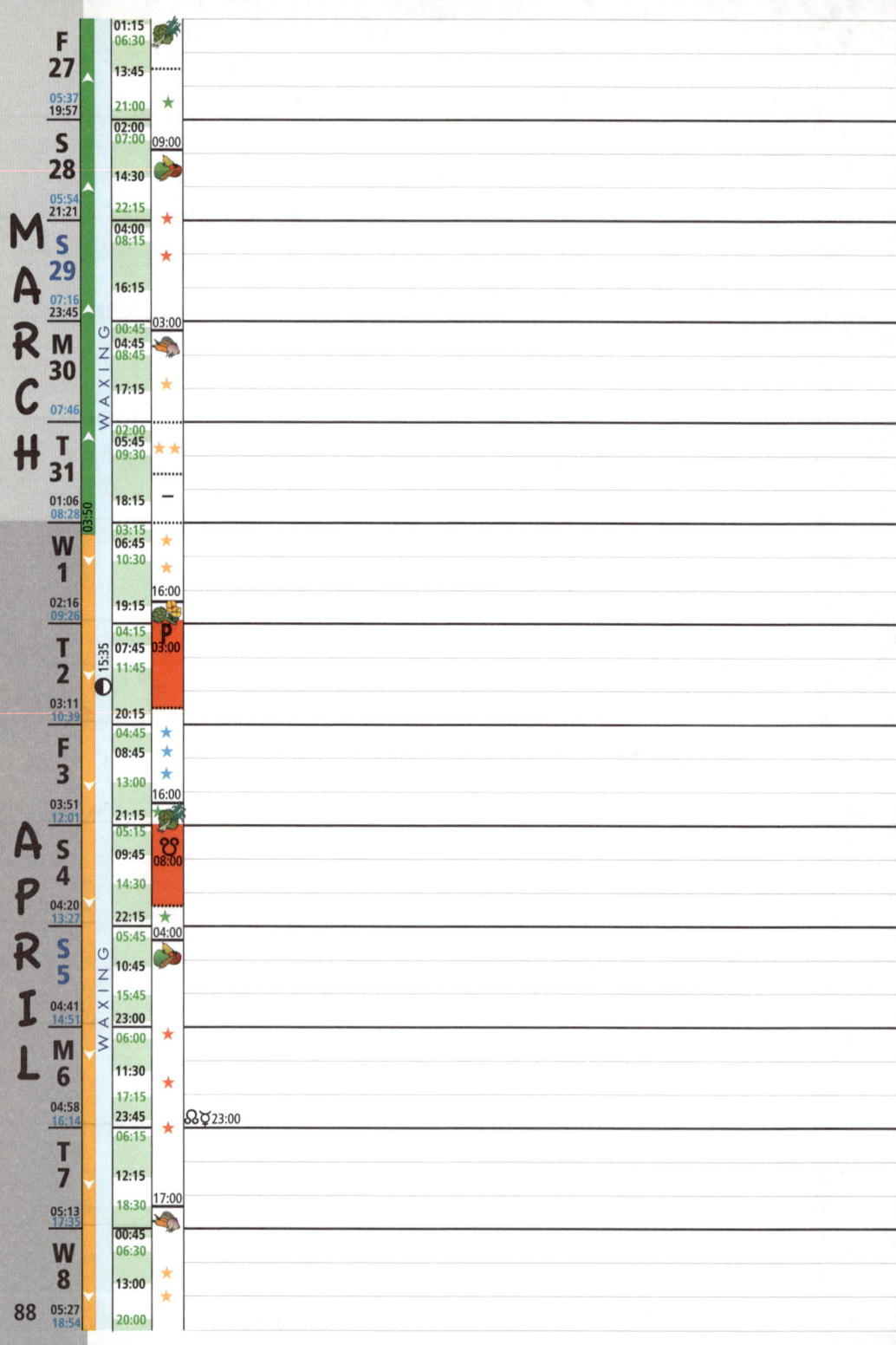

MARCH

F 27	05:37 19:57	01:15 06:30 13:45 21:00	
S 28	05:54 21:21	02:00 07:00 14:30 22:15	09:00
S 29	07:16 23:45	04:00 08:15 16:15	
M 30	07:46	00:45 04:45 08:45 17:15	03:00
T 31	01:06 08:28	02:00 05:45 09:30 18:15	

WAXING

03:50

APRIL

W 1	02:16 09:26	03:15 06:45 10:30 19:15	16:00
T 2	03:11 10:39	04:15 07:45 11:45 20:15	03:00
F 3	03:51 12:01	04:45 08:45 13:00 21:15	16:00
S 4	04:20 13:27	05:15 09:45 14:30 22:15	08:00
S 5	04:41 14:51	05:45 10:45 15:45 23:00	04:00
M 6	04:58 16:14	06:00 11:30 17:15 23:45	℞℞ 23:00
T 7	05:13 17:35	06:15 12:15 18:30	17:00
W 8	05:27 18:54	00:45 06:30 13:00 20:00	

15:35

WAXING

88

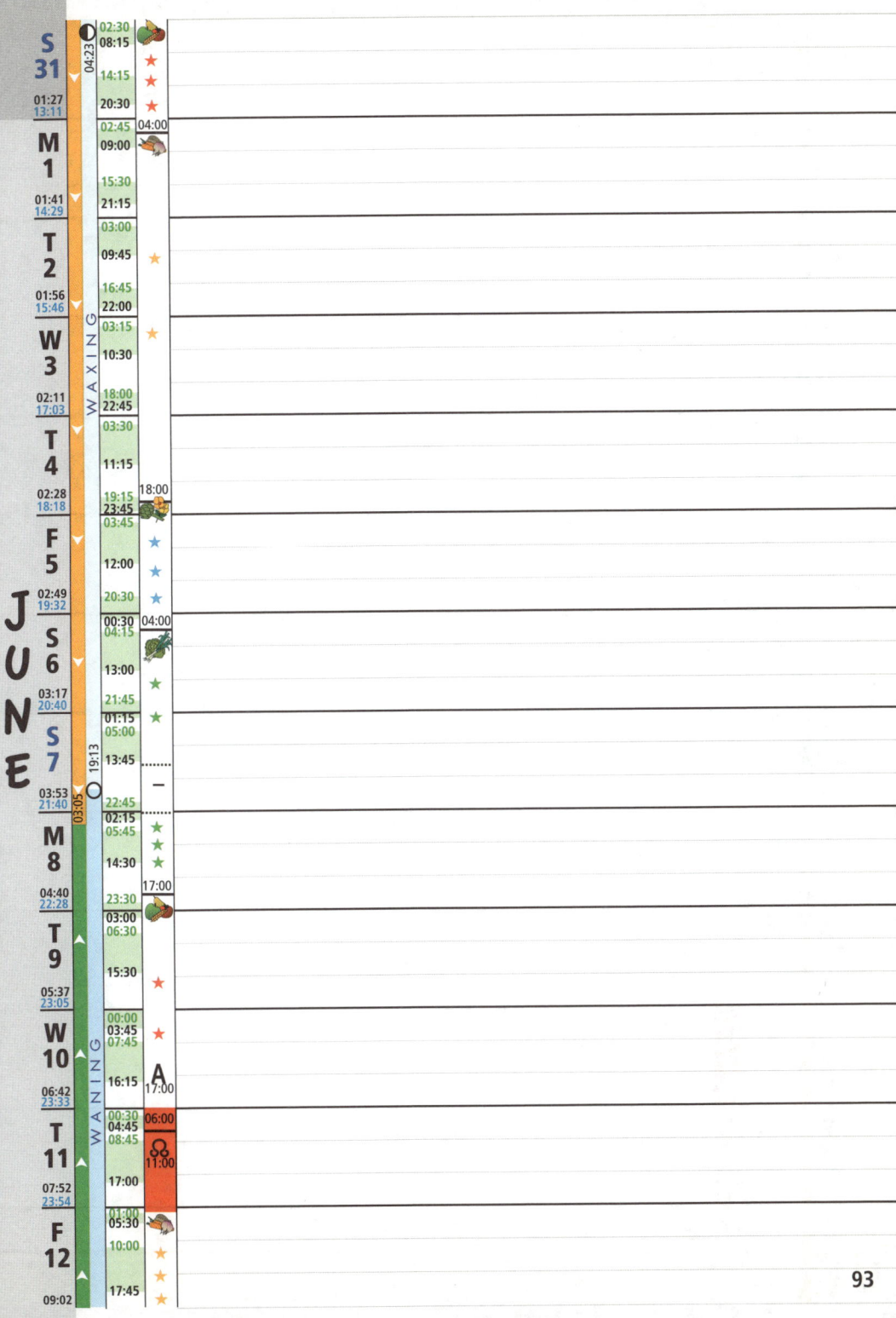

JUNE

S **31**	02:30 08:15 14:15 20:30	
04:23 01:27 13:11		
M **1**	02:45 09:00 15:30 21:15	04:00
01:41 14:29		
T **2**	03:00 09:45 16:45 22:00	
01:56 15:46		
W **3**	03:15 10:30 18:00 22:45	
02:11 17:03		
T **4**	03:30 11:15 19:15 23:45	18:00
02:28 18:18		
F **5**	03:45 12:00 20:30	
02:49 19:32		
S **6**	00:30 04:15 13:00 21:45	04:00
03:17 20:40		
S **7**	01:15 05:00 13:45 22:45	
03:53 21:40		
M **8**	02:15 05:45 14:30 23:30	
04:40 22:28		
T **9**	03:00 06:30 15:30	17:00
05:37 23:05		
W **10**	00:00 03:45 07:45 16:15	17:00
06:42 23:33		
T **11**	00:30 04:45 08:45 17:00	06:00 11:00
07:52 23:54		
F **12**	01:00 05:30 10:00 17:45	
09:02		

WAXING

WANING

04:23

19:13

03:05

93

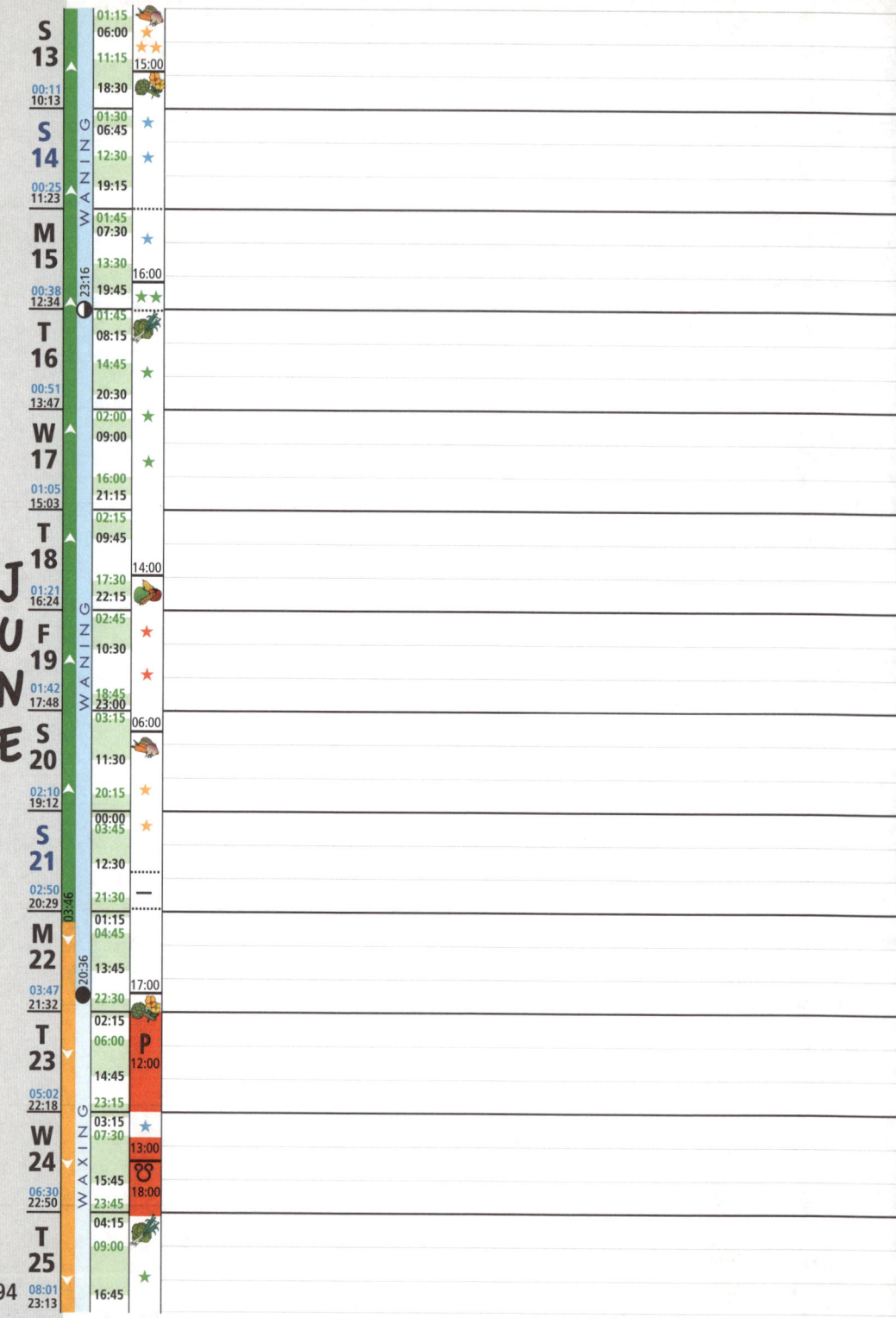

JUNE

S **13**	01:15 06:00 11:15 18:30	15:00	★ ★★
00:11 10:13			
S **14**	01:30 06:45 12:30 19:15		★ ★
00:25 11:23			
M **15**	01:45 07:30 13:30 19:45	16:00	★ ★★
00:38 12:34	23:16		
T **16**	01:45 08:15 14:45 20:30		★
00:51 13:47			
W **17**	02:00 09:00 16:00 21:15		★ ★
01:05 15:03			
T **18**	02:15 09:45 17:30 22:15	14:00	
01:21 16:24			
F **19**	02:45 10:30 18:45 23:00		★ ★
01:42 17:48			
S **20**	03:15 11:30 20:15	06:00	★
02:10 19:12			
S **21**	00:00 03:45 12:30 21:30		★ —
02:50 20:29	03:46		
M **22**	01:15 04:45 13:45 22:30	17:00	
03:47 21:32	20:36		
T **23**	02:15 06:00 14:45 23:15	**P** 12:00	
05:02 22:18			
W **24**	03:15 07:30 15:45 23:45	13:00 18:00	★
06:30 22:50			
T **25**	04:15 09:00 16:45		★
08:01 23:13			

WANING

WANING

WAXING

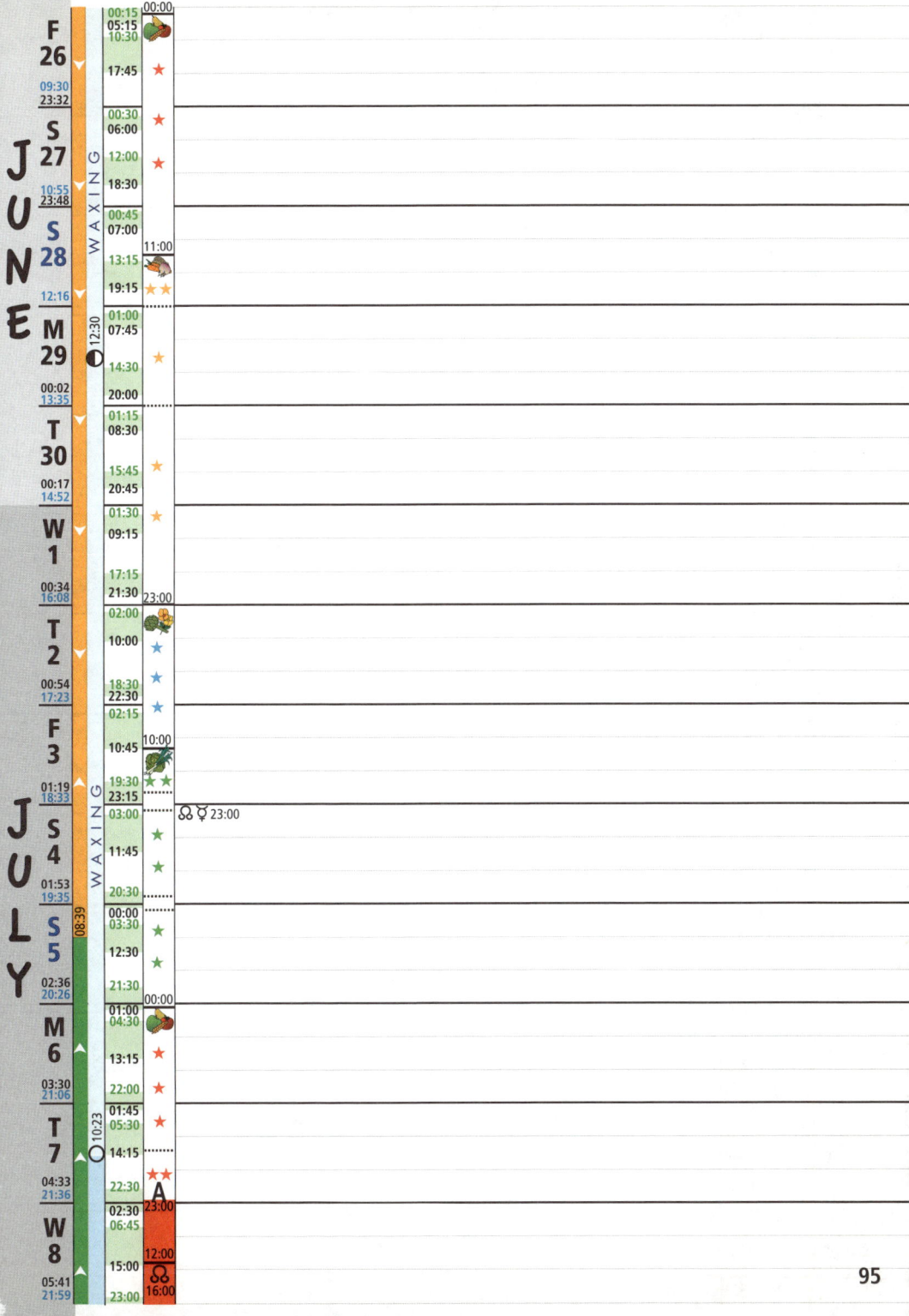

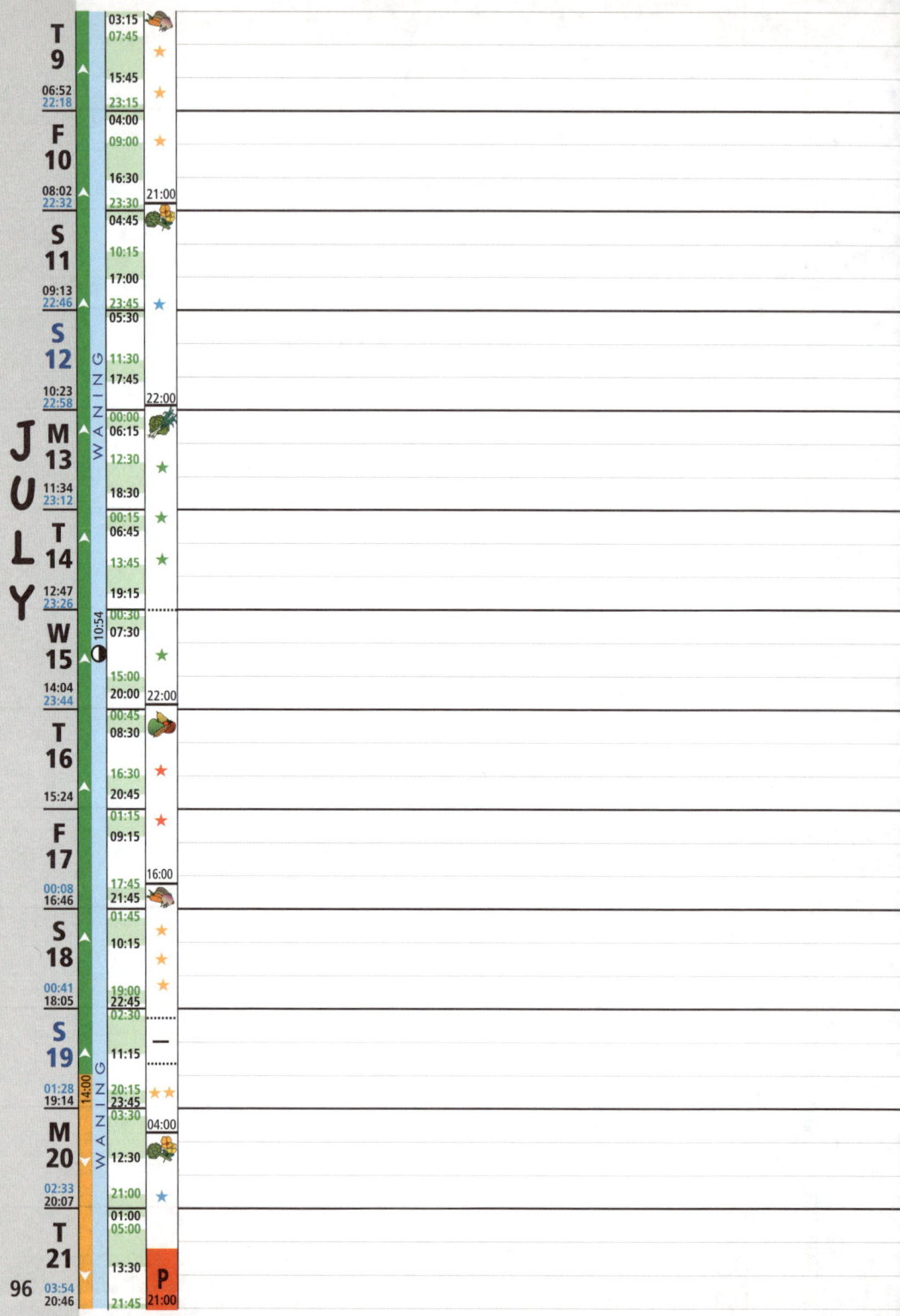

JULY

T 9 06:52 22:18	03:15 07:45 15:45 23:15	★ ★
F 10 08:02 22:32	04:00 09:00 16:30 23:30	★ 21:00
S 11 09:13 22:46	04:45 10:15 17:00 23:45	★
S 12 10:23 22:58	05:30 11:30 17:45	22:00
M 13 11:34 23:12	00:00 06:15 12:30 18:30	★
T 14 12:47 23:26	00:15 06:45 13:45 19:15	★ ★
W 15 14:04 23:44	00:30 07:30 15:00 20:00	★ 22:00
T 16 15:24	00:45 08:30 16:30 20:45	★
F 17 00:08 16:46	01:15 09:15 17:45 21:45	★ 16:00
S 18 00:41 18:05	01:45 10:15 19:00 22:45	★ ★ ★
S 19 01:28 19:14	02:30 11:15 20:15 23:45	— ★★
M 20 02:33 20:07	03:30 12:30 21:00	04:00 ★
T 21 03:54 20:46	01:00 05:00 13:30 21:45	**P** 21:00

WANING

10:54

WANING

14:00

96

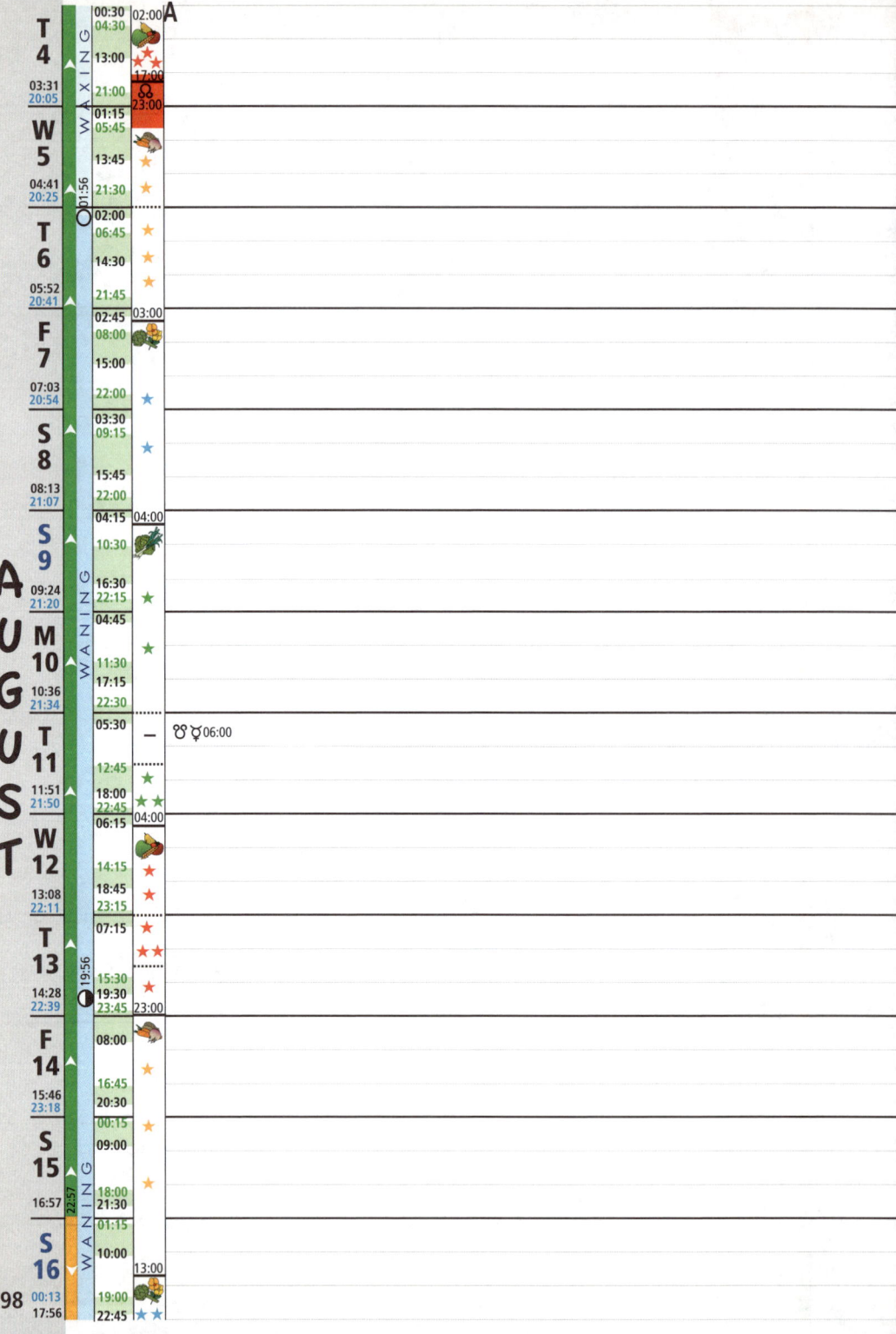

A

Day		Times		
T 4		00:30 / 04:30	02:00	
	WAXING	13:00		
03:31 / 20:05		21:00	17:00	
			23:00	
W 5		01:15 / 05:45		
		13:45		
04:41 / 20:25	01:56	21:30		
T 6	○	02:00 / 06:45		
		14:30		
05:52 / 20:41		21:45		
F 7		02:45 / 08:00	03:00	
		15:00		
07:03 / 20:54		22:00		
S 8		03:30 / 09:15		
		15:45		
08:13 / 21:07		22:00		
S 9		04:15 / 10:30	04:00	
	WANING	16:30 / 22:15		
09:24 / 21:20				
M 10		04:45		
		11:30 / 17:15		
10:36 / 21:34		22:30		
T 11		05:30	♊ ☿ 06:00	
		12:45		
11:51 / 21:50		18:00 / 22:45		
W 12		06:15	04:00	
		14:15		
13:08 / 22:11		18:45 / 23:15		
T 13		07:15		
	19:56	15:30 / 19:30 / 23:45	23:00	
14:28 / 22:39	◐			
F 14		08:00		
		16:45		
15:46 / 23:18		20:30		
S 15		00:15 / 09:00		
	WANING	18:00 / 21:30		
16:57	22:57			
S 16		01:15 / 10:00	13:00	
00:13 / 17:56		19:00 / 22:45		

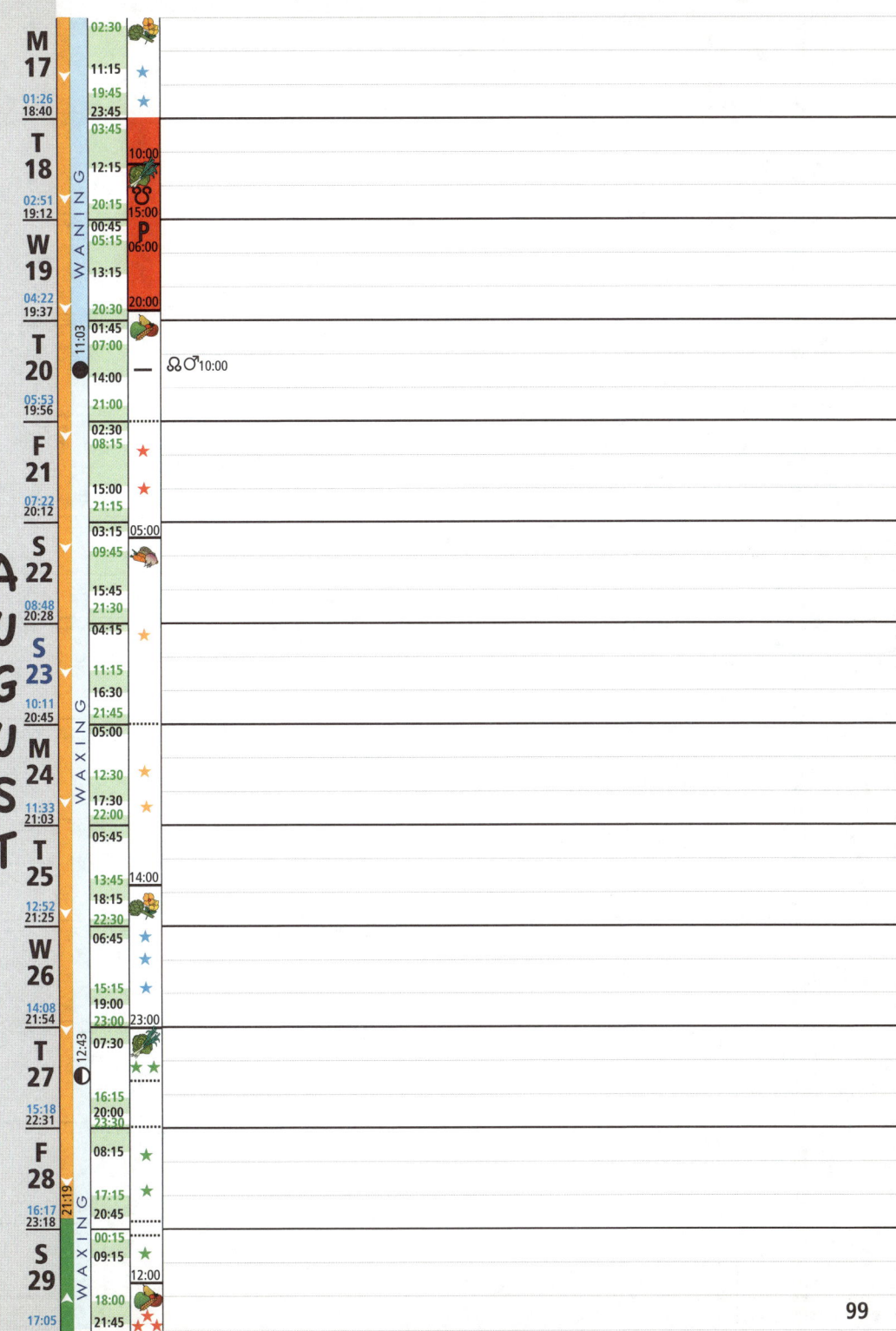

AUGUST

M 17		02:30	🐢
		11:15	⭐
01:26		19:45	⭐
18:40		23:45	
T 18		03:45	
	W	12:15	🐢 10:00
02:51	A	20:15	♉ 15:00
19:12	N	00:45	P
W 19	I	05:15	06:00
	N	13:15	
04:22	G	20:30	20:00
19:37		01:45	🌰
T 20	11:03	07:00	
	●	14:00	— ♋♂ 10:00
05:53		21:00	
19:56			
F 21		02:30	
		08:15	⭐
07:22		15:00	⭐
20:12		21:15	
S 22		03:15	05:00
		09:45	🐟
08:48		15:45	
20:28		21:30	
S 23		04:15	⭐
	W	11:15	
10:11	A	16:30	
20:45	X	21:45	
M 24	I	05:00	
	N	12:30	⭐
11:33	G	17:30	⭐
21:03		22:00	
T 25		05:45	
		13:45	14:00
12:52		18:15	🐢
21:25		22:30	
W 26		06:45	⭐
			⭐
14:08		15:15	⭐
21:54		19:00	
		23:00	23:00
T 27	12:43	07:30	🐢
	◐		⭐ ⭐
15:18		16:15	
22:31		20:00	
		23:30	
F 28		08:15	⭐
	W	17:15	⭐
16:17	A	20:45	
23:18	X	00:15	
S 29	I	09:15	⭐
	N		12:00
	G	18:00	🌰
17:05		21:45	⭐⭐

99

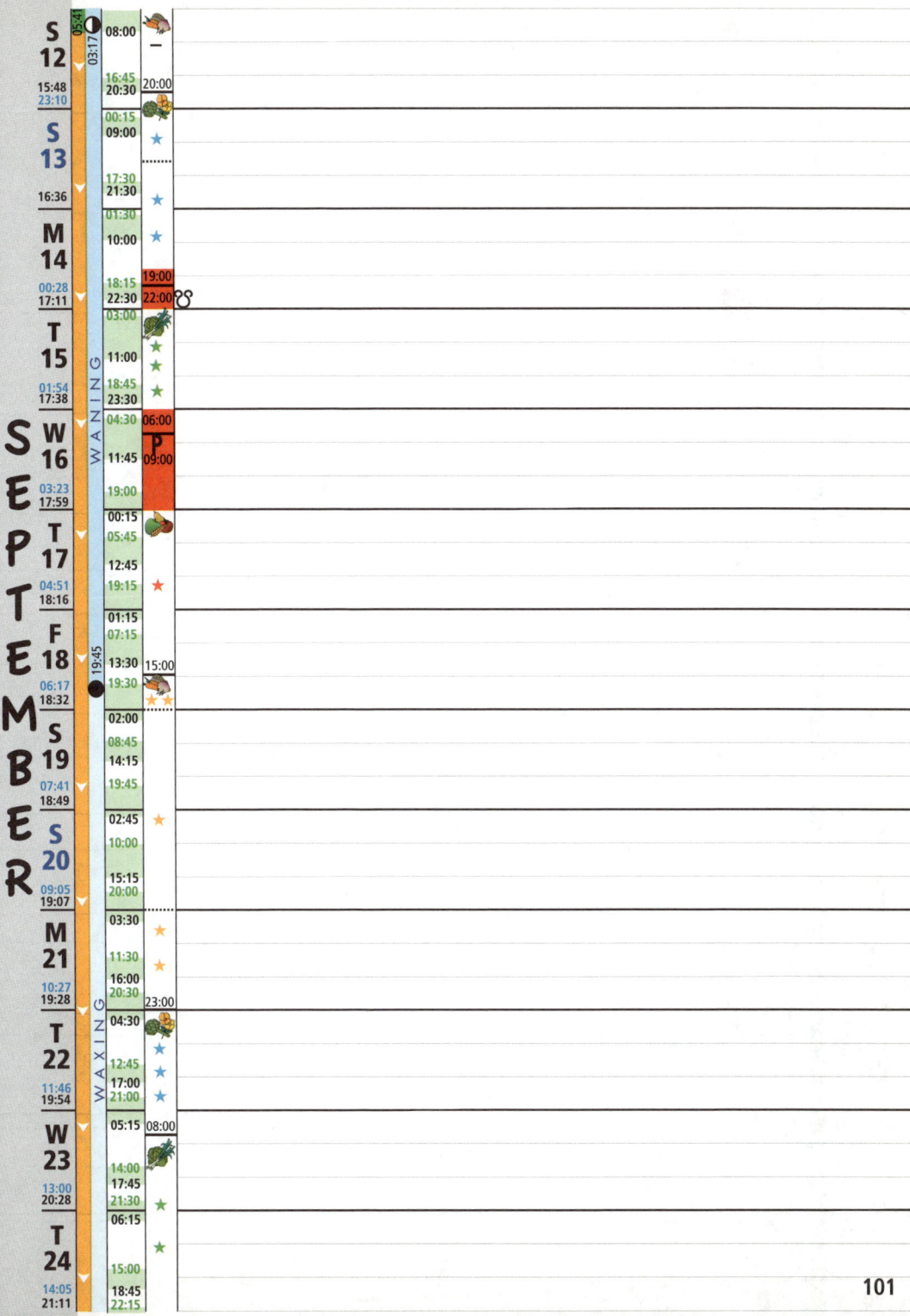

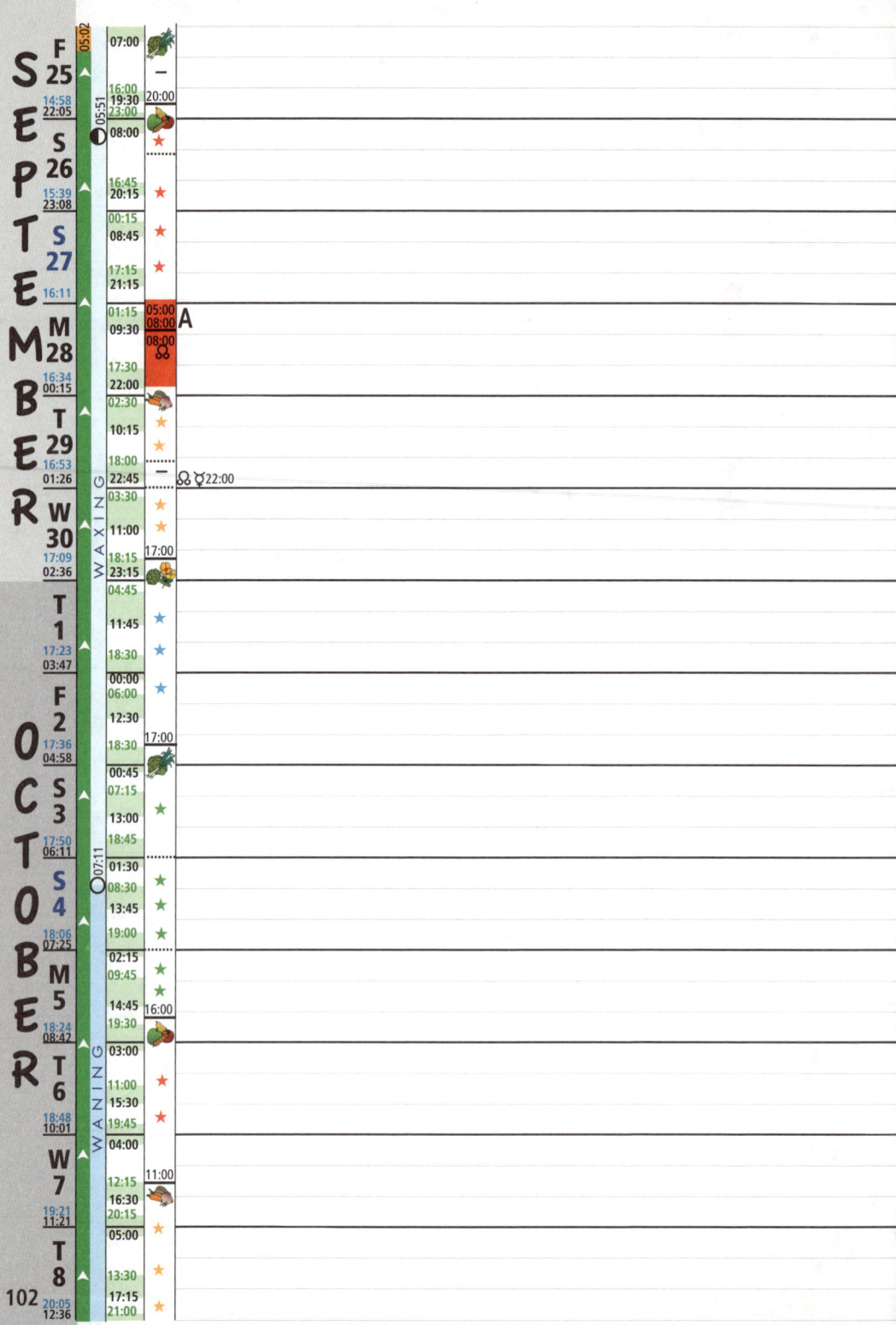

SEPTEMBER

F 25
05:02
07:00
—
14:58
22:05
16:00
19:30
20:00
23:00

S 26
05:51
08:00
★
16:45
20:15
★
00:15
08:45
★

S 27
15:39
23:08
17:15
21:15
★
16:11

M 28
01:15 05:00
09:30 08:00
08:00 A
17:30
22:00
16:34
00:15

SEPTEMBER

T 29
02:30
10:15 ★
★
18:00
22:45 — ☊ ☿22:00
16:53
01:26

W 30
03:30 ★
11:00 ★
18:15
23:15 17:00
17:09
02:36

OCTOBER

T 1
04:45
11:45 ★
18:30 ★
17:23
03:47

F 2
00:00
06:00 ★
12:30
18:30 17:00
17:36
04:58

S 3
00:45
07:15
13:00 ★
18:45
17:50
06:11

S 4
07:11
01:30
08:30 ★
13:45 ★
19:00 ★
18:06
07:25

M 5
02:15 ★
09:45 ★
14:45 16:00
19:30
18:24
08:42

T 6
03:00
11:00 ★
15:30
19:45 ★
18:48
10:01

W 7
04:00
12:15 11:00
16:30
20:15
19:21 ★
11:21

T 8
05:00
13:30 ★
17:15
21:00 ★
20:05
12:36

WANING WAXING

102

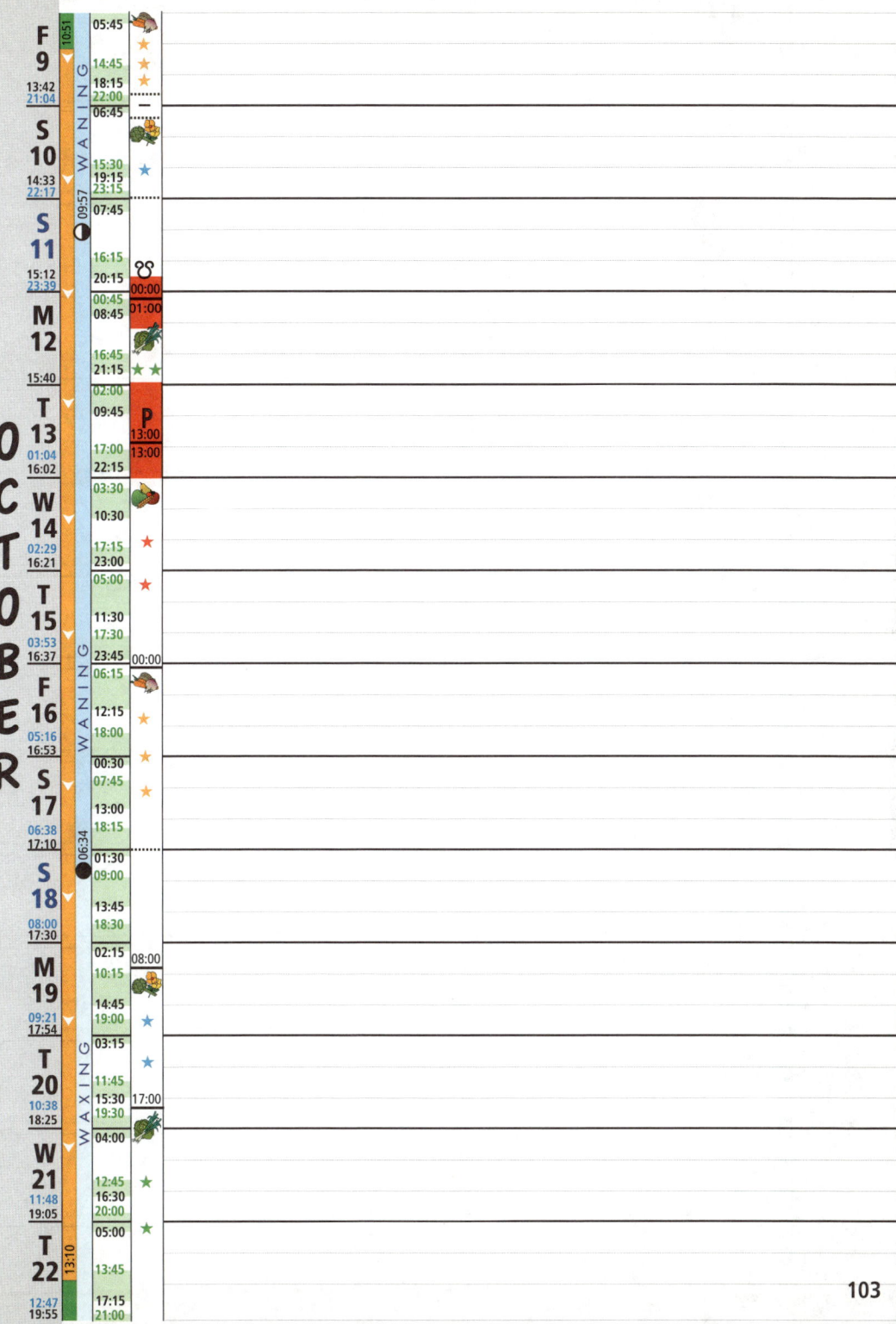

OCTOBER

F 9 13:42 21:04	1051 WANING 09:57	05:45 14:45 18:15 22:00	⭐ ⭐ ⭐
S 10 14:33 22:17		06:45 15:30 19:15 23:15	⭐
S 11 15:12 23:39		07:45 16:15 20:15	♊
M 12 15:40		00:00 01:00 16:45 21:15	⭐ ⭐
T 13 01:04 16:02		02:00 09:45 17:00 22:15	**P** 13:00 13:00
W 14 02:29 16:21		03:30 10:30 17:15 23:00	⭐
T 15 03:53 16:37	WANING	05:00 11:30 17:30 23:45	⭐ 00:00
F 16 05:16 16:53		06:15 12:15 18:00	⭐
S 17 06:38 17:10	06:34	00:30 07:45 13:00 18:15	⭐
S 18 08:00 17:30		01:30 09:00 13:45 18:30	
M 19 09:21 17:54	WAXING	02:15 10:15 14:45 19:00	08:00 ⭐
T 20 10:38 18:25		03:15 11:45 15:30 19:30	⭐ 17:00
W 21 11:48 19:05		04:00 12:45 16:30 20:00	⭐
T 22 12:47 19:55	13:10	05:00 13:45 17:15 21:00	⭐

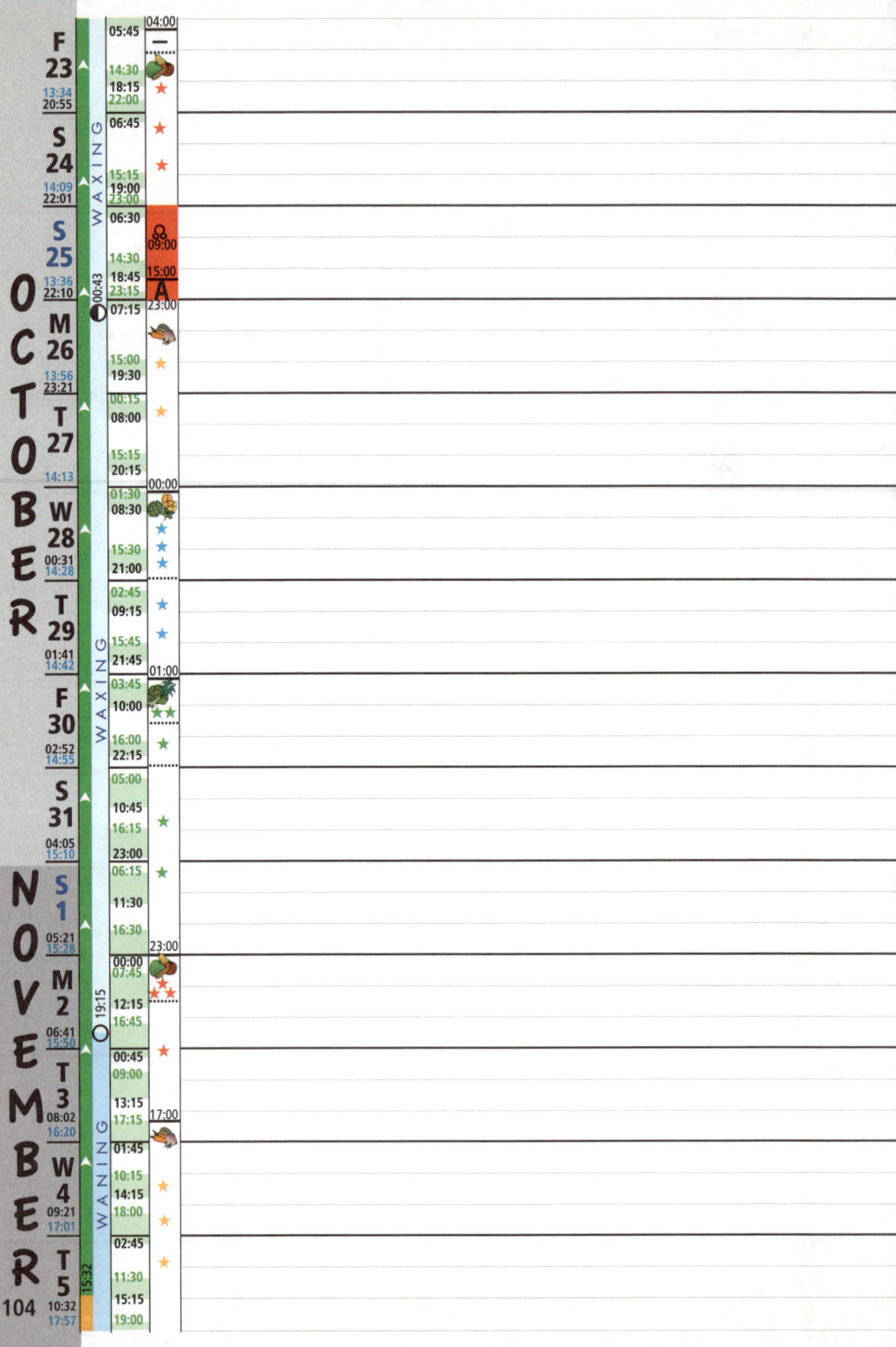

OCTOBER

F 23	05:45	04:00 —
13:34 20:55	14:30 18:15 22:00	★
S 24	06:45	★
14:09 22:01	15:15 19:00 23:00	★
S 25	06:30	09:00
13:36 22:10	14:30 18:45 23:15	15:00 A 23:00
M 26	07:15	
13:56 23:21	15:00 19:30	★
T 27	00:15 08:00	★
14:13	15:15 20:15	00:00
W 28	01:30 08:30	★ ★
00:31 14:28	15:30 21:00	★
T 29	02:45 09:15	★ ★
01:41 14:42	15:45 21:45	01:00
F 30	03:45 10:00	★ ★
02:52 14:55	16:00 22:15	★
S 31	05:00 10:45	
04:05 15:10	16:15 23:00	★

NOVEMBER

S 1	06:15 11:30	★
05:21 15:28	16:30	23:00
M 2	00:00 07:45	★ ★
06:41 15:50	12:15 16:45	
T 3	00:45 09:00	★
08:02 16:20	13:15 17:15	17:00
W 4	01:45 10:15	★
09:21 17:01	14:15 18:00	★
T 5	02:45 11:30	★
104 10:32 17:57	15:15 19:00	

WAXING

WAXING

WANING

104

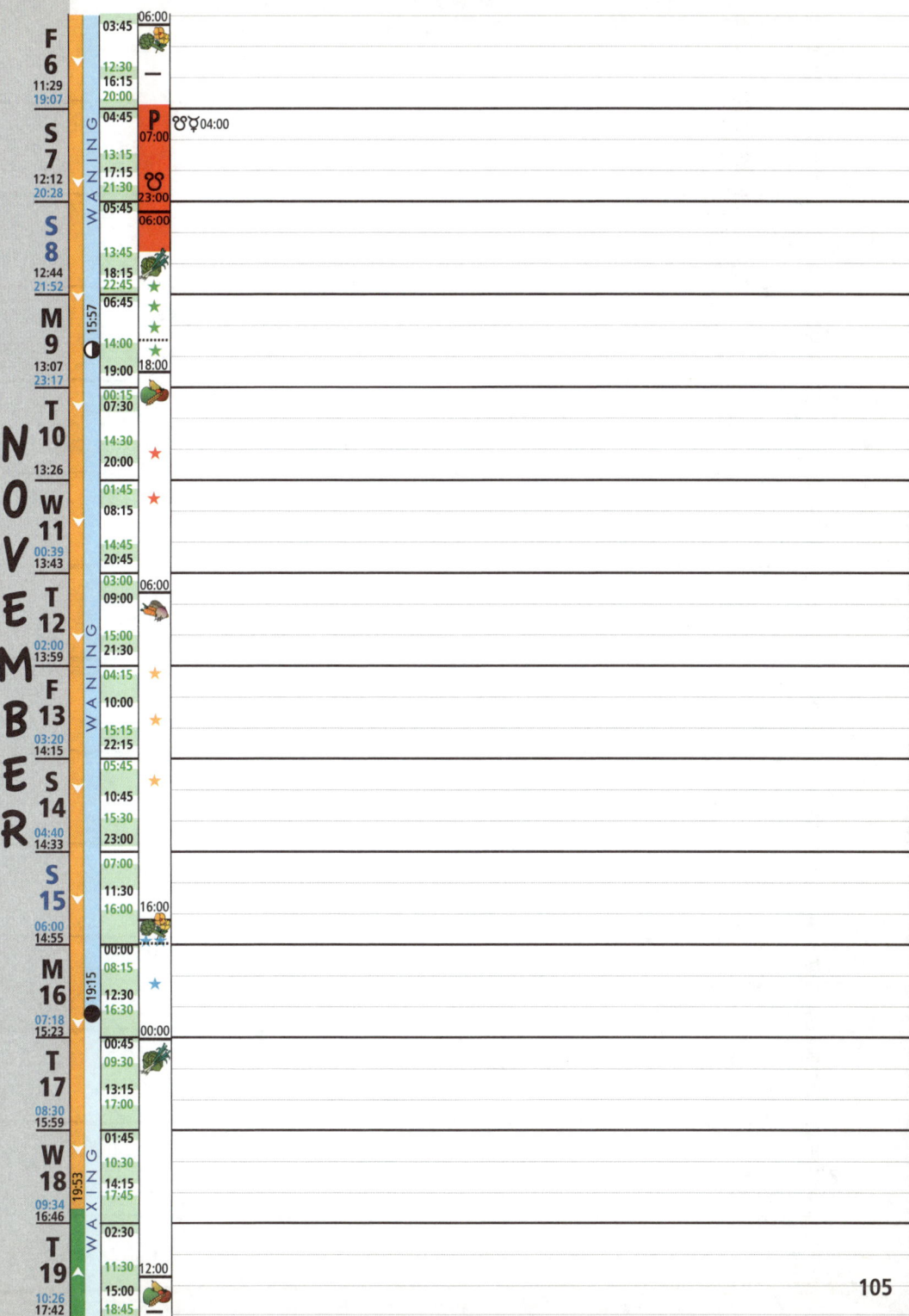

N
O
V
E
M
B
E
R

F 6
11:29
19:07

03:45
06:00

12:30
16:15
20:00

S 7
12:12
20:28

04:45
P 07:00 ☿♀04:00

13:15
17:15
21:30

♋ 23:00

S 8
12:44
21:52

05:45
06:00

13:45
18:15
22:45

M 9
13:07
23:17

06:45

14:00

19:00 18:00

T 10
13:26

00:15
07:30

14:30
20:00

W 11
00:39
13:43

01:45
08:15

14:45
20:45

T 12
02:00
13:59

03:00
06:00
09:00

15:00
21:30

F 13
03:20
14:15

04:15
10:00

15:15
22:15

S 14
04:40
14:33

05:45
10:45

15:30
23:00

S 15
06:00
14:55

07:00

11:30

16:00 16:00

M 16
07:18
15:23

00:00
08:15

12:30
16:30

00:00

T 17
08:30
15:59

00:45
09:30

13:15
17:00

W 18
09:34
16:46

01:45
10:30

14:15
17:45

T 19
10:26
17:42

02:30

11:30 12:00

15:00
18:45

WANING 15:57

WANING 19:15

WAXING 19:53

105

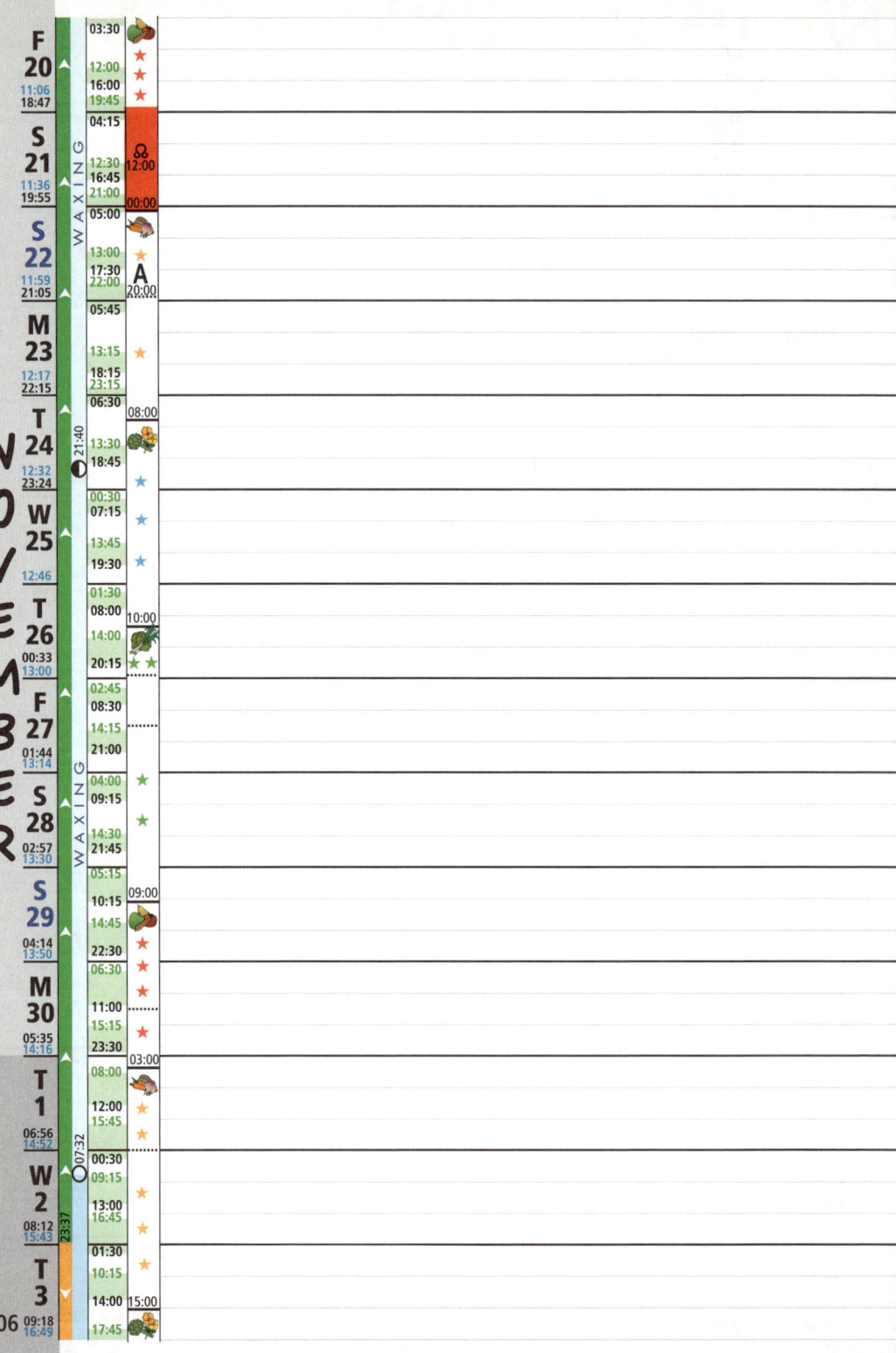

NOVEMBER

Day		Times
F 20	11:06 / 18:47	03:30 / 12:00 / 16:00 / 19:45
S 21	11:36 / 19:55	04:15 / 12:30 / 16:45 / 21:00
S 22	11:59 / 21:05	05:00 / 13:00 / 17:30 / 22:00
M 23	12:17 / 22:15	05:45 / 13:15 / 18:15 / 23:15
T 24	12:32 / 23:24	06:30 / 13:30 / 18:45
W 25	12:46	00:30 / 07:15 / 13:45 / 19:30
T 26	00:33 / 13:00	01:30 / 08:00 / 14:00 / 20:15
F 27	01:44 / 13:14	02:45 / 08:30 / 14:15 / 21:00
S 28	02:57 / 13:30	04:00 / 09:15 / 14:30 / 21:45
S 29	04:14 / 13:50	05:15 / 10:15 / 14:45 / 22:30
M 30	05:35 / 14:16	06:30 / 11:00 / 15:15 / 23:30
T 1	06:56 / 14:52	08:00 / 12:00 / 15:45
W 2	08:12 / 15:43	00:30 / 09:15 / 13:00 / 16:45
T 3	09:18 / 16:49	01:30 / 10:15 / 14:00 / 17:45

WAXING

21:40

23:37

07:32

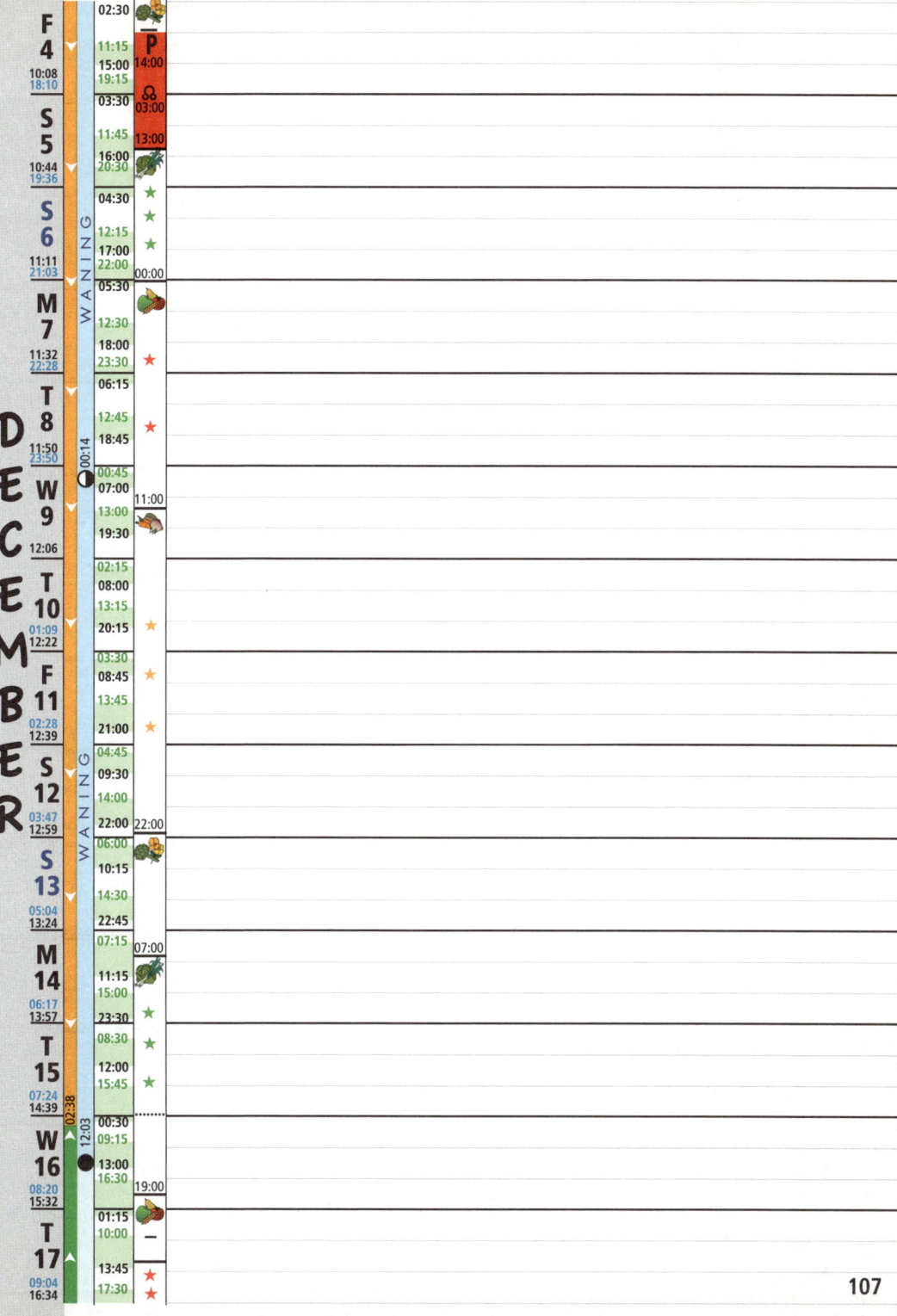

F 4 10:08 18:10		02:30	
		11:15	**P**
		15:00	14:00
		19:15	
S 5 10:44 19:36		03:30	03:00
		11:45	13:00
		16:00	
		20:30	
S 6 11:11 21:03	W A N I N G	04:30	★
			★
		12:15	★
		17:00	
		22:00	00:00
M 7 11:32 22:28		05:30	
		12:30	
		18:00	
		23:30	★
T 8 11:50 23:50	00:14	06:15	
		12:45	★
		18:45	
W 9 12:06		00:45	
		07:00	11:00
		13:00	
		19:30	
T 10 01:09 12:22		02:15	
		08:00	
		13:15	
		20:15	★
F 11 02:28 12:39		03:30	
		08:45	★
		13:45	
		21:00	★
S 12 03:47 12:59	W A N I N G	04:45	
		09:30	
		14:00	
		22:00	22:00
S 13 05:04 13:24		06:00	
		10:15	
		14:30	
		22:45	
M 14 06:17 13:57		07:15	07:00
		11:15	
		15:00	
		23:30	★
T 15 07:24 14:39	02:38	08:30	★
		12:00	
		15:45	★
W 16 08:20 15:32	12:03	00:30	
		09:15	
		13:00	
		16:30	19:00
T 17 09:04 16:34		01:15	
		10:00	—
		13:45	★
		17:30	★

D E C E M B E R

F
18
09:37
17:42

2:15
10:30
14:30
18:45
♌
17:00

S
19
10:02
18:51

3:00
07:00
11:00
15:15
19:45
★

S
20
10:22
20:01

3:45
11:15
A
15:00
16:00 ─
21:00
♋♀ 22:00

M
21
10:38
21:10

WAXING

4:30
★
11:45 ★
16:45 16:00
22:15

T
22
10:52
22:18

5:15
11:45 ★
17:30 ★
23:15

W
23
11:05
23:27

5:45 ★
12:00
18:15 18:00

T
24
11:19

17:37

0:30
6:30
12:15
☽ 18:45

F
25
00:37
11:34

1:30
7:15
12:30 ★
19:30

S
26
01:50
11:51

2:45
8:00
12:45
20:15 19:00 ♋ ☿ 20:00

S
27
03:07
12:13

4:00
8:45
13:15 ★
21:15 ★
★

M
28
04:27
12:43

WAXING

5:30
9:45 ★
13:45 13:00
22:00 ★

T
29
05:45
13:25

6:45
10:30
14:30 ★
23:15

W
30
06:57
14:24

10:07

8:00 ★
11:45
15:30
01:00

T
31
07:55
15:39

19:14

○

0:15
9:00
12:45 ─
16:45

108

D
E
C
E
M
B
E
R

Plan of your garden

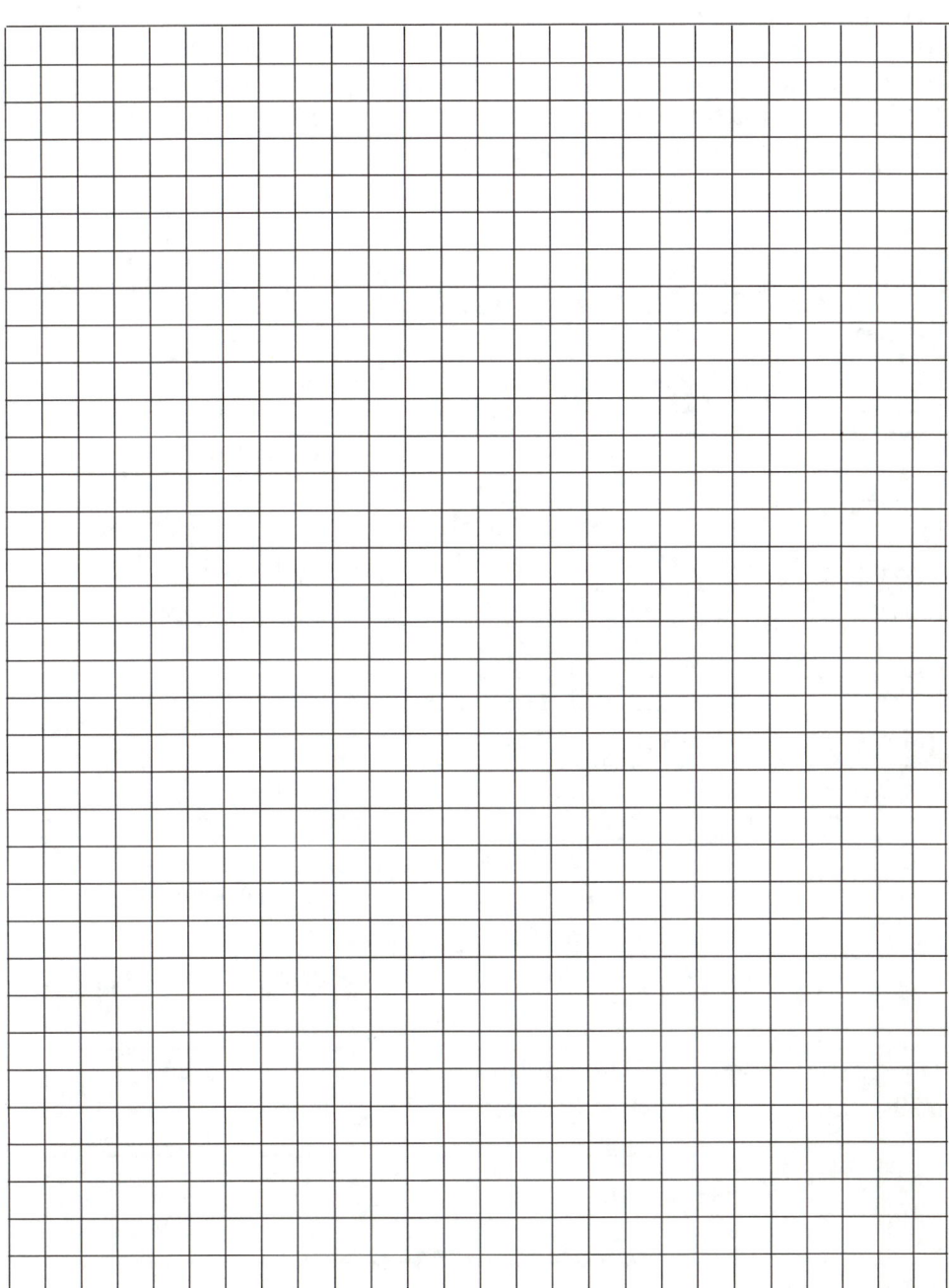

Companion planting

Plants release secretions into the soil via their roots so one plant can affect the growth of another nearby. The Chinese and the South American Indians have known about this and made good use of the knowledge for centuries. Organizing your garden so that you position those plants that have a beneficial effect on each other side by side is another way to help improve your gardening success. Try your own companion planting experiments; results will vary according to the type of soil.

Plant	Grows well with	Does not grow well with
Asparagus	Cucumber, leek, parsley, pea, tomato	Beetroot, garlic, onion
Aubergine	French bean	Potato
Beetroot	Cabbage, celery, lettuce, onion	Asparagus, carrot, leek, runner bean, tomato
Cabbage (except kohlrabi)	Beetroot, celery, corn salad, French bean, lettuce, onion, pea, potato, tomato	Chicory, fennel, garlic, leek, parsnip, radish
Carrot	Chervil, chive, dwarf French bean, lettuce, onion, leek, parsley, parsnip, pea, radish, tomato	Beetroot, Swiss chard
Celery	Beetroot, cabbage, cucurbitaceous plants, French bean, leek, pea, Swiss chard, tomato	Lettuce, maize, parsley
Chicory		Cabbage
Corn salad	Cabbage, leek, onion, strawberry	
Cucumber	Asparagus, basil, cabbage, celery, chive, French bean, lettuce, maize, pea	Potato, radish, tomato
Fennel	Celery, leek	Cabbage, French bean, parsnip, tomato
French bean	Aubergine, carrot, celery, cabbage, lettuce, maize, marigold, potato, spinach, radish, strawberry, turnip	Beetroot, garlic, fennel, onion, shallot, Swiss chard
Garlic	Potato, strawberry	Cabbage, French bean, marigold, pea

Plant	Grows well with	Does not grow well with
Kohlrabi	Beetroot, celery, leek, lettuce	Chicory, fennel, radish, strawberry
Leek	Asparagus, carrot, celery, fennel, lettuce, onion, strawberry, tomato	Beetroot, cabbage, parsley, pea, Swiss chard
Lettuce	Beetroot, cabbage, carrot, chervil, cucumber, broad bean, leek, onion, pea, strawberry, radish, turnip	Parsley
Maize	Cucurbitaceous plants, French beans, pea, potato, tomato	Beetroot, celery
Marrow and courgette	Basil, maize, nasturtium, potato	Potato, radish
Onion	Beetroot, carrot, cucumber, leek, lettuce, parsley, parsnip, strawberry, tomato	Cabbage, French bean, pea, potato
Parsnip	Carrot, onion	Fennel
Pea	Asparagus, cabbage, carrot, celery, cucumber, lettuce, maize, potato, radish, turnip	Garlic, leek, onion, parsley, shallot
Potato	Broad bean, cabbage, celery, French bean, garlic, marigold, nasturtium, pea, tomato	Aubergine, cucumber, maize, onion
Radish	Carrot, chervil, French bean, garlic, lettuce, pea, spinach, tomato	Cabbage, marrow
Spinach	Cabbage, French bean, radish, strawberry, turnip	Beetroot, Swiss chard
Strawberry	Chive, corn salad, French bean, garlic, leek, lettuce, marigold, onion, spinach, thyme, turnip	Cabbage
Swiss chard	Celery, lettuce, onion	Asparagus, basil, leek, tomato
Tomato	Asparagus, basil, carrot, garlic, cabbage, celery, leek, French marigold, nasturtium, marigold, onion, parsley, parsnip, potato, radish	Beetroot, fennel, kohlrabi, pea, Swiss chard
Turnip	French bean, lettuce, pea, spinach	

Index

Animals: 19, 34, 35
Asparagus: 40, 60

Beer: 38
Bees: 36
Blackcurrant bushes: 24
Boats (painting): 40
Bottling: 3, 38
Brambles: 32
Bread, sourdough: 41
Bulbs: 22
Bushes: 23, 24

Callouses: 47
Cattle: 34–35
Cereals: 33
Chicks: 35
Chimneys: 40
Christmas tree: 40
Chrysanthemums: 70
Cider: 38
Cladding: 39
Cleaning: 41
Clearing land: 32
Clothes: 41
Comfrey: 27, 28
Compost: 6, 16, 26, 28, 29, 71
Conifers: 23, 24
Corns: 47
Cows: 35
Cowshed: 34, 35
Cuttings: 24, 71
Convolvulus: 31
Covering (animals): 34
Cryptogramic diseases: 26, 28

Decanting: 38
Decoctions: 27
Depilation: 45
Dew: 25, 38, 46, 49
Digestion: 48, 49, 50
Disinfecting, cowshed: 34
Disbudding: 37, 70
Drainage, soil: 40

Earthing up: 21
Endives: 20
Ewes: 34

Fasting: 47
Fertilizers: 22, 27, 28, 32
Flowers: 10, 20, 22, 23, 24
Food: 48, 49, 50
Framework, wood for: 39
Fruit: 5, 10, 20, 23, 24, 25
Fungi: 28
Fungicides: 28

Gourds: 25
Grafting: 5, 16, 22, 24, 62
Grapes, cultivating: 37
Green manure: 30, 63

Hair: 44, 45
Harvesting: 7, 16, 17, 25, 37, 43, 72
Hay: 32
Hedges: 24
Hemisphere: 3, 4, 5, 58
Hoeing: 20
Honey: 36
Horsetail: 27, 67

Infusions: 43
Insecticides: 28

Jams: 3, 41

Lawn: 5, 41
Leaves: 15, 19, 24
Liquid fertilizer: 27, 28, 29

Manure: 29, 31
Mares: 34
Massage: 51
Medicinal plants: 43
Moon ascending-descending: 4, 5, 7, 23, 27, 54, 55
Moon waxing-waning: 2, 3, 4, 5, 23, 27
Moss, mould: 40
Mulching: 20

Nails: 47

Onions: 60, 62

Paths: 40
Planting: 20, 23, 27, 54
Ploughing: 6, 21, 31
Poplars: 23
Potatoes: 21, 62
Preserving: 3, 41, 73
Pricking out: 6, 17, 20, 21, 31, 67
Pruning: 6, 22, 23, 56, 66

Rabbits: 34
Repotting: 22
Roots: 6, 10, 20, 21, 23, 25, 77
Rosebushes: 22

Salad: 21
Sap (silver birch): 5, 7, 41
Sauerkraut: 41
Shallots: 60
Shoeing: 34
Shrubs: 23, 24
Skin: 46, 52
Slimming: 42, 48, 49, 50
Soil: 7, 15, 16, 27, 29, 31, 54
Sowing: 7, 16, 17, 20, 55
Springs: 40
Squashes: 25
Stinging nettles: 27, 29
Strawberry plants: 20
Surgical procedures: 52

Teeth: 51
Thistles: 31
Thorns: 32
Tides (influences of): 5, 16, 17, 25
Treatments: 46, 47, 51
Trees: 19, 23, 24
Trenches: 40
Trimming feet, livestock: 34

Warts: 46
Watering: 20, 23, 69
Weeds: 31
Wine: 3, 37
Wood: 6, 17, 38, 39, 40, 56, 78
Worms: 29, 47